THE
DARKEST
NIGHT

THE
DARKEST
NIGHT

22 WINTRY HORROR STORIES

EDITED BY LINDY RYAN

CROOKED
LANE

NEW YORK

Published in the United States by Crooked Lane Books, an imprint of The Quick Brown Fox & Company LLC.

Crooked Lane Books and its logo are trademarks of The Quick Brown Fox & Company LLC.

Library of Congress Catalog-in-Publication data available upon request.

ISBN (paperback): 978-1-63910-871-8
ISBN (ebook): 978-1-63910-872-5

Cover design by Nebojsa Zoric
Illustration by Mister Sam Shearon
Black-out poem art piece by Jessica McHugh

Printed in the United States.

www.crookedlanebooks.com

Crooked Lane Books
34 West 27th St., 10th Floor
New York, NY 10001

First Edition: September 2024

10 9 8 7 6 5 4 3 2 1

"Ah, distinctly I remember it was in the bleak December
And each separate dying ember wrought its ghost upon the floor."
—Edgar Allan Poe, "The Raven" (1845)

CONTENTS

INTRODUCTION

George C. Romero

SIR ARTHUR CONAN Doyle famously once said, "Where there is no imagination, there is no horror." One of the truest things I've ever heard, these words form the journey that has become my life—the constant pursuit of inspiration as the fuel for my imagination. Along the way, I've had the pleasure of sharing creative sessions with some of the most talented singers, poets, writers, filmmakers, and performers of our generation.

The interesting part: none of them were in any of the places we'd expect to meet such folks.

Don't get me wrong; there are plenty of brilliant creatives in all the places we *do* expect—Los Angeles, New York, Miami, Pittsburgh, and so on—but a homogenization often occurs in those areas. It's not immediate, and in rare cases, it never happens, but outside of these familiar cities with familiar artists, we find hundreds of small towns across the United States (and the world), each filled with raw talent unseen outside of a friend group or the local dive bar.

This inspired me long ago to seek out fresh talent and bring that talent together in any way I possibly could. You've never seen anything more inspiring than a room of total strangers come together over musical instruments to create a perfect song—one that might never be heard again; or, in the event it is ever recorded, will never be a perfect recreation of the moment that all those strangers vibed and clicked and created something, even if it's only a simple, profound moment of a deep sense of admiration, respect, and love.

But what does all this have to do with this anthology, you ask? Everything.

Five decades in this skinsuit have given me quite the ride, for sure. Ups, downs, and all-arounds have brought my life to places of darkness, light, fear, longing, loathing, loving, passion, anger, jealousy, derailment, laser focus, and finally to a place of pure joy as a husband, father, grandfather, and life and business partner.

This journey, however, has not been without its frigid and frozen moments.

I began my creative journey quite alone: hopping my first freight train in the dead of winter and at an age far too young and taking my first bullet to the gut not long after, then being packed in snow and kept alive over the Christmas holiday. An old-timer taught me the ways of the rails so that I could thrive in one of the most hostile, lonesome, and lonely environments one can navigate, filled with people who have chosen the career of invisibility and anonymity.

Those years spent in the isolation of boxcars clacking across the country and back, day-working on farms and oil fields and dive bars and carnivals (and any other damn place that would embrace my desire for anonymity) introduced me to some of the most talented, tortured, self-isolated people I've ever met. I rode through the seasons, and eventually winters became the "social" season on the rails. The uncertainty of the cold, snow, and ice kept trains off their regular schedule and left many of us to survive in harsh winter conditions. We formed small camps, shared resources, and worked together to stay warm until another train plowed through the baron, powdery landscape. I quickly realized that many of those who sought refuge on the rails had made a similar life choice to mine.

Together, we were on the fringes of humanity.

While I cannot play an instrument and have never participated in a musical jam like those I've witnessed, that time in my life was the closest I've ever experienced to creative nirvana. The philosophies, beliefs, and struggles with everything from self-displacement to fear of no more mornings came together in those snowy camps around fires and while tending to batches of hobo stew, forming our collective belief that what had led us to our current situation was born from the desire to chase the extremes in life—the only true way to ever understand what our inner creatives screamed to be heard. Creativity, like so many other life pursuits, requires a long-term commitment to an education that can sometimes only be earned outside the "safe" option—the ones others are afraid to pursue.

After decades of pursuing a life that would make Bukowski blush, Hemingway harrow, and Whitman witless, I have had an unparalleled and unexpected collection of experiences that has led me to the center of artist communities and the margins of the outliers. Holidays became bleak while celebratory moments became introspective. To this day, I am drawn to the cold of winter—the icy breath of wind, the crunch of snow underfoot, the sting of the wind on my face. While I've only just begun to enjoy the holidays, they have always been magnetic, calling me to the darker side of my past.

Beckoning me to give myself to the bleak of the cold.

There has been a common denominator throughout my journey: rooted in a lifelong pursuit of creativity in the belief that life is to be lived in extremes. From laughter to love, from struggle to pain.

It is because of these life experiences that I have the honor of introducing *The Darkest Night*, an anthology of winter horror tales—or, to be more a bit more accurate, a collection of *talent*—that has come together in a room that doesn't exist, to vibe and collaborate around a central theme. To write the perfect lyrics. To play the perfect harmonies, melodies, and notes until that perfect song—that perfect story—comes to life in a perfect creative moment.

The talent in this anthology makes the pages heavy to hold, loud to read, and powerful to hear.

Every page entertains. Every story intrigues, scares, amuses, and bewilders, and often these stories transport the ready back to the presence of childish wonderment, the birth of our collective fascination with horror—our love for storytelling and respect for a good storyteller.

These stories of winter dread will inspire nostalgia, ignite (or reignite) a passion, and coat the paintbrush of your mind's eye with the most vivid palette of horror, suspense, fear, and doubt. They will fill your quietness with auditory terror and nightmarish images made of mist and chills. They will haunt you long after you devour these pages.

—George C. Romero
Kentucky, 2023

EDITOR'S NOTE

Lindy Ryan

B EFORE TWINKLING LIGHTS and visits to shopping mall Santas, before stolen mistletoe kisses and gifts wrapped in bright paper and bows, even before Charles Dickens's *A Christmas Carol* and Washington Irving's *Old Christmas*, the Yuletide holiday has long been associated with ghosts and specters.

The origins of holiday ghost stories and hauntings have little to do with today's commercial celebrations. With its close proximity to pagan winter solstice festivals honoring the longest, darkest night of the year, Victorian-era Christmas celebrants would gather with family and friends to while away long, dark, cold winter nights in the company of ghost stories, séances, and greeting cards depicting macabre illustrations of frogs and anthropomorphic insects. In *Told After Supper*, humorist Jerome K. Jerome noted these beloved holiday traditions, saying,

> Whenever five or six English-speaking people meet round a fire on Christmas Eve, they start telling each other ghost stories . . . Nothing satisfies us on Christmas Eve but to hear each other tell authentic anecdotes about spectres. It is a genial, festive season, and we love to muse upon graves, and dead bodies, and murders, and blood.

In short, it's the merriest time of the year.

Today, the dark edge of the year is still a perfect time to find warmth on cold winter nights, and the authors and artists in this anthology continue the long-standing, hallowed tradition of spinning tales of monsters, malice, and malevolent spirits. From chilling folktales told around holiday hearths, to tales of prowling winter creatures, old gods, and sinister gift-givers, we invite you to gather round the fire and enjoy a season of short days, long nights, cold skies, and warm hearts.

Good Yule—and happy hauntings.

—Lindy Ryan
North Carolina, 2023

TO HELL WITH HIBERNATION *an illustration*
Mister Sam Shearon

THE MOUTHLESS BODY IN THE LAKE

Gwendolyn Kiste

O N Christmas morning, you discover your own body frozen beneath the ice in Lake Minton.

There's nobody else around when you find yourself there. Your cousins are building snowmen with carrot noses in the backyard, and the rest of your family is enjoying a potluck around an artificial tree in the living room.

Nobody notices when you sneak out the back door and steal into the forest. You're a ghost in your own life. You're only eight years old, but you feel so much older, the world already an unbearable weight on your back.

The air is glittering with cold as you cross the backyard and disappear among the trees. The horde of sugar pines closes in around you, the canopy casting long shadows across your face. It seems for a moment you're the only one left alive in the world. On days like this, that might even be preferable.

Your boots fall heavy in the dirt, and you keep going until the trees part, and you see it up ahead—the frozen water that's beckoning you.

It's called Lake Minton because that's your last name and it belongs to your grandparents. This is the sum total of everything your family has claim to: a lake, a house, and all the secrets dwelling within. For what it's worth, you don't live here full-time; you and your parents sequestered in a duplex across town, and for that at least, you're grateful. This place has always felt haunted.

Though you know you shouldn't, you creep across the frozen lake, each step more careful than the last. Most of the ice is frosted over, opaque as the past, but there's a spot up ahead where it's clear like glass, and you can gaze right down into the chilled water on the other side.

You inhale deeply and sneak a glance, expecting to see nothing but darkness waiting there.

You see yourself instead.

The eyes are closed, the cheeks are flushed, but it's unmistakable. The figure is exactly the same as you, except for one thing: it has no mouth, no lips, not even an outline where they belong.

Your breath fogging in front of you, you lean closer to the ice. "Hello?" you whisper. "Can you hear me?"

But of course, the version of you in the lake doesn't answer. Even if it were alive, it has no mouth to speak.

In this moment, part of you wants to scream for the both of you. Another part of you wants to race back to the house, the frozen pinecones crunching beneath your feet like broken bones, and tell the others what you've found. But somehow you already know they'll blame you. They'll tell you how you did something to deserve this.

So instead, you sit with yourself for a long while, the sun rising sullenly in the sky. The body never moves, never drifts an inch. It simply floats there beneath the ice.

With your heart in your throat, you trudge back to the family house. Inside, your parents, and aunts and uncles and cousins never noticed you were gone. The rest of the afternoon and evening dissolves around you. There are foil-wrapped gifts tied with curly red ribbons and shiny plates of cutout cookies and snickerdoodles and pecan tassies, enough sugar to make your teeth ache even from across the room.

Everything here looks perfect. Everyone here pretends it's perfect. Only you know better. You're the only one who seems to see the orange bottle of pills peeking out of your mother's leather purse or all the people with their glassy eyes and thin laughs and short tempers simmering with ancient grudges. A forgotten anniversary fifteen years ago. A snide word last Christmas. But you aren't allowed to say a word about it. The same way you can't say a word about what you discovered in the lake. You just sit back in the corner, by the Christmas tree, and nod politely and act like your parents didn't just rewrap one of the stuffed animals from your toybox and tell you that it's new.

"Did you have a nice Christmas?" your mom asks on the way home, but you only stare out the back-seat window, never answering her.

* * *

You don't visit the lake during the spring or summer or even the fall. You can't help but wonder if you're still there, trapped in the chill and the dark, but then you're not entirely sure you were ever there at all.

"It's all in your head," your mother says when you finally slip up and tell her about it, and she's probably right. In fact, you hope she is. It would be better if there wasn't a version of you out there, drowned and silenced and alone.

Besides, you have other things to occupy your time. Every weekend, your parents come stumbling in after midnight, Milwaukee's Best on their breath, resentment soaking through their voices.

You're always waiting up in bed, your Care Bears comforter pulled up to your chin. You tell yourself if you stay quiet, nobody will know you're here.

Sometimes, it works. Sometimes, it doesn't.

* * *

You're fourteen years old before you're brave enough to return to the lake. It's Christmas Eve this time, and you don't even want to take a walk outside.

But your mother is fighting with your aunt again, their words laced with venom and smiles, and your grandparents huddle in the corner, their eyes gone unfocused, their minds lost years ago.

Meanwhile, an uncle you only see on holidays, the one with the rancid milk breath, tries to ply you with a shot of whiskey.

"You'll like it," he slurs, and shoves a bottle of Southern Comfort at you.

"I'm not old enough yet," you murmur, but nobody hears you. You're used to that by now. In your family, it's better to be quiet than it is to tell them they're wrong.

You pretend to take a swig from the jug of Southern Comfort, and pass it back to him. Then you wait until you're sure your parents aren't looking before you grab your coat and slip out the back door.

The property doesn't look the same as before. A row of sugar pine trees near the lake has gone gray, the bark peeling off, the needles scattered in the dirt like confetti. You wonder what went wrong with them, why so many things die before their time.

But there's nobody around to ask, and more than that, there's nobody to answer. You keep walking instead, your chin tipped up, pretending you're not afraid.

On the lake, the ice is thick in the chilled winter night, and you tiptoe across it. There you are, bobbing in the frozen water like you never left at all.

The body looks older now. It's grown the same way you have.

You lean in, curious what your own skin feels like. Is it cool to the touch, as cool as the dead? Or is the version of you that lives in the dark filled with heat, with possibility? Is that why the cheeks are still flushed? Is that what keeps you from decaying—from becoming fodder for the fish, a victim of time?

Your hand curls into a fist, and you want to bring it down hard on the ice, cracking it in two, opening up the lake so you can reach inside and find out.

But then something tightens inside you, because you're not sure if those swimming lessons from the YMCA really took. The moment you hit the water, you might sink like a stone, sucked down into the dark before you even have a chance to meet yourself.

It's best to return to your family and their make-believe revelry. It's best to pretend none of this ever happened.

You're halfway back to the house when you see a shadow at the property line.

At once, you seize up. "Who's there?" you ask, trembling.

A girl your age emerges from behind a dead sugar pine.

You gape at her. "It's Christmas Eve," you say. "Why aren't you with your family?"

She lets out a harsh laugh. "Probably for the same reason you aren't."

Neither of you speaks again for a long time, a silent truth twisting between you.

"My name's Karla," she says finally.

You swallow a frozen breath. "I'm Taylor," you say.

You walk together a while, and she tells you all about herself, how she lives just a couple blocks away from the duplex you share with your parents. How she's strange and lonely just like you.

"I don't like Christmas," she says. "I don't like this town at all."

"Me neither," you say.

And you don't like what's hidden in the lake either. You want to take her out on the ice. You want to show her the version of you that's lingering in the dark.

Do you see it there? you're desperate to ask. *Do you see me?*

But you don't say a word about it. You're afraid the ice is too thin to support both of you and that she'll slip into the dark, stolen away forever.

When the moon hits its apex and you can't stall any longer, the two of you part ways at the edge of the forest. But at the last moment, Karla turns back and grins. It's the first time in a long time since anyone looked at you that way. Since anyone looked at you at all.

You can't help but smile back.

* * *

The years dissolve around you, and you're almost eighteen before you return to the lake.

By then, half the trees have vanished, a line of meager holes carved into the forest line.

"Probably some kind of disease," your mother says, but you know that's not true. Not unless your family counts as a special sort of disease.

You and Karla have tried to make the best of things here. You sneak away when you can, teaching each other how to drive, stealing your mothers' Virginia Slims, and smoking in the alley next to the school, where it feels like you're the only two people left on earth.

"It's okay," she always tells you. "We'll get out. We'll go somewhere."

You try to believe her. But she hasn't seen the things in the world that you have. She doesn't know what's waiting out there.

It's the day after Christmas, the detritus from the holiday strewn about the family property. A discarded tree on the curb, wads of wrapping paper from gifts you never asked for stuffed in gaping garbage bags.

You and Karla are standing in the front yard, no gloves, no coats, when you finally speak the words you wanted to tell her for years.

"There's something I want to show you," you say.

Without hesitating, she follows you through the forest and out onto the lake. Part of you is certain it won't be there, that somehow it's only visible when you're all alone.

But when you creep across the ice and gaze down, there you are, just like always, dreaming in the dark.

"It's you," she whispers, and the two of you stare down at your body for a long moment. It's almost eighteen years old too, everything identical except this version of you will never utter a word, even if it awakens.

Her face gone gray, Karla turns to you. "We need to do something," she says, and though you beg her not to, she tells whoever will listen: her parents, your parents, your teachers at school. It's like watching a wreck in slow motion, because you already know what will happen. They call you liars. They call you crazy. Nobody even bothers to come out to the lake and check. They're so convinced you're wrong that there isn't any reason to question it.

For the rest of your senior year, they have Karla sent away, and even after graduation, she doesn't return.

"Where did they take her?" you ask anyone who will listen, which is nobody at all.

She's the only one who believes you, and she's gone now. Your only witness vanished into thin air. All those years, you tried to protect her, tried to keep her from falling through the ice, but the world stole her away from you anyhow.

"She was nothing but a troublemaker," your mother says, and you hold your breath and wish you were someone else.

*   *   *

You're almost twenty-five when you return to the lake.

Most of your family is long gone, vanished into the road or into the grave. The uncle with the rancid milk breath, hitchhiking into a fog, never to be seen again. A cousin who found the end of the bottle until the end found him. Your grandparents, dead and buried, faded into oblivion. Death and decay are your birthright and your destiny.

With almost no one else left, you live at the family house full-time now. Last year, your mother shattered her ankle and demanded you move in and take care of her round the clock. With your father dead from heart failure, you were the only one around, so she sent you a dozen emails, all of them pleading and shaming, until you were too tired to argue about it anymore.

You're like a bug caught under glass. You'll never escape. You'll never be free.

Instead, you'll be a good daughter. You'll do the right thing—take care of what remains of your family. Take care of the house. Won't speak too loudly. In fact, won't speak at all. It's easier that way.

No.

That's a lie.

Nothing about this has ever been easy.

You've only done this because you never felt like you had any other choice.

On Christmas Day, there's no holiday tree. No foil-wrapped presents or table of pies and cookies and cakes. Just you and your mother and a dying hearth.

"You should get out more," she tells you that night.

"I don't have any friends left here."

At this, she curls up her nose. "You're still mad about that Karla girl, aren't you?"

You stand back in the corner, not speaking a word.

Your mother just shakes her head. "I never told you that you couldn't be friends with her," she says. "If you think I said that, then it's all in your head."

Barbed wire tightens in your chest. This is what she always claims. How every memory you have is just a figment of your imagination. The same way she told you that the body in the lake was in your imagination too. And because you're alone in this place with her, she always seems to be the one with the authority.

"Maybe I should just go away," you say at last.

A scoff. "And where would you go?"

Anywhere but here, you want to say. Anywhere that's far from this place, this family, and that body forever floating in the lake.

You only shrug. "I'm sure there's somewhere out there."

Your mother doesn't speak for a long time after that. You think she's mad at you, and maybe she is, but she's not scowling anymore. Instead, she's crying quietly in her La-Z-Boy recliner, her gray hair falling in her tired eyes, and you can't help yourself. You go to her and hold her, and you tell her how you won't ever leave.

"Promise?" she asks through salty tears, clinging tight to your collar.

"I promise," you whisper as everything goes cold inside you.

*   *   *

In an instant, the years blur together, and you're suddenly on the cusp of forty. Still living with your mother, still living near the lake.

Every morning, you gaze out the back window. All the trees in the forest have withered away, leaving a gaping wound in the landscape. And through that opening, you see it: the lake, waiting for you the same way it always has.

It's the middle of December, and you're in town to pick up this week's groceries when you hear the voice of a ghost.

"Hi, Taylor."

You whirl around to face her. Karla, barely having aged a day. You haven't seen each other in years. If someone had asked, you would have been convinced she'd forgotten you altogether.

"Hello," you say, and your voice splits in two.

"Can I buy you a cup of coffee?" she asks.

Together, you sit in the corner booth at the old diner, the wrap-around windows smudged with dark fingerprints, the scent of burnt coffee lingering on the air. It's nearly Christmastime again, and somebody has hung a rusted sleigh bell over the front door.

You want to ask where they took her, but she doesn't seem to care about the past anymore. She's only worried about the future.

"We could leave together," she says. "We could go anywhere."

But you only shake your head. "It's too late," you whisper.

You're nearly forty years old. You've wasted too much time. You can't make up for it now. Your whole life is an hourglass flipped over, and all you can do is watch the sand run out, grain by tiny grain.

"I'm only in town for the night," Karla says. "If you change your mind—"

She doesn't finish that sentence. She doesn't need to.

You finish your coffee, the bitter taste lingering in your mouth. "It was good to see you again," you say, and mean it. Then you head for the door.

Karla follows you out onto the sidewalk, the two of you lingering in the December chill. "You know you're wrong," she says. "It's never too late, Taylor."

You return home to your mother asking you about dinner, a bevy of shadows hanging over you. This haunted house you can never escape. Except there were never any ghosts here, only your family. It turns out the living can haunt a place just as easily as the dead.

That night, you cook meatloaf with onions, but you don't touch a bite of it, your gaze set on the windows and what lingers beyond.

"What are you looking at?" your mother asks, but you don't answer.

It's after midnight when your mother turns in for bed, and you wander barefoot out to the lake, your legs and heart going numb. In the water, you're waiting for yourself, your eyes closed, the shape of your mouth still missing.

This is all you've ever been—the silent one, the girl who does her best not to make a mess or make a sound.

Karla's words echo in your mind. *"It's not too late."*

You don't think about what happens next. You just raise your fist above your head the way you should have done years ago and bring it down hard on the frozen lake. The ice shatters at once, the entire earth trembling at your touch, your body slipping between the cracks.

The lake is even colder than you expect, and you're still not sure you remember how to swim. The dark water might swallow you whole, but in a way, that's still better than what your family has already done to you. How they've devoured you, piece by piece, not even bothering to spit back the bones.

You grab hold of yourself, and the body feels entirely different than you expect. It's soft and malleable, and it contorts in your hands like a second skin. And that's exactly what it is. This is the rest of you, the part of yourself you need to claim.

The part you need to stop running from.

You tear the flesh down the back, and without hesitating, you slip into it, into the shape of your own body, the two of you melding into one. It blends into you like butter, all of you twisting and contorting on your bones.

You buoy yourself back to the surface, but you still can't breathe, trapped inside the skin with no mouth. But that won't last. With both hands, you claw at your face, your fingers going raw, until your own lips tear through, and you take your first breath.

And with that breath, you let out a guttural scream, the reverberations ricocheting off the sky, loud enough to shake the earth and shake the town and wake your mother all the way back at the lonely house.

You aren't the same girl you once were. You hope Karla will recognize you. You think she will.

But either way, you know where you won't return. That lonely house will be even lonelier now, because you turn away, your eyes set on the darkened skyline, the stars gleaming with promise.

And in your new skin and your new self, you never look back.

COLD AS ICE

Tim Waggoner

ICE PELLETS STRIKE your windshield with *tic-tac-tic* sounds, like a barrage of tiny bullets, and form a continuous but shifting pattern of dark streaks slicing through your headlight beams. *Not bullets,* you think. *More like little meteors.* Strong winds buffet your car, seemingly from all directions, and you have to fight to keep your vehicle on the road.

You're gripping the steering wheel so tight your hands ache, and the defroster is blowing full blast. It's set on hot, and the dry air makes your eyes ache, stings the skin of your face. You'd love to turn it down, but you need it this hot to keep ice from forming on your windshield. The wipers are going fast—*thwop-thwop, thwop-thwop*—but they can't do the job alone. Without the defroster's help, ice would coat them within moments, rendering them useless. You glance at your speedometer. You're going twenty-three miles an hour on a fucking interstate, and it still feels as if you can barely keep your car on the road. You should pull off to the side of the highway, park, and wait for the worst of the storm to pass. That would be the smart thing to do. But no one's ever accused you of being smart before, and you keep driving.

It's Christmas—well, it's December 23rd, so close enough—and you're heading home after a bad first date. You're disappointed, angry, frustrated, embarrassed . . . but most of all, you're scared. Not because of what happened earlier tonight, but because of what's happening *now*. The storm and the road conditions, yes—you should've left her place earlier—but not just those. You're scared because, for the last several miles, something has been running alongside the highway, keeping pace with your vehicle—which, given your current rate of speed, isn't that difficult a feat. You don't want to look to see if it's still there. You've been trying to ignore it ever since you first saw it, to pretend it doesn't exist. You haven't been successful, though, and you aren't now. Despite yourself, you turn your head to the right and look through the passenger window.

You can't make out specific features in the dark, and the icefall doesn't help. The thing is white, has four legs, and generally resembles a dog, although it's larger, as large as a horse, and has a large rack of antlers, like an elk. If the creature makes any noise as it runs, the sounds of wind and ice hitting your car block it. But you think that even if there was no storm, the thing would move as silent as a midnight shadow. As you look at it, it turns its head to regard you, and although you can't see its face clearly, you can tell one thing.

It's smiling at you.

*   *   *

"I work at an insurance company. It's not exciting, but it pays the bills, you know?"

You nod, although her words barely make an impression on you. This is the second first date you've been on this week, and it's only Wednesday. And to make things worse, it's the night before Christmas Eve. *It really is the best night for me this week.* You weren't sure you believed her, wondered if it was an excuse so she'd have someone to go out with during the holidays—even if it was only a person she knew from email exchanges on a dating site and a couple phone calls. But you agreed. Now you wish you hadn't. The restaurant—an Italian place not far from her apartment—is decorated with cardboard Santas, reindeer, and snowmen taped to the walls, along with blinking Christmas tree lights hanging over doorways. There are a few families out for a holiday meal, but in general the place is filled with couples tonight, most in their thirties and forties, talking in hushed tones, no doubt sharing banalities as they wonder if they're going to get laid tonight. The atmosphere is less festive than one of quiet desperation, and you wish you suggested a different place to meet, or at least insisted on a different day.

It doesn't help that she lives almost an hour away from you and that the weather report for the night looks bleak—freezing rain accompanied by a sharp drop in temperature. Not a recipe for a fun drive home.

"So tell me about what you do," she says.

The two of you have already covered the basics about your jobs during previous conversations. You don't know why she wants to go over this ground again. But you dutifully talk about your work for a while, and then you move onto other topics, occasionally sipping wine and nibbling on garlic breadsticks while you wait for your entrées to come. They do—chicken parm for you, fettucine alfredo for her—and you're halfway through your meals when the discussion takes a more serious turn.

"You've been married before, right?"

You have to fight to keep from sighing. It's time for the Interrogation, the part of the date when the other person probes your past to assess whether or not it's worth taking things further with you. You hate this part.

"Yeah. Seven years. We didn't have any kids."

"How long has it been?"

"We split up almost two years ago. The divorce was finalized about a year after that."

"I hope it was amicable."

You recognize this statement as another probe. Will you start bitching about your ex? Or will you talk about how much you miss her and wish you could get back together? Either response will be a red flag and disqualify you as potential relationship material.

You decide to tell the truth.

"She needed more than I could give."

You hope your date will leave it at that. She doesn't, of course.

"How so?"

This time you do sigh.

"I grew up as an only child, and my parents weren't exactly what you'd call emotionally demonstrative. My ex used to say that I was too—"

cold

"—reserved."

* * *

There are more of them now. You're not sure how many. It's damn hard to see anything in this storm. A half dozen, maybe more. Some are larger, some smaller, but they're the same nameless species—huge, antlered, white-furred canids—and they share one additional attribute. Whenever they turn to look at you, they smile with mouths more human than animal. It's those smiles that really get to you.

You want to believe that the pack of creatures is an illusion of the storm—one part ice rain, one part darkness, and one part imagination—the problem is, you don't have much of an imagination. You prefer to watch documentaries and read nonfiction instead of consuming made-up stories, and you rarely lie, not because you're especially honest, but because you can't think of anything to say that isn't true. How could a mundane mind like yours create anything like the creatures running parallel with your car?

The storm has been worsening over the last several minutes. Visibility is near zero now, and you're crawling along at thirteen miles per hour. Earlier, you turned on the radio to listen to weather reports, scrolled through various channels, but everyone said the same basic thing: if you're out on the road, you're fucked. You turned off the radio then. You didn't need anyone to tell you *that*.

You haven't seen another vehicle on the highway—whether traveling the same direction as you or driving on the opposite side—for nearly thirty minutes. If you end up stuck in a ditch, there's no one around to help, and if you call for a tow truck, who the hell is going to venture out into this mess to help you? You still have plenty of gas, and you can keep the engine going and run the heater so you won't freeze to death. But if you *did* stop—voluntarily or not—what would your unearthly escort do? Would they continue running, leaving you behind until they were lost in the darkness? Or would they stop and approach your car, smiles fixed firmly on their inhuman faces? You hope you won't have to find out. It might take you another hour or two to get home at this speed, but if you keep plugging along, you should—

A white streak passes in front of your car, and without thinking you jam your foot down on the brake. Your car immediately fishtails, and if you were going any faster, you might start spinning, but you're going slow enough that the vehicle only slides a bit before coming under control again. *What the fuck?*

It happens again. And again. And *again*.

The creatures—the antler-wolves—are crossing the road in front of you, one after the other. Your sideview mirror is too covered by ice for you to see them, but you've got the back defroster going, and in the rearview you can see them curve around and pass behind your car. They are literally running circles around you as you drive. The thought is so absurd it almost makes you laugh, but a choked sob comes out instead. You can't tell yourself what's happening isn't real. You *know* it's real. If the road weren't so goddamned icy, you'd accelerate and try to pull away from these animals. Let's see the bastards try to keep up with you when you're doing fifty, sixty, seventy, eighty miles per hour. Hell, you'd go even faster, run the vehicle as hard as it would go until the fucking thing rattled itself to pieces. But the road *is* icy, and you're stuck at—another glance at the speedometer—*nine* miles per hour. You could probably go faster if you got out and walked. Not that you'd leave the safety of your car, not with the antler-wolves out there.

Forget about them. Just keep driving.

Maybe the storm had brought them out from wherever they normally lived, and they'd return once it was over. You just need to keep going and wait them out. Eventually they'll leave, for one reason or another—the end of the storm, you reaching town—and then you'll be safe. It'll be like this nightmare never happened.

The creatures increase their speed then, running so fast they're practically blurs. What's more, you realize their circle is contracting, but not evenly. It's moving inward more on your left, forcing you to angle toward the right. You understand then that the antler-wolves are trying to force you off the road. If that happens, you doubt you'll be able to get out of the ditch on your own. You'll be stuck in the ice storm, in the dark—

—with *them*.

Fuck that.

Normally, you'd never think of hurting an animal, but you're not sure these things actually *are* animals or that they *can* be hurt. But whatever they are, you can't allow them to stop you. You *have* to keep going, and if that means some of them get hurt, so be it. You press down slowly on the accelerator, try to pick up some speed, but it's useless. Your tires can't get enough traction on the icy road. You'll just have to see what you can do at nine mph. You turn your steering wheel to the left, grit your teeth in anticipation of hitting one of the antler-wolves. If you strike a couple, maybe that will scare the others off, and you won't have to hurt any more of them. At this speed, you won't really be hitting them, more like bumping into them hard.

You wait to hear and feel a *thump*, but instead there's a sudden impact of the driver's side door, the impact so hard that the side window cracks. The vehicle swerves to the right, and you yank the steering wheel to the left, attempting to keep your car on the road. *What the hell was—*

Another impact on the driver's side, this one on the rear quarter panel. Then another, this one on the driver's door again, and the cracked window shatters. The glass collapses into small bits, as it was designed to do, most of it falling outside, and you're not injured. *They're ramming the car,* you think, smashing into it like angry bulls, one after the other. The strikes become a barrage, and no matter how hard you fight to maintain control of your vehicle, there's nothing you can do. Eventually the rear swings around, the car spins, slides, and comes to a jarring stop in the ditch.

The engine is still going, icy pellets shoot through the broken window to hit your skin, and your headlights illuminate a dozen antler-wolves standing in a group, looking at you with cold blue eyes. Their lips draw back from sharp teeth in smiles as they start forward.

* * *

Dinner is over. You're in your date's apartment—you think her name is Vivian, but you can't remember for sure—both of you naked in bed, kissing, your combined breath smelling of wine, marinara sauce, garlic, and cheese. You're not surprised that she decided to come back to her place at the end of your meal. You didn't date a lot before you met your first wife, so you didn't have a lot of experience going out with women before your divorce. You've been surprised to discover many of them are interested in having sex on the first few dates, if not *the* first. If you cared about sex, this would be great, but as it is, it's something of a chore.

Still, you always try to take care of your partner's needs, and you do so now. She appears to enjoy herself, and after she climaxes, she wants to return the favor. There's no need, but you fear she'll feel rejected if you tell her this, so you let her go ahead. When it's over, you expect her to want to cuddle, but instead, she lies on her side, propped up on one arm, and looks at you intently.

"You weren't really here, were you?"

You don't ask her to explain the question. You know exactly what she means.

"I was here as much as I was able to be."

She nods slowly. "So when you said your ex said you were too *reserved*, this is what you meant."

"Yeah. Part of it, anyway."

"And it's not just sex, is it? It's the whole connecting to others part too."

Now it's your turn to nod.

"Why do you keep dating then?"

"I guess I keep hoping it will be different, that I'll finally be able to feel something."

"But it never has been different, has it?"

"No."

"And it wasn't this time, was it?"

"No."

She looks at you for several moments before speaking again.

"You should stop doing this. There's nothing wrong with being who you are, but it's not right to lead people on either. You're using us to try to fix something that can't be fixed. I don't like being used. No one does. You should go."

You want to say something to make this better, something that will allow you to part with her on better terms. But you can't think of anything, and even if you could, you know it wouldn't help.

You get out of bed and start to get dressed. She doesn't say a word as you finish, walk out of the bedroom, leave her apartment, and shut the door behind you.

Happy Holidays.

*   *   *

The antler-wolves stop when they're within a yard of your vehicle. Now that neither you nor the creatures are moving, you get a better look at them. They still appear much as you first perceived them, but their faces are disturbingly more human than canine, and what you took to be fur now seems more like frost. Their antlers are white too, and you get the impression that the creatures are made entirely of ice, which is impossible—you know that—but it *feels* right.

You hold your breath as one of the larger creatures leaves the pack and pads over to your open window. You fear the thing will lunge toward you, bury its teeth in your throat; or maybe turn its head sideways, thrust its antlers into the car, and stab you with them. But it does neither. It simply stands there, so close you could reach out and touch its white snout, its blue eyes glittering as they examine you.

The antler-wolf doesn't open its mouth, but you hear its voice inside your head.

You are us.

"I . . . I don't understand."

We dwell apart from this world. Our home is cold—far colder than this place could ever be—but when it is cold enough here, we can cross over, take shape, run, and play. Where we live, we are formless, and it is invigorating to be physical for a time. But only a time. In our natural state, we are pure thought. Calm, placid, content. We feel nothing but one another, for we are all there is, and it is wondrous. I started following you because I sensed your emptiness, so much like ours. The others joined me because they sensed it too. You do not belong here. You are not happy here. We are what you have been looking for. Join us and be free.

The others echo this thought.

Join us. Be free.

"I'm like you? I'm not . . . not broken?"

You are who you are meant to be. Decide quickly. The storm will soon grow weaker, our time here will end, and we will depart.

"And if that happens, I'll never see you again."

The antler-wolf doesn't answer. It doesn't need to.

You smile. "Let's go."

The creature smiles in return, then backs away from the vehicle. You feel a pulling, a tearing, a release, then you're outside the car. Ice crystals swirl upward from the ground, collect around you, give you your new temporary form. Your old one remains sitting in your car, silent and still, already beginning to grow cold.

We run, the antler-wolf says. It turns and darts off, the rest of the pack following. You follow too, slow and unsure on your four new legs, but you quickly gain speed and confidence until you are running with the rest of your new family, for as long as the ice storm lasts. When it's over, you will discard your body, and for the first time in your life, you'll go home.

CHILDREN AREN'T THE ONLY ONES WHO KNOW WHERE THE PRESENTS ARE HIDDEN

Josh Malerman

LYDIA RABINOWITZ HATED the holidays. That's how she'd put it to her friends: *"I hate the holidays. All of them."*

It used to be funny. Something punk to say. The first time she said it, she was a kid, and her two best friends were shocked to hear it. Years later, in college, people loved it. People would cheer her for speaking the truth. Truth to power and the corporations that ran holidays. Brass Lydia Rabinowitz and her bold statements. There was righteousness to be found in that, for her. And so, she continued, into the years following school. For as long as she could remember she'd been saying it. *"All of them."* That was the key. That was the punch. But, as declarations tend to do, this one started to turn on her. At some point, it seemed to make some people mad. Family, of course, but others too. They'd ask what she had against New Year's. A guy broke up with her over the Fourth of July. She wasn't so young when this happened, and it was the first time she didn't feel so funny saying it. Whether his reaction made her feel this way didn't matter. It was the first time she asked herself *why*. This was a decade ago. And she hadn't answered the question.

Because she didn't have an answer. She only had an image and a quote. For as long as she could remember, an annoying vision came to mind every time she said she hated the holidays. Whenever the phrase rose up within her, it came accompanied by a closet. Off-white sliding doors. It wasn't the closet from her childhood bedroom, and so she didn't know what it was. And the quote, too, an echo of a voice, yelled:

"WHERE IS SHE?"

It sounded perhaps like her mother, and it came from somewhere deeper in a house.

What house?

This was all dreamish, and frustrating for that. A memory, maybe.

I hate the holidays. All of them.

Then: the image of the closet. And the yell:

"WHERE IS SHE?"

These thoughts came upon the pumpkins of Halloween and the white meat of Thanksgiving. The red of Valentine's Day and the green of St. Patrick's. But never was Lydia Rabinowitz's distaste for the holiday season as strong as it was in December.

And nothing made her feel as sick as Christmas.

For that, the vague thoughts of the closet and the yell lingered during the winter months whether she spoke her declaration or not. They bothered her, and often a friend would ask why she was frowning at a moment when everyone else was not. More than once, Lydia asked to sleep at a friend's house, unsure why she felt so uneasy with these thoughts. Sometimes she didn't even know these particular thoughts had come. They'd arrived so commonly, sneaking behind whatever current event was on her mind. But at some point, whether on the couch at Fiona's or in her own bed at home, the vision of the closet and the distant, angry question would come. Eventually, Lydia left town.

She'd come to connect the winter months with the major holiday season and, foolishly or not, she thought perhaps California wouldn't feel as Christmas-y as Michigan. At thirty-five, she moved alone, citing a thirst for adventure. But close friends and family are often able to sense something unsettled in loved ones, and those she left behind did wonder. Her parents were long divorced, which only bolstered her Christian mother's staunch desire to celebrate Christmas, a want that was present but not as loud when she was married to Lydia's Jewish father. Still, they did celebrate Christmas when Lydia was a child. A thing she successfully didn't think about on her drive west. Nor did she think of it much over the course of her first seven months living in the Golden State. She made a new friend, an odd, shy man named Marvin, and she tried things she considered to be California-esque. Like fish tacos and yoga. She even surfed once, but the darkness of the sea gave her a familiar unsettled sense, and for the first time she thought of the closet again. And the angry yell.

"WHERE IS SHE?"

Years after her parents' divorce, Lydia's mother confessed she believed Lydia's father had cheated on her. This was a shock to Lydia, who wasted no time asking her father if this was true. His frustration with the question could've meant two very different things, Lydia thought: either he had cheated and was upset Lydia now knew, or he had not, and this accusation then had something to do with a divorce he did not think he deserved. Following Lydia's failed attempt at surfing in California, years after asking her father this question, the echo of that accusation gave new meaning and breadth to the angry yell:

"WHERE IS SHE?"

A memory started to form then. Lydia felt pieces had come together to make a picture she did not wish to see. December in California was upon her, and while she'd been right to think it would feel different out West, bereft of snow and evergreens, she was wrong to think the old feelings wouldn't come. The only place she could think that might be less Christmas-y than California was Las Vegas, and so on December first of that year, not even a full year since she'd moved, Lydia packed a small suitcase, gassed up her small Volvo, and headed for the desert, where she hoped the garish city would obliterate all sense of Christmas, if only by swallowing whole the spirit of the season.

Her GPS told her it was just over two hundred and eighty miles to Las Vegas, and she'd arrive after dark. That would put her in the middle of nowhere at twilight, an idea that comforted her, being as far from society and its holiday traditions as she could get. She did not think of her parents as she drove, did not allow herself to imagine her mother's disappointment when she would eventually tell her she had no plans to return to Michigan by year's end. She played an album of Grateful Dead covers loud (Marvin had tried to turn her on), and she tried not to wonder as to what she was doing. Someone might consider her now *going to lengths* to avoid an uncomfortable feeling. She wore sunglasses for the first hour of the ride and rarely looked at her phone on the passenger seat beside her. She kept the windows down despite the growing coolness in the air (windows up were for states that got real cold, like Michigan, states that looked like Christmas cards five months of the year). She drove fast, and the sound of the desert rippling past was just what she'd been looking for back in Los Angeles. A constant drone to cloak the angry yell, a consistent flowing hum that wove in and out of the (surprisingly, but covers after all) conservative music, and an expanse of desert so wide, there would be no room for an unwanted memory to come sneaking up on her.

But one did.

And when she saw the closet on the side of the road, freestanding, with no home to support it, her first reaction was frustration. The vision, it seemed, had found her anyway, despite the lengths to which she had gone. There seemed no escaping the closet and the yell. But it wasn't until she was coming up on it, slowing down unintentionally, her eyes on the off-white sliding doors, that she understood this was no vision, no memory, no thought.

It was a closet. An actual closet. On the side of the road.

She pressed the brakes hard after rolling past the oblong thing. She eyed it in the mirrors. She stuck her head out the open window and reversed, slowly, along the desert road's shoulder.

A closet. With no home to support it, no explanation for it at all.

Lydia put the Volvo in park and let its engine idle as she eyed the rectangular impossibility from across the two lanes.

"What the *fuck*," she said.

She undid her seat belt. She got out of the car. She stood with one hand on the open door and felt an uneasiness that dwarfed the uneasiness she'd become accustomed to this time of year. Yet, that dark swilling was accompanied by a sense of progress. A crack in the case. A case she wasn't sure she wanted to crack.

She eyed the bottom left corner of the left sliding door. A word there in Sharpie. A word Lydia recognized because Lydia had written it herself.

Her name, written when she was still a child.

She felt breathless then. And the desert sky pressed in on her.

The progress she felt was the fact she now knew what the closet was, where it had been, how she knew it. All these years, that vision wasn't random after all. This very closet had popped into her head a hundred thousand times, never with a word of how it knew her. But she knew it now.

This was the closet in the basement of her childhood home.

This was where her parents kept her Christmas presents in the wintry months of the holiday season.

Lydia started to cross the two-lane highway without looking both ways. A car came whipping by, and she leaped back, her eyes on the face of the driver. Did they see the closet on the side of the road? Were they distracted by her, Lydia, a lone woman unsafely crossing the road?

How could they not have seen the closet?

The car continued on its way, driving without slowing, toward the same horizon Lydia was fleeing. She watched it recede long enough to know it wasn't going to turn around. Not even for a woman who might be having car trouble on the side of the road. And certainly not for any closet.

Now she did look both ways and crossed the empty highway.

Yes, her name. The sight so familiar to her now. And with it, a flood of memories: the stuffy smell of that carpeted basement room. Scattered toys. Wood-paneled walls that didn't reach the ceiling. Hadn't she thrown a toy over that wall once? Hadn't her father got upset about it?

She stepped to the side of the closet and saw the off white continue there, a sight she'd never seen as a child. A sight nobody had ever seen or ever sees: the outside of the closet walls. She stepped far enough to see the back of it too. Then, moving instinctually, thinking this closet must suddenly vanish, must suddenly be revealed to be something else, she circled the entire thing.

"*WHERE IS SHE?*"

Lydia almost ducked at the sound. This was more than a memory, more than a thought. These were words, shouted. She stepped back from the closet and looked up. It sounded like the voice had come from the sky.

Like the shout had come from upstairs.

Standing in front of the closet again, beginning to feel a chill she did not ascribe to the twilight that had arrived, she heard more. For the first time since perhaps the actual day she'd heard it in real time, she heard more than just the angry yell:

"*I saw her! When I pulled into the driveway! I saw her walking through the house!*"

Lydia's stomach sank. Yes. She had been too young at the time to understand what this could've meant.

"She saw the other woman through the front windows . . ."

Mother's accusation of cheating. And Father's response that she was nuts.

An argument, yes, upstairs in the living room, as Lydia, a child, stood before the off-white doors, wondering if she should slide them open, if she should sneak a peek at the presents waiting for her, just like she'd done the past few years.

There wasn't much to it. You pulled the presents out quietly, sure not to rip the paper, and you shook them. By their size and sound, you could determine what they were. You'd asked for them, after all, and if there was one thing Lydia Rabinowitz had learned already, it was that parents didn't like to make these types of decisions on their own.

Was Mother yelling about her? Did she know Lydia was in the basement, at the closet door, reaching out with flat palms to slide the off-white doors apart?

This was what she'd thought back then. Mother yelling about her. Now, she looked up and down the desert highway. She knew now her mother hadn't been yelling about her. Mother had seen someone in the house.

And where was that other woman now?

Lydia looked to the closet doors again.

"Hello?" she asked.

Was it possible? Had her father's mistress hidden herself in the basement closet? Had she seen Lydia's mother arrive, then hurried herself down the carpeted stairs? Had Lydia's father told her to hide down here?

"Hey?" she said. "Is anybody in there?"

But this was crazy. Lydia wasn't in the basement of her childhood home. She was on the side of the road between Los Angeles and Las Vegas. It was December and there was no snow on the ground, and there never would be out here. Still . . . more of the memory came back to her. The smell, yes, but it was a little different this time. The stuffiness of the basement, the lingering scent of a recent vacuuming. And something else. Something like the bathroom down here had been stopped up.

"WHERE IS SHE?"

Like lightning across the desert sky.

No, this wasn't a case Lydia wanted to crack. The way the pieces of this memory made her feel, the uneasiness as they slid together.

She heard her parents yelling in the sky.

She eyed the closed closet doors.

And, partially thinking of shaking presents, *remembering* thinking that, and also partially now thinking of a grown woman hiding in a desert closet, she put her palms to the left door and slid it to the right.

"Oh . . ."

The smell was stronger now. That sewage smell.

But it was eclipsed by what she saw.

Clothes. Her father's suit coats. Her mother's faux fur. Hanging just as they had, long ago, their hems just barely above the small stack of wrapped presents on the carpeted closet floor.

Lydia tried to breathe through her nose as she went to her knees. As she eyed the presents and remembered the exact wrapping paper. Remembered the day she saw all this exactly as it was now. And with these sensory landmarks, the uneasiness grew. She thought then that whatever this was, whatever she was experiencing here in the middle of the desert, it was exactly why she hated the holidays. All of them. It was exactly why she'd moved to California, and why she had no plans on returning home.

She split the clothes hanging over the presents. She removed the top one.

No cars came as she shook it, as she listened, as she remembered having asked for the set of five construction vehicles that transformed into one giant robot. She remembered feeling no joy at this discovery.

Because of the smell.

And because of a sense of being watched.

Now, here, on her knees on the side of the road in Nevada, Lydia slowly lowered the present and leaned forward, looking deeper into the shadows of the side of the closet that was still hidden by the closed off-white doors.

And just above the last of the hanging coats, eyes there, looking back.

"*WHERE IS SHE?*"

Lydia hurried to her feet and stepped back from the closet. Half breathless, feeling unsafe, unsound, she looked to the half of the closet still closed.

Someone was standing on the other side of those doors. Someone flat to the back wall.

Beyond the closet . . . all open desert at dusk.

She looked to the open half and imagined those eyes, peering out from the darkness of hanging coats, the mustiness, the bad smell in there.

"Come out!" she yelled. Because she couldn't think of what else to say.

Had her mother been right? Was this her father's mistress?

But Lydia thought she knew the answer. The details of the event filling in . . .

And it was the last of the suppressed memory's elements to be had.

A case she did not want to crack.

Still . . .

She moved fast toward the off-white doors and flattened her palms to them and slid them to the left, even as the eyes she'd seen now appeared, at the bottom of a face, as the suggestion in the darkness became a figure, yes, hidden no more, a figure with long dark hair, eyes on its chin, half crouching to fit its enormous height into the confines of the basement closet of the Rabinowitz home.

This was no mistress, Lydia knew. This was no woman at all.

"I saw her through the window! I saw her in the house!"

Mother's voice in the desert sky. But Mother hadn't seen a woman. And somewhere in Lydia's trembling mind, she understood that her father had never seen this thing at all.

But Lydia had. Yes. As a child. The day her mother yelled about what she'd seen. The thing she'd seen crossing the living room through the home's front windows. The thing she couldn't have known was no woman, no man.

Lydia backed up without looking, and a car whipped by unseen. She cried out as the thrust from the passing vehicle made the dust rise so that the thing stepping forth from the closet appeared to be stepping through dark parting curtains.

Lydia ran to her car. She got behind the wheel.

She looked once and saw it, crossing the highway, its height, its walk, its impossible face.

A face she hadn't allowed herself to remember.

And she knew then, as she put the car in drive, as she told herself to *drive*, she knew then the reason she hated the holidays was because of this, this monster, this thing she'd seen in the basement closet of her childhood home.

She moved by instinct, stepping on the gas, and did not look to make sure no cars were coming. But none were.

Within seconds the thing was in her rearview mirror, still stepping toward her, still emerging, it seemed, from the closet, and from whatever opaque place she'd kept its memory for so many years.

Unable to stop herself from shaking, unable to calm down, Lydia lifted her phone from the passenger seat and swerved as she found her mother's number.

"Lydia?"

"I'm heading home," Lydia said, too loud, too fast, sure her mother could hear the terror in her voice. "I'm driving home."

"That's wonderful. Are you okay?"

"Yes," Lydia said. "Maybe. I don't know. I'm just coming home is all. I had it wrong for so long."

And she thought of all the times she'd made people laugh when she told them she hated the holidays. And she wondered how many of them would've laughed had she told them her home was haunted. That in the carpeted basement closet, a thing had been hiding by the presents, a thing so horrible her mind hadn't allowed her to remember it.

"Well, okay," her mother said. "I'm very glad to hear it. We can find a tree together. Though I know you don't care for—"

"No," Lydia said. "I was wrong, I had it all wrong. I'd love to find a tree. I'm on my way."

A wife believing she'd seen another woman through a window. A divorce. A home left behind by a family who did not know it was haunted.

Lydia drove.

Toward Michigan.

Toward snow and evergreens.

Toward Christmas she drove.

THE VERMIN MOON

Hailey Piper

A YEAR AFTER HER daughter's funeral, Melanie Jones holds a
burial for a rat.

Snowfall has been light so far this year, nothing like the white
hell that draped the town and slickened the streets while Riley was
walking home from middle school last January. Melanie only has to
clear an inch off the matted wet grass before jamming the iron-
headed shovel into the backyard soil. Hard earth shrugs off each
blow—she's a gaunt woman, never had much muscle—but she can
chip at it until there's a shoebox-deep hole, where Hopper will rest
beside Punchy, who died six weeks ago.

Hank stands on the porch above, hugging a dark robe around
himself. His cheeks are pink with cold, and his graying hair echoes
the overcast sky.

"Come inside, Mel," he says, annoyed. "Ground's frozen solid."

"Things don't stop dying to wait for springtime," Melanie says,
wiping dark hair from her sweat-dotted forehead.

Hank should already know winter is a mean season. Melanie
will never again mistake Christmas and New Year's for times of
warmth and cheer. She instead recalls the hospital's sickening clean
scent, its ticking machines as they failed to save Riley's life, and the
white-coated cemetery. The ground was frozen that day too.

If gravediggers could bury Riley six feet down, Melanie can
manage a fraction of that depth for the last of Riley's little friends.

* * *

The nightmare at first pretends to be a kindly dream. It shows Riley's eleventh birthday. Her pleading promise of being a responsible girl. Heading to Pet Pros and plucking up two squirmy blond rats—Punchy and Hopper. Little more than babies, thin and sickly, but a veterinarian instructs how to help them. Riley tricks them into drinking their medicine by letting them lick it off her fingers, makes sure they have plenty of cardboard and fabric for nesting, and keeps them clean and entertained.

She is responsible, exactly as promised. A little lady in every way.

Melanie never saw the car skid from the road—no one did—but her nightmare exhales an amorphous ice cloud that might be a pickup truck, a minivan, a white Cadillac. Hell on wheels to steal Riley away.

The sound of screaming tires melts into squealing rodents. A great verminous chittering eats at the core of Melanie's dreams, where grief chews a hole through some secret place within her. The stink of decay breathes through it. She claws at her insides, a Melanie digging through a greater rotted Melanie, as if she's dead and her body won't let go of her soul.

The death-stink fades. In comes the honey-sweet scent of Punchy and Hopper, their fur coated in musky oil after rodent puberty.

And then another scent. Too human. Too familiar. A scent Melanie thought she lost a year ago when she looked at Riley's unmoving face, caked in the sterile odors of a funeral home.

Her baby girl.

* * *

Melanie gasps awake and trembles. The house is cold around her—maybe the heater has died along with Hopper.

Except she's heard of this, hasn't she? Sudden cold can be a symptom of the dead.

Melanie peers into the darkness, not wanting to turn a light on and wake Hank, not wanting to confirm the room is empty. With the lights off, she can at least pretend a narrow eleven-year-old girl stands in the bedroom doorway, looking for her parents in the aftermath of a bad dream.

"Riley?"

The darkness is absolute, same as the chill. If Melanie turns a light on, will she see her breath? Will she see Riley, asking why her pets are dead?

"I took care of them, baby, like I promised," Melanie says. "They were old for little creatures."

Unlike Riley. Eleven years would have been ancient for a rat, but it's nothing for a daughter. Riley might have come looking for time owed. Time due. And her pets too.

Melanie keeps awake, waiting for something to happen in the night.

But nothing does.

*   *   *

Nothing happens in the day either. Melanie heads to work at the hardware store while Hank heads to the office. He's home when she gets home, and yet the house is an empty animal, hollowed of every organ the way Hank has been hollowed of concern. He's almost jovial at times, maybe excited to have the rats gone. No more reminders of Riley.

Why doesn't her absence hurt him anymore?

Melanie glances at the vacant cage, emptied of the rats' tangled nests and chewed-up toys. She's wiped everything down and plans to donate it to a small animal shelter.

But it's another reminder of Riley, isn't it? In her bizarre eleven-year-old paranoia, she made her mother promise that if she wasn't around, Melanie would care for the animals. Neither of them could be blamed when fate slid across the icy street and jumped the curb.

The rats became Melanie's responsibility, a promise kept. And now they're gone. She tells herself that isn't a promise broken.

So why does guilt haunt her thoughts?

*   *   *

She doesn't mean to visit Pet Pros on her next day off. It's somewhere to go, something to do, a refuge from winter's chill, and better than lingering at home, where Hopper rests beside Punchy in the backyard, and Hank moseys through an unburdened life. Strange that she sees the pets' burial site more often than her child's. If only Riley could have been buried at home.

Melanie squats on her haunches, at level with the rats behind finger-smudged glass. Most are thin furry noodles with fresh pink tails, but there's an older one as well, a victim of pet store purgatory. Melanie wishes she could set him free, but domesticated rats are little more than fluffy sausages on tiny legs. They have few survival skills.

She could rescue him—she knows that—but she would have to get at least two, and it wouldn't be the same as Punchy and Hopper. Different personalities, untouched by Riley. The new rats would be Melanie's pets, not her daughter's.

"Anything I can help you with?" a scratchy voice asks. A pale young woman with tattooed arms and spiky green hair stands in a dark purple vest, the nametag reading "KAY."

"No, that's alright," Melanie says, but then she looks to the elder rat, lying on his side. His head bobs up and down in hopes of understanding new sounds, new smells. "How long's he been here?"

"The big guy?" Kay jangles a key from the key ring at her side and turns a lock beneath the glass. The display for the big rat pops open. Her black-painted fingernails scratch behind his ear. "That's complicated. He was here, and then adopted, and then they returned him four weeks later. I think he's a year old now. It's weird here— pets go away, you think you'll never see them again, but every now and then, somebody comes back."

Melanie knows the feeling. She doesn't mean to be here herself.

"The kids at his last home weren't too friendly, so he bit one." Kay lets the big rat sniff her fingers, curious about her nail polish. "Animals are just animals though, being themselves. People call these guys vermin, but you know what the problem is? A child. They can show kindness, sure, but there's nothing crueler either. You ask me, kids are the real vermin."

Melanie stares at the big rat for another moment. And then she leaves the store.

* * *

A wintery wind assaults the house in the night, its cold fingers pawing at the shingles, windows, and outer walls. Scattered ice ticks against wood and glass.

Hank snores, unbothered through every blow. His sleeping sounds used to comfort Melanie, same as when she would listen to infant Riley snoozing in her crib, but tonight Melanie can't distinguish Hank's wheezing from the wind whistling through the trees.

All this air courses through the world, but none for Riley's lungs. Not since last January.

At the drowsy edge of another nightmare, something claws up from the grief hole in the back of Melanie's mind. Not the icy wind, but clumsy infant hands, little more than balls of dough. And then sticky kindergartner fingers grasping a candy cane. And then an eleven-year-old's gentle touch as she lets pink rodent tongues lick water droplets off her pale fingertips.

"Don't tease me that you're coming back," Melanie whispers. "It's cruel."

But children can be cruel, she remembers. Especially one intent on haunting her mother over dead rats instead of letting her move on.

"I did everything I could," Melanie snaps, fighting sleep and dreams.

Hank stirs beside her and mutters something. Melanie presses a hand to her lips, watching for him to rouse and ask her what's wrong.

But he settles again. Another snore soon quakes from his side of the bed.

Only when she lies back down and lets sleep blanket her mind does she hear another sound. It's a strange wind, blowing not through lungs or trees, but through some kind of musical instrument.

A single forlorn note haunts Melanie's thoughts until it fades into the night.

* * *

The sky spits flurries into the streets, slowing Melanie's journey to J&J Music Center since no one knows how to drive in even the lightest snow anymore. That's what coworkers used to tell her after Riley's funeral, her death inevitable when winter robs every driver of their competence.

And their compassion. The vehicle that struck Riley sped off, no witnesses, no suspects, leaving only a broken girl on the sidewalk, never to regain consciousness.

On grim days, Melanie imagines the vehicle existed solely to destroy her daughter, rocketing out from a portal in thin air and then vanishing into some vehicular homicide Narnia, where another winter could welcome the murderous driver.

Melanie barely steps past J&J Music Center's sliding doors when a cheerful voice calls out to her.

"Can I help you?"

No one can, yet people keep asking, Melanie wants to say. She bites her lip against unwarranted bitterness.

An older man approaches in a sweater and slacks, a smile gleaming between his deep brown cheeks. "Mohan," he says, shaking Melanie's hand.

"Melanie. I'm looking for an instrument, but I don't know anything about music. And I don't know how to describe the sound in my head."

"I can help. Process of elimination, that's all." Mohan points at one wall after another, where musical instruments reflect fluorescent lighting. "You have your strings, woodwinds, percussion, brass, keys, and guitar, although certain categories overlap. There's some classification debate."

Melanie dredges the nightmare's note into her mind. "Woodwinds?"

Mohan snaps his fingers. "See? Getting somewhere already. This way."

He leads her past shelves of piping that wouldn't look out of place at the hardware store, and then they reach a corner where the assembled instruments are mounted for display. Mohan pulls out his phone and queues up melodies played on different wind instruments.

"A recorder," he says, and a flat tune bleats from his phone.

Melanie shakes her head. "Something else."

Mohan nods and tries another. "Clarinet."

"Too deep."

"Flute."

Melanie pauses. "That's close, but—" She grips her head, fingers aching to plunge through her skull and dig the sound out of her brain. "An old sound. And rich."

"The material might be different," Mohan says. He reaches for a wooden flute about the length of Melanie's forearm. "This might do it. An ordinary C flute by design, based on early Yamaha models, with a walnut make. Not genuinely old, but strong and resonant. Isn't it beautiful?"

Melanie gets the sense that Mohan isn't saying this to convince her to buy the flute. There's genuine adoration in his voice, his eyes. Melanie almost forgot what fondness looks like in a man. Too much time has passed since she's felt any semblance of it in Hank. She wonders if less love means less pain at Riley's absence, a choice he's made to protect his heart. It must be easier that way.

Melanie almost envies him.

Mohan cleans the mouthpiece with an alcohol wipe and then plays a brief melody. The sound whistles in the back of Melanie's thoughts, wind through branches, breath through lungs, music through a grief hole that might resonate with a wooden flute.

"I think that's the one," she says. At least she hopes so as she pulls out her credit card.

*   *   *

Another nightmare visits her in the cold and windy darkness. There's no scent or feeling this time.

Instead, there is sight. Of Riley.

Her narrow frame rises through the grief hole and stands at the center of Melanie's mind. Skeletal trees brace the snow-coated backyard around her, as if Riley has returned to the living world not to visit her parents, but to pay respects to the pets she left behind. Above her shines a half-moon, one side hidden by the world's shadow, the other a glowing ivory tooth in the sky.

And in the wind, a forlorn note carries through the night.

* * *

Melanie wakes with a start. And with understanding.

This is not a haunting—it's an opportunity for reunion.

Melanie doubts Riley can point out the vehicle that killed her, or its driver, but if a mother can hold her daughter one last time, say she kept a promise, that will be enough.

The conditions have to match the vision Riley has brought. Outside in the winter night, snow on the ground, beneath the half-moon, playing a certain note on the wooden flute.

"I'll be there, baby," Melanie whispers.

She doesn't care that Hank stirs beside her. His ungrieving mind is ignorant of the world. People go away sometimes, they break your heart, and you think you'll never see them again.

But every now and then, someone you love comes back.

* * *

Melanie calls in sick from the hardware store the next day. "Caught a cold," she says, faking a cough. "Something's going around. This damn weather."

She then drags the empty rat cage over to the couch, where she lies down and stares at the living room's white plaster ceiling, imagining a glittering snowfield beneath bright moonlight. Tonight is the moon's first quarter phase, when it's cut perfectly in half between light and shadow.

"I kept my promise," Melanie whispers, running her fingers down the cage bars like she's strumming guitar strings. "And I'll make another—to see you soon, baby."

She touches her lips. Always whispering. Why? Hank isn't home, and even if he returns right now, who fucking cares? "See you soon, baby," Melanie says, and then raises her voice. "See you soon, baby. See you soon, very soon—SEE YOU SOON, BABY!"

She shouts so loud that her throat scratches and tears gush down her cheeks. Again, who cares? She's going to see her little girl again, and nothing can stop her unless the moon clouds over. She furiously checks and cross-checks the weather between sources.

Snow will fall briefly this evening, blanketing the town, but then the wind will clear the clouds and harden the white fluff into a glittering landscape.

The kind to shine beneath the half-moon.

*   *   *

A slamming door wakes Melanie from the living room couch. It's nearly five in the afternoon.

"Mel?" Hank calls. He appears from the foyer, bundled in his coat, forehead creasing in concern. "Didn't you go to work?" Before she can answer, his gaze settles on the empty rat cage. "Oh, Mel. You can't seriously still be upset about those things."

Melanie blinks at him. Has he noticed nothing that's gone on this past week? This past year?

Hank unbuttons his coat, every movement laced with impatience. "This isn't practical. There's a line between grief and obsession, and you're crossing it." He gives a wan smile. "But I guess it's your nature to care for things. Even if they don't deserve it."

The last bit is his idea of an olive branch. He doesn't want to fight tonight, already regrets what he's said. He wants to carry on with his jovial post-grief existence, no hole in his heart, his mind; no trouble from his wife.

Melanie sits up and fixes him with a dead-eyed stare. "What about a child? Does a child deserve my care?"

Hank's fingers freeze at the last coat button. "What?"

"Children can be kind or wild or cruel," Melanie says. "No matter how much you love them, they can break your heart. But you still care for them—and the things they care about. You don't pretend they're unimportant just because they belong to a child."

"That's not fair." Hank points a finger, either at Melanie or the cage. "This is about the rats? Mel, they're a couple of animals. We move on."

Melanie grits her teeth. "They were Riley's."

"You're not upset about *them*," Hank says, rolling his eyes. "You're upset about *her*. You got wires crossed between daughter and vermin so badly that you don't even know what you're sad about anymore."

"Riley loved them," Melanie says. "You didn't promise her, but I did, and—"

I need to show her that Mommy kept her word, Melanie wants to say.

"We broke promises to her before," Hank says. "All the time. Girl Scout cookie sales. Disneyland."

"But this promise was about something alive," Melanie snaps. "It mattered to me because I'm not unfeeling like you."

Hank's face crumples, and a dark curtain closes behind his eyes. At last, there's some hurt in him. Maybe even some heartbreak.

Melanie wishes she could grab those last few words and stuff them back in her mouth. Even if they're true.

"Hank—"

"Think I'll head out for dinner tonight. And maybe longer." Hank turns from the living room, rebuttoning his coat. "Take care of yourself, Mel."

He steps into the dark outdoors as the first flakes of snow drift from the sky.

* * *

The snowfall ends shortly after dark, and a biting wind slides over the house. Hank hasn't returned home, but this was never about him. This is between a mother and her daughter, and about the promise one kept to the other.

Melanie crosses the back porch, where the mean season's chill nips at her face. She doesn't mind, for once. Winter is an animal, less conscious than an infant, than a rat. It can only be itself.

The half-moon shines from the clear blue-black sky, the same tooth Melanie saw floating in her nightmare—no, her dream. Her premonition, if she does everything right. She hurries down the porch steps, where fresh-fallen snow crunches underfoot, clumping where she buried Hopper beside Punchy last week. She pauses at their unmarked graves and imagines Riley standing beside her.

"Soon," Melanie says, her breath misting. She clutches the wooden flute from J&J Music Center. "Very soon."

Only, now what? Does she play right away? Wait for a sign? She supposes so—the dreams have come to her unbidden. She should wait for the right moment.

The wind slices under her skin, painting ice down her muscles. Her naked fingers begin to ache, and she alternates holding the flute in one hand and stuffing the other in her coat pocket. Too much waiting and she might damage her blood vessels, even get frostbite.

Dark thoughts bubble from the grief hole—is Hank right? Has she mixed up her lingering grief for Riley with guilt over the rats' deaths?

Melanie couldn't keep them alive forever—that would have been an impossible promise, so what's causing this wretched clawing inside her then? Why can't she grieve like a normal person? Normal people don't wait in the moonlight for a child's ghost. Normal people don't snap at their husbands over dreams and superstition. She might've hurt Hank this evening for nothing.

But hasn't he been hurting her? Not a snapping bite like she took out of him. More a slow gnawing, mirroring the rats as they nibbled at nuts and seeds.

Hank could've given Melanie a divorce after the funeral if he stopped loving her then, an emotional mercy killing, but no;

instead, he's dragged this out across a year of emotional barbed wire and broken glass. He's put her through the kind of pain that makes someone stop caring about normal expectations. Normal is apathetic. Passive. It sits on its high horse, absorbing unearned praise for inherent righteousness it has never earned.

Melanie's love is a verminous thing beneath hateful normal. A cockroach. A rat. Maybe even a child, easily disregarded by everyone but her mother.

She shouldn't have had to weather this nightmare alone.

A chittering noise fills Melanie's head, the sound of rodents—or her husband. She shudders at the idea of Punchy and Hopper crawling up from their graves, not actually dead, Mommy fucked up; or worse, Hank coming home now, finding her frozen in the yard and judging her again.

But then the cacophony dies and another sound emerges from the grief hole. It is familiar music in the back of Melanie's mind.

The one-note theme of Riley's homecoming.

Melanie laughs into her free hand. It's so simple—if she were asleep right now, she would be hearing the sound in her dreams. But she's awake tonight to hear it, which means she's ready. The wind rakes thin tree branches and scatters snowy flakes. It's time.

Melanie takes a deep breath and blows into the flute as hard as she can.

The sound is a dying animal cry.

Melanie rips the mouthpiece out and gapes at the flute's shaft. She never asked Mohan how to play the damn thing. Part of her assumed the moment's magic would take care of it, that she would know what to do by motherly instinct.

She tries placing the balls of her fingertips over every other hole. The note is gentle this time, but too high. She alternates which holes are covered and which are open. She tries covering all of them, and then one, and then two.

Wrong, wrong, wrong, wrong. She should have asked for help in the music store or practiced through the day to find the right sound, instead of sleeping on the couch until Hank came home.

The back of her mind clenches, and the note weakens like a fading wind. Melanie's terror smothers the grief hole. She's going to miss her chance.

Don't you dare, she thinks. *I made another promise, and Mommy's keeping it.*

She forces herself to take a slow, calming breath. It shakes with wintery mist. She needs a blanket and hot tea, and probably a warm shower.

But more than that, she needs to see Riley again. No matter what.

Melanie covers the top flute hole and blows a note. The next hole, another try. And the next, the next. Two fingers here, two fingers there.

Down the flute. Other hand.

Try again. Closer.

There.

She finally breathes the right note. It swells at the back of her mind, and she gasps in brief delight. She then takes another deep breath, stiffens her shoulders, and blows the forlorn note through the wooden flute.

The wind thrashes around her, wafting snow into her eyes. She keeps going. Even as her lungs deflate, and her breath runs short, and her head dizzies, she keeps hoping that somewhere in the haze, she'll see Riley.

A blurry silhouette breaches the scattering snow, a standing shadow in the night. Maybe Hank has come home? Except this isn't the right size or shape for him.

And it isn't the right size or shape for Riley either.

The world blurs as Melanie at last runs out of breath. She sucks in frosted air and blinks over and over. Winter's wind ebbs around her, letting the snow settle onto the white backyard surrounding the standing shadow. Melanie blinks again, trying to discern the strangeness ahead. In the moonlight, she understands part of her mistake in guessing the figure ahead might be Hank or Riley.

Because there is no figure. An absence cuts through the air as if someone's opened a door atop the snow, cut from the air itself.

But there is no backyard through the doorway.

A deep blue sky hangs within the opening. Here the half-moon has reversed its shadowy and shiny sides, as if a lunar face has switched which eye it keeps shut and which it keeps open. Bright moonlight caresses sleek stony towers of intertwining black castles. They reach far into the gloomy distance, mounted by crumbling balconies and parapets, where child-sized figures skitter down steep inclines and winding staircases.

But they are not children. Not like Riley.

Barbed hair juts from their spines, and coarse fur covers their lengthy torsos and narrow limbs, stopping only around their beady black eyes, pale fingers, and naked pink tails. On every level of each castle, these child-sized rats scuttle on two legs. Some of them paw at stonework and glass. Others clutch iron hooks and cleaver-like swords in their thin hands.

Melanie's teeth chatter, and her breath chugs in smoky white clouds. This isn't right. She called for Riley, her child who loved rats, not children who *are* rats.

Where the hell is Riley?

The doorway clenches like a muscly orifice, and the grief hole in Melanie's mind does the same. Grief for child and guilt over rats might've crossed wires to become twin infections, eating away some enigmatic resilience inside her that separates her nightmares from the real.

Or maybe something cruel once left the world, a crossbreeding of types of vermin, and that should've been the end of it.

But every now and then, something comes back.

Through a grief hole. Through a doorway.

A looming silhouette breaches the gap, and Melanie staggers backward on crunching footsteps. The figure is larger than the rat-children, its face too human.

Melanie pauses as a grown man steps into the snow. He wears a dark green tunic and leather jerkin, and a narrow green cap sits atop his head. One hand is raised palm out, as if to calm her. Moonlight glints in his bright blue eyes, and white rat-like teeth gleam from his red beard.

Melanie can't stop shivering. "Who—" she begins, but her chattering teeth cut her off.

The grinning man steps closer. His breath crosses Melanie's cheek, unclouded with cold. She could reach out and touch his beard, but he reaches for her first, closing a gentle hand over the wooden flute.

"Dankeschön, mein liebling." His slow, friendly voice carries a grim edge. "Dankeschön."

Before Melanie can ask what that means, the man pries the flute from her wind-stiffened hands. Moonlight vanishes from one eye as he winks at her, and the cheer in his expression thrusts an icicle through her heart.

He glances over his shoulder, at the aging castles and skittering rat-children, and then he closes his beard-rimmed lips around the wooden flute's mouthpiece. Spidery hands dance down the shaft with expert quickness, and fluttering notes sing into the chill wind.

It's a charming melody. Melanie almost likes it.

But she has no time to admire the music. Squirming silhouettes fill the opening between the castle-filled otherworld and the one Melanie knows, and then a legion of rat-children pour into her backyard.

She stumbles back, hands covering her mouth against a scream. They are not children like Riley, not rats like Punchy or Hopper. These are old creatures, forgotten and lost, no kindness or curiosity in their dark eyes. Only thoughtless attention to a melody and a cruelty that stretches from their clutching hands into their crude weapons.

"Who—" Melanie tries again, and then, "What—"

But the question she can't begin, let alone speak, is *"Where's Riley?"* And the thought that she might have been mistaken, even tricked at her unusual intersection of child and pet mourning, barely flits through her mind before panic stretches the grief hole wide open and swallows everything she knows. There's no sense of Riley anymore. No sense of any thought.

There is only the castle dust Melanie smells pouring off the rat-children's fur, and the chittering she hears in their teeth, and the swelling horde she sees as they spill into the world. Pink tails slash behind their legs, and the vermin moon gleams along their vicious hooks and swords before they skitter into shadows, chasing a piper's song.

Spreading beyond the yard, past the trees. Over the neighborhood, and then the town.

Into the night.

THE BODY OF LEONORA JAMES

Stephanie M. Wytovich

THE EARLY MORNING sky was a massacre of cardinals, their red wings like blood clots sifting through clouds. It was early yet, the part of morning when it's still dark, still quiet, and the earth vibrates with rage, but the cardinals flew down to the forest floor in a conclave of slaughter, their feathers like crimson scalpels slicing through branches and leaves.

Despite the winter chill, the scent of pine and rot ran rapid through the forest, the decaying perfume a new skin for what had slept in the belly of the night. A gentle layer of frost dusted the ground, and the pitter-patter crunch of paws weighing on ice echoed through the copse of trees and settled near a wooden hovel, a modest home untouched for years. That is, unless you count the children who entered it on dares, or the women who heard about the body of Leonora James and needed to run their hands across the stained floor to see if the legend was true.

The birds circled a makeshift grave behind the house—a loose patch of dirt that never quite settled, no matter how many years she'd been buried, and they collectively pecked at the soil, their beaks sharp, desperate against the mournful cries of the woods. Never properly buried, her bones weren't deep. Instead, her body had become one with the earth when the weight of her death snapped the rope around her neck, her womanhood dragging her down, down, down to fester with the maggots and the worms.

Red wings fluttered madly as the cardinals got closer to her body. They frantically shifted dirt, dusted at loose soil, but it was their chirps, their gentle squawking that began to guide her spirit back into her remains, her teeth rattling, clacking against one another as the winter solstice licked them alive. Her messengers stood like sentient guards, impatiently waiting as they made a red circle around an unfortunate tomb, hoping for a quick awakening.

It was midafternoon when her skin started to regenerate, all those patches of porcelain flesh wrapping across wet, taut muscle like a piece of stretched canvas. It hurt, this rebirth. All the stretching, the way her muscles tensed together and cramped. Each step came unbalanced at first—a wobble here, a limp there—but eventually her pace evened, and she was able to appreciate the subtle wind against her naked gait. Even still, the reanimating hurt. Every nineteen years, Leonora woke up to red, to the crackle of blood to bone, meat to membrane. It was exhausting and painful, and the growing left her hungry, her stomach a barren desert, her tongue a shriveled husk.

As she walked toward her house, a trail of blood formed in her wake. The cardinals followed, their feathers thickening the red line as they walked single file behind her, entranced. The house was a reminder of memories she savored and moments she longed to forget, but there was no denying her pull to it. She needed its bones as much as it needed hers.

The forest watched her, the air quiet, still.

Snow fell in clumps and collected in the strings of black hair that fell down Leonora's back. She stood at her front door, her bare breasts two full moons, her nipples cracked and bleeding. She reached for the rusted knob and turned it while she pushed against the door with her shoulder. Dust erupted in hazy clouds as the wood scratched along the floor and welcomed her back.

She opened her mouth in a thin smile, and a centipede crawled out, then disappeared again through her right nostril. She coughed hard and stretched, her shoulders popping and dislocating as she tried to center herself and gain some balance. The cardinals collected inside, roosting on windowsills, rafters, and turned-over chairs, their beady black eyes never leaving her as she acclimated to her current state.

Near the windowsill sat three jugs of water, and next to them was a modest collection of food. Some of it was relatively fresh, others preserved in vinegar, and the remaining few were the leftover soldiers of canning season. She saw beets and pickles, honey, salted pork. A basket of sugared apples. The people of this town feared her—that much was clear—and even if most of them thought hers was only a scary story, a cautionary tale passed down from generation to generation, it seemed it was better to be safe than sorry. After all, the offerings were always there.

Hunger ripped through her body, a feral beast. Leonora reached for a loaf of bread. She tore off a hunk and jammed it into a jar of what looked like strawberry preserves. Saliva jammed down her chin as more of her teeth pushed through her gums. She moaned as she ate, the sweetness coursing through her mouth, down her throat, and into her stomach in swells of pleasure.

She devoured it all, scooped out the rest of the fruit with her fingers, and licked the jars clean. In an almost fugue state, she ate the meager feast in minutes, her jaw tired, her lips stained.

Leonora limped toward a bed near the back of the cottage. Unlike the rest of the house, the blankets weren't covered in dust. *Teenagers.* She sat down and pulled the cloth around her shoulders, savoring the warmth. For a moment, she thought about what it would be like to lay her head on the pillow and use this time to simply relax, to breathe and exist, quiet and still. It would be just her and the birds, maybe a daydream or two, but she knew those were foolish thoughts. If she wanted to keep cheating death, the bloodletting had to happen.

By sunrise tomorrow, the first girl would be dead.

* * *

Next to the hearth, there was a small hideaway almost invisible to the human eye. Leonora had found it as a child and had stashed her treasures there for as long as she could remember. She bent down on fragile knees and dusted off layers of sticks, ash, and dead spider carcasses that had accumulated in the space. She knocked on the surrounding area of floor until she heard a hollow *plunk*. Leonora grabbed the poker from its stand and used it to pull up a piece of the floorboard, then hurriedly stuck her hand in the hole.

Nineteen years' worth of cobwebs enveloped her hand. She patted the ground, ignoring the creatures and insects that crawled and slithered over her wrists and arms. When she felt the handle of the mirror and the string of her leather pouch, she pulled them out, eager to see them again.

The silver hand mirror wasn't anything special, at least not at first glance. It didn't have any ornate trimmings, wasn't handsomely polished, but what it lacked in aesthetic, it made up for in power. Leonora bit down on her tongue, waited for blood to fill her mouth. She licked the face of the mirror, her saliva and lifeforce mixing with the reflection of a ghastly woman, a woman who worshipped the very blood she'd been known for spilling.

Bloody 'Nora in the woods, hunting girls who are not good . . .

The mirror showed her snippets of the past, allowed her to revel in her kills. She watched as she slit the heels of teenage girls, how she washed their hair in honey and locked them in basements to starve. On one occasion, she'd collected their menstrual blood on a full moon and painted her face with it before falling asleep in the arms of an older maid, a beautiful woman with black hair down to her waist, who'd been dead for sixteen days. By the time she'd been caught, she'd killed nineteen women and drunk over thirty quarts of blood.

She takes their bodies, drinks their wine, licks the sinew from their spines . . .

Leonora reached for the leather pouch and pulled out three vials of dark, coagulated blood. She caught her now-toothy grin in the mirror as she removed the corks and placed one drop from each vial on her tongue. *Marion. Penny. Lucy.* Their essence tasted like copper keys, like iron horseshoes, her daughter's deaths a source of immense pain and unspeakable pleasure. Memories of the way they ran from her, how they barricaded themselves in their rooms surged through her mind. She recalled their screams, the way their chests opened like flowers, their wine spilling, collecting into her hands. Leonora's pupils dilated at the thought, a lightness lifting her, filling her with a mixture of lust and rage.

Her eyes went gray as a soft mist rolled through her vision. Like a bloodhound, she smelled her before she saw her. A young girl. Twelve maybe? Thirteen? The blood dripping between the girl's legs was cherries and honeysuckle, plums, and jasmine. Leonora salivated, thin strands of drool hanging from her chin. The girl walked along the edge of the forest, teetering the lines of safety as she moved through the soft snow, blissfully unaware of watchful eyes and century-long promises that acted more like curses.

Leonora laughed.

It was sad how easy this would be.

* * *

The birds got there first.

They sat in trees, left tracks in the snow. A few of them dropped feathers that landed in the young girl's hair. She would think it was luck, that her ancestors were looking out for her, gifting her something to let her know they were close by. *Foolish child.* The girl picked them out of her braids and smiled, her cheeks rosy, a sparkle in her eye.

Leonora watched from behind a briar bush, the red, frost-covered berries masquerading as her eyes. Thorns reached around her head, and she stood there, half naked and shaking, not from the cold, but from the anticipation of the child's flesh. She could already taste its warmth, the way it would wrap around her, take the years off her back.

And her blood . . .

A cardinal flew down and rested on the girl's shoulder, as if summoned by magic. In the distance, Leonora hummed, her voice a scratched record, a broken glass, but as it carried in the wind, the howls of her long-devoured daughters caught shape and turned her voice to crushed velvet. By the time it slid into the young girl's ears, it was all cinnamon and nutmeg, an invitation to self-soothe, to close her eyes, to rest her head . . .

When she fell onto the white blanket of earth, one arm crossed over the forest line, and it was just enough for Leonora to reach out and grab her, to drag her deep into the forest. Leonora's long brittle nails traced the veins of the young girl's wrist, her heartbeat quickening with excitement. She'd get creative with this one. String her up like a starfish, feed from one limb at a time. She'd drop to her knees and worship at the girl's altar, sucking blood clots from her sex, painting the snow red with her mouth. If she was lucky, the girl wouldn't lose consciousness too fast.

Leonora preferred not to dine alone.

* * *

It was dark by the time they got home. The girl was still asleep, woefully oblivious to the fate that awaited her. Leonora hauled the child's body to the back of the cottage to warm her by the meager fire. The girl's blond hair collected in pools of ash near the hearth as sweat blossomed on her brow like tiny diamonds, like fresh tears.

Leonora went to the hole beneath the floorboards to get the rope. A creature of habit, she preferred to reminisce in the ritual, and this cord was stained from years of use, the rust-colored lines and blotches a tease, a reminder of what awaited. But first, she picked up the mirror. She walked it over to the child and let its gaze sweep the girl's face and body. She wanted to remember every detail of what she was about to do.

She propped the mirror up against the windowsill and went to grab the rope, when her left heel erupted in pain, bringing her to her knees.

"What—"

The young girl stood up, strong and collected as she stared the old woman down. Her cherub face was scratched and bleeding, her knees and legs blackened from the wet earth.

"That was for my sister," she said.

Leonora reached for the wound to stop the bleeding, but the girl moved fast and slashed the blade once across her face and then back against her throat. The birds squawked and erupted in a frenzy as they flew throughout the room, some of them slamming into walls, others into glass.

Blood poured onto the floor in lakes of garnets, in small groupings of pomegranate seeds.

She had gotten cocky, careless. She watched as the child removed pansies from her ears, berated herself for not noticing the talon around her neck, the thorns pushed into the palms of her hands. The blade was concealed—*such a clever little cunt*—but part of her admired the child for her fight. It would make the girl's blood sweeter in the end.

A smirk broke out across Leonora's face.

"Don't even think about touching me," the young girl said. "I'll gut you faster than those birds could ever resurrect you."

Leonora stared into the child's eyes, her dark pupils channeling the demons she'd shaken hands with centuries ago. A hiss slid out of the gash in her throat as a black snake reared its head beneath the open flaps of skin.

The young girl acted fast, the thorns in her hands piercing the snake mere inches from her face. She slid her hand down its belly, vivisecting the serpent before throwing its corpse in the flames.

"That one was for me," she said. "I hate snakes about as much as I hate old hags who don't know when to quit." The girl picked up the rope and tied it around Leonora's wrists, then her ankles. Centuries worth of blood continued to leak from her wounds.

"Father said they found my sister bled dry in the woods, her body broken and left in a shallow grave. One of her eyes was missing," the young girl said. Leonora froze as the girl moved closer to her face, her soured breath ragged, rushed. "I don't know if you had something to do with the latter, but either way . . ."

The girl reached into her pocket and pulled out the frozen body of a cardinal. "Respectfully, I know these are your favorite," she said before shoving the bird, beak first, deep into the socket of Leonora's right eye.

Leonora moaned, her wails unholy, profane. She thrashed in her imprisonment, her body rocking back and forth as half of her world went black.

The young girl laughed.

"You know, my parents never got over her death. Mother killed herself shortly after I was born, and Father? He went mad with grief. Said the cardinals talked to him, told him to do horrible things," she said. "Thing is, the cardinals spoke to me too, but unlike him, I listened."

Leonora quieted. Fear crept across her face.

The girl leaned in and licked a stream of blood from Leonora's cheek.

"You were right about one thing, though, I'll give you that. Fight does make the blood taste sweeter, but between us girls, I much prefer the taste of fear."

Lenora watched as the young girl—a mere child—grabbed the mirror from the windowsill. The girl bit down on her tongue and when she licked the glass, the mirror sang the screams of countless murdered girls.

It was too much to bear.

Leonora spat at the child, her mumbles turning to spells that turned to curses. She tried to concentrate, but the bird in her eye threw off her balance, her sense of direction, and the blood of her victims drained from her faster than she could speak, her body weakening, decaying, stiffening.

"You know, the thing about curses is you can't cast them if you don't have a tongue," the young girl said. "But it's probably better to play it safe," she said.

And then she cut off Leonora's head.

* * *

The faint light of sunrise glowed in the horizon. Leonora watched from the house as the young girl dragged her headless corpse back to the grave she'd climbed out of mere hours ago. The child staked her body in the earth with long spears of sharpened birch, stuffed her neck wound with feathers. When it was done, she came back, tired but triumphant, and picked up Leonora's head.

Leonora couldn't talk, could barely see. The pain radiating behind her right eye was immeasurable. It sent knives through her temples, blurred the world around her. But still she watched, watched as the young girl eased herself into the grave, how she lay next to the headless body, slowly rooting herself into the earth, Leonora's head by her side.

Then she took out her knife.

"This ends tonight. No matter where you go, no matter how long it takes, just know, I'll be there, forever by your side, there to kill you, time and time again."

And with that, the child slid her knife against her own throat, her gore a river of rubies over both her and Leonora's chests, the two of them bound in blood, together in death, in life, and everywhere in between.

Leonora closed her eyes as the sun came up, as the young girl sputtered her last breath.

Beneath them, the snow-covered earth turned red.

MR. BUTLER

Clay McLeod Chapman

M<small>R. B</small>UTLER CAME back.

    He was waiting for me, left on our doorstep nearly thirty years later, as if he'd been delivered at an abysmal hour by some midnight Amazonian while my family—Christ, *my son*—slept inside.

How long had he been out here? Sitting in the cold?

I didn't find him until I went to pick up our paper. We're still subscribers, firm believers in print media and all that. I woke up before everyone else in our house, as usual. Nothing new there. I carried my coffee mug onto the front porch, to grab the morning edition, and was immediately met by the breath-clenching cold. Twenty degrees, easy. Maybe less. Enough of a drop for my lungs to lock with that first inhale. My T-shirt and boxers clearly weren't enough of a defensive measure against the dregs of January. Looked like we'd gotten six or seven inches during the night. I'd have to excavate our car from underneath that thick blanket of white if we wanted to drive anywhere. The sun had barely risen, an ashen pallor cast across the horizon, less light and more of a wintry gray haze.

That's when I noticed our newspaper wasn't where it normally was. Usually, it's tossed onto our front porch—somewhere near it, at least—a rolled up bone bound by a rubber band.

Instead, I spotted a box. A corrugated cardboard box.

We weren't expecting any packages. Neither my wife nor I had ordered anything online. Christmas had already come and gone. We were completely gifted out by now. Our family had entered a dead zone for home deliveries, all the duplicate presents returned and refunded.

This box shouldn't be here. *He* shouldn't be here.

"Albeeeeee . . ."

The coffee mug slipped from my fingers. Ceramic fangs scattered across the porch steps the second the cup shattered, sending a splatter pattern of milky brown liquid across the snow.

It had been so long since I'd heard his voice. The stiff glottal stop could've easily been the bitter breeze blowing in from farther down the block. *"Just the wind,"* as they say. Just a . . .

box.

That's all this was. *Just a box.* An uninhabited cardboard container, abandoned on my doorstep in the middle of the night, its auburn bulk sitting in stark contrast to the bland canvas of white all around us.

So . . . where were the footprints? Our front walkway was a smooth, untouched white plane of snow. Not a single track on it. Whoever delivered this package must've dropped it off before the flakes started to fall, I figured. Then why wasn't the box covered in snow too?

It's really him, I thought, immediately feeling a shiver not caused by the cold.

Mr. Butler once carried a Black+Decker countertop microwave. I say *once* because there was no microwave inside this particular container. The Black+Decker brand name was printed across its broadside, the stenciled letters scuffed into a blurry oblivion, barely legible, but I still knew what it was. *Who* it was. Mr. Butler had found me. After all these years.

He's come home, I thought. *To me.*

The packing tape had peeled away, husking some of the cardboard's skin along with it. One flap was flung out, bobbing in the breeze, while the remaining three curled inward—wilted petals on a browning flower—obscuring whatever might've been hidden within.

I kicked the box with my slipper; it limply skidded an inch without any resistance. The faint scrape of cardboard across the concrete steps set my teeth on edge, digging in my molars.

I leaned over, held my breath, and peered inside.

Empty. Completely empty.

Just a box. Just a . . .

a . . .

"It's me, Albeeeeee . . . your friend . . ."

What does a box *become* if it no longer contains the item that it originally carried? What do you call it then? Is a TV box still *technically* a TV box without the television tucked inside? Can a fridge container still be considered a fridge container without the fridge itself? Can a box still call itself anything other than *just a box* after its innards have been C-sectioned from its cardboard womb, all bundled in an amniotic sac of bubble wrap? Nothing more than a barren box now?

What is it? Tell me. I wanted—*needed*—to know: *What was he now?*

Just a box, right? Just a . . .

friend.

It didn't matter how many decades had passed since Mr. Butler last took me into his flaps . . . He hadn't changed at all. Not one bit. Exactly the same as the last time I laid eyes on him. Held him.

Whereas me? I looked nothing like that timid little boy he'd cradled within his comforting cardboard embrace. I can't even imagine what he must've seen. A man, not a child, all old now. A father myself. I was almost embarrassed—ashamed, really—of what I had become.

Could I even fit inside him anymore?

"Look how much you've grown, Albeeee . . ." The longer Mr. Butler whispered, the warmer his cardboard voice became, losing a bit of its rigidity with each word that drifted up from his stiffened lips. All four of them. Softening, almost. Becoming something tender again. Fleshy. A wisp of loose packing tape flickered in the wind, reminding me of a tongue lapping at the air.

"I've looked everywhere for you . . ."

I hadn't realized how much I'd yearned for him. Hadn't thought about him in years, to be honest—*years*—but glancing at that flap flitting in the wind, nearly waving at me, I couldn't help but lapse back to my sixth Christmas, when I'd first met Mr. Butler. My one and only friend . . .

"Did you miss me, Albeee?"

I had. I truly had.

"Then climb in . . ."

I don't know why I was so hesitant to pick Mr. Butler up. Was I afraid of him? I was, wasn't I? The cardboard was no longer stiff, softened since it'd been sitting out on our stoop overnight, spending countless hours huddled in the cold. Moisture had seeped in, its corners gone all soggy. He even felt like flesh when I finally touched him. Cold skin. A cardboard corpse.

There was some heft to the receptacle, surprisingly. Much heavier than I'd expected.

Was something inside?

Tilting the box slightly to one side, I heard that corrugated *zzzip* of a single loose toy skidding over its brown belly. I could've sworn it was empty. Had been positive it was. Wasn't it?

"I brought you something, Albeeeee . . ."

Just a box. It was just a box.

"A present . . ."

I peeled back its flaps, like picking the petals off a flower—*Mr. Butler loves me, Mr. Butler loves me not*—and peered inside once more.

Optimus Prime. I recognized the toy straight away, out of its packaging, poseable arms reaching up for me. Where in the hell had he come from? He hadn't been in there when I first peeked, and now there he suddenly was, as if this were all some kind of magic trick: *Watch me pull a rabbit out of my hat, ladies and gents . . .* Only this was different: *Watch me pull my childhood toy out from some soggy ol' cardboard box . . .*

I hadn't seen Optimus since . . .

Since . . .

The box started to slip from my fingers, but I kept my grip. One corner pitched forward, sending teeth all across the stoop. They showered across the icy steps: *tink-tink-tink-tink-tink . . .*

Not teeth. Legos. Loose plastic bricks of all colors tumbled out
from the box, hailing over our front porch. There had to be hundreds of interlocking bits falling at my feet.

"Bring me inside, Albee . . . please . . . it's been so long . . ."

Too long.

"Hold me."

I broke Mr. Butler down right there on the front stoop. It didn't
matter how cold it was; it didn't matter that I could barely feel my
own legs anymore, the numbness reaching all the way down to the
bone, I wasn't stepping back inside our house until I'd stripped this
box of its packing tape and collapsed the cardboard into a flattened
heap and tossed the whole goddamn thing into our recycling bin. I
was brutal about it—cruel about it—tearing him apart.

"What are you doing, Albeeee?"

"I can't, I'm sorry, I just can't . . ." I know how that made me
sound. How heartless. Mr. Butler had come back for me—found
me, somehow, after all these years—and this was how I treated an
old friend? After everything we'd been through together? After he'd
saved me?

"Why? Why are you doing this to me, Albeeeee?"

"I can't let you in." Near my son. That's what I was afraid of,
wasn't it? I didn't want Mr. Butler to know I had a boy of my own.
Didn't want the two of them to befriend one another.

"Why, Albeeeeeee?"

"I'm so sorry . . ."

* * *

What can I tell you about Mr. Butler? He was meant to be a lesson.
"A teachable moment," my stepdad told my mom. "Your son needs
to learn how to clean up after himself."

I was six, officially entering my Lego era. Mom went overboard
on this particular Christmas—my sixth—overcompensating for
the abrupt shift in our family dynamic by spoiling me with gifts.
Ever since Hank had moved in earlier that year, our routine had
drastically changed. Rules changed. Life changed. No amount of
toys was going to alter the fact that there was a new head of our

house, sprouting out from the stump my biological father had left behind.

Hank didn't like me. Even I knew that. He saw me as some vestigial remnant of my mother's previous marriage that either needed to be tucked away where nobody could see . . . or cut off completely. It became his mission to make up for lost time and teach me some long overdue manners. *"We'll make a man out of you yet, Albee. Mark my words."* I was another project for him to tackle around the house: Fix the loose window shutter. Fix the leaking faucet.

Fix this fucking kid.

Try picturing our first holiday as a freshly sutured family: Mom, on holiday overdrive, living in a state of denial that had her decorating everything. Silver tinsel dribbled from just about every corner of our house, reminding me of a runny nose. Jesus, a hundred runny noses, trails of snot everywhere. Our tree oozed metallic mucous. The living room glistened in it.

Here I am, some blissed-out boy in the middle of all that snot, unwrapping my very first Star Wars Lego set. The floor is a battlefield of wrapping paper, shreds spread everywhere. I've barely begun the arduous task of assembling my AT-AT Walker, which was all I'd wanted from Santa, and boy, had he delivered. It would take hours—days, maybe—to put this thing together, and I'd unwisely chosen the living room floor as my assembly line. The sprawl of Lego pieces was overwhelming, a minefield of off-gray bricks scattered across the carpet. One misstep and a toothsome shard would dig directly into an unsuspecting foot.

Seems like destiny that it would be Hank's heel. He'd been making his way across the room, toward the kitchen, when he abruptly halted and let out a shrill hiss. Seething, almost. He gritted his teeth and clasped his bare foot, hopping on the other in a bitter pogo.

"Goddamn it, Albee! What'd I say about your toys?"

Hank was never going to be a father to me. That's just a simple fact. His tightly wound-up temperament didn't permit loose ends— and what was I but the ultimate loose end?

It's weird to think back to him now, as a father myself, but Hank would play these head games and pass them off as *"raising me right."* Less of a corporal punishment-type and more an absolute mindfucker of a stepfather, Hank thought it best to give me the choice of how I wanted to discipline myself. Somehow that made it worse, letting me pick my punishment. What's the opposite of a *Choose Your Own Adventure* novel? *Choose Your Own Abuse?* Would I prefer twenty spanks or a month of no TV? No dinner for one night or no toys for a whole week? He'd offer me either physical punishment or the emotional toll. What would leave more of a mark on my psyche: Something quick and painful or long, drawn-out torment?

The choice was mine. Always mine.

I'll give Hank this, though: if it weren't for him, Mr. Butler would never have come into my life in the first place. Never saved me. In that respect, I guess, I owe Hank some thanks.

In his Lego-blind rage, Hank seized the nearest thing he could get his hands on—a Black+Decker microwave box—top of the line for 1984—and dragged the empty vessel over to me. A fresh box. All stiff. Rigid. Thirty by twenty-four by thirty inches, barely big enough for me to slip my scrawny body inside, I realized. The microwave had been a gift from Hank to my mom, but now there was the empty cardboard container to contend with. Tiny torn scraps of wrapping paper still clung to it, adhered to the box's broadside with Scotch tape, like flecks of loose flesh peeling away. The Styrofoam padding inserts had been pulled out. One corner was slightly dented, the crushed cardboard sinking into itself, a bit softer than the rest of the receptacle.

"Alright, Albee," Hank started in. I could even hear him gearing up for a lecture, his tone shifting into the low drone of Parental Mode. "Time for you to meet Mr. Butler . . ."

I had no idea who he was talking about. Did he mean the box? Who—or what—*was* Mr. Butler? There was nothing special about the container as far as I could tell, no pictures of grinning families emblazoned on its broadside or text beyond the Black+Decker brand name.

It was just a box. A bland, brown box.

"Mr. Butler is here to make sure we keep our house nice and clean," Hank continued. "He lives in our closet, okay? He only comes out when there's a mess somebody forgot to pick up." One by one, Hank plucked up every last Christmas present I had opened and plopped them inside the empty vessel's gullet. I could hear the plastic clatter of Transformers clashing against He-Man figurines. What had been hollow only moments ago filled up fast with my entire holiday bounty. There wasn't a single present left on the floor. Hank even picked up the Legos, pinching each plastic brick and depositing them all inside the box's hollow grotto.

"If Mr. Butler ever finds one of your toys where it's not supposed to be, guess what? It's his toy now. Mr. Butler will hold onto it until you learn how to pick up after yourself."

"Hank . . ." My mom started; her voice tentative, always uncertain of herself. She sat on the sidelines of my most recent *teachable moment*. Couch-side seats. "It's Christmas, hon . . ."

"He's never going to grow up if you keep mollycoddling him," Hank practically spat back at her. I swear I saw the silver tinsel shiver. "The boy needs to learn some responsibility."

Responsibility. That was Hank's big thing: instilling some responsibility in this feral child who'd been raised in the wild of this household without a proper father figure. He would straighten me out if it killed him. Whenever Mom tried to stand up for me— protect me from the man she'd brought into our house—Hank would shoot her down. Put her in her place. She'd fold so easily, like wrapping paper, always kowtowing to his strict disposition. There was no stopping Hank now. Our house was all his, and we had to make sure it was eternally spic and span, nary a toy out from its proper place, wherever that might've been. I sure as hell didn't know. All I knew was this wasn't my home anymore. Wasn't my family.

I was all alone.

"When you finally show a bit of *incentive* to do something *good*," Hank said, kneeling before me so that we were eye to eye, "then—and only then—will Mr. Butler *consider* giving you back one of your toys. You have to show *respect* to be given respect—do you understand?"

I stared back at him, fidgeting in my footed pajamas, feeling the need to pee. Mr. Butler sat between us, holding every last Christmas present I had just opened, like some mass grave of Transformers and G.I. Joes and Legos, all buried together in this grim cardboard crater.

"Tell me you understand, Albee. *Tell me.*"

I nodded without a word, knowing right then and there that I would never get to play with any of my Christmas presents. They were already gone.

"Mr. Butler can be a friend to you, Albee. He's here to help you, okay? Teach you. I've tried. Maybe he'll get through. If you're good to him, well, I bet he'll be good to you."

It was a box. Just a cardboard box. Why was Henry talking like it was alive? Real?

What even *was* Mr. Butler?

That night, after sleep took my stepfather, I slipped out from bed and tiptoed back into the living room. I tried to be quiet about it, but the plastic padding of my footed pajamas clung to the cold floorboards, peeled away with every step, released a tacky shucking sound. Every step sounded like I was tugging a thin strip of Scotch tape off from its dispenser.

It felt cold in the living room. Colder than the rest of the house. The Christmas tree lights had been left on; a buckshot of blinking colors spattered across the walls. The smell of pine hung in the air. Tinsel quivered when the furnace kicked on in the basement, this slight exhale of heat seeping through the vents and pressing against the silver strands dangling all around the house. Mother of pearl effluvia swayed all on its own, coming alive.

I did my best to maneuver over the creaking floorboards, taking every sticky step slowly, *slowly*, holding my breath as I reached the closet and opened the door. Praying it didn't squeal.

I was met by a padded wall of jackets. Nothing but a barricade of puffy coats and blazers, each gently rocking on its own hanger. I got down on my knees and parted the curtain of empty sleeves with both hands, hearing the high-pitched skid of thin wire hooks scraping over the rod just above my head. I peered deep into the shadowed alcove of our closet. For a moment, I could've sworn the cubby somehow reached farther than its architectural dimensions should have allowed, opening into some kind of clearing that went beyond the walls of our house. Had I just stumbled upon a darkened dell? The lingering glow from the Christmas lights couldn't reach this far into the closet, creating a blackened tidepool.

There he was—not a he, *it*. It was just a box, nestled at the center of our closet.

Mr. Butler.

Stop calling him that, I thought to myself. *It's just a box. A dumb box.* Hank could call it whatever he wanted. It wasn't alive—or whatever he pretended it was. It wasn't a butler at all.

It was just a box.

Besides, I had a job to do—I was on a mission. I'd come to break out my toys. Liberate them from their cardboard incarceration. Hank could take my gifts away, but he couldn't stop me from sneaking out in the middle of the night and playing with them while everyone else slept. All I had to do was peel back the four folded flaps from up top and . . .

The box was empty.

All my toys—*gone.* Every last one. Not a single Lego left behind. The entire container was vacant. Where were they? I didn't understand. They had been in here just that morning. I'd watched Hank dump them all in with my own eyes. Had he hidden them somewhere else?

I picked the box up with both hands and shook. Hard. *Harder.* Nothing tumbled out.

Empty. Absolutely empty.

Tears rose up in my eyes. I bit my bottom lip, trying to hold myself back from crying, but the best I could do was swallow my sobs, push them deep into my stomach, where nobody could hear me. Not Mom. Definitely not Hank. If he caught me bawling in the closet, I was sure he'd make another *stupid* teachable moment out of all this. This was just another one of his *stupid* abuses, I knew it. He'd probably planned this all along, knowing I'd come for my *stupid* Christmas gifts. I could just picture him in bed right then, wide awake, grinning to himself as he listened to me sniffle, as if this had been the plan all along.

I still gripped the box with both hands. My grasp tightened around its cardboard lips, squeezing. I wanted to tear Mr. Butler to pieces. *That'll show Hank,* I thought, letting tears dribble down my face and fall right inside the box's barren reservoir. Let the saltwater soak through the cardboard, softening it. *I'm gonna rip his stupid box to shreds with my bare—*

The cardboard flap caressed the back of my hand. Just the slightest corrugated graze against my skin.

I yanked my hands back. The box dropped to the closet floor. Nothing moved.

I held my breath, waiting. For what? Mr. Butler to move? That's what had just happened, right? I felt the flap flex. It touched me. Stroked my hand. *Tenderly.*

Cardboard, that's all. Stiff cardboard. Solid and unyielding. Just a box.

I slowly brought my hand back out and pressed my palm against its broadside. I rubbed my fingertips across its rough, woody-textured surface, feeling the subtle fuzziness of its grain.

Just a box, I kept repeating to myself. *It's just a box, just a box, just a—*

Then it flexed.

What had been rigid only a breath before suddenly contracted, the cardboard expanding beneath my palm, as if my fingers were pressed against someone's chest and they had just taken the deepest inhale. It *moved.* I swear the box stirred on its own, inching closer.

"Albeeeeee . . ."

Rather than run, rather than be afraid of this thing—this breathing box—I remained right where I was. I brought up my other hand and patted its bristled surface. I felt it ripple under my fingers, its corners contorting. Mr. Butler's lid was like lips, all four flaps whispering:

"Hold meee . . ."

"Hold?" I squeaked, the thinnest croak from my throat. So I tried again. "Hold . . . you?"

"*Pleeeeease . . .*"

"Like this?"

"*Yessss . . .*"

Mom found me in the closet the following morning, inside the box, curled into the cozy confines of its cardboard, a slumbering puppy nestled within its stiffened dimensions.

Mom didn't tell Hank. She was sure to scooch me back into bed before he woke and found me where I wasn't supposed to be. Our little secret.

Things started to go missing around the house after that. Small items at first. Silverware. Office supplies. It was barely noticeable, but over time, the number of cutlery thinned itself down. No one ever said anything about it—not to me, at least—but it became harder to find things. Inconsequential things. Staplers or tape dispensers or paper clips.

Mom worried about me. She knew something was wrong, even if she didn't do anything to help. I had wet my bed before Mr. Butler, but now she'd find me asleep in the closet. Nestled in a microwave box.

Just a boy in a box, all curled up. Eyes shut.

Christmas had come and gone. We were still in that postholiday gloaming, that liminal space between Christmas and New Year's, where it's far too early to take down the tree. You could feel the holiday cheer receding from our house as the decorations started to disappear. Where had all the tinsel gone? Where were the votive candles suddenly slipping off to? Did anybody else notice how our tree was losing all of its ornaments, one by one, as time went on?

Our house so felt clean. So empty of clutter.

Spic and span.

At night, once everyone else had gone to bed, I would lie awake for an hour or so before slipping out from the covers and sneaking out of my room, quietly making my way down the hall and toward the living room, to the closet, where I would open the door, gingerly twisting the knob so that it didn't squeal, and slipping behind the shadowed curtain of our coats.

Mr. Butler waited for me with open flaps.

I'd place one foot in at a time, stepping into that blackened tidepool. I fit just right. The box was the perfect size for my scraggly frame, as if it had been assembled just for me. We were meant for one another. *Made* for each other. I was the item and he was my vessel. A boy and his box.

"How's that?" I asked, rubbing Mr. Butler's corrugated tummy. I'd just fed him a pewter candlestick pilfered from the dining room. There were plenty more where that came from.

"More . . ." His appetite was growing, always hungry. *"More, Albeeee, more . . ."*

"Slow down," I whispered. "We don't want to get caught."

"Pleeease, Albeeeeeeeeee . . ."

"Tomorrow, I promise."

It wasn't until Hank's Rolex disappeared that he went on the war path. He tore our house apart, top to bottom, searching for it. He suspected I had stolen it, but of course I hadn't. What did I need with a watch? Mr. Butler was just hungry, and I was running out of options.

Our Christmas tree hadn't been watered in a while. Its needles began to brown and fall to the floor. I felt the thinnest prickle under my bare feet that night as I tiptoed into the living room, my hands full with Mom's fondue set. I pulled the pot out from the cabinet, along with all its miniature pitchforks. When was the last time our family had eaten fondue?

"I got you something," I whispered through the closet door. "You're gonna love this—"

The light flipped on.

Hank reclined on the couch. He must've been waiting, sitting in the dark for lord knows how long. A late-night stakeout. He was wearing his silk bathrobe. I hated that bathrobe.

"So. Albee. What've we got here?"

I instinctively stepped back, away from Hank, clutching the fondue pot as he rose from the couch and approached. He took his steps carefully, not rushing toward me. Closing in. "Where are you taking that?"

I felt the doorknob to the closet press against my back.

"In there?" Hank's arm shot out. At first, I thought he was going to hit me, but he only reached for the door. He opened it, sweeping me out of the way.

"*Don't,*" I started. I didn't want him to see.

Too late. Hank was already leaning into the closet. "What the hell—"

Mr. Butler was full. Everything that had gone missing around the house, inside him. Toys and dishware and small appliances. Even Hank's Rolex, a cherry on top of all this junk.

"Look at you . . ." Hank got down on his knees and started rummaging through the box. The clatter of pans filled the living room. The tinkle of silverware. "You little hoarder!"

Hank leaned in further, his head hovering above Mr. Butler's gaping maw. All four flaps fanned out, a cardboard chasm, inert and stiff. Just a box. Nothing more.

"I don't care what your mom says, I'm going to make sure you—"

It's hard to remember if Hank shouted or not. I don't think he did. I simply sunk one of the fondue forks into his shoulder. The slender stem stuck straight out of the nape, like an antenna protruding from his body. A weathervane at the base of his neck. His shoulder pinched as he tilted his head toward the fork. It must've hurt, but Hank looked more confused than anything. He stared back at me with this strange expression on his face, utterly flummoxed. *"Did you just stab me with a fucking fondue fork?"*

There was a breath between us before I knocked him flat in the face with the fondue pot. I heard—felt in my wrist—this resonate *tunk* when metal met his nose. Never much of a sportsman, this was as close to baseball as I was ever going to get. *Home run.*

Hank's upper body sprawled across the top of the box. His back now rested on top of the mound of missing houseware, arms fanning at his sides. Blood oozed from his nostril—I think it was the right? Maybe the left. He tried to pick himself up but was having a difficult time of it. He kept blinking. He looked so confused, eyes fluttering open and shut. He didn't understand what I'd done. He needed help, reaching his hand out for me.

"Albee . . .?" It sounded like a question, like he didn't understand who I was anymore.

Didn't know me.

"Now," I said.

Nothing happened. Hank just stared dumbly back at me, blinking repeatedly.

"Now!" I shouted.

"What're you . . ." Hank's body started to slip into a sitting position. His back remained pressed against the cardboard box, his head level to Mr. Butler's lid. "What're you doing?"

"Now now NOW!"

The quartet of cardboard flaps folded over Hank's head. Leathery lips sealed around his face, a stiffened rictus enveloping his skull.

That's when I know for certain that Hank screamed. Screamed with all the air he had left in his lungs. His shouts were muffled, muted by Mr. Butler. No matter how loud he shrieked, there was just no pushing through that cardboard Venus fly trap as it worked its lips over the circumference of Hank's entire head, the flaps wrapping their way down to his throat.

Then his shoulders.

His chest.

I watched as Hank's whole body slid down the corrugated gullet. Those thinly crenelated muscles kept working my stepfather deeper and deeper within Mr. Butler's stomach, a python passing a rat through its slender esophagus. It was a slow process, but I watched it all.

Inch by inch.

I don't know how Mom slept through all the screaming. Maybe she didn't. Maybe she stayed in her room, listening to Hank's muffled shrieks ebb into digestion. Maybe she knew. Maybe she's known this whole time and has never said a word to me. I don't know.

All I know is Mr. Butler made my stepfather disappear.

*   *   *

Can a cardboard box be haunted? Softwood trees, pine or fir—Christmas trees—have longer fibers than hardwood trees. Perfect for pulping. Shorter-fibered trees are used for paper, but the stronger filaments found within wood have the strength for corrugated cartons. An entirely different process, apparently, pulping for cardboard than pulping for paper.

Is that what Mr. Butler is? The ghost of Christmas trees past? Or is he the displaced spirit of some assembly line worker who passed away at the pulping plant, whose soul is now seeped into this particular microwave box, blended together forever in this cardboard vessel?

What is he?

Mr. Butler was my friend. That's all I know. He had been there for me when no one else in our house was. We played together after everyone else fell asleep. I told him things I never told anyone else. Not even my mom. To this day, nobody knows the secrets I shared with him.

Then why am I so afraid to see him now?

"Bring me in, Albeeeee . . ."

The box keeps coming back. Pops up on my doorstep. Every morning, I wake up and there it is—right where it was the morning before, on our front porch—waiting for me.

"I need you, Albeeeeee . . ."

I've thrown him away. I've burned the box in our backyard, but burning doesn't work. Tearing it to pieces doesn't work. Recycling doesn't work. Mr. Butler just keeps coming back.

"Hold me . . ."

What becomes of cardboard? If you have kids, an empty box quickly contorts into a pirate ship. A rocket ship. A battleship. My son could easily spend his morning converting this box into a corrugated submarine or tawny tank or lord knows what. Whatever his imagination wanted. Cardboard is a malleable substance, much like modeling clay. Its corners and flaps have the magical capacity to meld into the tail fins of a space shuttle ready to launch into the cosmos, its empty reservoir now a cockpit full of blinking controls and levers. A box like this can become just about anything in the mind of a child, as if that's what its cardboard is truly meant for. Whatever it carried is no longer important. It never was. Not to children, at least. Kids don't care about blenders or microwaves. They want the box.

A box is never just a box. Not for a boy. Not for me. Mr. Butler held something much darker. He contained my rage when I had nowhere else to put it, a receptacle for all the anger I felt for my stepfather. That man had given me a box, *just a box*, a vessel for my own punishment, and I filled it to the cardboard brim with all the fury a six-year-old could muster.

So, what is Mr. Butler now? What does he hold now?

I can't bring Mr. Butler inside. I can't keep feeding him. It doesn't matter if he's come back after all these years. I don't want him in my home. Near my family. My son.

He's hungry. I know he is.

Maybe that's what I'm afraid of. Lately I've found myself echoing Hank every so often. Things that he would say to me when I was a kid suddenly come slipping out from my mouth.

We just got through Christmas. Our house is a mess. There are toys everywhere. The living room floor is littered with junk. It's practically impossible to walk through our house without stepping on something. I finally hit my limit and told my son that if he didn't clean up after himself, I would introduce him to someone. Someone who lives in our closet. Someone who helps pick up after little boys who don't do it themselves. An old friend.

Maybe it's my turn. Maybe Mr. Butler is here to clean me up.

I open the front door to pick up our newspaper, but of course it isn't there. Just Mr. Butler squatting on the front stoop, all four flaps pulled back, flitting in the bitter wind. Waving.

"Hold me, Albeeeee . . . pleeease . . ."

One last time. What's it going to hurt? It's still early. No one's awake. Just once more. Me and my old friend. Me and Mr. Butler . . . I'm freezing my ass off out here, but what the hell. I only pray that none of our neighbors are watching me through their windows right now.

I step inside the box. Left foot first. Then the right.

I'm standing in the box. The lid barely reaches my knees. I'm far too tall to fit. How is this supposed to work? I must look so stupid, doing this, but I owe it to him to try.

"Ready?" I ask. I can see my breath fog in front of my face. I'm shivering, it's so cold out here. It's bound to be in the teens, and all I'm wearing is a bathrobe and slippers.

There's a warm swell around my ankles.

The heat rises up my shins.

I crouch down, squatting in the box. I barely fit. The best I can do is force my rump in. I'm crushing the cardboard with my rear end. I'm afraid it's about to tear. I'm too big for this.

"Sorry," I say.

"It's okay . . ."

Just then, one flap flips upright and wraps itself around my forearm. Another presses against my back. Then another. Suddenly all four flaps embrace me, pin me in place.

I can feel the corrugated ripples of its fibrous muscle tissue working over my arms, tugging me down. Pushing me deeper inside. *Deeper.* Somehow there's more space within the box than the actual dimensions could—should—allow.

The flaps find my shoulders. Each lid ripples against my skin and eases me in deeper. *Deeper.* The cardboard surface now reaches my neck, Mr. Butler's lips working their way over my throat. Suckling on my chin. I take one last breath of cold January air before plunging my head underneath the cardboard's surface, all four flaps now sealing me in its warm embrace.

All wrapped up.

FEAST OF GRAY

Lindy Ryan and Christopher Brooks

H E RUBS BARE hands in the dirt until he can't make the ground more flat, then lifts the bottle out of the paper bag and stands it there. A little cloud of dirt rises when he claps, and the way it warms his hands, he gets caught up in rubbing them together, breathing into them to increase the burn. Dim clouds of his breath vanish faster than the dirt from the air.

He reaches back into the bag and stretches his fingers around three round objects, takes them out together, as if he plans to juggle. He stands the three cylinders in an arc beside the bottle, the white one taller than the two darker ones with their matching silver tops. The Hostess pie package crinkles when he pulls it out of the bag, and he puts that farther from him, on winter-brittle grass as stiff as the pastry's wrapper. Dessert. It will come last. The flimsy plastic takeaway utensils he lays down side by side as if he were setting a table—fork on one side, knife and spoon on the other.

With no plate, there's just a blank spot in the center of the dead grass.

Greg flinches at a noise, whirls up into a crouch. It's all but silent this late at night in the small town—the snow muffles the sound even more—except for the voices behind him.

Two birds argue over a garbage can. The bigger crow dips his head in, comes up empty. The smaller one squawks, then swoops down from a granite obelisk and into the can. It hops out and waves a piece of paper like a flag. The wrapper looks too clean to do much for the bird, which springs across the pavement before it sheds the wrapper and launches into the air.

With a loud cry, the bigger one follows. The snow is flat and patchy where mourners stood that morning, and the crows steer wide of the dark spot in the snow where Greg has laid out his feast. Frost-hardened fabric sticks to his skin where cold seeped through his dress pants, and he only then notices how his knees ache.

The pair of birds soar low over granite markers and disappear into the trees that line the backside of the graveyard. *It should be two turtle doves, not crows,* he thinks. A halo of mist rings the bottom of the trees, and Greg imagines the birds going to play in the marsh beyond.

No birds will come bother him, he thinks to himself.

"Scarecrow," he mutters, and the top button of his shirt rubs his neck. His hands are cold when he fingers the collar. He took his tie off in the meeting, then left it in the motel room, he's pretty sure.

"Went to a meeting after the service," he says. No headstone marks his mother's grave—not yet. He kneels at the foot of a long narrow slip of dirt and pulls a folded postcard from his jacket pocket. "Someone, some stranger, gave me this."

The card shows a painting of a stormy sky, the sun barely able to break through. He sets it away from him, next to the pie. This morning the dark spot in the snow had yawned for the graveside service, a full-sized hole, even though all they had to plant, all that remained of her, fit in a fake-marble urn, the whole performance so unsatisfying. His stepfather, Mom's final husband, cried in the arms of his kids, crowding the hole in the ground so Greg had to hang back. Mom had never treated her stepchildren like she'd treated Gregory and Joseph. As bad as Greg's stepfather might have been, he wouldn't let her do her work on his kids. So, Greg needed to return tonight for his own service.

The way the card is folded, it makes a tent on the dirt, like a seating assignment. The first half of the word across the painted clouds faces away from him.

"The card says *Grateful*," he tells his mother. "She gave it to me because I didn't share, I guess." He pats the pockets of the coat, then reaches back into the bag, under the warm main course, and pulls out the pack of smokes. "You always said that was all crap—acts of contrition. Anyone too weak to stop drinking on their own would be useless sober anyway."

He pinches a cigarette between his lips and stands the pack on top of the silver lid of the cranberry sauce. It falls over, and he leans the pack against the can. The lighter is in a pants pocket. He has to flick it over and over, the other hand cupped around the end of the cigarette, before he gets a spark. He draws in a long breath, so much warmer than rubbing hands together. He coughs a cloud out over the feast, then lets the next warm inhale out a little faster.

"The thing is," he says, "the drinking isn't even the problem. Drinking is a *symptom* of the problem. My sponsor, Chelsea, told me that. The problem is your behavior, the things you say and do, like hitting your wife. The problem's you. I mean yourself." He takes the cigarette in his hand and shakes his head hard, wincing. "I take it back." He points the cigarette at the patch of dirt. "It's you, Mom. *You* at the end of that table in the New Hampshire house, holding court over me and Joe." He stares at his hand, remembers the way she'd point one of those impossibly long cigarettes of hers at them, bottle of beer in the other hand.

With no tombstone to glare at, he pictures his mother's face in the trees at the edge of the marsh. Her face rising from the snow and the mist, like a Rorschach test, like a dragon or Snoopy seen in the clouds overhead. "Thank god none of the other places we lived had a dining room table. Something so perverse about you sitting at the head of a table, Ma, your face getting meaner the thinner it got. But this . . ." Greg bites the cigarette and kneels back down, reaches both hands into the grocery bag.

"You get what this is, right?" The large package from the deli warms his hands. The plastic pops and crinkles when he grips it. "I mean, that time of year. Christmas dinner for Mom. The big show." The barbecue smell cuts through the frigid air as he lifts the package. The paper bag pulls at his wrists. A tear runs down through the Market Basket logo, the sound of paper ripping loud in the cemetery. He sets the chicken where a plate should go and snaps the tape on one side of the package so he can flip it open like a clamshell.

"A final Christmas feast, Mom, to make up for the last one." He laughs. The can opener lies with the knife and fork beside the chicken. He takes that, and the can of cranberry sauce from next to the white candle, and struggles to open it.

"You always made such a fuss about it when we were little," he says, setting the open can down. "We couldn't do anything in the house for weeks while you put on your pageant, the one time of year you'd do the whole pretense of being a mom," he says, "until you'd blame us for however you fucked it up. Like Joe made too much noise and distracted you, and *he* burned the turkey, when really you just didn't have the brains to set a timer."

The wick lays flat across the top of the fat white candle, and he has to force a thumbnail under to stick it upright. He bites the filter and sucks hard enough that the glow of the cherry fills the inside of his cupped hand. Stars fill his eyes as he holds the wick there, but it won't catch, and he doubles over.

"Then when he got sick," Greg says between coughs. "Then when he got sick." The cold air wreaks havoc on his lungs. "One more Christmas dinner. One more for Joey." He pulls it together and wipes tears from his eyes, then draws deep on the cigarette again. This time the tip of the wick glows but goes out as soon as he takes the cupped hand away. He goes to kneel but has to sit. The candle falls over between the two cans when he tries to set it down, and coughs wrack his chest and throat and head.

"Remember that motel room? Maybe not." He laughs, and it turns into a cough. "You got so hammered. Who could blame you. We'd already opened our presents, those books of Lifesaver candies? You could hardly stand up." He shakes his head. "I should talk." He'd been the one who took the chicken out of the oven and diced it up to drop in that big plastic bowl with a bunch of fifty-cent packs of ramen. "I threw everything together into this horrid, mushy mess, and I said, 'Mom, I don't think this is done,' and you screamed. You shrieked. 'Stove's already cool!' you said. 'What'm I

supposed to do!' And I said, 'Oven, it was in the oven,' and you—"
Greg laughs. "Bam!" He slaps the side of his head and glares at his
mother's face in those trees the birds had flown into.

"You made us eat it," he says. "Then we all got to go to the
hospital. I tell you, watching your mom nodding off as she shits
herself. That left a mark. The doctor asking me about the cut on
my head, and you coming to just enough to blame Joe." She'd
waved her finger, no cigarette, at her eldest son, that wasted child,
as the doctors tried to keep him alive, pumping fluids in him as the
salmonella outran the cancer. "Yeah, that zombie with the dead
eyes—he threw the can of cranberry sauce!"

The cigarette in Greg's hand is almost gone. "Oh shit," he says.
"Am I doing your fifth step for you? Am I rattling off your amends?
First meeting I ever went to, there's this little guy there—older guy.
Talking about how excited he was when he heard about the promises, how he instantly bought the whole thing, thought he could
save his girlfriend too—he says, 'I can do her fifth step for her!' Like
Jesus was in the room. But the program doesn't really work if you
have nothing to be grateful for. My sponsor, she says that's dangerous thinking, but it's not like she's rock solid."

He drops the filter at the foot of his mother's grave and grinds
what's left of the cigarette into the dirt. Already he feels colder,
inside and out. "I was so scared going home with you, Joey stuck in
the hospital. But you acted like nothing ever happened." He sits
down and reaches for the Hostess pie. "You pulled out those nasty
little single-serve frostbite pies," he says. "Not like this." He tears
the wrapper and takes a bite of the ice-cold filling. "They'd been in
the freezer since clearance last year." The pie she'd set out for Joe
had thawed, making a puddle on the Formica table. "Just another
Christmas dinner for the books."

The wind that wouldn't let him light the candle kicks up, and
the *Grateful* card dances across the cemetery, vanishing in the snow.

"Thing is, Mom, you're in there." He glares across the empty
cemetery, points his finger between his own eyes, and still smells
the cigarette on his hand. He breathes it in. "Even when I don't
drink, doesn't matter. I want to be better; I *try* to be better. Joey and

I used to talk about it—but you are in there. When I'd fight with my wife, my first wife, no blow was too low because you're in there saying, 'Go for it'; the most important thing is to win the argument, or at least end it—even if all you have is the back of your hand." Apple filling sprays from his lips, onto the chicken, onto the dirt. "Whatever stops other people from hitting their kids, their wife, that was never in you, was it?"

He sits with his legs sprawled on either side of the graveside Christmas dinner as the cold slices up through his body, fogs out of his mouth as he chews. When he exhales, it's only his own breath.

The whites of his eyes freeze in the night air. "You taught me so much." It's that look, that hate glare, he learned from her. The look he gave his own wife and children more than once. More than a lot.

"Oh, you taught me, like a Buddhist: no attachments. That's how I could go the last six years without seeing you." His eyes shoot darts, shoot laser beams, but the face he imagines for his mother in those distant trees, they've got no eyes to fire back.

He digs his nails into the dirt. "It's why you're here, two states away from the son you buried. Why I don't know my own son's last address or where my daughter and ex-wife live. Yeah, they stopped sending Christmas cards way before I stopped sending child support."

The face in the trees moves, his mother's face, and part of it breaks off. The mist swirls away from it as it slides away from the trees.

Not just a face, the whole of her, her figure, his mother's figure, steps through the mist.

Greg scrambles to his feet while reaching for the bottle and almost falls back to the ground. He waves the bottle like a club. Across the cemetery near the marsh, the figure weaves between gravestones, getting bigger.

But the gait is wrong. Whatever death might transform in his mother, it would not give her the strut of a teenaged boy. The young man crosses the cemetery toward Greg.

So, he thinks, *the kids in small towns still haunt boneyards.* The black figure crosses the cemetery in the dark, like Greg used to do in other towns.

He raises the bottle for the kid to see. He'll have to open the thing after all, offer the kid a drink.

"How much you hear me telling off my mom?" Greg mutters. Maybe the kid will give him a wide berth.

Unlike those crows, this young man does not steer clear. Greg looks down at the open can of cranberry sauce, the candle he couldn't light, the chicken that must already be cold. When he looks back up, this guest has come closer—close enough for Greg to recognize him, to recognize the wasted and thin face he hasn't seen in twenty-five years.

When he'd told his sponsor he had to come back for the funeral, she'd said to be careful, she'd said the veil between the worlds is thinner—for him, she meant, with his mother dying and the time of year—but Chelsea had been hitting the pipe again.

"Joey," he whispers.

It makes sense. While Greg had stood at the edge of the service this afternoon like any other guest, Joe missed it altogether.

Greg wipes a tear from his cheek. "Come to pay your respects?"

He stands the bottle in its place and picks up the cranberry sauce and the spoon and says his brother's name again. "You get what this is, right?" he says. "That time of year!"

The last Christmas dinner the three of them had together was worst of all for poor Joe.

The figure stands where their mother's headstone should stand. The flesh of his face so full, so healthy. He'd died when Greg was fourteen, their age difference just enough that Joe always looked like a man to his little brother. Now, at eighteen, he's every bit the baby.

"I must look so old," Greg says. Looking at his brother, frozen at eighteen, it's like looking at himself at that age. He never realized how much they looked alike. He had no one to point it out to him.

The child's face shows no expression. A ridiculous memory springs to Greg's mind, a TV show in which the hero returns, terrified to find herself walking the earth again. Without putting the can or spoon down, Greg holds his arms open wide and steps across the Christmas dinner, onto the cold earth of their mother's grave.

But his brother raises both hands, rock hard, into Greg's chest. It surprises him on a lot of levels. The chicken slides under his shoe as he stumbles but doesn't fall.

"You're worse than her," Joe says, his voice like winter wind, like crows' wings. Greg stutters, drops the cranberry sauce. "You have a son of your own," Joe says, "and you don't even—"

"You heard all that?"

"Heard it?" the ghost says. "We always said we'd never be like her." His face changes, the way the sickness changed it. "You promised—"

"You made me promise!" Greg shouts.

"We promised each other every day that we'd grow up to be good guys!" Joe screams, his face twisted like Greg's own son's, the last time he saw him. "If I wasn't going to get to grow up, you'd carry that for both of us!" Joe's face twists, so he looks older, darker, the way Greg imagines he looked at thirty, screaming at his first wife when she'd called him out for sneaking money for motel rooms he had no business in. "You were supposed to live the life I wouldn't get to!"

Greg trips again, and the chicken shoots out from underfoot. He spins, catches his balance, but falls to all fours when something hammers at his back. He scrambles away from the feast, realizes he still has the spoon, and drops that as he reaches the car path. The spoon rattles across the asphalt, and Greg unlocks his frozen knees from the ground, from the slacks, and sprints. Something rips, louder than the sound of the grocery bag, and his back is ice cold, so cold it feels wet. Something even more cold pierces his shoulder, then shivers across the back of his neck, down the length of his spine.

Greg screams, not words now, but shrieks like his mother, the harpy. The wind whips his screams from his mouth, but the tight grip on his throat cuts off his cries just as he reaches the gap in the iron fence, the threshold of the cemetery. This vise around his neck—it doesn't so much stop him in his tracks as lift him up from them. One shoe kicks the top of the gate, then both feet scramble in the air as the frost-crackled grass disappears beneath.

He tries to twist free, twist around, but icicles dig into his back, and he can't breathe. He reaches behind him, grabs at the thing as it clings to him, claws into him, and he finally cranes his head around enough to see a long, thin face and black eyes, as the grip on his neck loosens and he can breathe again, and the ground races up at him.

He slams onto ice-hard dirt. And something else. Neither arm will move, but the hand he can see from where he lies holds a bunch of black fur. Warm fluid soaks his shoulder where he feels his heartbeat.

Greg tries to sit up, and all the pain in his body centers on his shoulder. A black pool spreads, sticking his arm to the dirt, and he can see the stuff in his hand is feathers. He turns his head, and the broken glass of the whiskey bottle sticks out of his arm, so close he's afraid he'll cut his face. The cranberry sauce holds its shape, frozen in the mouth of the can.

The only light is moonlit snow stretching across the cemetery, broken up by other people's headstones. The snow fades to black as a figure walks away from him, toward the marsh, blowing rings of smoke in the air above its head.

I HOPE THIS FINDS YOU WELL

Eric LaRocca

I WAS ASTONISHED, TO say the least, when I first received correspondence from Mr. Alexander Kettering after only meeting with him once before at the private club.

Not only was I surprised to receive a message from him that was delivered by my valet on a snowy day in December, seeing as how I knew so little about the man, but I was even more bewildered to receive correspondence via an old-fashioned handwritten letter. I couldn't help but marvel at the formality of the custom—the devastatingly poetic antiquity I considered when I entertained the fanciful thought of stout and prematurely balding Mr. Kettering sitting down at his desk to write a letter.

Surely, he could have easily obtained my information from those in charge at the club and have sent me an email. I wondered why he had strained to be so decidedly formal—why he had endeavored to make such a ceremonial inquiry? Before even opening the envelope, I knew there was something gravely serious about his communication—an omen that told me there was the presence of calamity and misfortune lingering in the air like the presence of a heartsick specter. Naturally, it was one thing to send an email and initiate polite conversation; however, it was apparent to me immediately that Mr. Kettering's correspondence was prompted by an entirely different matter from the prospect of pleasantries to be exchanged.

After all, Mr. Kettering and I had already issued enough civilities the other evening when I encountered him at the private club. It was told to me in the strictest confidence by one of my associates that Mr. Kettering was a new member of the club and, in fact, had been recruited to join based on his enthusiasm as opposed to his financial abilities to contribute. While most of the patrons of the Lorimar Club were enrolled by those in charge, Mr. Kettering was touted to most of us as a very distinguished newcomer who would apparently change some of the club's dynamics with his youthfulness and vitality.

It of course had shocked some of the older, more conservative patrons of the Lorimar Club that Mr. Kettering did not own a chalet in the Swiss Alps, nor did he vacation in Mozambique during Christmastime, as did most other club members. However, the more accepting patrons of the crowd seemed overjoyed to welcome Mr. Kettering and most likely hoped his youthfulness would instill some verve into the activities we often indulged in. Customs had become somewhat tedious for most at the club, and even the stuffier, more traditionalist members of the club accepted Mr. Kettering with a politeness that was certainly not afforded to everyone who was accepted. No, certainly not.

In fact, it was usually customary for most first-timers to be subjected to a series of tests—a special course of endurance—in order to discern whether or not they were the right fit for our private coterie. Usually, these tests were the best method to root out those who were looking to advance their social status as opposed to really and truly reveling in the prospect of the wonderful community we had established.

What surprised me most about Mr. Kettering's indoctrination to our association was that he was never given the test that all others must endure. When I asked one of the chief executives from our board of directors why Mr. Kettering hadn't been tested like the rest, I was met with a frown and a stern warning to never question Mr. Kettering's status ever again. Naturally, I found it rather peculiar that such care, such dedication went into making certain that Mr. Kettering was awarded membership without going through the once-mandatory protocol. But I simply figured that the club was desperate for newer, younger blood, and those in charge were willing to sacrifice tradition in favor of remarkable applicants.

It wasn't until I received the letter from Mr. Kettering five days before Christmas that I realized something was dreadfully wrong.

I could feel it.

I could sense the threat of something approaching the same way harbor tides swell and churn violently when a cruise liner arrives at port.

Once my valet had abandoned me with the letter, I took the gilded letter opener that had been gifted to me several Christmases ago by one of the more affectionate and tender members of our club, Mr. Cedric Anton. I slid the sharp end underneath the crease and snapped the envelope open. Unfolding the letter, I began to read:

Dear Mr. Sutcliffe,

I hope this finds you well.

I also sincerely hope that you will pardon the forwardness of this letter.

It took great confidence to write to you in the first place, as I am told you are one of the most trusted and reputable members at the prestigious Lorimar Club.

I hope you will remember that we briefly met the other evening in the club's main dining room and enjoyed a pleasant conversation about my recipe for lamb chops with a cognac Dijon cream sauce. You had asked me for the recipe, and I promised that I would supply a readable list of ingredients as soon as I returned from my business trip to Cherbourg. I returned late last night and wanted to send across the recipe as soon as possible. You will find it attached to this letter.

However, I must confess: I did not write to you merely to share my recipe for lamb chops. Instead, I write to you with the hope that I may call upon you for your trustworthiness. I hope you will not think it presumptuous of me to think you would be inclined to aid me in any way given that I am such a new and inexperienced member of the Lorimar Club. I know for certain that you are busily engaged, and I do not wish to waste more of your time than I already have.

I write to you today with a great trepidation in my heart. I'm fearful of something, and I do not know how I can possibly define my fear to you so that you can understand how this fear has already begun to eat away at the patchwork of my life. Not only my life, but the life of my wife as well. I cannot pretend to claim I'm sophisticated when it comes to explaining what ails me. I'm a poor patient when I am routinely seen by doctors and others in the medical profession. Although I may be underdeveloped when it concerns explaining what exactly is wrong, I can say with certainty that something, in fact, is wrong. I believe that something truly reprehensible will occur at the Lorimar Club before Christmas.

As you most likely already know, I joined the prestigious Lorimar Club with the intent of satisfying some of my more unconventional curiosities and predilections. (I hope you will excuse the vulgarity that I must adopt in order to fully explain myself.) While I understand that some of the club members keep their membership private from their families, my wife is fully aware of my involvement and has never made an attempt to impede my participation.

In fact, she was ecstatic when I was first accepted to the organization and had made numerous comments with the hope that my involvement with some of the members from the club might satisfy some of the intense urges I've been experiencing for the past several years—urges that have undoubtedly weighed heavily on my relationship with her.

Of course, some might find it exceptionally odd for a wife to willingly go along with her husband's sexual escapades with other gentlemen. But my darling Valerie has always been so trusting and benevolent when it comes to our marital arrangement. She knows in her heart that I will never be hers fully, and how I love her and care for her differently than I do the gentlemen I seek out for sexual companionship. There's an

*obvious difference between the attachment I feel toward Val-
erie and the intense hunger I feel for camaraderie with people
of the same sex.*

*I needn't bore you with the details or make an effort to
justify my involvement with the Lorimar Club while being
married to a woman. I know full well there are countless other
gentlemen who belong to the organization who are in similar
heterosexual relationships to mine. I don't expect you to accept
me or judge me. However, I greatly wish to impress upon you
the feeling I have that something terrible will happen at the
club before Christmas. In less than five days.*

*To better understand my suspicion, I will need to explain
to you how I came to this sudden realization.*

*When I was first accepted to the Lorimar Club, the asso-
ciation was flaunted to me as an organization where gentlemen of a certain pedigree can make significant connections
with other compatible men. These associations may, of course,
lead to sexual relationships, as is very common. I was, naturally, excited for this opportunity, as I had felt starved from so
many of my cravings over the past few years. As you know full
well, it's nearly impossible to engage in this kind of secretive
activity without risk of being outed.*

*Although the association was promoted as an organiza-
tion dedicated to preserving sexual relationships between the
more distinguished gentlemen in our city, as well as bonding
over a shared love of expensive, uncommon cuisine, I fear
something far more sinister is occurring.*

*Without insulting you with the graphic details of my most
recent sexual transaction with one of the club members, I can
simply tell you how unsettled I was by the whole ordeal. Naturally, I don't expect the activity to be similar to the lovemaking
I practice with my wife; however, there was something distinctly odd about the way in which the fellow club member
solicited and consequently engaged with me. I feel queasy even
writing this, but it felt as though he had every intention of
devouring me whole.*

The gentleman ordered me to permit him to nibble and chew on certain areas of my person—to pretend to consume my fingers, my toes, my nose, even my eyes. Of course, I felt obliged to obey him, seeing as he was one of the more senior members of the club. However, it caused me tremendous anxiety. More to the point, it made me wonder if this particular gentleman was acting out some secret fantasy with me that I wasn't aware of—something he hadn't told me. I was especially unnerved—"disgusted" is probably the more appropriate word—when he confessed to me how he wished I tasted better. "It's not your fault," he told me. "Infants and small children usually taste more filling."

I wish I could tell you that this was an isolated incident.

However, it was not.

Instead, over the course of one evening, I became sexually engaged with several other older gentlemen—all senior members of the association—and our physical interactions ranged from basic foreplay to full penetration. Each gentleman I became involved with seemed to treat me as if I were some imported delicacy—a strange kind of meal to be savored. I became possessed with the all-consuming suspicion that they were using me for some perverted fantasy that they wouldn't dare share with anyone else.

When I asked one of them if it was typical for the older members to ask the newer members to engage in this kind of unusual behavior, they simply waved me off and told me not to breathe a word of what we had done together. Of course, I found it peculiar when the first gentleman ordered me to keep quiet. But I found it somewhat dangerous to the integrity of this organization when three other gentlemen ordered me to keep the details of our engagement private as well.

I hope this provides some insight as to why I feel the need to write you. Perhaps I've overstepped my bounds, and perhaps you're cross with me for being so vulnerable, so open with you. But I recalled the other evening when we met how you had said you hoped we would have the opportunity to chat again.

You seemed so sincere. Far more sincere and trustworthy than the other club members I've had the pleasure of dining and sleeping with. I wonder if perhaps I feel so intrinsically drawn to you as someone safe because we haven't coupled with one another. You've never asked it of me.

I do sincerely apologize if I've overstepped or offended you in any way.

There's a point to all of this, I assure you.

My presence has been requested at the Lorimar Club tomorrow afternoon at three thirty p.m. Although I found it unusual that I would be requested to be present so early in the afternoon, that's not what shocked me most of all. No. What truly disturbed me was that the senior officers of the club have requested my wife, Valerie, to be present for the meeting as well.

I suspect something horrible will happen at this meeting. Something truly unspeakable.

Although I do not intend to neglect this meeting, nor do I intend to deprive them of my wife's presence, I am hopeful that you might be kind enough to meet with us as well. It would mean a great deal to me. Of course, I completely understand if prior commitments keep you occupied.

Regardless, I thank you for reading this letter and for humoring some of my concerns. Perhaps I am incorrect. Perhaps I am needlessly worrying.

I hope I am.

God, I hope I am.

Would you be kind enough to burn this letter after reading?

I do hope that I have not intruded too heavily upon your time. Thank you for your attention and your kindness.

> *With very best wishes,*
> *Alexander Kettering*

My eyes went over his name again and again for what felt like hours.

I could scarcely believe he had the confidence to send such a letter. After all, we hadn't talked in depth. Of course, I thought he was attractive, and I had designs to engage with him at some point while he was a member of our club; however, it felt so strange to think a complete stranger like Alexander Kettering would confide in me something so devastatingly personal.

My mind began to race. I had several options. The first option: I could have my valet send for a courier to dispatch Mr. Kettering's letter to the senior officers at the club so that they were aware of his misgivings. But could I really be so callous and unfeelingly cruel? Especially to a brand-new club member with so much untouched potential. The second option: I could dictate a letter to my valet and tell Mr. Kettering in no uncertain terms that I was occupied tomorrow afternoon at three thirty PM and did not wish to be involved in his affairs with the association. Once again, am I capable of being so uncaring and inconsiderate? It pained me to think how likely it could be that I am, by definition, a cruel, unforgiving person. The third and final option: I could write to Mr. Kettering and comfort him with the knowledge that I would attend the meeting tomorrow at three thirty PM at the Lorimar Club.

With much hesitation, I called for my valet and asked him to bring one of my fountain pens to my desk so that I could write a letter to be sent by courier at once.

* * *

The following day, I ordered my valet to send a car for me, as I would be going to the Lorimar Club. When he asked me if I had mentioned the proper destination—given how early it was—I told him that I was not mistaken.

He sent for the car, and in a matter of minutes I was being whisked away to the club downtown. I sat in the back seat, nervously wringing my hands together as I anticipated what was to come. I watched the windshield wipers snap back and forth; the clogged roadway ahead was blurred beyond a screen of snow that seemed, all at once, to appear and then hammer away at us.

Finally, we arrived in front of the club, and I climbed out of the back seat. Mr. Kettering was already standing there on the front steps of the entrance. He was surrounded by several senior officers—their hats dusted with freshly fallen snow. I came upon them, and they parted for my arrival.

"My dear Sutcliffe," one of the senior officers said, greeting me with a halfhearted wave. "I didn't realize you were going to be here."

I noticed how many of the officers wrinkled their faces at my appearance, clearly bewildered by my presence.

"I invited him," Mr. Kettering volunteered reluctantly, eyeing me for some semblance of approval, as if I were the one in charge. "I had such a lovely chat with him the other night. I thought it would be good to have him here while we met."

The senior officers shrugged and began filing inside the entryway to the club.

Just then, I noticed a young woman pull on Mr. Kettering's sleeve as she seemed to appear from out of the snow, like some kind of Yuletide spirit.

"You were going to wait for me, weren't you, darling?" the young lady said to him.

"Yes, of course, dear," Mr. Kettering said, glancing at me. "Mr. Sutcliffe, I'd like to introduce you to my wife, Valerie."

The young lady's chestnut-colored eyes flashed at me unreservedly while she adjusted a small pendant on her winter coat that bore an etching of a cherub from an Italian fresco.

"Delighted to meet you, Mr. Sutcliffe," she said to me.

I offered her my hand, and we remained tethered there for an instant before we eventually broke apart and filed inside the private club's foyer.

I watched her as Mr. Kettering removed her coat, and it was then I noticed something that immediately explained to me the poor man's apprehension, his nervousness.

Mrs. Kettering rubbed her distended stomach—the unborn child she carried there.

"Oh," I exclaimed, nearly forgetting myself. "How much longer?"

Mrs. Kettering's lips curled when she smiled at her husband.

"The doctor says we can expect him very soon," she told me, looping her arm around her husband's. "We're terribly excited."

It was then I noticed how some of the senior officers seemed to circle around Mrs. Kettering, eyeing her stomach's hidden and precious cargo, and it was then I truly understood the fear etched across poor Mr. Kettering's face—the horror that seemed to churn relentlessly in both his eyes.

The older men congregated around us and regarded both Mr. and Mrs. Kettering as if the two of them were about to deliver a consecrated and divine gift—a hallowed and almost divine kind of feast.

"Perhaps we should retire to the board room," one of the older officers suggested, pulling Mrs. Kettering along by the arm and farther away from the protection of her beloved husband.

"I'm positively famished," he said.

THE BURIED CHILD

M. Rickert

AN EARLY FROST sparked rumors of a hard winter. The once-resplendent morning glories withered into brown blossoms on black vines; the mums, expected to brighten doorsteps for weeks, shriveled into corpse bouquets, but just when Marlene had grown accustomed to the coldest September on record, summer made its riotous return. Ground bees swarmed in grass that shot up like a threat in the night, and the star moss grew, once again, celestial. Even the roses bloomed well into October, clotted red sprouted like fairy-tale wounds from thorned branches. Yet, only death is said to last forever. One November night the temperature fell. A thunderstorm cut the sky with shards of light, and a howling wind tore the leaves from their branches, littering yards with the bright confusion of red, yellow, and gold that glittered in the morning with a whisper of snow.

* * *

When sirens screamed in the distance, Marlene paused in her raking, to face the juniper tree in her backyard, before looking up at the salty snow that had fallen intermittently. *Blah, winter!* She stuck out her tongue, and a flake landed there, melted before her lips were even closed.

Such a simple thing! Nothing, really. A single snowflake when she would soon be surrounded by so many. Still, it felt like she'd swallowed a secret. Not the rancid kind from her past. A secret filled with light.

Hope, even.

Marlene went about doing her errands (the Piggly Wiggly for groceries, the mill for ice salt) in a state of enchantment she attributed to winter's surreal arrival—crimson petals in the snow, asters encased in ice, geese flying north instead of south—pretending no interest in the murmuring buzz of gossip that reverberated around her, the same word repeated over and over again.

Bones.

Only after Marlene was home, settled with her tea by the fire, did she indulge her curiosity, as if it didn't matter. But, when she upset her cup as she leaned over to extract her phone from the purse set by her feet, spilling brown liquid onto the arm of the chair, she ignored it in order to scroll through the community Facebook page.

Bones. Found by a child walking with her father who had ascended the small hill on the south side of town to restore what he thought was a Halloween decoration upset by the storm. The property looked abandoned but clearly wasn't. What other reason could there be for toy bones to be scattered there? He stood for a while, brushing his thumb across a gritty spot on the thing, his reverie broken by the sound of a child singing.

"Something about that," he'd said. "I don't know how to explain it. The voice . . . I don't know. All of a sudden I realized it wasn't plastic at all."

He'd scrambled down the hill to scoop up his silent daughter, cleaving her to his chest as he scanned their surroundings for signs of danger.

"Who's there?" he'd asked, but no one answered.

You can listen to the 911 recording and hear for yourself the fear in his voice.

*   *   *

Marlene walked through her snow-dusted backyard. It wasn't possible. The world didn't work this way. But when she got to the juniper tree, she peered into a ragged hole beneath it, rimmed with snow like some kind of Middle-earth margarita. Empty.

*   *   *

Before Marlene buried the bones under the Juniper tree, she had carried them for years in a bag sewn from red cloth with black thread. They rattled when she moved them and sometimes when she didn't. On the day she learned her mother had died, Marlene snuck out of her apartment to cut the strings of her neighbor's wind chime, which, made of wood, did not chime at all, but clamored like the bones.

* * *

Marlene had never escaped the terrible thing she did. But had it escaped her?

* * *

She didn't worry about visiting the site. It would have been strange if she hadn't joined her neighbors to stand at the border of yellow tape that held them back from the mounds of roots and stones, chips of glass and old pennies. Marlene knew that would be all they would find. There were no more bones. Only the hands that had scuttled across town, under cover of the storm, seeking freedom or reunification or something only the dead know about.

Marlene didn't even realize she was smiling until she heard the soft, dreamy sound of a child singing, and her foolish grin collapsed. A little boy of six, staring at her.

He was there, and then he was gone.

No matter how wondrous the journey of the bones had been, no matter how profoundly it had expanded the possibilities of reality, what was lost was lost forever.

* * *

The first thing Marlene noticed the next morning was the silence. Snowing again, and snowing hard. She slid into her slippers, pulling the old brown sweater over her pajamas as she walked carefully down the stairs to the kitchen, where she put the teakettle on. How welcome the silence! How lovely the juniper tree's coated branches, how white the ground beneath it. How gray the sky.

Is it magic? Marlene wondered.

The only answer, a piercing scream. The teakettle.

*   *   *

A funeral for hands.
The small box, empty.
The grave marked "J," as in Jane or John Doe.
"Precious child," in script beneath the lone initial.
Beyond the dark gathering, Christmas lights shimmered gold and white, blue and red. Snow fell on the frozen ground. They would come back in spring to dig a real grave.

*   *   *

Snow!
It pelted the windows.
It drifted softly.
It hardened to ice.
It blew in angry swirls like the dust of ghosts.
It came with a howling wind.
It arrived in the night, hushed as whispers.

*   *   *

Cleave: "To split or sever. To adhere firmly, remain faithful."

*   *   *

She is lying in bed when a light cracks through the door, arriving with the silhouette of her mother, whose long robe murmurs like the sound of secrets as she walks across the floor. Marlene knows what is going to happen. She tries to make it stop, but her entire body is paralyzed, as if she has eaten poisoned berries.

Her mother sits on the side of the bed, to thread the needle. She pulls a black thread from dark air and draws it through the tiny hole, knots it with her long fingers. Marlene tries to speak, but the words won't form. She has lost the power of her own voice. Her body. Her will. Cold fingers lift Marlene's lip to press the sharp point into resistant flesh.

How can such a small thing cause the whole body to suffer?

The thread pulls through. Strangely, that part feels almost good. A relief for a moment before the needle darts in again. Top lip to bottom.

*   *   *

"Get your brother," her mother said. "He's playing in the basement. It's time for him to come up now."

Marlene wondered why he would play in the dark he feared. "You need to come with me. Why are you sitting so still, like a doll?"

Her mother hollered, "If he doesn't listen, you will have to hit him. Sometimes that's all that works."

Marlene said, "Why is there a red ribbon wrapped around your throat?"

"Don't make me come down there, or you will both be in trouble."

Marlene said, "You need to come now. Why aren't you listening to me? Do as I say!" Then she smacked her little brother so hard his head fell off and rolled across the floor.

She screamed.

Her mother came down the stairs with the soup pot and said, "Bring me the cleaver."

Marlene brought her the cleaver.

The basement was very dark, but Marlene closed her eyes.

That night Marlene's mother spoon-fed the distraught child stew, in bed.

"Oh, Mother," Marlene cried, "can't you put him back together again?"

Her mother pursed her lips and drew an imaginary needle through her red lips. "This is something we will never speak of again," she said. "You must never tell anyone what you did, or they will take you away from me forever."

Marlene thought that besides being a horrible, disgusting sister, she was a terrible daughter, but the next morning her mother said, "I can't deal with all your mess by myself. Because of what you did, we're moving. Wrap these bones in newspaper, put them in this bag, and take it to the river. Fill it with rocks and throw it off the bridge."

And that was that.

Marlene did almost everything as she was told.

*   *   *

Her brother's hands, mottled with purple and stiff as stone.

*   *   *

Marlene, the murderer.

*   *   *

Marlene loved her job in the library. She enjoyed the hushed space. The sound of pages turning. She did not appreciate the clattered click of keyboards but grew to tolerate it. There were many perks to working in the library—the cupcakes in the break room on employees' birthdays. The children looking up at her in anticipation during story hour. The way books came across her desk that she might never have discovered on her own, like the tattered volume of fairy tales that turned up later that winter, after almost all talk of bones had been replaced with complaints of the weather.

Marlene loved stories, especially the ones with horror. Why had she avoided fairy tales so long? Probably because her mother had loved them. But after the bones' astonishing journey, Marlene decided it was time to claim some wonder for herself.

She took a walk around the block after dinner that night, as she often did, to help her digestion, which had been poor ever since she was a child. When a car slowed past, Marlene tensed up, prepared to fight against all sorts of dangerous creatures, but the car continued on its way, and when a shadow flickered from the edge of the road, Marlene wondered if it might have been a fairy.

The fire was still burning when she returned, her house toasty warm. She put on her flannel pajamas, made hot chocolate, and sat by the fire, holding the slender volume, prepared for her life to change.

*   *   *

Once upon a time, in a village made of stone, there lived a child with a cruel mother. The father traveled frequently to distant lands, returning with a bounty of green and dirt, root vegetables and milk in canisters. He implored his wife to agree to move, to raise their child in a land of flowers, but the mother had a fear of other people and places. She'd seen a stranger once when she was a child herself, a weeping woman who arrived on a dusty horse, begging for water. The stream was on the other side of town, and the villagers were tired from their own work. After the creature collapsed, the stranger tried to cup her own tears in her hands, to pour into the horse's foaming mouth, but the creature was dead. When the villagers began to carve up the animal to roast over a fire, the woman became hysterical and called everyone barbarians.

"I will never live with people so stupid as that," the mother said. "What must it be like to not understand how life works?"

"Mila," the father said, settling his daughter on his lap. "Do you know what I saw?"

Mila shook her head no.

"Snow."

What's this now? the mother thought. She'd seen that look on her husband's face years before. It was the look he used to have for her. *Who was Snow?*

"Looks like flowers," he said. "Very tiny white flowers falling from the sky. But cold."

Falling flowers, the mother thought, *the man is an idiot.*

"Please bring me some, father," Mila said.

He shook his head. "Daughter, I cannot. It melts. It disappears. Like a dream. It would be gone long before I return. Unless . . ."

"Yes, Papa?"

"You come see for yourself."

The mother screamed. "That you would do this to me! Take away the only thing I have left. Here," she thrust an imaginary blade toward her chest. "Just cut my heart out and eat it. You might as well."

That night Mila was awoken by her father softly brushing the dust from her face. "Shh," he whispered. "I'm taking you away from her."

"To snow?"

"Yes."

She was happy. She was terrified. She was only a child and did not know what to do with the storm that formed inside her. She opened her mouth and screamed. Her father's eyes grew wide as saucers. He shook his head no. But it was too late. Her mother burst into the room. Silver plunged into her father's back. He fell beside Mila and did not blink.

"Oh no," her mother said, her voice strangely flat. "I thought he was an intruder."

"Help him, please," Mila cried.

"Yes, yes," her mother sighed. "Now, go sleep by the fire. I have to think for a while."

It was still dark when Mila was awoken by her mother. "You need to leave before anyone sees you," she said. "First, go to the root cellar and bring me the sack of potatoes, six onions, and all the carrots. Then go to the stream and bathe yourself. Don't talk to anyone about what you did, or they will take you away from me. After that, walk upriver, fill the bucket with clean water, and bring it back here. Do this several times. You will work up an appetite. But don't worry. Tonight, we are having stew."

"And Papa?" the child asked.

"Gone," the mother said.

"To snow?"

"To snow, to ash, to dust. What's the difference?"

Mila took the long walk to the stream, where she watched the cold water blossom red around her. Then she went upstream to fill the bucket, which she carried home. Her mother dumped the water into the big pot over the fire. Mila took so many trips to the river that she wore holes into her little slippers. The villagers called to her as she passed, "Little girl, why are you doing this big person's job?"

"Tonight we're having stew," Mila said.

"Stew?" the villagers said. "We would like some of that."

Mila thought she should tell them they weren't invited, but remembering she had been instructed not to speak at all, said nothing further. Her mother was angry when so many arrived for supper, but there was plenty to share, and in the end, she enjoyed the power of being admired.

The stew was delicious. Though Mila was almost too tired to eat, she managed to finish three bowls, her eyes growing heavier with every bite. Her bed had been stripped, but no matter. She was so tired she curled up onto the itchy mattress, dreaming of tiny white flowers falling on stone. When she awoke in the morning, the scent of stew hung heavy in the air, and the rooms were dreary.

A feeling poked in her gut, sharp as a bone.

"Mother," the child asked, "when will father return?"

The woman laughed. "Ha," she said. "You still haven't figured it out?" She pointed at the soup pot, still simmering over the low fire, her father's boots on the hearth, and finally at the girl's belly.

* * *

Marlene ran to the bathroom. She threw up her dinner of palak paneer, her lunch of peanut butter on whole wheat, her breakfast oats. She had eaten nothing more that day, so what else could possibly come? She retched saliva until it burned and then, with a great heave, a putrid lumpy brown liquid, clotted with flesh and tinged with blood. She tried to pretend she didn't know what it was. Her brother.

* * *

Snow is not white, but translucent.

Snowflakes reflect the light and scatter it in many directions.

The sound of crunching snow is caused by its crystal branches breaking.

All snowflakes are formed around a single particle, either a piece of pollen or a speck of dust.

* * *

The next morning Marlene called in sick. It snowed heavy wet flakes for hours, and she wandered through the rooms, occasionally sitting in a chair, as if she'd never tried it before, like Goldilocks. Late in the day, the snow stopped, and the sky became a shroud.

When night fell, it was so cold, even the stars shivered. Only then did Marlene walk across her glimmering yard, stumbling on the uneven terrain, to stare at the place beneath the juniper tree where the hole had been. "How long did it take," she whispered, "to claw your way out?"

As if punched in the gut by a ghost, she gasped and bent over, small flakes spewing from her mouth. First there were just a few, but soon there were many. Snowflakes swirled around her face and drifted down to join the others, both wondrous and terrible. She would never be able to separate what belonged to her mother, what belonged to her brother, what belonged to her, and what belonged to the dust.

At the sound, faint but unmistakable, Marlene slowly turned to face the house where two figures stood, silhouettes in the window, waiting for her, one softly singing, the other threading a needle.

With appreciation for:

"The Juniper Tree," Brothers Grimm
The Juniper Tree, Barbara Comyns
"The Juniper Tree," Peter Straub

FATHER'S LAST CHRISTMAS

Lee Murray

PULLING HER SHAWL tighter around her shoulders, Kate slipped into the Great Hall behind a serving maid and a drabble of tardy courtiers. She shivered. The salle was near freezing, despite the festoon of brocade and velvet covering the walls, and the lick of the fire in the hearth. It seemed as if the winter's rawness were reaching up from the aging flagstones, through her threadbare cast-off slippers, to creep into her bones. Yet it wasn't merely the seeping cold of the stone nor the castle's icy draughts that chilled her: the King was dying. Cursed by the witch he'd had burned at Michaelmas; he'd been stricken with a strange malady ever since. His healers had been whispering all day that the old man would be lucky to see the morrow, much less the feast of Saint Stephen, and Kate could believe it, given his deathly pallor and the labored rattle of his lungs.

Now, on the eve of Christmas, his twelve children had been summoned before him for what would surely be the King's final Réveillon. Except that princely dozen had not attended his table to eat his stuffed pheasant, drink his ale, and wile away the midwinter eve with tales of their beloved monarch; they had come to hear him announce who among them might succeed him on the throne.

As the thirteenth child, a bastard girl, the issue of the King's dalliance with the late queen's sister, Kate had never been in the running, but she would not miss this for all the world. The King's choice was still to be determined. Whichever of his offspring offered him a gift deemed worthy of his legacy would be the next to wear the crown. The future of the kingdom, and Kate's own livelihood, were in play. She could barely contain her anticipation. Indeed, no one in the castle had talked of anything else for the past sennight while the princes made their secret preparations.

Kate pushed her way through the throng, to a corner, where she leaned her back to the stone sill. She grinned. All the wolves were here. Her half brothers. Circling for the prize. And all of them so competitive, the night's revelry was bound to be interesting.

To the King's right was Arthur, the eldest, already graying at his temples, his black tunic glittering with jewels. Arrogant and assured, he was feigning interest in his platter, but in truth his attention was on the King's milk-skinned page boy.

To the King's left, the twins, Dale and Dunstan, cruel pranksters, fenced one another with their skewered poussin, and next to them, Edwin, also rumored to have been a twin until he ate his brother in the womb, flicked a bone to the hound snapping near his heels.

Francis, the family cleric, was brushing snowmelt off his shoulders and drying his boots near the hearth, while Christian, the dullard, was hunched at the table, slurping on giblets and dripping juice down his front.

Kate squirmed. On the opposite side of the table, Marcus, her nearest in age, was staring right at her. Marcus was a weird one. If she could help it, Kate didn't like to be the subject of his interest. As a child, he liked to drop things from the castle gates, just to see them burst on the road. It had started with fruit—ripened apples and plums—but when the excitement faded, he'd moved on to dropping hedgehogs and puppies, and then there was the toddler, the son of the stable master who had fallen to his death, the child's cranium dented like cheese and oozing whey on the gravel, and Marcus, loitering on the ramparts, the only one to see, although he swore it was an accident.

"You!" Kate's attention was dragged away from Marcus. It was Harald. Also a bastard, but male and handy with a blade, so one their father acknowledged. He grasped her rudely by the forearm and thrust his ruddy face in hers. "Don't idle there in the corner. Bring more wine, girl," he demanded, and he waggled an empty cup in her direction.

Kate bristled beneath her shawl—he knew very well she wasn't one of the castle drudges, even if she spent her days in the kitchen— but then, she knew better than to deny Harald, having suffered his beatings more than once. A rib on her left side, broken in one of Harald's rages when she was nine, had knitted poorly and still pained her in the cold.

Dropping her head meekly, Kate slipped off the sill, claimed a jug from a passing servant, and poured a draught into his cup, taking care not to spill it on his finery. Harald eyed her suspiciously, then grunted and turned away to take his place at the table. Kate sighed.

"Did I miss anything?"

Startled, Kate gave a squeak, but it was only Lisbet, Kate's old nurse and her sole ally since the King had tired of Kate's mother and banished her from the castle a decade ago. She'd been whipped off to an abbey in the north, or so people said, but why then had she never said goodbye?

"Not yet," Kate replied, still holding the jug of wine.

At that moment, her father's advisor, a hook-nosed sycophant, rapped his knife against his platter, the clang carrying over the chatter of the courtiers. "At the King's pleasure, we will begin the gift-giving ceremony."

The crowd hushed.

Lisbet took the jug from Kate, and they scuttled to the sill.

The King lifted his head and coughed, his thin shoulders shaking with the effort, then spat a gob of thready white liquid on the floor. The spasm over, he nodded for the advisor to proceed.

"As the King wishes." The man bowed his head, his hook nose almost scraping on the floor. "Remember, the most princely gift shall be rewarded with the keys to our fair kingdom. We shall begin with—"

"Me! Me first. I have a gift for the King," Christian shouted. He clambered to his feet, wiped his greasy hands clumsily on his tunic, then rummaged in his purse. He pulled out a grisly rabbit's foot and thrust it into the air. A stringy sinew trailed from the knuckle and the animal's fur was matted with dark black blood. "I offer this rabbit's foot, so the kingdom will have good luck for hereafter," the fool proclaimed. He beamed with pride, but his face fell when the crowd around him crowed with laughter. Harald guffawed so hard that he sloshed his wine on the table. Even Hooknose raised his eyebrows.

Still hovering near the hearth, Francis stepped across to Christian, cuffed him on the shoulder, and pushed him back to his bench. "A fine sentiment, dear Christian, and a worthy gift, I'm sure. Your brothers will be hard-pressed to best such an auspicious offering."

Christian grinned broadly, too dim to realize the praise was false. The court tittered at his expense. Everyone knew the King was never going to relinquish his throne to a man who barely knew his letters. All the kingdom's princes would have to die first.

"Since you have the floor, Prince Francis, perhaps you would like to present your gift?" the advisor asked.

The tremble of his jaw betrayed Francis's annoyance. No doubt he'd hoped to be among the last to present his gift and thereby create a more lasting impact. But everyone was waiting, so he strode to the middle of the room and stripped off his cloak and tunic.

The courtiers gasped. A lady seated nearby gave a nervous giggle. Even Kate was surprised. Underneath his tunic, Francis wore a hairshirt, not of the usual sackcloth, but woven of thorns and brambles. In a theatrical flourish, he lifted the shirt off his shoulders, revealing the bloody ruin of his back. His skin was crisscrossed with grazes and gouges, some still dribbling blood and pus and others scabbed over with dark crusts. Kate clucked her tongue at his ambition. Francis must have been wearing the shirt since the moment the throne went up for grabs. He turned a slow circle, his arms raised, displaying his wounds on his goose-fleshed skin, as if he were the Savior himself.

"But that's not a gift," Christian whined, still clutching the pitiful rabbit's foot.

"It is a *symbol*, Christian," Francis chided. "A display of the suffering I am willing to endure in service of the kingdom, as our father, the King, has done these past forty years."

Sacrifice. Kate almost choked on her own spittle. Her *father's* sacrifice. What of the sacrifice of Kate's mother, his sister-in-law? And the late queen? And what of the King's elder brother, the rightful heir to this accursed realm? The lad had stepped aside in favor of his brother (arguably at the tip of a blade), running for France when he was scarce old enough to sit a horse and the late king was still hale on the throne. A posse had been sent to France to recover him—who ordered it done, no one knows—but it seems the young prince had died. People whispered of the flux or possibly the pox, though none could say for sure. Whatever had befallen the lad, he had certainly never come back, and the King had not uttered his name since . . .

Lisbet laid her arm on Kate's and shook her head gently. A warning. Now was not the moment for Kate to call attention to herself. Kate covered her displeasure by retying her shawl.

Hooknose interrupted Francis's posturing. "An honorable gift, Prince Francis, which no doubt the King appreciates."

In fact, the King hadn't bothered to lift his head, much less his eyes. Nor did he move for Gavin's fatted calf, nor the queue of black hair that James insisted had come from an exotic land far to the east, nor even for John's Viking goblet carved from a walrus's tusk. Only Thomas's gift, the mummified finger of John the Baptist in its gilded reliquary, warranted a flicker, but then again, the King's amination might simply have been a prelude to the coughing fit that caused Hooknose to demand more logs be added to the fire, and blankets carried from the King's bedchamber.

It was only after that, when Dale and Dunstan took the floor, that things started to heat up. Dale began by sweeping away the King's platter. The metal rang out on the flagstones, which woke the old boy up, so it was not such a silly move. Then, clutching an end each (though it hardly needed it), the pair lifted their gift onto the table.

Dunstan unwrapped the parchment packaging.

Hooknose stared in puzzlement "What exactly is—"

"It's a Bible," Dale said, pushing back the wrapping.

"Transcribed by monks," Dunstan added.

"And bound in whore-skin leather," his twin finished.

The advisor peered into the blossom of parchment and wrinkled his nose. "Indeed."

The King mewled. He gave a weak wave.

Ever attentive, Hooknose hurried over to his liege. He lowered his ear to the King's crusted lips, listened a moment, then turned to the twins. "While this is a fine gift," he said, "and worthy of the wager, there are two of you. The King would know which of you claims it."

Dale and Dunstan looked at one another, understanding dawning beneath their winter beards. If their gift were chosen, only one of them might rule.

There was a split second of stillness, then a shrill twang resonated through the chamber as Dunstan unsheathed his sword and lunged headlong at his brother.

Courtiers scattered. Benches rolled.

But Dale twisted, arching his back, so Dunstan's blade pierced, not flesh, but the table, biting a gouge out of the wood.

Dunstan howled. Seething with fury, he whirled and lunged again, but Dale had already jumped away, snatching up a silver tray to bunt away the attack.

The crowd roared, urging them on as they swapped blows— strike and parry, strike and parry—neither man making ground. Hardly surprising; the pair had been dueling one another in jest since they were still in swaddling. Yet, the hardness of their expressions told Kate this was no jest.

Tiring of the exchange, Harald threw his sword to Dale, who caught it, releasing the tray even as Dunstan pivoted. Dale did not waste the advantage; he dragged the steel through his brother's hamstrings.

Dunstan screamed. He stumbled. Fell. Blood glutted the stones. Unable to rise, he stabbed wildly. Dale moved in to finish it but slipped on the blood-slick and fell forward onto Dunstan's blade. It slid between his ribs, even as his own sword skewered his brother's arm, slicing through the artery.

The fire dampened, cold licking through the hall once more. Dead or dying, the twins lay humped before the throne, their blood slowly freezing on the flagstones.

The crowd fell quiet. Kate rubbed at her arms. It was a shame. They weren't the worst of her brothers.

Hooknose nodded to a pair of the King's guards, who ran in and dragged away the bodies, creating a garland of blood on the floor.

The ceremony continued.

Edwin was next up. The prince stepped to the dais, his wolf-hound bounding at his heels. But in a flash, the prince whirled, plunging his knife into the animal's hide. The dog yelped and struggled, but Edwin held fast, pushing the spike home. When the dog had ceased its flailing, Edwin sliced it from throat to queue, cutting away the straggly vessels to expose the animal's heart. He lifted it pulsing from its bony cage, curls of steam spooling from the organ as it cooled in the hall's midwinter chill. "I offer the heart of a loyal subject," Edwin said, while the blood ran down his arm and onto the floor.

Christian chortled in glee.

"We should stop this at once," Francis thundered. "It is inhuman."

Harald snorted. "So you would have us stop now, would you, Brother? Now that a dog has been put to death. Yet you said nothing about the demise of your poor brothers."

Francis lifted his chin. "Dale and Dunstan fought of their free will. This slaughter of innocents is beyond the pale."

Harald's eyes narrowed. "Perhaps it is your own gift that pales."

The cleric glowered.

"Let him be, Harald. His back is itchy," Edwin quipped.

While they were bickering, Hooknose gestured to the King's guards with a sweep of his arm. A soldier broke away and pulled the dog's limp corpse through the aisle and out of the hall. By now, there would be a small heap congealing in the castle courtyard.

"Let's away, love. I smell a bad portent," Lisbet murmured into Kate's ear. She would know; it was Lisbet's sister burned on the pyre at Michaelmas. But Kate shushed her former nurse. Despite her affection for her, they could not leave now. There was too much at stake.

Hooknose looked to Harald, who took his sweet time strutting to the center of the room. Harald looked over his father's subjects. Cleared his throat. "I have journeyed the four corners of the earth in service of the King. And I have seen many wonderful things: palaces, ships, and even a mighty elephant. Today, I offer my Lord a token from my travels."

Opening his fist, Harald circled the room, so all could witness his offering. Kate stood on her tiptoes and swayed this way and that for a glance of it amid the courtiers' heads.

Is that all?

Laid across Harald's palm were a dozen tiny gold nuggets.

Thomas snorted with derision. "There isn't enough gold there to fashion even the smallest bauble."

"The gold is of no import, Thomas," Harald retorted. "It is their source that is significant."

"How so, Brother?" Gavin called.

Harald did not speak at once. Instead, he juggled the gold kernels, throwing them up and catching them again, filling the air before him with a golden circlet.

Eventually, he said, "These are the teeth of a Moor, extracted by my own hand—and a bloody exercise it proved too."

"Do you mean to give the King a new smile?" Christian asked, setting up chorus of chuckles.

Harald grinned and poured the nuggets in a pile near the other gifts. "I do indeed, Brother, for I offer my pledge to seize our prosperity whenever and however the kingdom may require it. I will not shy from it. Be it grain or gold, I will pluck it from our enemies' mouths."

The King grunted. Acknowledgement or approval? Approval, no doubt. The King had never baulked at plunder when his coffers were dwindling. And Harald clearly saw it as a positive sign, because he bowed low and grinned before moving back to his place at the table.

Only two gifts remained.

"Prince Marcus!" Hooknose said. "We await your gift."

Kate scanned the salle. Where was Marcus?

Suddenly the doors to the Great Hall blast opened, and Marcus swept in, bringing with him a glacial gust from the outer hall, and a snowy package tucked under his arm. Several candles flickered out.

"It is appropriate that I should follow Harald," Marcus bellowed as he stalked down the aisle, "since I too bring a gift from beyond our boundaries." He upturned the sack, sending a severed head bowling toward the throne.

Nearby courtiers drew back their slippered feet.

The head slowed to a stop. Face down.

"Although, mine cleaves a little closer to home." He bent to lift it, dangling the bloody head aloft by its scalp. "I give you our good neighbor, come to join the evening's merriment."

Arthur scoffed. "He does not look so merry."

Marcus giggled. "No? And yet giving is a reward in itself. Our neighbor's Yuletide wish was to surrender his lands to our care, an idea, I'll admit, I put into his head, but only after it was cleaved from his shoulders."

The King sighed deeply.

Edwin spat. Harald dashed his cup on the floor.

Kate couldn't believe it. It was Marcus who'd lost his head. Did he not see what he had done? He'd gone too far this time. Some things could be covered up, but this? The owner of the head had sons—and a far larger army than their own. Now, the King's successor must go to war before the body of this head had stiffened from mortis.

The alarmed courtiers whispered among themselves. It wasn't the response Marcus had expected. Disgusted, he tossed the head away and slunk back to his bench to sulk.

With this blunder, surely their father would choose Harald?

But there was still Arthur to come, and as the firstborn, his claim was the greatest.

Kate wiggled with impatience against the cold stone of the sill, but Arthur, it seemed, had no intention of prolonging the proceedings. He rose from his seat beside the King and strode around the table.

"It goes without saying that our children are our legacy." He smiled fondly at the milk-skinned page boy as the child passed him with a fresh basket of buns.

Kate held her breath. Where was he going with this? Was Arthur's wife pregnant with the King's first grandchild? That might change everything . . .

"Each new generation assures our kingdom's progress." Arthur bent and pulled the page boy to him, kissing the youth on the top of his head. Confused, the child pulled away, a deep red gash bubbling at his throat. He slumped into Arthur's arms.

Cradling the child, the prince picked up a goblet from the table and held it under the gushing wound. "But the purity of our bloodline is key," he said, the goblet almost full now. He fixed Harald with a stony glare. "And only the purest among us must be allowed to ascend to a role anointed by God." He released the dying boy, got to his feet, and thrust the bloody beverage before the King.

A woman cried out. Another fainted. Lisbet squeezed Kate's hand.

"My gift," Arthur said. "A virgin's blood, a symbol of purity, and my heartfelt pledge that forevermore, only noble blood will sit this throne."

Through the clamor, Kate heard Harald's low growl. He stood up, about to draw his sword, but Francis grasped his tunic and pulled him back. "He means to rile you. It is father's choice."

The hook-nosed advisor grimaced, nodding once again at the guards to clear the body. He then waved his hand at the gifts lined up on the table, with the exception of the neighbor's severed head, which still lolled about the floor somewhere. "The King will now consider your gifts."

The courtiers huddled in groups, exclaiming over the events of the evening while they waited for the King's verdict. Marcus, who must have been feeling bolder after seeing the page boy dragged out, joined the others at the table.

Kate slipped off the sill.

This time it was Francis who grabbed her arm. "Fetch wine for Harald," he barked. "If we can't calm him, he's likely to rip Arthur's limbs off."

Kate and Lisbet exchanged glances. With a sly look, the nurse picked up the jug she'd set down earlier and handed it carefully to Kate. "I'll find another and help you, love. Since everyone's on edge." She hurried away.

Kate filled a cup from the jug and tapped Francis on the shoulder. When the pair parted, she passed the wine to Harald. The cleric held out his goblet, so she filled that too. Then she poured a cup for Edwin and Arthur, and she even filled John's Viking cup and set it before the King—alongside Arthur's goblet, with its blood still tepid and frothy—not that the King had the strength to lift either.

By the time Kate had filled the cups of the princes on one side of the table, Lisbet had completed the other, and the jug was empty. She set it down.

Hooknose rapped on the platter again. "The King has made his decision." The advisor lifted his head and considered the hall's occupants, his eyes falling on Harald.

The prince was shaking. His face was pale, and sweat beaded on his forehead. But it wasn't the pending announcement that had provoked Harald's anxiety, and it wasn't Arthur's insults either. In fact, the King's firstborn was staggering about the Great Hall, clutching at this throat and cawing like a crow, the result of the poison root that Lisbet had sprinkled in the wine.

"Wait, I can't feel my fingers!" Edwin gasped.

"It'll be the cold, pet," Lisbet said.

"I feel dizzy," James said as he collapsed against the table.

"The wine," Lisbet replied.

Harald said nothing, too busy retching up his insides.

"What's happening?" Hooknose cried.

"They're dying," Kate said quietly. Well, there was no point in denying it. The princes were writhing in pain, grabbing at their throats and their hearts, clamoring for help.

The courtiers either ran from the hall or pressed against the walls, out of reach.

Only Francis and Christian were still at the table. Christian gaped in confusion. He wiped his tongue with his hand, the action so childlike that, for a moment, Kate felt a surge pity for him, but then she remembered his merriment over the hound, and she shook it off. He was no less cruel than the others. Francis was wavering now. Kate saw one side of his face droop with the palsy, and soon after, his entire face fell in his platter.

The King lifted his rheumy lids, coughed again, then surveyed the hall. "What have you done?" he gurgled.

A gob of sputum rolled off his lower lip.

"It's my gift to you, Father," Kate said. "You wished for an heir worthy of your legacy. Have I not done exactly that? Did you not have your own brother killed? Am I not your sole surviving"—Christian fell sideways off the bench—"off-spring?"

"I'm not dead yet," the King croaked.

Lisbet giggled. "You will be. You have hours at best. You've been taking the same thing as these others, albeit in smaller doses, in your daily tinctures."

The King's eyes bulged.

"It's the root of women's bane," Kate explained. "Lisbet borrowed it from her sister's cache."

Lisbet wiped the spittle from the King's mouth with a corner of her apron. "It's my Christmas gift to her, since you torched her, and I cannot bring her back."

"Witches!" the advisor breathed.

Kate smiled. "Most vengeful women are, Advisor."

The man moved to call the guards, but Kate scooped the Moor's golden teeth from the table, and stepping close, she placed them in his hand. "No need for that," she said folding his fingers over the gold. "That is, assuming you desire a role in my new court?"

Hooknose stared down at bounty in his hand. "I . . . I'd be honored to serve you, Lady." His kept his voice quiet and did not meet the King's glare.

Kate took Arthur's seat next to her father. She carved a slice off Gavin's roasted calf, releasing runnels of golden fat from the meat. She waved the morsel underneath the King's nose an instant, then popped it in her mouth. "I appreciate that. Would you be good enough to cut off Marcus's head and carry it to our neighbors with our compliments? I would avoid a war at such a merry time."

THE WARMTH OF SNOW

Cynthia Pelayo

M OTHER DIDN'T BELIEVE we should have a television, and so we didn't. Mother also didn't believe in love. She believed in cold and snow and mistletoe. She believed our hearts should hold still, unbeating, unflinching to the love of another.

Because what was romantic love after all?

I had never experienced it, yet I longed to, even on a winter's day. It was just after dinner, and as we were accustomed to do, we retreated to the library in our home to read. The snow had just begun to fall.

I asked Mother again, "If we aren't to believe in love, then what are we meant to believe?"

She didn't look up from what she was reading. She turned the page and said: "You will love books. Turn to the books. You'll find feeling and meaning in the books, or in the plays." She lowered her voice. "And nothing else."

So I did, and so we did, because there was nowhere to go, nothing to do, and no one to speak with. I took up my evening's reading and dove into the words.

Hamlet
Act 1, Scene 1

Bernardo: "Who's there?"
Francisco: "Nay, answer me: stand, and unfold yourself."

I notice my fingers are stained red. I hope Mother didn't notice. I woke much earlier than she did and made preparations. I read the directions, gathered the ingredients, mixed and folded items, and then set it all to bake. Afterward, I worked in the garden. As my fingers grew numb against the handle of the shovel, all I could think of was love, or the lack thereof in this house. I knew this recipe would bring us resolution, because what was the point of waiting for the end of our story?

Each time I asked Mother of love, her answers only ever left me wanting to know more. Recently, I had pressed her to further elaborate on love, and all she said was that she had never known true romantic love, but she imagined it was like being caught in a thorn bush in a winter storm: stinging pain, stinging cold, layered in blood-stained snow. When she spoke of how void her life had been of love, I pictured a frozen, dead landscape, dotted with mistletoe, those translucent white berries glistening across the ground like sparkling diamonds. I imagined rows and rows of mistletoe bushes, delightfully waiting to poison the next person overcome with hunger and longing. Because all of us longed for something, didn't we? Who really ever got all they wanted in this life? Very few, I believed, especially in the area of love.

"There is no love for people like you and me," Mother would say. "Romantic love only exists in books and poetry or plays, and even then, is it real? For we are the readers, and these are just parts playing through our minds, parts we'll never perform, of people loved tenderly. No one will ever love us. Even the sun refuses to shine on us, so how could we ever expect to be loved with what we are?"

And so, this is where we find love, in pages written long ago by poets and scorned lovers. We did our most reading when the tendrils of winter wrapped around our necks. We read fairy tales and novels, thick leather-bound tomes, and when the deep December wind howled outside of our window, we turned to the works of William Shakespeare. Why Shakespeare in winter? Perhaps because he brought a bit of drama and emotion to our already stale and unfulfilled lives. I longed to feel something—anything—and Shakespeare allowed me to feel it all and more.

Mother sits in her big blue velvet chair in our library, slowly turning the pages of *Much Ado About Nothing*. I look to the window out of habit, as I do. It's nighttime so the heavy black-out curtains are pulled back. While the sun shames us, at least the moon welcomes us, its fellow nocturnal children. The window looks down over the desolate moonlit street. In my hands I hold two books, one placed inside the other, nestled like Russian dolls. The first is *A Midsummer Night's Dream*, and that is what faces Mother, but set inside is *Hamlet*, and that is what I read, again and again when the nights grow longer.

"Why *A Midsummer Night's Dream*?" Mother asked.

I quote:

Act 5, Scene 1

Puck: "If we shadows have offended, think but this, and all is mended."

Without setting eyes on me, Mother nods and turns another page. "We are shadows, you and I."

She'd be upset if she found me reading *Hamlet* again. She said I should stay away from it after I had grown accustomed to quoting the macabre parts of the play throughout my day:

Act IV, Scene 5

Ophelia: "There's rosemary, that's for remembrance. Pray you, love remember. And there is pansies, that's for thoughts."

I look across the room, admiring the bookshelves that reach to the ceiling, and then slowly scan the rows of books until my eyes settle on the expansive hardwood floor. The room smells of wood polish from our regular polishing of the house's woodwork, and warm vanilla from the tall white pillar candles mother regularly burns. She likes making candles and does so in the basement, mixing essential oils and pouring melted soy wax into molds. Once I asked her why she enjoyed candle making so much, and she said, "It gives me some power to be able to create something that emits light and warmth inside, since we don't have access to it on the outside."

She in turn asked me, "Why do you like baking?"

I thought of what she said, of bringing light and warmth inside, and I echoed that: "Because baking brings warmth to this cold house."

I continued reading *Hamlet*. I pictured the words being acted out by players on a stage. I enjoyed reading the stage directions because in my head I could see where the performers belonged in space.

There are five stage directions in theater: upstage, downstage, center stage, stage left, stage right.

For a long time, I thought of the outside and of roles, the types of roles people play: husband and wife, daughter and son, lover and mistress. More. I believed the role I was meant to play in life was that of Hamlet, the melancholic prince.

Act 3, Scene 1

Hamlet: "To sleep, perchance to dream—ay, there's the rub:
For in that sleep of death what dreams may come."

I was meant to play the role of someone who could never truly know love.

Mother says art is our heartbeat, and in order to continue on, we must keep creating, because if we are not creating, we are withering and fading along the edges. So we dedicate much of our time to art, to reading, and she to making her lovely candles, and I to baking breads and sweets.

Whatever other time I have is spent in my room, wandering the halls, or sitting on the stairs and looking out the great window with stained glass detailing—of blues and reds, yellows and greens, beautiful wintery landscapes with birds perched on snow-covered branches, and lush green vines with red berries in the corners of the frame. I'd imagine that if the sun were to ever touch the stained glass, it would splash watercolor shadows across the wooden floors.

We hope that creating gives us meaning. I often wonder if Mother feels she has value. Sometimes I feel as though whatever value I do have here is slim. My days are on repeat. I study what lessons Mother has set before me. We eat our meals. I bake our bread or tarts or cookies. Then we read. Then we close the curtains as we shuffle off to bed, so we are not shocked by the morning sun. Then we sleep—and then we do it all over again. We work our way through this dark house, through our work, feeling little to nothing. All through this cycle I think and think that all I want to do is feel something for someone, but there is no one to feel for.

The condition that keeps me inside is called polymorphous light eruption. When I am exposed to the sun, my skin develops tiny bumps that merge into itchy, raised red patches. Blisters and hives soon develop, and then comes the stinging, scratching, screaming, and pain. I am allergic to the orange orb that hangs in the daytime sky, and so my sun is the moon. Light is my pain, and night is my only comfort, even though the darkness is my constant reminder that I cannot live out there in the world with people. I will never be in situations where I can enjoy fleeting moments of serendipity, the smile from a handsome stranger from across the room. I am trapped in this house, and I belong only and ever to the night. This is why I have never set foot in a classroom. Mother homeschools me, and it is this time at night that we sit and read. She has the same condition. And I wonder sometimes about Father: Who was he, how did they meet, and did they love one another—if even for a moment? Mother never speaks of Father. She only ever speaks of books, of poetry and prose and of longing to be free from this great brownstone she says she knows we will die in one day.

I turn another page, and it comes to me that it isn't Hamlet whom I was meant to play, but Ophelia. This makes sense because I've only ever dreamed of her. I thought of her begging and pleading, in her way, to be loved. I saw her in my mind, in ethereal dresses of silk and chiffon, situated against the moonlight. I heard her small voice, sweet like honey. And then I heard her words again and again, and each punctuation came with a beesting: "Pray you, love, remember."

This is when I think of her most, in winter, and this winter I think of her more. I think of her words even now.

Act 3, Scene 1

Ophelia: "And I, of ladies most deject and wretched . . .
        Blasted with ecstasy. O, woe is me. T' have seen what I
        have seen, see what I see!"

Perhaps it's because I am around the age she was in the play, and perhaps I think about love often as I sit in this sad house. And I know that there is no one within these walls that could love me, and while she loved him, truly did love him, he did not love her. I imagine that's the greatest of heartbreaks: loving greatly and not feeling that love returned. So I wonder, what is the point of love on a summer's day or in a winter's night, when it can be so fickle, extinguishing with a thought or a word, or with a look toward another? Or worse, never having had a chance to meet and bloom?

All I wish for sometimes is that, in the end, I meant something, if even for a fleeting moment—like the gentle journey of a cold water droplet freezing in the sky and descending to the ground as a snowflake, where it will eventually melt and disappear. Yet, I wonder, if I have no one in this life to love and in turn to love me, then am I just like a beautiful holly bush, pretty as decoration, but poisonous to hold and consume?

When I imagined her death, it always occurred downstage right. I can see her now, dressed in white satin, a spotlight only on her. Her smooth, long, dark hair hanging down in front of her shoulders. Her eyes trained up to the ceiling, in her world, to the heavens, wondering why he didn't love her. I wished for her to break that fourth wall because then I could tell her to forget him and love me instead. I would be kinder.

But we can't love fiction.

She dies in Act 5, Scene 1.

Enter Gravedigger and Another

In this act, it's always watery, and am I the Gravedigger in this reality, or am I Another? Either way, it's like I'm there, seeing the act play and play again—the Gravedigger, Another, Hamlet, the Queen, the Doctor, and her Brother. And it's her Brother who says over her grave: "And from her fair and unpolluted flesh, may violets spring!"

The melancholic prince says, "What, the fair Ophelia?" As if in shock that it is the young and beautiful Ophelia dead in the grave. How was he not surprised that death was her chosen spouse instead of him, for Hamlet disregarded her in life, and so Death pulled her in lovingly.

The Queen stands over the grave and says: "Sweets to the sweet, farewell."

Sweets to the sweet. A touch of sweetness as Ophelia was covered in her grave. Perhaps sweetness eases a burial.

I think of the graves I dug out back, and I think of how the snow fills them inch by inch. Soft, cold, and white. Then I think of Ophelia and how she suffered, all for love. She loved him and he did not reciprocate, and so she chose the fate that would pain her less— the one with fallen snow.

When I ordered from the market, I inquired if they sold live mistletoe, but unfortunately they didn't. For some reason I thought those would be easier to acquire. I thought the little white pearls would taste lovely in the tart I had baked. But after more searching, I located a holly bush, and those little red pearls like rubies would go lovely into the desert and scattered atop as decoration.

It's believed William Shakespeare wrote at least thirty-nine plays, one hundred and fifty-four sonnets, and three narrative poems during his lifetime. One of those poems he wrote was "Holly Song." It begins like this:

> Blow, blow, thou winter wind,
> Thou art not so unkind
> As man's ingratitude;
> Thy tooth is not so keen,
> Because thou are not seen.

This poem made me think of Ophelia, and Mother; and I, hidden away in this house, locked in these rooms, away from the warmth of the sun. It made me think of beginnings and ends, of things wrapping 'round, of twists and turns. I thought of the stained glass in our house, those green leaves and those red berries painted on the surface, and I thought of the pits outside filling with soft white, and the sweet smells emanating from the oven early this morning.

"Mother."

She dropped her book on her lap, startled by my voice. She was reading *Macbeth*, a play about witches and curses, shifts, and betrayal.

"I made us dessert," I said.

She closed the book and set it on the stand beside her. "You did?"

"I didn't mention it after dinner, because I thought it would be a nice surprise to take our dessert after our reading, to look out the window as we watch the snow fall."

"That's very kind of you," she said.

"Maybe we could step outside after dessert. There's a very pretty spot I'd like to show you that I've discovered in the garden."

"It's winter. Nothing is in bloom," she said.

"Right, nothing is bloom, but there's a surprise outside for you and me," I said. "Like a surprise ending to a story."

I thought of this house, and I thought of how love didn't love here, and I thought of these books and stories, and I thought of the little red holly berries I had baked into the tart as well as scattered over what would soon be our graves.

I thought of Ophelia, how she knew she'd never be loved, and so she chose death—her only true love. I know too, that Mother and I cannot ever truly be loved.

Like Ophelia, I have chosen, but for us both.

I have selected a blanket of snow, a few sprigs of holy, small red gems that will mark our final resting spot, and the eternal promise of mourning things we were never meant to know, the warmth of sun and the warmth of love.

WINTRY BLUE

Christopher Golden and Tim Lebbon

C HRISTMAS EVE IN the mountains. The night turned blue and the woods were quiet stillness, with an icy chill in the air. It was near to perfection. All they needed now was—

"Yay, Daddy, it's snowing!"

Oliver glanced into the back seat, where Katie had pressed her face to the passenger window, smiling as her breath steamed up the glass. He turned on the windshield wipers as the first fat flakes began to land. His daughter had turned nine just after Thanksgiving, and some days she seemed more like twenty. She'd been trying to act all grown up ever since they'd lost her mother, but times like this, when she grew too excited to put on that act, she was his little girl again, with magic in her eyes.

"Look up," he said. "You'll see a lot more snow soon."

"So cool!" The road snaked up into the thickly forested, snow-covered mountains. "We're driving all the way up there?"

"All the way," Oliver said, glancing back at her. "Grandma and Grandpa are excited to see us. She made cookies, and he wants you to help him build a fire."

"Isn't that dangerous?" Katie frowned, and the quizzical line between her eyes broke his heart. It did every time. She looked so much like Emma, and he was glad of that . . . but still. Sometimes the reminder hit him like a bullet.

"In their fireplace, silly. It's big. So big you can walk into it."

"Grandma and Grandpa do everything big," Katie said with the weighty wisdom that so often accompanied the proclamations of the very young.

"That's for sure."

Oliver thought of the house where they were spending Christmas. Everything about his late wife's parents was big. Their cars, the vacations they planned, their Christmas trees. Thankfully, their hearts were even bigger. They'd lost a daughter, but they still treated him like a son, and that meant the world.

Katie went quiet, staring out at the changing landscape. They'd left the low valleys behind, and copses of trees clung to the hillsides, tumbles of rocks piled here and there like giants' playthings cast aside. They'd soon be entering the dense woods above the snowline, and from there Emma's folks' expansive mountain house was just over an hour's drive. That was if this snow didn't start coming down too heavy. Oliver was prepared; the car had snow tires—and shovels, food, and warm clothes in the trunk—but he still felt a flutter of nerves. He hadn't driven in conditions like this for a while.

"What is it, Katie?"

She was frowning again, her bottom lip protruding a little. He glanced at her, to the road, back again. "Kate?"

"It's Santa," she said, voice barely above a whisper.

"Santa?"

"How will he know where I am?"

Oliver chuckled. She might want to act all grown up, but she was still only nine. His little girl still believed. "You think Santa doesn't have a way of knowing where *all* children are on Christmas Eve?"

"But how? That film *Arthur Christmas* was made up. Elves don't have iPads!"

"They don't—you're right," Oliver said. He glanced around, thinking, thinking, and then he saw a small white mound beside the road, leftover from the previous snowfall that had mostly melted away. "It's the snowmen," he said. "Up here in the hills, anyway. Other places, it might be scarecrows or butterflies or certain breeds of dog, but here it's the snowmen who tell Santa how to find all the kids who are away from home for Christmas. And it looks like there's going to be plenty of snow!"

"So we have to build a snowman called Frosty, and he can tell Santa where I am?"

"Yeah, sweetie. You'll have to ask Grandpa to help you."

"Yay! Yaaaaaayyyy!" Katie danced in her seat, and Oliver smiled. *Good call,* he imagined Emma saying. *Thinking on the run. I like it.*

"Good call," he muttered, and as the car wound its way up into the hillside forests, the snow began to fall heavier.

* * *

Two days, over twenty miles hiked, Nadia complaining about blisters on her toes and being cold and every little thing that bothered her, and now they'd found the cabin at last, and it was a bust. The stuff Dan had read about this place was bullshit—there was barely a wall left standing, undergrowth had smothered most of it years or decades ago, and there was nothing special here. Nothing . . . other.

"It's just a ruin, Dan," she said.

"I see that."

"So can't we just—"

"Let's make a fire and eat," he said. "I'm tired—and cold. You?"

Nadia nodded, smiling in relief.

"I'll go find us some wood." He dumped his big backpack, tugged out the small axe from the outer pocket, and stomped away into the trees.

It had started snowing heavily an hour before, and Dan loved it. It wasn't too cold; it deadened the sound through the trees, and it brought a sense of peace down across the landscape. And a sense of peace in him too. They had hiked up here filled with a sense of adventure, excited by the possibility of unearthing grim secrets. Until ten minutes ago, he'd been sure the truth of what had happened here was about to be revealed. Then they'd found the cabin.

Legend had it all sorts of crazy shit had unfolded here a century ago—sacrifices, disappearances, a family living in the cabin who'd murdered and maimed. The stories said all of that horror had attracted the attention of *other* things. Dark things, malignant and full of malice.

So it was said.

But as Nadia had observed, the cabin was a ruin, and nothing about it felt different from anywhere else on the mountain.

"Don't mean it ain't still there," the voice said. Dan called that voice Silas, and it was an old man in his head, busy translating the information and research Dan had been absorbing for years, and bestowing wisdom upon him. That's who Silas was—a wise old man. He was the person Dan thought he might have become had he not messed up his life. The person his father had never been.

"I'm better that my father," he muttered, and his voice died in the snow. No echo to argue back.

"Sure, much better," Silas said. *"So don't worry about the cabin not being there. It's just a damn place, that's all. It's not a feeling. It's not* them. *"*

He trudged through the snow, circling several old trees and hacking at branches that had fallen from them over the years. As he collected kindling, he listened for noises in the snow and looked for movement between the trees.

He had done everything he could to lure the monsters in. The previous day, he and Nadia had walked through the site of an old burial ground. He was quite certain she hadn't even been aware of where they were—there was little visible evidence, and anything left was buried beneath layers of leaf fall and soil. But his maps were detailed and accurate, as was his research, and as he'd pissed against the foot of the ancient trees, he'd silently mocked the spirits that haunted these woods.

He wanted them to come so that he could kill them.

Nothing had happened. Yesterday evening, he had talked Nadia into making love against an old tree that had fallen years before. She'd been cautious and hesitant at first, and he'd reassured her there was no one around. Soon they were at it against the tree, the scent of their lovemaking on their skin and breath, and he'd been sure to spill his seed on the ground.

Panting, sweating, still naked, he'd watched the shadows, waiting for the beasts to arrive and censure him for his vileness. None came.

"Teasing me," he said, hugging a load of chopped wood to his chest. "Laughing at me."

"They ain't laughing at you," Silas said. *"Who the fuck d'ya think you are? You know these things! The Tsi-Noo, the Chinook, all those others known and unknown. You've studied them, absorbed their stories, an' you're doin' everything you can to draw them in. It'll happen. They'll come. Then you kill 'em and become the man who killed a monster. Everyone will love you. You know that."*

"I know that," Dan said. He pocketed the axe and headed back toward the ruined cabin, where Nadia was already digging a small pit for their fire.

"An' if they don't come," Silas whispered, *"there's always plan B."*

* * *

Oliver fought to keep his eyes open. A part of him knew he should pull over, shake it off, get himself fully awake. Driving up a mountain road in the middle of a snowstorm was dangerous enough, but doing it while struggling to stay awake behind the wheel was sheer idiocy. Doing it with his daughter in the back seat probably made him a shitty father.

He sat up straighter. Gripped the wheel. Cracked his window and let the cold air howl through the gap. It did the trick, for now.

"Daddy?" Katie said, sounding confused. "Daddy, there's a lady!"

Lady? Oliver frowned. He glanced over his shoulder, saw that Katie had her face to the glass again, cheek to window, gaze locked on something ahead of them, in the trees off to the right.

Oliver craned his neck over the steering wheel, trying to see what had caught her attention. He spotted movement in the trees, thought it must be a deer, and began to tap the brakes just before a wild-eyed woman burst over the snowpack at the roadside and hurled herself in front of the car. Long hair flying, face etched with panic, she waved her arms to stop him. As he slammed on the brakes, all he could see were those eyes, wide with terror, and the bloody spatter across her pale face in the glare of his headlights.

In the new-fallen snow, the car slewed sideways. He had turned the wheel. The last thing he should have done in a snowstorm while stomping on his brakes, but his reflexes had taken over, and now he felt a sinking certainty that he would run this woman over.

In the back seat, Katie screamed. He had just a flicker of a moment to understand that this moment would be seared into her memory forever.

The car had gone completely sideways in the road, still skidding in the snow. The passenger side thumped into the woman, and he glimpsed her flailing backward, arms flying, smashing down onto the road.

"Oh my God, Daddy!"

The car had come to a halt, headlights buried in the snowpack on the left side of the road. His foot was still on the brake. His heartbeat thundered in his ears, and he wondered if he'd killed her. Not who she was or what she was doing in the woods on the mountain in the middle of a snowstorm—he wondered only if she was still alive.

The interior light came on with a ding. Oliver blinked. Disoriented by shock, it took him a moment to realize Katie had opened her door, unsnapped her seat belt, and jumped out of the car.

"Katie, wait! No!"

He slammed the gearshift into park. Engine still running, heat still blasting, radio playing Frank Sinatra Christmas songs, he opened his door and practically fell out into the snow. Lurching to his feet, he ran around the back of the car, through the wash of red taillights, and watched as his daughter knelt by the motionless woman.

And then she moved.

Thank God.

The woman sat up. Katie helped her, then turned to look back at her father, stricken with the bottomless empathy of children. "Dad, she's bleeding. She's really hurt."

Dad. Not Daddy.

In this instant, Katie had left childhood behind.

The woman looked at Oliver through her bloodied fringe. "I'm okay. It wasn't the car. You didn't hit me that hard and I . . . I landed in the snow. But please, you've got to help me."

"I'm so sorry," Oliver said, going to her. Katie had taken her by one elbow, and Oliver held her other side, helping her stand. "My God, look at your hand!"

His thoughts were chaos. Christmas Eve forgotten. Katie's grandparents forgotten. Where was the nearest hospital? Would it be faster to take her himself or call an ambulance? With the shitty cell service up here, could he even call 911?

But mostly, he was staring at her left hand. The last two fingers had been torn off, leaving bleeding, ragged stumps. Blood trickled from them into the snow. In the strange gray light of the storm, it looked unreal.

"No, no," she said, shaking her head, voice turning more frantic. "You didn't do that. It wasn't the car. Please, we have to go! He's *coming*!" Bleeding, stumbling, blood spatter on her face, she lurched toward the car. Her words were almost erased by the wind, her voice ghostly in that moment. "He started with my fingers, but he says he'll eat my heart!"

She slid in the snow and collided with the car almost in the same spot where it had struck her. Steadying herself, she ripped open the door and turned to him.

"Let's go!" she screamed.

Wild. Primal. Desperate to survive.

Katie took Oliver's hand. He flinched. He'd been frozen, still in shock, but now his daughter tugged him toward the car.

"Dad, come on!"

"Shit," Oliver muttered. "Holy shit."

Hand in hand with Katie, he ran back toward his car, toward the bleeding woman who even now piled into the passenger seat.

From up in the woods on the side of the road, there came a long, animal howl.

* * *

"Why is she looking at you like that, Dan?" Silas asked, inside his head.

"That's a great fucking question," Dan said.

Nadia flinched at the sound of his voice. She took a step backward, caught her boot on a log jutting from the snow, and pinwheeled her arms in order to stay upright. Dan reached for her hand to help steady her, but she yanked it backward to avoid contact with him. Her recoiling like that sent a chill through him.

But his insides were already turning to ice.

"I didn't ask a question," Nadia said, her gaze darting around as if searching for a path home.

Dan smiled. He knew she would see the disdain and anger in that smile, that his teeth would be bared, but he no longer cared.

"I wasn't talking to you," he said. "I was talking to Silas."

She backed up another step and bumped into the remaining wall of the cabin. "Who the fuck is Silas?"

"That's all you need to hear, isn't it?" Silas whispered in his skull. *"You've been with her this long but never trusted her enough to tell her about me. Your oldest friend."*

"True," Dan said aloud.

Nadia threw up her hands. "That's it. I'm done. You're acting like a lunatic. I came up here in the middle of a snowstorm with you because—"

"You wanted an adventure."

"Yes! I wanted an adventure." She searched his face for some sign that they were connecting. "I love the folklore, the spooky stories—all of that. I thought it would be romantic and creepy, us doing this hike together. But now you're just being an asshole."

"She doesn't understand," Silas said.

"She will," Dan replied.

Nadia's face flushed with anger. Lighting quick, she slapped his face. "Stop it! Focus on me. What the fuck is wrong with you?"

Dan softened. He smiled. "I'm frightening you, aren't I?"

"Yes!"

He sighed. Nodded. "Nadia, I told you why I wanted to come up here. All the stories about this cabin, about this part of the mountain. We're looking for a monster."

"You said if we spent time here, if we found the cabin, maybe we could understand why people lost their minds up here."

"And you said," Dan reminded her, "that maybe we'd feel the evil spirits."

Nadia slipped out from between him and the wall of the cabin, getting a bit of distance from him. "I was joking. Being spooky. It was fun to think about it, but I don't believe in any of that stuff. Not really!"

"But I do," Dan replied.

Her laugh echoed with bitterness. "I can see that now."

"Nadia," he said. His voice had turned strange. Deeper. Raspy with emotion. He could hear all of that himself, but he did not try to hide what he felt. It was too late for that. "I've told you why I want to find a monster."

She froze. Eyes narrowed. It seemed almost as if she were seeing him for the first time.

"Maybe she is," Silas said.

Dan had done terrible things as a boy. To Mrs. Perini's cat. To his own sister's puppy. Eventually, to his sister. He'd been angry and resentful, and hurting things felt like the relief of exhaling a long-held breath. In school he had been an instigator, bullying and nudging others to start fights so that he could finish them. When he had killed the bird his biology teacher had brought to class, he had been expelled. She'd called him a monster. He'd been forced to receive psychiatric counseling, but by then he hadn't needed it.

That one word had done it. *Monster.*

"I thought it was a metaphor," Nadia said, studying him now.

Dan smirked. "I did awful things when I was a kid. I turned myself around, but I always knew the only way I'd ever really feel like I'd put it behind me is by becoming a hero. Slaying monsters."

"Babe, no. It's all *metaphor*," she'd insisted.

"What if it isn't? I told you about them. Tsi-Noo and the rest. So many legends around the world."

"The Wendigo. Sure. But if you think that's real . . ."

"She's not listening," Silas said.

"You're not listening, Nadia. The Tsi-Noo. The Chinook. The Wendigo. They're all variations on the same thing. Like vampires—"

"Vampires, now?" She rolled her eyes.

That broke something in him.

He lurched across the eight feet separating them. Nadia tried to run, but too late. He grabbed her by the arms and hurled her to the ground. She could have started screaming then, but instead of fearful, she looked furious. She started to shout at him, but Dan loomed over her, pointed a finger.

"Listen!" he boomed.

She did. Anger in her eyes. And a flicker of fear. Silas thought that showed a bit of wisdom.

"I'm not saying vampires existed. I'm saying that for the legends to be as pervasive as they were, sprouting up in every corner of the world at a time when those cultures were not yet influencing one another . . . There had to have been something that inspired societies across the globe to tell stories about creatures like that. This is the same. Something inspired these monster stories. About people trapped in winter storms, starving and lost, who turned to cannibalism, and once they broke that taboo, it loosed the evil spirit inside them."

"Look at her eyes," Silas said.

Dan obeyed. Silas had spoken with glee, and Dan understood why. The anger had fled from Nadia's eyes. As she listened to his words, fear took over.

"I want to go," she said. "No more hiking, Dan. I'm cold and hungry, and I'm tired of being on this mountain. I want to go back to the Jeep, right now."

Nadia started to rise.

With his boot, Dan shoved her sprawling to the ground.

"The one I believe in," he said, "says that once you succumb to the evil spirit, your heart turns to ice. And then you *are* the monster."

"Look at her eyes," Silas said, relishing the words. *"It's just hit her."*

Dan smiled.

Nadia tried to rise again, holding both hands in front of her, to ward him off. "Stop it, Dan. You're not a hero. You're not a monster. You're just a man who needs help. I didn't realize it had gotten this bad, but you're confused, babe. There are no evil spirits. No monsters—"

He grabbed both of her wrists. "You're so wrong."

"Now!" Silas screamed in his ears. *"Now, now, now, now!"*

Nadia screamed too, but Dan could no longer hear anything but Silas in his skull.

He darted his head forward. His jaws snapped down on her left hand. Teeth dug into flesh and cracked bone. He whipped his head right to left, and then tore two fingers off. Blood sprayed his face.

Nadia cracked him in the head with a snow-crusted rock her fingers had found. Dan staggered backward, grinning, blood dripping down his chin as he chewed her fingers and swallowed the first bits. Sharp little bones cut his throat going down, but his grin only widened.

He felt his heart begin to freeze, not just frosting over, but replaced entirely by ice. Joy overtook him. He wanted to laugh and cry.

But more than that, he wanted another bite.

Nadia lifted her hand to stare at the stumps of her fingers. Her own blood spattered her cheeks and lips. She couldn't speak as she looked up at him. Dan felt himself growing larger, felt his teeth sharpening, lengthening. Ice crusted around his eyes.

He laughed.

She ran.

* * *

The woman in the passenger seat was shivering so hard that her elbow struck the door, her teeth clattered, and her boots stamped on the floor.

"Seat belt," Oliver said, but if she heard him, it didn't register.

"Drrr . . . drrrr . . ." the woman said.

"Dad?" Katie said from the back seat.

"It's okay." He caught her eye in the mirror, smiling, desperately wishing he could hug her tight. "She's just cold and—"

"Dad, what about the police?"

Damn it, my daughter's thinking straighter than me, Oliver thought. He snatched up his phone from the console and held it to his face to open the screen.

The woman knocked the phone from his hand, still shivering but glaring at him now, bloodied and terrified and quite possibly out of her mind.

"Drrr . . . *drive!*"

From outside there came another howl, long and high. The woman's eyes went wider.

"He . . . he's . . ." She held up her hand again, showing Oliver the mutilated fingers. "He's coming to . . . eat my . . . *heart.*" And she looked at Katie in the back seat.

That was enough for Oliver. He turned the key, and for a few seconds the engine turned over without catching. *Now we're stuck with whatever's out there,* he thought. *"Crazy boyfriend or escaped killer or fucking wolf, we're trapped and even if there is phone reception—"*

Then another voice whispered to him from the past, and it gave him a valuable moment of calm and clarity. *"Deep breath,"* Emma said. *"Close your eyes and breathe, breathe . . ."*

Oliver closed his eyes, took a deep breath, and turned the key again.

The engine caught. He touched the gas and they moved forward, tires spinning for a second before catching on the icy road. The wind gusted, moving the thickly falling snow as if the storm were a living, breathing thing.

"Your fingers must really hurt," Katie said.

Oliver frowned, glancing into the rearview mirror. Katie wore her seat belt. She couldn't see the woman's ruined hand from there, but she'd gotten a good view moments ago, and Oliver was sure the memory would remain with her. Something like this, the aftermath of some kind of violence . . . it was the kind of thing that stayed with a child for a lifetime.

Their new passenger shifted in her seat, skittish and frightened, watching the road and the woods for whatever she thought pursued her. Whatever had torn off those fingers. She cupped her ruined hand with her whole one, breathing hard. Oliver realized she hadn't even heard Katie speak to her.

"Hey," Oliver said, hands tight on the steering wheel. She looked at him as if she'd forgotten he was there. "You're safe now. We'll be at my in-laws' place soon. What's your name?"

The tires skidded a bit in the snow, hit a bump, but he kept them moving, car climbing the mountain. The woman blinked a few times, as if clearing things she had seen from the screen of her memory.

"Nadia," she said. "I'm Nadia."

The snow buffeted the car, falling harder. "What happened, Nadia? Who's after you?"

Her eyes changed. For a moment they lost their panic, their sense of terror, and they focused properly on Oliver for the first time. He glanced at the road, then back at Nadia, and she was still looking at him.

"A monster," she said.

In the back seat, Katie drew a sharp breath. Anger sent a warm rush through him. This stranger they were helping, this bloodied victim of some unknown encounter, was scaring his daughter. And whatever awful thing had happened, Katie was Oliver's top and only priority.

"You're all right now, Nadia," he said. "Soon as we reach the house we can call—"

"Daddy!" Katie shouted. "It's Frosty! Look! Up in the woods, it's Frosty the snowman come to see where I am, just like you said!"

Oliver glanced up through the trees to the right, wary of taking his attention from the road again. Snow fell, and the trees stood thick and dark, huddled together. Nothing out of the ordinary.

Nadia jerked back in her seat, staring into the storm, and then Oliver spotted the shape barreling down the hillside toward them.

"Why is he running?" Katie asked, uncertainty splintering her happiness.

The thing coming downhill appeared bigger than a man, yet it walked on two legs. It bounded through the deepening snow.

It was white and red.

Nadia screamed.

*　　*　　*

He had never felt so whole. So powerful. So free.

Silas had gone silent. Dan had not spent a moment wondering why—he understood immediately. Silas had been his real voice, his real soul. The man he had pretended to be on the outside had been nothing but a mask, and now that he had ripped off that mask, he didn't need to pretend anymore that Silas was some separate creature, some other man. Dan had no more doubts about whether he was better than his father. There was no turning over the past, nor planning for the future. There was only an ecstatic, beautiful present.

When Nadia had run, he'd tripped and fallen, writhing as the pains of growth and change twisted his body in the snow. Even as he shrugged the pains away—as he felt his ice-forged heart flushing cool power and strength through his lengthening limbs, his pulsing muscles, his expanding chest and teeth and claws—he'd known that she would not get far. In a way, he had been glad for her head start. The thrill of the chase gave sparkling life to the thing he had become. His hunger had become his engine.

He loped downhill toward the road and saw the car passing between snowbanks. He could smell her inside. Her scent was familiar to the old Dan, and it ignited in him desires and lusts that surged like fire, setting his nerves aflame and bringing a deep, animal howl from his lungs. Trees shook at the sound of his voice, shedding accumulated snow. Birds took flight. To his right a deer broke cover, and he considered running it down and gutting it and bathing in its blood and fluids.

But he would soon be doing that to Nadia, and human blood was richer. He could still taste her meat on his tongue and stuck between his aching teeth.

He bounded down the slope, cutting a silent path through the falling snow, and as he closed in on the vehicle, he leaped, clawed hands outstretched.

He landed on the car's roof and heard the loud crack of a window breaking from the impact. The vehicle slewed to the left and back again as the driver attempted to maintain control, and Dan gripped onto the roof's edges and strained his whole body, raising his head, bringing an ebullient roar from deep down and letting it fly.

It flew between trees and swept across the hillsides, singing of freedom and a voracious hunger.

As his roar echoed away, the triumphant beast he had become leaned forward and smashed at the car's windscreen with one fisted hand. He hammered again and again until he made a hole, the rest of the shatterproof glass becoming a puzzle with a million little pieces. He grabbed the edges of the hole and tore the spiderwebbed glass out in handfuls. The car skidded again, and the driver stomped on the brakes in an attempt to throw him from the roof.

Dan hung on as the car skidded sidelong across the road, heading for a snowbank and a long, rolling drop down a rocky hillside. Its wheels jammed into the roadside ditch, and Dan loosened his hold, slipping to the right so he could bring his heavy fist down against the rear passenger window.

His hand smashed straight through, and he felt something that brought out another roar, this one filled with hunger.

Warm skin, smooth hair.

Food.

* * *

"*Daddyyyyyy!*" Katie's scream tore into his heart, and as Oliver twisted in the seat and reached back for her, his whole world narrowed to a single, awful focus.

The hand and arm reaching through the smashed window and grasping Katie in its bloodied claw. His daughter fighting and screaming as she was lifted and pulled toward the ragged opening. The inhuman voice of the thing on the car's roof.

Oliver grabbed Katie's legs and held on, pulling, refusing to let go as he played a tug of war with his precious girl. She screamed and bit into the monster's hand, trying to force it to let her go.

"Help me!" he shouted at Nadia in the passenger seat.

Her face was freckled with a hundred tiny cuts inflicted by the smashed windshield. Blood smudged her pale skin, her eyes wide with shock.

"Help me!"

Nadia reached behind her, opened the door, and tumbled out into the snow. Silently cursing her, Oliver turned back to Katie, thrusting himself between the front seats. He let go of her leg and grabbed at the thing's arm, drove it upward into the sharp-toothed remains of the smashed side window, and raked back and forth. Skin split, blood flowed, and he heard an angry grunt from the creature on the car's roof. It let go of Katie, and its fingers flexed. Before it could grab again, she clambered into the front with her father and hunkered down in the driver's seat. Oliver did the opposite, sliding fully into the back seat, placing himself between the smashed window and his daughter.

What the hell do I fight this thing with? he thought.

It reached in again, and he grabbed the hand, wincing as long nails slashed at his palm. He turned it against its elbow pivot and pushed it up toward the ceiling, and its howl of pain gave him a flush of hope.

He heard the snick of a car door opening, a rush of cool air against his back, and he looked back over his shoulder and saw Katie crawling out into the storm.

"Katie, *no!*" he said, and the muscle-knotted arm in his hands thrashed, and slashed nails across his face as it withdrew. He heard the thudding movement of the thing on the roof shifting, and it dove for Katie, reaching with long arms and screeching in delight as it fell toward the frightened girl.

Then Nadia was there, darting in from the side, tackling the creature in midair.

Oliver scrabbled across the back seat and out into the snow, ignoring the shapes fighting to his left, and protecting Katie with his body. As he left the car, his feet caught on a plastic box in the footwell, and he tumbled with it into the snow.

Flares! he thought. They were only road flares, but they burned hot and fast, and perhaps they would scare this thing off.

"Daddy!" Katie said, and she reached for him, slinging her arms around his neck. He sat up and hugged her tight, turning toward Nadia and the creature.

Oliver narrowed his eyes against the gusting snow, trying to make out the shape of the thing. The cold stung his face, but for just a moment the wind quieted, and he saw it in full for the first time.

"What the fuck?" Oliver said.

Anger flooded his veins. He let go of his daughter, and she slid down to stand beside him, trying to hang onto him. Snowflakes landed on her lashes as she watched the bloody Nadia trying not to die. The bastard choked her with one hand, bent down with bared teeth, and Oliver saw that this would not be a kiss, but a bite. Torn lips, or a chunk of flesh from her cheek.

Katie screamed, no longer in fear, but in horror.

Oliver crouched in front of her, eye to eye. "Run, baby! I'll shout for you!"

He shoved his own daughter, sent her reeling through the snow. She landed on her knees but kept moving, rising, one boot left behind in the deep snow. Katie headed for the trees.

Oliver opened the box of road flares, grabbed one, let the box drop to the snow. He snapped the cap off the one in his hand, and it flamed to life, burning fiercely, hissing like a thing alive.

"Motherfucker, get off her!" he shouted.

Bloodstained teeth clacked; jaws clamping shut an inch above Nadia's lips. The thing on top of her whipped around, madness in its eyes, and lunged for Oliver with a cry that sounded like anguish and hunger and fury all bound up together.

Oliver couldn't be sure, but he thought the thing was smiling.

*   *   *

The thing that Dan had become gathered all its fury and hunger and roared, its powerful voice vibrating in its ribs, shimmering in its aching teeth and claws, pulsing in its skull and jaws. It left behind the woman whose flesh it had already tasted and hurled itself through the falling snow at the man daring to stand against it. The woman had bled too much to run very far. It would catch her again if she tried. But this man—it would eat his heart and his eyes.

Fingers hooked into claws, it reached for him. The man's eyes reflected back the burning light of the road flare, and the thing heard a warning voice in its head. Not Silas's voice, for it had become something like Silas had always been. This was the other voice, the original Dan, perhaps the child he had been before Silas began to whisper inside him. It warned him, tried to overrule the primal urge to rip and tear, to kill, to sate its hunger.

Too late.

It felt a sudden blazing pain in its throat. It stumbled, lashing out with both arms, staggering to the left. It grabbed at its throat, felt the road flare jutting there, and tried to tug it out. Pain sent the thing to its knees as it tried to scream. Fire burned the inside of its throat; heat flooded its insides. Sacrificing Nadia, eating her flesh, had turned him into the monster he'd always wanted to kill—or to be—and his heart had frozen to solid, jagged ice. Now the flames from the flare sucked down inside the thing as it tried to breathe, and the icy rock of its heart melted.

Silently screaming, it ripped the broken flare from its punctured throat. Blood and sparks arced out across the snow.

And it fell.

Voices whispered in its head—in his head—as the last breath rattled in its chest.

Then, silence, inside and out.

*   *   *

In the quiet, Oliver could hear only the wind and the low rumble of his car engine. Its nose still in the ditch, it had kept running. Somewhere in the back of his mind, he knew he ought to shut it off, conserve gas while they waited for help. He felt numb, not with cold, but with shock.

Fifteen feet away, Nadia cradled her ruined hand as she rose unsteadily to her feet. Their eyes met through the veil of snow. Her hand seemed to have stopped bleeding, but she had other wounds. She would live, he thought, but help had best arrive soon.

Small footsteps crunched in the snow behind him.

Oliver turned.

Katie held her lost boot in one hand. She had dug it out of the snow but seemed to have forgotten its purpose. Her face had gone deathly pale. For the first time, he saw the scratches on her cheek where the thing had clawed at her. Blood trickled down her chin.

A shudder went through him, and Oliver rushed to her, bundled her into his arms. She hung onto her loose boot.

"Baby girl, oh my God!" he said. Warmth flooded back into him. Tears welled in his eyes.

He'd almost lost her. They'd almost lost each other.

That thing . . .

That fucking lunatic had nearly killed them.

"Daddy?" she whispered in his ear, grave and wise. "That wasn't Frosty."

"No, baby. Frosty's still out there. He'll tell Santa you've been the bravest, bravest girl."

"I'm very brave," Katie agreed.

Oliver held her and tried not to cry as love and relief overwhelmed him.

"Daddy, my chest hurts," Katie whispered in his ear. "It's hard to breathe."

He froze. Took a deep breath and pulled away from his daughter, holding her at arm's length. Studying her. Thinking the impossible. In his mind's eye, he could see the moment when the madman had smashed in her car window and tried to drag Katie out into the storm. The moment when she had bitten his hand, teeth sinking deep, breaking skin, drawing blood.

Katie put both hands over her heart and frowned. She looked confused and a bit scared.

"It feels like the snow's on the inside," she said. "My chest is cold."

Oliver stared at her; sure his daughter's eyes had always been green.

Tonight, with the snow dancing around her, those eyes were icy, wintry blue.

CAROL OF THE HELLS

Kelsea Yu

Say your goodbyes,
Watch as he dies.
All up in flames,
Nothing remains.

Should have been you.
What did you do?
Why did you shriek?
You are so weak.

"DAMNIT, HOLLY, SHUT up." Holly Chang felt twice the fool, first for scolding herself like a child, then for speaking aloud when she was alone in her car. But sometimes the startling sound of her own voice was the only thing that disrupted her runaway mind. It loved to sing along with various Christmas carols, using the wretched replacement lyrics her teenaged self had thought up.

Holly took a deep breath and repeated three phrases from her therapist. "I was young. It wasn't my fault. There's nothing I could have done differently."

She reached for the knob to switch tracks. "Carol of the Bells" cut off abruptly, replaced by "Deck the Halls."

Holly sighed. Her horrid brain had special lyrics for that song too. Still, she didn't turn the music off. She really did want to get better, yet she couldn't help punishing herself through small, needle-sharp reminders. Tonight, on the least wonderful night of the year, her self-loathing was always at its strongest.

She reminded herself of the things she had to look forward to. Her neighbor had gifted her a box of homemade Christmas sweets, and she'd saved one last mouthwatering eggnog cookie for tomorrow. She and a coworker had tickets to see a musical in two weeks. And everything would look better in the spring, when the weather warmed.

Her breathing eased a little.

The next neighborhood was quite the spectacle. Holly drove slowly, looking through her window at each house. Most had simple, tasteful decorations—waterfall Christmas lights on the porch rail, a pair of light-up deer on the lawn, a tree wrapped in rainbow tinsel—but a few had gone all out. One yard was a cross between a manger scene and a rave, complete with a light-up baby Jesus. Two houses down from neon Mary and Joseph, a pretty brown cottage was decorated to resemble a gingerbread house. Near the end of the street, Holly found her favorite: a house styled after *The Nightmare Before Christmas*.

Her dad would've loved the movie if he hadn't died the year before it came out.

She wiped the tears from her eyes. They always seemed to sneak up on her. At least they were proof she might not be all bad.

As if to refute that thought, "Deck the Halls" cut out, and the *Jaws* theme song began playing; the ringtone Holly reserved for one particular person. She clicked a button on her dashboard, and Gina Chang's voice boomed through the car speakers.

"Where are you?" Gina's words were slurred but recognizable. She'd only started drinking, then.

"Driving, Mom."

Gina snarled. "You're looking at those goddamned Christmas lights again, aren't you. I don't know why you have to do that every year."

"It makes me think of them." Holly left the last house in the well-decorated neighborhood behind, speeding up as she turned onto the main road through town.

"That's kid shit. You shouldn't need to drive around town, gawking at people's houses as some childless creep, to think of your brother and your father. You should be thinking about them every goddamned moment of every goddamned day. I know I do."

"Cody loved the lights."

"Cody was too old for it."

Gina was wrong. Holly might only have been nine at the time, but Cody had been her world. She remembered seeing her older brother's expression as they drove past the lights that last December. The way he drank in each scene, hiding his delight each time their mother looked in the rearview mirror, since fifteen-year-olds weren't supposed to think light displays were cool. He'd loved those lights almost as much as their dad had.

"Merry Christmas Eve to you too, Mom."

"It's your fault. You deserve to live with that."

"I know."

They'd had this conversation a million times. Sometimes Gina broke down sobbing by the end. Sometimes she screamed drunken curses, reminding Holly she was never meant to be born. Holly could live with either of those reactions; at least they were something. Like the cool relief of pinching the soft skin of your underarm until the pain was too sharp to think of anything else. They felt like what Holly deserved.

But tonight Gina simply let Holly's last words hang between them. Though they were thousands of miles apart, the distance didn't matter. Gina's words cut through state lines, through decades. Always aimed straight for Holly's heart.

"Good. At least you know." There was something in Gina's voice. Something more than the usual meanness waiting to reveal itself.

Holly realized her lower lip was bleeding; she'd been biting it, hard. She knew her therapist would say she didn't have to pick up the phone, didn't have to reinforce her mother's version of events. But Holly couldn't help herself. Every year she hoped it would be different, that her mother would be calling to wish her happy birthday. To remind Holly that she'd been named for the little sprig of mistletoe someone had hung from the hospital birthing room's ceiling. To tell Holly she was sorry and to forgive her.

Hope was a hellish beast.

Holly sighed. "What do you want, Mom?"

On the other side of the line, there was a swish, then a gulp and a satisfied sigh. She pictured her mother clutching the neck of the bottle, downing more whiskey.

"Mom?"

Gina laughed—a mean, hollow sound. "I figured it out. They—they helped me figure it out. It'll work this time."

Holly's heart sank. "I thought we were done with this." As far as Holly could tell, the money she'd sent Gina for the past few years had ended up in the hands of various people who claimed to be occult specialists—swindlers promising the impossible.

"You never did—" Gina burped. "You . . . awful child. You never believed in me. But I figured it out."

"Mom, those people are all charlatans. They prey on your deepest hopes, your darkest dreams."

Something smashed on the other side of the phone, and Holly flinched. It sounded like a shattering window. Or . . . Gina had smashed her glass bottle into the wall. Shit. Holly had underestimated how drunk her mother was.

"Mom? Are you okay?" Holly kept her eyes on the road. Just a few more streets and she'd be home.

Gina laughed again, something triumphant simmering beneath the surface. Holly shuddered. Anything that made her mom this pleased couldn't be good. "I'm about to be. But I need *you.*"

Holly hated the way the words made her hopeful. *She's toying with you again. Stop fucking falling for it.*

"I need you to be—to be good for once," Gina slurred. "Be a good girl, Hollyyyy. All you have to do is stay quiet."

"Mom, what are you talking about?" Holly's heart was racing now. This time, something was different, wrong. Off.

"All you have to do is—is stay quiet," Gina said again. Then Holly heard a click, like the cock of a gun, and then Gina laughing,

laughing, until the awful laugh was cut off by the deafening crack of a gunshot ringing clear through the speakers of Holly's car.

Holly screamed and screamed and screamed, and nothing made sense, and the road ahead was dark as a void, and she couldn't see or think or feel, and her head hurt, and everything was wrong, and she needed a moment to pause and *breathe*, and—

Her foot slammed on the brakes so hard they screeched. Her tires hit a patch of ice and spun out of control, and then there was the dizzying whirl of street lights moving fast, too fast, and the beam of her headlights illuminated a woman crossing the road, and she turned and it was Gina, the face belonged to *Gina*, and her eyes were red and bloodshot, and she was cackling, cackling, and someone slammed on their horn, and then there was the crunch of metal and the punch of an airbag and shock and pain, and one last thought skittered across Holly's mind before everything went black—that it was thirty years too late, but she was finally, finally going to get what she deserved.

*　*　*

The world was still and dark, the silence punctuated only by the wild drumbeat of Holly's heart.

She was horribly, impossibly alive.

Holly waited for someone to start screaming at her, for the groan of someone in need of aid, for the flash of sirens. She'd hit a car, or she'd run someone over, or—she didn't know what'd happened, but it had to be bad. Surely, someone would come to investigate the noise.

She waited, but no one came.

At last, Holly dared open her eyes.

She was greeted by a row of candy canes, red and white lights alternating as they danced, oblivious to her distress.

She *knew* those candy canes.

She blinked as the rest came into focus. Past the dancing confections sat a row of hedges, swaddled in glowing green. Behind them, a large window looked into a dining room her younger self had sat in countless times.

This can't be.

Holly stumbled out of the car onto a lawn, ice-tipped blades of grass crunching beneath her sneakers. Her car was mangled, and she felt like she'd been shaken up in a snow globe, but she could walk, sort of.

Head spinning, she lurched toward the front door of the impossible, achingly familiar house on unsteady legs, feeling like the survivor of a horror film. A wave of dizziness hit her, and she fell. She looked up to see a six-foot-tall jolly snowman with a crooked carrot nose and purple bowler. She could've sworn it hadn't been there a moment before. Her head pounded.

Holly knew what she'd find beyond the snowman: a polar bear wearing a Santa hat and sitting beside a pile of gigantic gifts, its belly marked in Sharpie with a screaming stick figure. She'd told Cody it was someone the bear had eaten. Cody had thought it hilarious. He'd also taken the blame for the offending drawing when their father had discovered it.

Holly looked up to see the roof lined with icicle lights. There was no figure atop the tiles. She gulped, wondering what this meant.

She made her way to the front door, past the gnome family— three cute, matching figures and one smaller, uglier one, purchased when Holly was born. And then she was staring at the fresh holly wreath on the door. For years Cody had convinced Holly that their mother had bought it as an unspoken way to honor her birthday. She'd only learned after his death that he'd secretly been buying them with his allowance.

Holly turned the knob, wondering if this was when she'd wake up from this vivid hallucination. Maybe her physical body was stuck in the car now, dying, and her mind had chosen *that* day to return to. It made more sense than what was happening now. This house was impossible, after all.

The door opened and she stepped inside.

The scent of chocolate pecan pie, mid-bake, greeted her. Despite everything, her mouth watered. The foyer looked surreal in the way of stepping into a place you'd imagined going to for years.

She knew, then, that this was no dream. There were too many details she hadn't recalled in her mental tape of this day. Too many things she'd forgotten until this moment. The four stockings hanging on the front railing, Cody's torn in one spot from the year he'd been too eager to pry his new Swiss army knife out, and the box had caught on the yarn. The chandelier above, half the bulbs gone out. Holly's bright red rainboots on the shoe rack, dripping melted snow.

She thought of something her therapist had said years ago. About how holidays seem to exist outside the normal time stream. The way we never quite get over the nostalgia of childhood memories, how each year we use the next holiday to try to enter that elusive past.

Holly stepped forward; her tread felt strangely soft. She looked down. Instead of her Sketchers, she had on the fuzzy, red-nosed reindeer slippers Aunt Grace had sent for her ninth birthday-slash-Christmas gift. Instead of jeans and a sweater, she was in her blue snowflake pajamas. Her legs no longer hurt; her neck pain was gone. And she was small, barely any meat or muscle to pad her thin frame.

Then she heard *his* voice, newly deep with the occasional break, and all concerns fled her mind as she ran toward the one person she'd ached to see again.

"Cody!" Holly's slippers thumped on the worn beige carpet. Seconds later, she was in his arms, enveloped in a warm hug. He swung her in the air, and she squealed in delight. For a moment, she was the carefree nine-year-old she'd been whenever she'd had his full attention.

"Hey, birthday girl!" He set her back down, and she felt immediately forlorn. But he knelt down to her level and smiled wide, and she couldn't help smiling back.

Holly knew something wasn't right. She noticed the cut on his chin and thought—with the clarity of a thirty-nine-year-old—that he must still be learning to shave. She noticed the acne spots, the braces, how impossibly young he looked. The strain in his smile.

"What was that for?" he asked in the gentle voice he reserved for her.

Holly's mind felt jumbled. There was something she was meant to be asking. Or telling.

"I finished wrapping Dad's gift. Wanna help me haul it over?" He didn't wait for an answer, bounding up the hall. Holly followed him.

Dad's gift. *That* was it.

"Wait!" Holly shook her head trying to clear it, to get the words straight, to convince him not to do this. Maybe that was why she was here—a second chance. For thirty years, she'd wished for a do-over. She ran into his room.

Cody lowered the giant gift-wrapped box he was holding. "Everything okay, kiddo?"

She wanted to please him so badly it hurt, but she forced the words out. "No. We can't give it to Dad. It's dangerous!" Too many things crowded her head at once, dominated by the pull of her nine-year-old self's instincts. Adult Holly felt like a parasite nestled into child Holly's mind, trying desperately to turn things her way.

Cody laughed, a bright, happy sound that made her heart leap.

But she had to make him understand how serious this was. "No! It'll catch fire!"

"Oh, it'll be fine. It's store-bought. There are safety regulations when it comes to this stuff! And Dad probably won't even put it up until next year."

No, he won't. He'll put it up now, and everything will go wrong.

From down the hall, Gina hollered. "Cody? Holly? We're about to open gifts!"

Holly stopped, startled. Her mother's voice sounded different. Not carefree exactly, but less burdened. Sober in a way Holly had forgotten.

Cody was halfway out the door when Holly grabbed his arm. "Wait! Let's give him something else."

"Holly, come on. I saved up all month for this, and we got the one you picked. Let's go join Mom and Dad. After gifts and pie, we can make hot cocoa and play *Mario Kart*, okay?" He left the room, box in hand.

All alone, Holly's head cleared a bit. No one listened to nine-year-olds, damnit. What could she say to convince them, to change things?

"Of course you're hiding in Cody's room." Gina appeared. She grabbed Holly's spindly nine-year-old arm, grip like a vise as she dragged her daughter back down the hall.

"Mommy, that *hurts*." Holly hadn't meant for the words to come out.

"Quit whining." Gina yanked Holly down the three steps from the hallway to the sunken living room. Holly stumbled, landing hard on the worn wood flooring.

"There you are!" Eddie Chang boomed, looking up at them. Holly saw the flicker of something cross her father's face before his usual, vacuous smile replaced it. She'd always figured he'd been oblivious to the way Gina treated her, but . . .

"Open yours first, Dad!" Cody sounded eager.

"No—wait!" Holly said.

Her father was already tearing through the grinning wrapping paper Santas. With each rip, Holly's heart skipped a beat. She imagined him climbing up a ladder to the rooftop. Plugging it in. She couldn't let that happen. But no one was listening to her. She had to find another way.

She stood, and Gina's eyes cut to her.

"Bathroom," Holly mumbled as she slipped out. She slapped the side of her head, trying to *think*. The pull of the room, of her family, of Cody was so strong. The temptation to spend a few more moments with them before everything went to hell.

No. I have to save them.

Holly needed to find something sharp enough to cut through a power cord.

Her craft scissors weren't strong enough, and the box cutter in the front closet was too high up for her nine-year-old self to reach. Then she remembered the scissors on Cody's desk, sitting beside the tape dispenser and wrapping paper roll. She crept into his room, plucked the scissors off his desk, and tucked them into the elastic waistband of her pajamas.

Holly padded back down the hall, lurking in the shadows until her dad pulled the newest inflatable decoration out of its box. One reindeer, two reindeer, three reindeer, then Santa's sleigh. Without air filling out their blobby bodies, they looked like they'd been run over by a steam roller.

"We don't have room on the lawn," Gina said. "You have too many of these ridiculous characters already, Eddie. You'll have to replace something!"

"It's not for the lawn, Mom! It's for the roof. We even got an extension cord that'll reach all the way!" Cody turned to their dad. "The whole thing lights up. Holly picked it out for you."

At Cody's mention of her, Holly went rigid. But Eddie didn't look around, didn't wait for his daughter to return.

Though she knew she should be glad, a little stab of hurt lanced her heart. She watched her dad and Cody each pull one side of the inflatable, stretching it out between them while Gina read the instructions. They looked like a picture-perfect family of three. Mom, Dad, and their beloved child.

Holly tore herself away from the scene and tiptoed past the living room, heading for the front door. She heard the electric air pump start running. Between its earsplitting sound and her parents arguing over where to put the new decoration, she was able to slip outside, scissors digging into her side.

Holly shivered in the frigid air. She grabbed the scissors and looked for the power outlet as icy wind nipped her cheeks. Warmth leaked from every chunk of her exposed skin. She needed to do this quickly or her limbs would freeze.

Inside the house, it was warm and cozy.

No. If you don't do this, he'll die.

Holly found the power cord from the candy cane lights and traced it to an extension cord plugged into the side of the house. The extension cord was plugged into another extension cord, and every outlet was filled. Her reindeer slippers were wet and squishy from the snow, and water seeped through her pajama bottoms as she knelt by the cord.

The front door swung open. "Holly?"

Shit.

She flipped the switch, and all the lights went out.

"Holly!"

She could hear rage building in her mother's voice, but Gina wouldn't cuss her daughter out where others could hear. Or maybe she hadn't started cussing at her until after the incident. Holly couldn't remember, couldn't think about that now. She began to cut. Her fingers were so stiff with cold that it was hard to line everything up, to move them, but she managed.

Snip. The cord was thicker than a super jumbo candy cane—the kind she'd seen at a store, looking ripe for bludgeoning an elf with—and the scissors, sharp as they were, barely made a dent in the insulation. She tried again.

"You wicked child," Gina grabbed Holly, her whispered breath painfully hot against Holly's frozen cheek. "You are *not* going to ruin Christmas Eve. Get back inside."

No. This can't be happening.

Adult Holly knew what she was about to do was monstrous, but she had to save them all. She stabbed her mother's arm, and Gina screeched, letting go.

Eddie burst outside. "Gina?"

"She cut me!" Gina was too angry to keep her voice down.

Eddie grimaced, glancing at the neighboring houses. But he said nothing as he headed straight for Holly.

She knelt in the grass, fumbling for the cord. It was hard to see now that the decorative lights were out, and she'd lost her spot. She'd have to make a new cut. She sniffled, trying not to despair. Her fingers were so cold they felt like they'd fall off any minute now.

Before Holly could do any real damage, solid arms wrapped around her. She wriggled and fought to get away, but Eddie was so much stronger and so much warmer. He took the scissors and carried her inside.

Find another way. You still have time.

But she didn't.

Inside, Eddie headed for Holly's room. "You messed up, kid. Gotta face consequences."

"Dad, no!" She couldn't let him lock her up. She had to convince him. "Please. I'll say sorry to Mom. I'll do extra time-out this week. I'll wash all the dishes. I'll give up my allowance forever! Just let me stay to open presents."

"Sorry, kid."

"But it's my birthday!"

Eddie shook his head, looking sad. "Mom's orders."

Holly tried to argue, to fight, but it was no use. For years, she had seen her father as a poor sod under her mother's iron rule. Now she recognized his complicity.

It didn't matter. What did matter was the lock on her door, keeping her from getting out.

What mattered was the window in her room, too high for her to climb.

What mattered was that no one listened to nine-year-olds.

She pounded on the door, but no one came. She could imagine what was happening outside her room, the events of that fateful day painstakingly pieced together over the years. Cody was down in the daylight basement, digging through the special-occasion boxes for the Christmas dessert plates. Eddie was outside, setting up his new decoration. And Gina was whipping cream to accompany her pie.

Any minute now, Eddie would plug the inflatable sleigh into their overburdened network of extension cords, and the power would surge, starting the fire.

The lights went out.

Holly began to shake. It was happening all over again.

Eddie would be frantic now, searching for his wife and children. He would find Cody first and help pry open the basement window so Cody could climb out. Then the two of them would look for Holly, unaware that Gina had locked her in her room for some offense she'd committed. Gina would find her own way out, narrowly avoiding flames and burning debris as she escaped the house.

If it weren't for Holly, all three of them would make their way safely out, with no reason to go back inside.

I need you to be good for once. Be a good girl, Holly. All you have to do is stay quiet.

Holly's breath quickened. Had her mother's last words come to her now because she was at the end of her own life?

Holly could still be good.

She closed her eyes and prepared for the end. She imagined flames licking her cheek, the friendly face of death welcoming her at last. This time, she would not scream. Her scream would tell Cody where she was. He would break her window from the outside, climb up the trellis, and jump in. Then he would lift her out, saving her. He'd still be there when part of the ceiling caved, pinning him. Eddie would follow Cody inside, screaming his name just as the roof collapsed, burying them both in the rubble.

None of that would happen this time because Holly wasn't going to scream.

Except.

Except . . . something was different this go-round, wasn't it?

This time, Gina hadn't been the one to lock her up. Eddie had done it. Which meant that he knew where Holly was.

Hope bloomed in her chest. Her father would rescue her first. It would be the logical decision. After all, Cody was a teen, and Gina an adult; they both had better chances of making it out on their own than Holly did. Plus, Eddie might be compelled by guilt since he'd been the one to lock her up.

Once he and Holly were out, they could help Cody. Maybe, miraculously, all four of them would make it out alive.

Holly waited.

The smell of char filled the air, and Eddie did not come.

For thirty long years, Gina had told Holly that the deaths had been her fault. Holly had been young—so young—and desperate for any scrap of parental love. She hadn't questioned her mother's assertions until well into adulthood. By then, the accusations were rooted too deep, Holly's trust in herself too shallow.

Holly had directed all her rage inward for so long that she'd rarely allowed its direction to slip.

It began to slip out now.

Her father knew where she was, and still he did not come for her.

She imagined him prying open the basement window now, reaching out a hand to the child who was not only Gina's favorite, but also his favorite.

Didn't Holly deserve at least one parent who loved her?

It didn't matter. Cody was good. Cody deserved to live.

But didn't she deserve to live too?

All you have to do is stay quiet.

As Holly's throat grew dry and she began to cough, she reminded herself of all those times she'd wished for a chance to go back and change that day. She tried to hold onto her mental picture of Cody, grown up and smiling, picking up his daughter and swinging her in the air. Cody, in a trendy, big-city apartment, hanging up a canvas print of him and Holly. Cody and Eddie rewatching *Nightmare Before Christmas* and wishing they could share it with her.

It would be enough to save Cody and to be remembered. He *would* remember her. And he deserved to live.

Holly finally had a chance to right all her wrongs. All she had to do was let him live. All—she—had—to—do—was—keep—quiet.

She opened her eyes to see the brass doorknob to the room melting. To see the haze of smoke as death came for her.

She opened her mouth, and she screamed.

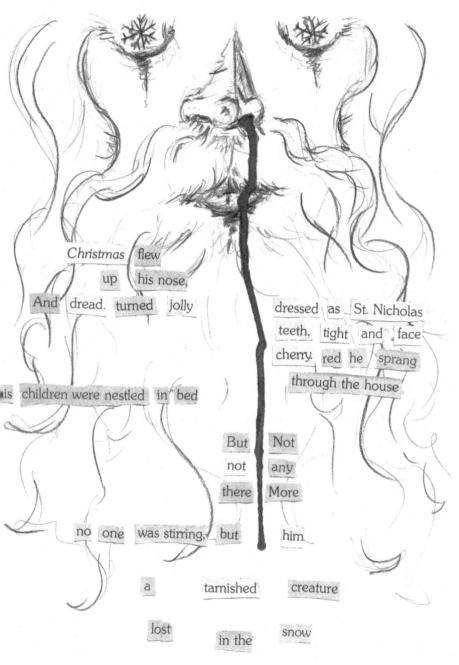

Christmas flew up his nose, And dread. turned jolly

dressed as St. Nicholas teeth, tight and face cherry. red he sprang through the house

is children were nestled in bed

But Not not any there More

no one was stirring, but him

a tarnished creature lost in the snow

FULL OF TOYS, *a black-out poem*
Jessica McHugh

NICE

Nat Cassidy

MITCHELL'S FOOTSTEPS TORE through the house like muffled machine-gun fire. *Thumpathumpathumpathump.*

"I made another one, Daddy—I made another one!" He launched himself from the foot of the stairs onto his father in the easy chair.

Daddy—also known as Kevin—let out a great *oof* as his six-year-old son landed on his lap (narrowly missing real estate that would've gotten a much different reaction). "That's great, buddy."

"I think it's my best one!" Mitchell held out the ornament he'd been working on upstairs—a hand-painted portrait of Santa splashed across its surface.

"I think so too!" Kevin exchanged looks with Andrea from across the room. Andrea was pouring herself another glass of Grüner.

Between them stood their Christmas tree, trimmed, lit up . . . and practically sagging under the amount of Mitchell's hand-painted, Santa-revering ornaments.

"Do you think he'll like it?" Mitchell asked Kevin.

"I'm sure he will."

"Promise?"

"*Mitchell*," Andrea said over her wineglass, "do you think your father knows what's going on in Santa's head?"

Kevin opened his mouth to remind Andrea to play nice, when Mitchell, suddenly abashed, said:

"At school? Eric said that Santa is really just your parents. Is that true?"

Andrea growled: "Oh, that little piece of—"

"Hon." Kevin cut her off. He turned to Mitchell, whose face was wide open, ready to receive the best news . . . or the worst. "Didn't Eric get in trouble for swallowing rocks for pocket change a few months ago? Does that sound like someone who knows anything about anything?"

Mitchell giggled, relieved. "No."

"Why don't you go upstairs and get ready for bed, and we'll find a good spot on the tree for your newest masterpiece?"

Mitchell hopped off Kevin's lap. *"Nine more sleeps until Christmas!"*

Another volley of machine-gun footfalls as Mitchell tore his way back upstairs.

"Stop running or you'll go on the naughty list!" Andrea called after him. The running stopped immediately.

In the silence that followed, the adults let out a breath together.

Kevin got up and went to the tree, ornament in hand.

"Would it kill you to have just a little more holiday cheer?" he asked his wife.

"It might."

"Baby."

Andrea sighed and put the bottle back in the fridge. "I'm just . . . I'm so over all this Christmas stuff. He gets so obsessive."

"All kids are superfans of something! For some, it's Batman or Star Wars. He loves Santa."

"Yeah, but he's so . . ."

She didn't finish. They both knew how uniquely intense their son could get. It wasn't just the ornaments. Drawings of Santa were Scotch-taped all over the living room. And kitchen. And hallway. And his bedroom. Santa was the inevitable subject of every conversation. All Mitchell cared about was pleasing some made-up commercial mascot who lived in the friggin' Arctic. Or was it the Antarctic? Andrea didn't know. It was all so stupid.

Kevin gave up and added the ornament to an already cluttered branch. Then he left the innumerable Santas leering at him, to go to his wife and kiss her forehead. "Remember what he was like with dinosaurs? Or learning how to tie knots? He'll find something new soon."

"Yeah . . ."

"Besides, I think it's great how enthusiastic he gets! He makes *me* love these things all over again too! I bet he'll be one hell of a salesman someday. Or a politician."

"Or a serial killer," Andrea muttered into her glass. "Or a cult leader."

"Andrea."

"Yeah, I know. 'Bah, humbug.' Sorry. You know how I get this time of year."

Another kiss. They held there for a moment, letting the tension deflate a little. Then Kevin yawned. "I'll go tuck him in."

Andrea stared at her glass. Before Kevin disappeared down the hall she said, "Hey. I'll . . . I'll find the Christmas spirit soon. Promise."

"I know you will." Kevin gave her a smile. "I noticed you put that little Elf on the Shelf in his room. The Christmas spirit gets everyone in the end."

Then he was gone, leaving Andrea with her wine. She had no idea what he meant about an Elf on the Shelf, but by the time they reconnected later that night, she'd already forgotten it.

* * *

It was just past midnight when a pair of tiny hands shook Mitchell awake.

His eyes fluttered open.

Standing on the bed was the elf that had mysteriously appeared on his bookcase this morning. About a foot tall, a sparkly, red conical hat on his impish little face.

Being six years old, Mitchell didn't question it. His face lit up like—well, a Christmas tree. "Hi!"

The elf put a white-gloved finger to his own lips. Then, in a whisper: "Hi, Mitchell. Gotta keep it quiet, okay? Otherwise your parents'll be on us like crabs on a Williamsburg toilet seat."

"I don't know what that means!"

"Doesn't matter. Just hush, okay?"

Mitchell nodded, smiling a huge smile. The elf's voice was high and sweet, but there was a rasp to it. An adult might have heard it and thought of a smoker's voice. Mitchell just thought it sounded delightfully silly.

"Cool." The elf began to pace a little over the bedspread. "So—"

"What's your name?" Mitchell asked at full volume.

"Ugh. It's . . . Twinklebottom."

Mitchell giggled. The elf's face drew down in a sneer. "Oh, like 'Mitchell' makes any fucking sense? Listen, we don't have a lot of time. I need to talk to you about something very important, okay? So, just, shh."

Mitchell did his best to keep his voice quiet. "I've been good all year, right? I've tried so, so, so hard, and—"

"Yeah, yeah, you've been great. That's . . . heh, well, that's kinda the problem. I couldn't help but notice you've got a bit of a Santa thing going on here and so—"

"I *love* Santa!"

Twinklebottom seethed through gritted teeth. "Kid! Shut your tit-hole and listen!"

Something flashed in Mitchell's eyes that made the elf pause for the briefest of moments. Something hard and cold. Gone as quickly as it arrived.

"Thanks, buddy!" Twinklebottom said, backing up, trying to sound syrupy sweet. "I'm sorry, it's just . . . well, I'm a little stressed right now, Mitchell. This is a stressful time, okay?"

Mitchell nodded. "Daddy says Mommy is stressed too. I wish I could make her feel happier."

"Yeah. Lotta stress in the air. But that's why I'm here, bud. I need your help."

"My help?"

"Mitch? *I need you to help me save Christmas.*"

Mitchell's eyes went wide. "Tell me," he whispered.

So Twinklebottom did.

"It didn't used to be this way," he began. "A long, long time ago, things were soooo much easier." He described how, for generations, being one of Santa's elves was a great gig. Toys were fun to make—even the complex ones. But with every year, the orders got more and more complicated. Electronics. Microchips. The workshop stank of toxic chemicals, burning plastic, frying wires. "And there are so many more goddamn kids now! And each kid wants so many goddamn things! You know what exponential means, Mitchell?"

Mitchell shook his head.

"It means arthritis! It means back spasms! It means stress ulcers and nervous breakdowns and all kinds of shit magical beings aren't supposed to be fucking worried about!"

"You sure do swear a lot," Mitchell said, grimacing.

"'Cuz I'm in *pain*, Mitchell!" the tiny creature hissed.

Mitchell looked genuinely distressed. "So . . . what can I do?"

"Well, you're not gonna like it. But remember, I'm saying this as a representative of Christmas, right?"

"A representative." Pronouncing the word with a solemn nod. "Right."

Twinklebottom took a breath, then stared Mitchell right in the eyes. "I need you to be naughty, bud."

Mitchell recoiled like he'd been gutshot. "What? N-naughty?"

"I know what you're thinking. You *can't* be naughty. Right?"

Mitchell's eyes darted to the portraits he'd taped all over his room. "Santa—"

"Santa hates naughty! I know! But I've got news for you, kid. Santa's not the saint you think he is! He's a boss, just like any other boss. He only cares about one thing: the bottom line. Check this shit out."

Twinklebottom pulled out a little phone from his green pants, then pulled up some pictures to show Mitchell. The images were small but undeniable. Cramped workspaces. Miserable faces. Elves frozen in misery.

Mitchell started to cry.

"I know, right? It's bleak shit." Twinklebottom took the phone back, put it away. "Lemme put it this way, kid. Things are so hard for us because of all the work we've gotta do, right? And we've gotta do all this work because . . ."

"Because you make toys?" Mitchell blubbered.

Twinklebottom nodded. "For?"

"The good boys and girls?"

"That's right. The 'Nice' list. So we'd have *less* work to do if the Nice list was . . .?"

The word problem helped Mitchell calm down. He sniffed back a sinus cavity full of snot and thought. "Shorter."

"Exactamundo, Mitch, ol' pal. When you think about it, the Nice kids are the ones who are being bad, because look what they're doing to us!" Now it was Twinklebottom's turn to cry. His voice cracked with emotion. He fought it valiantly. "Mitchell, my friend . . . if you could just be naughty . . . and maybe get some of your friends to be naughty . . . well, it'd be the Nicest thing you could ever do."

Mitchell's brow knit as he tried to work through the paradox. "O-okay. So . . . if I'm naughty . . . then that's good . . . because it helps the elves."

"Now you're getting it!" Twinklebottom jubilantly smacked one of Mitchell's comforter-covered legs. "Because you wanna be nice, right?"

"More than anything!"

"*So stop being nice, Mitchy.* Please. For us."

Now, Twinklebottom reached out and touched Mitchell's hand tenderly. The six-year-old's hand dwarfed the elf's, but it curled around Twinklebottom's all the same.

When Twinklebottom looked back up, he noticed that coldness had again crept into the boy's eyes. It made Twinklebottom's elf stomach cramp a little. What was going on in that kid's head? No time to dwell on it, though, because Mitchell gave a short, definitive nod and sighed.

"Okay, Twinklebottom."

Twinklebottom sagged with relief. "For real?!"

"I'll be naughty, Twinklebottom."

"Holy shit, Mitch! You're the best! The elves thank you! And, hey"—he gestured to the drawings on the wall—"happy elves mean happy Santa, right? So, even if you still got a hard-on for ol' Jelly Guts over there, you're still doing him a solid too. Aw, shit, speaking of, I gotta get back to the Pole before he notices I'm gone. Time and Yuletide waits for no one, am I right?"

*   *   *

After that, Mitchell couldn't fall back asleep. He calmly took down each of his paintings of Santa, stacking them on top of one another, and put them face down on his little desk, under a yellow plastic stegosaurus.

His head swam. Could he really be naughty? Wasn't that breaking The Rules? Or was it really following The Rules? That day Daddy had caught him playing with one of Mrs. Gresham's cats and that lighter he'd found in the kitchen drawer, Daddy had told him how important it was to be Nice.

Don't you know you have to be Nice, Mitchell?

Those were The Rules.

How could he be Naughty?

How would he even start?

Then he remembered that box under the bed.

*   *   *

Two nights later, Twinklebottom was on top of the fucking world. Which, he supposed, was kind of an ironic turn of phrase considering he wasn't at the North Pole right now. He was heading back to his dear buddy Mitchy-poo's boxy suburban house to let him know the good news.

He'd managed to sneak a peek at the numbers. Mitchell's Naughtiness was off the charts. Hell, even some of numbers of the other kids on the block seemed to be going down too. The kid was a Naughty savant. Twinklebottom *had* to know his secrets.

When he'd initially had the idea for this little pilot program, he'd figured a Santa superfan would be an ideal first candidate. Obviously, whatever results he'd get would be too late to affect the demands for this year, but if he could get some movement out of a kid *that* hardcore, during the height of Christmas fever no less?

Well, there would be some motherfucking proof in the figgy pudding, right there. And he appeared to have succeeded beyond his wildest sugarplum dreams. There were gonna be some real changes afoot starting next year. This would teach that fat, monopolistic fuck a thing or two about using his workforce as chattel.

Twinklebottom sauntered up the side of the house to Mitchell's second-floor window. It wasn't midnight like before, but it was definitely past bedtime. Sure enough, Mitchell was in bed. Under the covers, but not asleep.

Twinklebottom tapped on the window.

Mitchell didn't look as excited to see him, but he did smile.

That smile got a little bigger as Twinklebottom jumped up and down on the bed, letting Mitchell know how great he'd done so far, how all the elves were *sooo* grateful, how they had hope for the first time in years, all because of one brave little human moppet.

Total bullshit—Twinklebottom hadn't told his plans to anyone else, and honestly, the conditions weren't *that* bad; all the photos he'd shown had been photoshopped—but Mitchell didn't need to know any of that.

Mitchell's smile seemed to falter, though. And it never quite reached his eyes.

Twinklebottom noticed the kid was pretty dirty. Stains all over his hands like he'd been rooting around in dirt and mud.

"Someone hasn't been taking a bath, I see. Pretty naughty," Twinklebottom said with a teasing grin.

"Yeah . . ."

"And your room is so messy! I bet Mommy asked you to clean it, and you said no."

"Not really . . ."

"Oh. Kay." The kid's aloofness was already starting to get annoying. "You're squashing my high a little here, kid."

"Sorry," Mitchell replied, looking down at his feet. "I don't feel very good. My stomach hurts a little."

Little shit's probably been sent to bed without supper twice now, Twinklebottom thought jubilantly.

"Why don't you take me through what you've done so far, huh? Then we'll see about scrounging up some food for ya? Just keep it quiet so we don't wake your parents."

"Okay."

Mitchell took a breath and started recounting all he'd done to be Naughty. It was in that halting, scattershot way all kids of that age have of telling stories—no chronology, no build, all kinds of doubling back and digressions—but at least he started to come out of his stupor a bit as he talked.

"I did everything I could think of. Like, Mommy always told me not to play with the plants, so I played with the plants. And I ran around a lot. That was fun. I even ran with the knives. Mommy and Daddy both told me never to do that, so I did it. And up and down the stairs. And I turned the TV up real loud. And the screaming."

A few minutes more of this detailed some picayune transgressions—none of which sounded bad enough to juice the kid's Naughty numbers up so high. Twinklebottom was about to get impatient when Mitchell said:

"Then I found my ropes from my magic kit and then . . ." His eyes expanded. "Can I just show you? It's downstairs." Without waiting for an answer, he spun on his heels and ran out of the room. *Thumpathumpathumpathump.*

Twinklebottom followed. Before he could stop the kid and remind him to be quiet—last thing he needed was to wake the kid's parents up—he noticed a stretch of rope tied across his bedroom doorway.

Almost looked like a trip wire.

Just beyond, in the hallway, lay a plastic stegosaur toy. The toy was yellow, but the sharp plates lining its back appeared coated in something dark and crusty. Some of the plates were bent, like something heavy had fallen onto the toy from a great height.

Twinklebottom felt a strange rumbling in his gut. Dread.

Mitchell's voice continued, loud and heedless, at the top of the stairs.

"Come on downstairs—I wanna show you!" he called.

Twinklebottom climbed over the rope and hurried down the hall to catch up . . . but then something else caught his eye as he passed the doorway of what appeared to be the largest bedroom. The grown-ups' room.

He couldn't be sure what he was seeing—he'd have to actually go into the room for a better look—but from this vantage point outside, it almost looked like a pair of legs were trussed to the bed-frame, with the same kind of rope that had been stretched across the doorframe.

Those legs were very still. Inanimately still. But . . . did he also hear moaning coming from further inside the room? A barely audible voice? The words *Help* and *me*?

"Come *on*, Twinklebottom!" Mitchell urged from the landing, sounding more animated and excited than at any point so far this evening.

Thumpathumpathumpathump down the stairs.

Twinklebottom tore his eyes away from the bedroom and followed. He suddenly didn't want to see anything more.

The air was starting to feel very thin. He wished he were back at the North Pole.

Mitchell's litany of achieved naughtiness continued downstairs. He was rambling about how Mommy had always told him not to sing so loudly inside, so he'd been singing Christmas carols at the top of his lungs; and also he'd tried to pour milk into his cereal without help, and the milk got everywhere. And he'd turned the TV remote into a drumstick—*parumpapumpum*.

Except Twinklebottom had stopped listening by the time he also reached the living room.

He was too stunned by what he was seeing to even know how to listen anymore.

When he'd first cased this house, he'd noticed the family's giant tree. It had been impossible to miss, the way it glowed with lights and sagged with all the ornaments dedicated to Santa.

Most of those ornaments were shattered on the floor now. Fallen from the tree like overripe fruit.

Instead, the tree sagged under a different weight. Human organs hung from the branches—conspicuously only at a height a child could easily reach. Ropes of intestines twined around like tinsel. A heart was speared messily on one branch. Other organs, sloppily removed and even more sloppily hung, smeared across the evergreen in unrecognizable clumps. A spleen, a gallbladder, a lung—who the fuck knew?

The tree still glowed too. Mitchell hadn't taken down any of the lights. The blood cast the bottom half of the tree into a sick emergency red.

"Kid . . ." the elf wheezed. "What did you do?"

On one of the branches, he saw the viscous globe of an eyeball hung from its shredded optic nerve, like a traditional bulb.

Mitchell stood in the middle of the living room. Only now did Twinklebottom understand that wasn't just dirt that smeared his pajamas. His hair. "I did what you said! I was as Naughty as I could be!"

Twinklebottom thought he might faint. The periphery of his vision sparkled with dark stars.

He mustn't faint. Not here. He had to get out of here. But he couldn't get his legs to work. He was concentrating too hard on not throwing up, not passing out. He bent down and noticed all the dirty footprints all over the floor.

Mitchell took a step toward him.

"There's just one problem, Twinklebottom."

"Oh, kid," the elf managed to say in between panicked gasps. "You got plenty of problems, all right."

Mitchell took another step closer. "My problem is . . . I tried everything I could that was Naughty, but I'm scared I did it wrong. Because even though I knew I was being Naughty? It all just felt so . . . Nice."

The kid sounded genuinely, almost innocently conflicted. Twinklebottom looked up in horror to see how close Mitchell now was. And how *huge*.

Before the elf could say anything, though, a knock came from the front door.

Twinklebottom whirled around. "Oh fuck, who's—"

"Be right there!" Mitchell called to whoever was outside. In response, Twinklebottom could hear the giggle of delighted children. Then he remembered the Naughty numbers. Even the other kids on the block had begun to trend downward.

"That's my friends," Mitchell said. "I told them all about what you told me and how they need to be as naughty as can be. They're here to help me finish with Mommy."

The interruption helped Twinklebottom find his motor skills again. He began to back away. "Hey, that's great, kid. I'll—I'll leave you to it, then."

"But what about my problem?"

Twinklebottom tried to laugh through a throat as dry as year-old gingerbread. "I wouldn't worry about that. You're good. You did good work! I mean, bad work! Naughty work!"

Mitchell advanced, closing the distance between them easily. God, humans were so fucking *big*.

"But is it really Naughty if it feels Nice? Do I need to do something I don't like for it to be *really* bad?"

"Nah, don't sweat that, kiddo, it's all—*ah, fuck!*"

Pain rocketed through his foot. In his backing away, he'd accidentally stepped on a shard of ornament. It tore through his little elf boot and lodged into his flesh, going all the way to the bone. He fell, hard. Without wasting a second, he tried to pull the shard out so he could run.

More knocking on the door. The impatience of children.

Mitchell loomed over him, as huge and imposing as a god.

"Wait a minute," Mitchell said, not to the elf or the kids outside, but to himself. "Maybe, if I want to be *really* Naughty, maybe I need to do something bad to *Christmas*. Because I care about Christmas the most."

"Nah, you aced the test—you really don't have to worry about it!" Twinklebottom babbled. His hands were slick with blood and sweat. He couldn't get the damn shard out.

Outside, the kids began singing. Carols, atonal and insane—or maybe the elf's brain just couldn't comprehend anything anymore.

"Yeah," Mitchell continued, piecing it together. "Yeah, maybe if I want to be *really* Naughty . . . what could be naughtier than doing something to"—he found the word waiting for him like a present—"a *representative?*"

"No! No, kid, wait—!"

Mitchell's hand easily wrapped around Twinklebottom's head, muffling the elf's screams. He scooped the elf up and went to answer the door.

THAW

Rachel Harrison

THERE ARE PINE needles in my hair, under my fingernails. Tinsel in my mouth, somehow. There's a pot on the stove with simmering sugar, cloves, cinnamon sticks, and cranberries—some concoction I found online—wafting the scent of holiday cheer through the cabin. There are cookies cooling on the counter, almost ready for frosting. From the speakers, some crooner sings about a wintery landscape.

"Isn't this romantic?" I ask him. "Much better than spending the holidays with my family."

"Or mine," he says, throwing another log on the fire.

"Just us," I say.

"Just us," he echoes, stepping back from the hearth.

"Hey. You changed. You're wearing the shirt I got you." A red and black flannel I'd bought him specifically for this trip.

"What do you think?" he asks, hands on his hips, trotting around the wagon-wheel coffee table that's so tacky it's hard not to love.

"You look . . . hot. Like, smokin' hot. You look like a lumberjack," I say. "Like a nature guy."

He laughs. "Nature guy?"

"Don't laugh!" I say, wrapping my arms around him. "I'm being serious."

"Yeah?" He puts his face near my face but doesn't kiss me. Such a tease.

"Dead serious."

"Ooh," he says, giving me a quick peck. "Come here. I want to show you something."

He takes my hand and leads me to the corner, near the tree we lugged up here and decorated this afternoon.

"Look," he says, pointing out the frosty window.

I lean closer, but my breath fogs the glass. "What is it?"

He reaches across me to open the window. I wince at the punch of bitter wind.

"You see it? Over there on the hill?"

The cold stings my eyes. I squint, and I recognize a shape off in the distance, near the line of trees, like it's just emerged from the forest or is standing guard. A snowman. Classic snowman. Button eyes. Carrot nose. Branches for arms. Striped scarf. Black top hat.

"That's random," I say. I don't remember seeing it when we got here. It's possible I missed it, with where it is. I stare at it now. It's almost too perfect. Entirely symmetrical. Seamlessly round. The proportions exact. Like an illustration. A cartoon. "Is it real?"

"What do you mean?"

"Is it a decoration, or is it a legit snowman?"

"Aren't all snowmen decorations?" he says, his tone dangerously close to condescending.

"I mean, is it, like, made of plastic? It doesn't look . . ."

"Doesn't look what?"

"Real," I say, shivering. "Can we close the window?"

He reaches across me again and pulls the windowpane down hard. He doesn't lock it, so I do. "I thought you'd be charmed."

"I just . . . I don't know. I guess I find it weird that it's out there, not in front of the cabin. And who built it? There are no other houses around here."

"The owners, before we came," he says. "They're after that Airbnb superhost status or whatever."

"Yeah," I say, uneasy. The smell of cinnamon and cloves is now cloying, making me nauseous.

"I have an idea," he says, taking my hands in his. "Let's open that bottle of champagne and get in the hot tub."

"I was . . . never mind. Yes, let's do it," I say.

"You were what?"

"I was saving the champagne for tomorrow night, but . . . fuck it."

"Fuck it," he says, spinning me around. "It's Christmas vacation!"

I steal another look out the window at the snowman, the wind blowing his branch arms so it looks like he's waving.

* * *

Half an hour later, we step into the hot tub on the back deck. I hold the bottle of champagne and two Solo cups.

"We're so classy," I say, teeth chattering. My body is confused. Hot water. Cold air. I thought it would feel better than it does.

"You have tinsel in your hair," he says, picking some out. It catches on my earing, and I wince. He keeps pulling until it's free, tossing the silver strands onto the deck. Glimmering litter in snow. "Here, pass me the bottle. I'll pop it."

"I hate this part," I say, setting the cups down on the edge of the hot tub so I can cover my ears. I turn away, anticipating the sound.

"This is the fun part," he says. The cork comes rocketing out. I scream, he laughs.

I grab the cups and hold them out so he can fill them. "I startle easily."

"I know," he says, setting the bottle of champagne on the deck. "Okay! Cheers to our first trip together. Our first holiday together."

Officially, yes. We were dating last year, but it wasn't serious. On Christmas night, we stayed up late drunk texting from our respective childhood bedrooms, bitching about our families and ranking seasonal candy, and then talking about what we'd do to each other if we were in bed together. He stopped responding at around two AM, so I snuck downstairs to eat sugar cookies and stare at the lights in the neighbor's yard, which they always left on all night. They had an eclectic mix of decorations—string lights, a nativity, inflatables, elves, wooden cutouts of Disney characters, an assortment of Santas, multiple American flags.

I thought about how much effort it must take to put out all those decorations. I thought about the electric bill. I wondered if they were ridiculous or whether I was cynical. To me, the holidays were always more of a hassle than a celebration. A trip home to passive-aggressive parents who didn't love each other but were too stubborn to get divorced. My younger siblings who shut themselves in their rooms to play video games and scroll through social media. Visits to extended family who would steer the conversation to politics so they had an audience to grandstand to about their narrow-minded beliefs. My aunt who, without fail, would ask me if I had lost weight, despite knowing I spent time in the hospital my senior year of high school for an eating disorder.

"Leaving me hanging?" he says, splashing me.

"Sorry," I say. "To our first holiday. Our first trip. To us."

"To us!" he says, tapping my Solo cup with his. "Cheers."

"Cheers."

He takes a sip of champagne and then kisses me. He smells like fire. Like smoke. He tastes of peppermint.

"We could do this every year," he says. "A new tradition."

His family is similarly difficult, and it's nice to have that in common. To not have to explain the complicated array of emotions. To have somewhere else to go, someone to be with. Someone I could see a potential future with.

"It is pretty dreamy," I say, shifting to the other side of the hot tub so I have a view of the snow-covered hills, the evergreens that texture the horizon. "So peaceful."

As soon as the words leave my mouth, they become untrue, like fruit rotting the minute you bring it home. Because I see it. The snowman. And he's somewhere else. He has moved.

"Look," I say. "Look!"

"What?" he asks, following my gaze out toward the trees. "Oh. Another one."

"It's not another one. It's the same one. Same hat, same scarf . . ."

"There's more than one top hat in the world," he says. "Why are you freaking out? It's a snowman."

The way he says it, there's no way I can answer. How do I justify my fear? This strange, bone-deep unease at the sight of something so sweet and harmless.

Only, it's not just the hat and the scarf that are the same. It's
the same exact shape, the same size. Even the branches are the
same, I swear. There's just something about it I can't put my
finger on. How it was around the side of the house, toward the
front, and now it's at the back. And there's a disturbance in the
snow. A trail.

I want to ask him if he sees it, but I don't want to harp on this
and risk ruining the night. The trip. A holiday that there's still some
hope to actually enjoy.

He once told me about the time he brought his college ex home
for Christmas, and she spent the whole day irritated that his mother
was insensitive to her peanut allergy. The way he told the story, it
was clear that he sided with his ex, acknowledging her complaints
were valid and his mother was being ridiculous for lamenting that
she couldn't make her famous peanut brittle. But he also said something along the lines of how he wished his then-girlfriend could
have just let it go, not made such a big deal of it.

They were broken up by Valentine's Day. After the holidays, he
said he knew she wasn't the one, and didn't want to go through the
motions, give her false hope in the form of chocolates in a heart-
shaped box.

"Never mind," I say, downing my champagne and putting my
back to the snowman. "Forget I said anything. Let's . . . let's talk
about something else."

"Or not talk at all," he says, pulling me toward him.

I let him kiss me, even though I can't be present in the kiss
because I can't shake the feeling we're being watched. That, out
there, two big button eyes see us. Observe with intention. Slowly
move closer.

*   *   *

We come in from the hot tub, take a shower, put on our pajamas.
We frost the cookies while singing along to carols, making up our

own lyrics, laughing until we're doubled over, breathless, making wild sounds like donkeys, like hyenas.

We finish the champagne and transition to eggnog, heavy on the bourbon. He drinks himself to sleep on the couch as we watch the fire, and I go into the kitchen to clean up.

I wash the dishes as quietly as possible so I don't wake him. The sound of his snores and the fire crackling drift in from the other room. He's probably out for the night. I wonder if I should leave him or try to coax him off the couch and into bed. Selfishly, I don't want to sleep alone.

Not here.

It's a nice rental. Classic log cabin. Rustic. Newer amenities. Clean. But it's still a cabin in the woods, miles away from anything. Anyone.

Except for the snowman, says a mean voice in my head.

Why is it bothering me so much? Why does it freak me out?

I wipe my hands on the dishrag and slink toward the tree, toward the window just behind it. I take a deep breath, inhaling the scent of pine needles and the dying fire. I exhale, and I cup my hands around my eyes as I lean into the window, press up against the cool glass.

I expected the snowman to be there, but he isn't. He's gone.

Which means, the snowman did move. I wasn't imagining it.

I stagger back from the window, bumping into the tree, knocking an ornament to the floor. It shatters, and I wince, certain I've just woken him. He grunts and I hold my breath. But then he goes on snoring, even louder now, so loud that I don't even notice the crunch beneath my feet, so loud I don't even hear myself yelp. I carefully lower myself to the floor, remove my socks and examine my skin, scanning for shards of the broken ornament. My fingers find a sliver of glittery silver glass stuck in my left heel. I pick it out. There's no blood, just a dull throbbing.

My back to the wall, I scooch over until I'm a safe distance from the wreckage, then stand, tiptoeing to the bathroom to take a better look at my feet. I flip the light on and sit on the cold tile floor, quickly finding another shard wedged into the arch of my right foot. I extract it and toss it in the trash. A shock of red lingers on my fingers, drips onto the green tile. Panicked, I grab some toilet paper, attempt to wipe it up. It doesn't absorb—it dissolves, leaving an even bigger mess.

My heart beats hard and fast—*rum-pum-pum, rum-pum-pum*. I part my dry lips to cry for help, but I'm still hesitant to wake him. What if he asks me what I was doing over by the tree near the window? I'm too embarrassed to admit that I was looking for the snowman.

The snowman who is not where he was. The snowman who is on the move.

Where is he now?

I put my socks on, ignoring the blood dripping from the cut on the bottom of my right foot, and shuffle out toward the back deck. I can't see out the door—the angle isn't right—so I slip into the bedroom and crawl across the mattress, to the window on the other side. From here, I should be able to see the snowman. At least if he were in the same spot as when we were out in the hot tub. He's not. No—not anymore. There's a divot in the snow, evidence of his presence, and there's the trail. Stretching from the side of the cabin, back around the deck, to the other side. It's moving closer. Coming toward us.

I slide off the bed and hobble back to the kitchen, to where I was. There's a window there, behind the table. What if the snowman was there, watching me as I cleaned up? The thought of its black button eyes turns my stomach.

But there's nothing out the kitchen window. Just the snowy hillside and the forest beyond.

Maybe it's the eggnog, the champagne, the excessive consumption of sugar. Maybe it's nerves. Maybe I am seeing things, imagining things. Making something out of nothing.

I should just let it go. Allow myself to enjoy this time, this happy season. Maybe I'm so used to it being ruined for me—by my family, by exes who aren't looking to commit, by work, by the balance in my bank account, by a general sense of loneliness—that I can't help but expect for something to go wrong.

I sweep up the ornament, cover him in a blanket, and then put myself to bed, avoiding the windows. I leave the door open but pull the curtains closed. I shut my eyes and wait for sleep. For visions of sugar plums. For warm fuzzies.

All I see in the dark are button eyes, and all I feel is cold. Cold and alone.

There's a rapping at the window. I tell myself it's the wind.

*   *   *

"Good morning," he says, snuggling up to me, kissing my neck.

"Morning," I say, a reluctant little spoon. I didn't sleep much, and I'm not thrilled to be woken up, especially after I was so careful not to disturb him last night.

"Merry Christmas," he says.

"Mm," I say. "Merry Christmas."

"Where's the coffee?"

"I left it out," I say, yawning. "On the counter."

"You didn't. I looked," he says. "You did leave the window open."

"What?"

"In the kitchen. You left the window open."

I sit up. "No, I didn't."

He raises his eyebrows. "I'm not mad. Some snow got in, but it's no big deal. A wet floor."

"Okay, but I didn't open the window." Right? Or did I? When I went into the kitchen to see if the snowman had moved, did I open the window?

"Well, I didn't open it," he says.

I kick off the covers, teeth chattering at the cold as I stumble out of bed and down the hall into the kitchen. The coffee is out on the counter. And the window is open. There's a small mound of snow on the sill, a twig sticking straight up out of it.

A finger, I think. Then I chastise myself. Not a finger, not a snowman extremity. A twig. Just a twig. Blown in from outside.

I close the window and lock it. I grab a paper towel and mop up the snow, wondering why he couldn't have done it.

"Oh, shit. Sorry. I didn't see it," he says, picking up the coffee. "You want some? I think there's only a French press, though. You know I always mess it up. One scoop? Two? I can never remember."

"I can do it," I say, wondering if he really didn't see the bag of coffee grounds, or if he did and just needed an excuse to wake me because he wanted coffee and knew I would make it for him.

I fill the kettle with water from the tap, put it on the stove. Light the burner. Watch the blue and orange flame.

"Should I start a fire?" he asks. "Then we can have coffee and breakfast?"

"Sure. Okay."

He pulls some mistletoe out from behind his back and holds it over our heads, kisses me. It's sweet, and his arms are so warm around me. My frosty disposition thaws. I giggle and push him away. "Mister Jolly over here."

"The jolliest," he says, walking over to the fireplace with a box of matches.

I feel guilty for getting annoyed with him. For doubting him. So what if he wanted me to make him coffee? Maybe he just wanted my company on Christmas Day. To spend time together. To celebrate.

"I brought peppermint creamer," I call from the kitchen.

"Genius woman!" he says. "A visionary!"

Is he being sarcastic?

Am I doing it again? I'm doing it again. Trying to sabotage the holiday, to pull out the rug before it's pulled out from under me.

I scoop some grounds into the French press, and I wait patiently for the kettle to scream.

* * *

After a breakfast of eggs and bacon and coffee and mimosas, he goes to the bathroom, and I put the dishes in the sink. The same holiday playlist we had on yesterday comes through the speakers, and even though I'm sick of these songs by now, I let them play because I don't want to be a Grinch. A humbug.

"Baby, It's Cold Outside" comes on, right as he walks in wearing jeans and a flannel. Not the one I got him. A different one. One I've never seen him wear before. I wonder if it's new. If he got it before or after the flannel I gifted him, which he wore yesterday for maybe forty-five minutes before we got in the hot tub.

"Ah, the holiday rape song," he says flippantly. "Honestly, I don't think it's that rapey."

He goes over and kneels in front of the fire, poking it with the iron. I watch him.

Did he really just say that?

"Did you really just say that?"

"What?" he says. "I don't. Do you?"

"I . . ."

"It's flirty," he says. "People are too sensitive. Some of it, I understand. But this?"

Not knowing what to say, I say nothing.

"Are you offended?" he asks. "I'm only joking."

"I know." I tell the lie as I turn toward the double window, the one between the kitchen and the front door. What I see outside doesn't surprise me. It scares me, but it validates me.

"Ow," he says. "Fuck. I burned myself."

"Are you okay?"

"Yeah, I'll live."

"Mm."

"What are you looking at?"

"The snowman," I say.

"Again with the snowman?" he says. "Want me to go knock it over? Decapitate Frosty? Pour hot water over its head?"

"You could try, but I don't know what would happen."

"I have a pretty good idea. Do you think I should put something on this burn? It's not *bad* bad, but it kind of hurts."

He shows me his hand. There's a patch of heat-warped skin at the base of his thumb, already blistering, red and shiny as a holly berry. "Can you go see if there's a first aid kit?"

I think of last night, pulling glass out of my feet. Should I let this go?

"Hey," he says. "Hello . . .?"

"You asked me why the snowman freaked me out. Maybe it's because I just can't help myself. I'm constantly wondering if a good thing is bad. I guess I'm a cynic, but . . . sometimes it is. Sometimes the good thing is bad."

The wind howls outside the cabin, rattles the door.

"Or maybe I was afraid because my intuition told me I needed to be. My intuition is never wrong, but I don't always listen to it. I should have listened. And you should have listened to me."

He gets up, wordlessly, and walks over. He pushes me aside so he can see out the window.

"What the . . ." he says. "Did you . . .?"

He gets his boots, which are on the mat by the door, near the presents, near the pile of fallen pine needles under the tree. He slips them on, pulls his coat off the hook.

"You shouldn't go out there," I say.

"It's just a fucking snowman," he says, walking back into the room, grabbing the fire iron from the hearth.

"I don't think it is. I really don't think it is."

"Stay here," he tells me, as if I'd follow him without specific instruction. I'm not going outside. Baby, it's cold outside.

He opens the door, and again I warn him, but he's already gone. Stomping down the porch steps, holding the poker like a baseball bat, approaching where it waits, at the foot of the stairs. Bigger than I remember. Or maybe just closer.

Closer. Definitely closer.

Because I can see its button eyes aren't black. I can see they aren't buttons at all.

When the screaming starts, and crimson streaks the white, white snow, I lock the door, and for a while I don't look, so I almost don't see the long branch arms drag his halves off into the woods, leaving behind a trail of blood and a fire iron.

Soon the snow starts to fall, and it covers the red, and it covers the iron, and I help myself to more eggnog, and I put another log on the fire, and I put on the flannel I bought him that was balled up in his suitcase, and I listen to some crooner sing about wintery landscapes, and I wonder why I was ever so scared of spending the holidays alone.

"Just me," I say to myself. "Just me."

At some point, I know I will have to look out the window, to open the door. The snowman could be out there. Could be waiting.

Or . . . I could draw all the curtains. Keep the doors locked. Stay forever.

For now, I'll just keep the fire burning. I'll keep myself warm.

CANDY CANE

Thommy Hutson

S HE RUNS, EVEN though I can see, almost feel, that it hurts her.
Poor thing. Gashes on the leg, at least two holes in her side, and
I'm pretty sure I got a good, clean slice down her back. She stumbles, and it becomes quite easy, almost relaxing, to follow. I do so
much prefer it when they put real effort into the getting-away por-
tion of the program, but you win some, you—*whatever*. The bottom of her dress billows, its lilac pattern fluttering with every
stuttered kick of her leg. I focus on her backside, where the fabric
clings tight and heavy, matted with blood, the ends of her auburn
hair sticky with dripping, dropping red.

She staggers through the trees, her head turning like a broken
robot's, as if she might find someone in the park this late, a strange
passerby who would help instead of sending her to the promised
land like I already told her I will. The moon throws beams of white,
accentuating the red that pours from her wounds in the most precious way. Red and white make pink, after all. She really should
thank me.

As her life drip-drops, it tickles to recall how the tip of my blade
went through and in, sideways and out. This one displayed a forti-
tude more than most; I won't lie and say that when she kicked me in
the face, it didn't both hurt and thrill me. *Toughytoughytoughy*.

But all good things come to an end. Lilac slows, turning her
head and flailing her arms as I pull the syringe from my right jacket
pocket. I rub my thumb along its plastic covering, a rhythmic
caressing that signals that the real fun is about to start.

She stops, turns, and looks at me in a pathetic, mournful way. *Someone needs their medicine,* I think as she opens her mouth to speak through broken teeth. (I never meant for her to fall down the stairs; I'm not a monster.) The words sound like *"I love you."*

Indeed, they all do.

The needle goes in easily. An act of intercourse, I always think, the pain and pleasure. The nape of the neck is always so easy to get, so easy to see. There is no more modesty. Used to be, you could barely see below the chin. Now, I have to turn away while walking down the street because someone's cleavage and, dare I say, in some cases, their nipples, scream at me.

She crumples in my arms. I cradle her and stroke her hair, look into her hazel eyes and tell her everything will be all right. Then, I gently lay her down on a thick patch of soft, cool grass (see? not a monster).

I stare at her as the moonlight shines down, coming and going through thick but broken clouds. I wait and I watch, and I watch and I wait. Soon her eyes will open, but that will be the only movement the medicine allows. Yet, she will feel. Oh, how she will feel! Each and every delicious, glorious cut I've meticulously planned. Sawing and stabbing and ripping and tearing, her blood spraying in a rain of excitement. It's almost too much—and yet never enough.

I know Lilac will cherish it (they all cherish it) when I noticed the flutter of her eyelids, the peeking softness of the haze, the single tear that runs down the side of her head. That signal of intense *joyjoyjoy.*

The time has come.

I grab my bag, reach in, and run my fingertips along the cool edge of the hatchet's blade—

Knock! Knock! Knock!

* * *

The noise startled the author. Brow furrowed with annoyance, he grimaced and looked at the door. The last thing he needed was an interruption to shackle his imagination. Inspiration only holds for so long, and his publisher didn't care about how or when or why, just that the manuscript be delivered on time.

The noise rattled, almost scratched through the author, like a gust of icy wind had broken free from the clutches of the blizzard outside and found its way in—not because the sound raked through his ears like dried branches on paint-chipped wood, but because he wanted to be alone. *Should* be alone. That was the point of buying this place bounded by woods. No neighbors. No interruptions. One road in, one road out.

Pound! Pound! Pound! The desperation on the other side of the door, the very one with red chipped paint, grew from a whisper to a roar.

"I see the fire," a man's voice said, deep but plaintive. "Please, let me in."

Jesus Christ, the author thought. He looked around, smoothed his hair in a subconscious and ridiculous display of vanity. *They can see in?* he wondered, even though the curtains were drawn. He shook his head. Yes, he should have had the decorator hang the red velour window coverings instead of the lacy vanilla, but the red felt so thick and heavy. *Like blood,* he thought.

Hindsight.

The author removed his fingers from the typewriter keys, frozen since the audible intrusion. The memory function on the machine wouldn't let him forget where he'd meant to insert the period, though what his next words might have been was another story. He quite liked the IBM Memory Typewriter, a gift from his publisher when his third novel, *Daisy's Delight,* hit the bestseller list. Victor Blackrock, the serial killer lead of the author's burgeoning franchise, had already captured (some would say sickened, even poisoned) the hearts and minds of many a reader, but Daisy pulled at them more than what Victor did to, say, Lily or Rose in books one and two. Maybe Victor's ability to stay ahead of and outsmart the police won readers over, though book three introduced the character's most formidable foe, Detective Comox. Still, even the detective couldn't catch Victor. No one could. No one even knew his true identity, that slinky, shadowy killer.

At least not yet.

The year 1974 had been a good year for the author, but a better year for the publisher as four other writers in their stable had also received the expensive typing machine. Now, he toyed with upgrading to the newer version; it had a "100" in the name, so it must be even fancier. Three years of technology upgrades meant more memory, which meant more writing—or at least that's what the author tried to believe. He couldn't help but wonder how many other novelists used the machine, relied on its recall, or if writers on hit television shows like *Happy Days* or *Three's Company* hammered out their inane situations on them. He giggled when he thought about what Chrissy or Janet would do if they met Victor. He knew for sure there would be blood. And that Jack would still go for a laugh by falling over the couch after slipping on one of his roommates' innards.

With the muster of Clark Kent, the author pushed his black-framed glasses up the bridge of his nose. He wheeled his chair back, rolling silently over the cowhide rug that matched the various trophy animal heads the previous owner had left hung on the walls. There were too many eyes, the author always thought, glass as they may be, staring at him. Judging him. Still, he enjoyed putting on paper the internal horrors of his mind, so why not a little external ambiance to keep the mood set.

He walked—almost tiptoed—to the door, clenching his teeth in hopes there would be no further knocking or pounding or scratching or calling from outside. *Let the icy winds carry them away,* he thought. His silent shuffle seemed futile as his heavy frame lumbered across old, creaky floorboards. He knew he should lose weight. He also knew he loved snacks while writing after midnight—a "big no-no" as every diet guru would say. Calling Black Beauties!

After crossing the curtained window as fast as he could, the author placed his cheek against the door—just like one of Victor Blackwood's victims would have done, only to be answered by a knife jammed through the jaw, spearing the tongue if the popular killer were feeling especially nasty. At this, the author pulled back and waited—hoped—that the sounds on the other side of the door would be footsteps crunching in the hardening snow, followed by a car revving and driving away. Even better, perhaps just the rush of wind on a stormy winter's night.

But "It's freezing, please!" the phantom voice bellowed from the other side of the door.

The author jumped back. He couldn't stop the yelp from escaping his lips, nor could he stop the racket his shock cost him as he backed into the buffet table. A lamp tipped over, its leaded glass shade clanking against a cerulean ceramic ashtray probably made in some art nouveau sculpting class.

GoAwayGoAwayGoAway. The author ran fingers through thinning hair. He closed his eyes, scrunching them together until he felt pressure behind the orbs.

"My car broke down near the main turnoff, and you're the only place I saw."

The author believed everyone, the interloper outside included, could hear the screams of annoyance and frustration inside his head.

"I just need to warm up. Please."

The author's shoulders slumped. Clearly, the man wasn't going anywhere. He stepped toward the door with the muster of a death row inmate marching toward their final seat.

* * *

The author watched the man rub his hands together by the fire. He studied him, trying to get a read. Since he couldn't create this character, he would at least work to understand him. His coat, covered in snow, was not expensive. His black hair was thick, but erratic unevenness proved it hadn't been trimmed in some time. He wished he had seen the man's eyes better. You can tell so much from the eyes.

The author got what he wanted when the man stood up.

"That's nice and warm." He turned to the author. "I can't thank you—"

The man stopped, his eyes dark enough to almost match his hair, and stared the author up and down. A small smile, one it seemed he tried to stifle, formed. "I know you."

The author stood up a bit straighter. This happened often enough that he went into PR mode. He let out a huff of air through his nose. "You're that writer," the man said. "Yeah." He looked more excited now as he clocked the author up, down, all around.

The author nodded and bowed his head in a symbol of both acknowledgment and humility.

"I am," the author answered, "*that* writer." He saw no point in hiding it, not like he used to. When he would try to play it off to avoid being seen, to avoid having to talk to too many strangers who asked too many questions and wanted too many autographs. Or, worse, when they had the best idea for a story ever. Fame, he thought, really was a bitch. But here he was, in the middle of the woods, in the middle of a winter storm, seeking peace and quiet to write his new novel after a particularly juicy inspiration—and some fan pretending not to be a fan had fucking found him.

The man stepped back and put his hands up. "I'm sorry—I didn't mean it like that. I just don't know names well, I guess. But I know your work." He clenched his teeth and pulled his head back. "Scary stuff."

The author raised his eyebrows. *Thanks—I think.* "Do you need to make a call?" he asked, more statement than a question. He motioned to the phone.

The man trained his eyes on the author, watching him more closely than the callous and inert glass orbs of the dead animals around him. Death seemed to follow him even here in his expected but only perceived seclusion.

"Full confession," the man said, stepping closer. "I've read all your books."

The author wasn't prepared for this, nor the moment the man stepped to the couch and sat down. *He fucking sat down.* The author couldn't believe it.

"What gets me is how death is so real, the way you write it. The pain. You could feel the pain of the victims." He looked to the author. At him, almost through him. "Yikes."

The author had heard all this before and was tired of it. He leaned back on his desk, trying to find the right words to snatch from those swirling in his mind. "It's not real," he said. "They're not real."

The man leaned forward, squinting. "Aren't they, though?"

The comment put a moment of nausea through the author, though he wasn't sure why. Something about the way the man said it. Lilting. Accusatory. Hopeful.

"It makes you wonder—well not *you*, but me. Anybody," the man said. "What does it feel like to take a life?" He kept staring as he shrugged, and let out another smile, this time more deliberate. "Have you ever wondered that?"

The author twitched at the question. In some strange, uncomfortable yet recognizable way, he felt as if he'd been punched in the stomach, then patted on the back. He wanted this man—this intruder for sure—to leave.

Now.

The man stood and stepped toward the author, who shifted to the side, a bit more behind the desk. The author grabbed the glass bulb knob of the top right drawer, something that always reminded him of a mini crystal ball. He noticed the man in front of him saw it too.

"Words on paper might as well make you God," the man said. "Creating a life, taking it away, wrapped in blood and the lust for it. It's power. Maybe the ultimate power." The man stopped talking, but not staring.

The author gazed back, his heart beating, and he felt the smallest droplet of perspiration trickle down his back. It was not the temperature in the room, that's for sure, though if one measured, it would have chilled since the exchange began.

The man traced the raised paisley patterns that filled the golden velvet covering of the sofa. Then he laughed, loud and fast.

The author shook at the outburst, hand bumping against the desk. It hurt, but he didn't let the man know.

"Imagine that—me scaring you." The man chuckled. "Do you have anything to drink?"

"No," the author replied curtly. *Dear God, please leave.*

The man bobbed his head back and forth. "Probably better. We want to have our faculties at a time like this."

The author smiled, hoping to diffuse the tension while the man looked around the cabin.

"This is a nice place." The man stared up at one of the deer heads. "Hunters." He let the word hang out in the universe for anyone who heard it to decide what it meant. If it were a celebration or a judgment.

The author tried to steady his breathing, pictured his heart moving like a rabbit's, then visualized it slowing down, and saw himself on a beach, relaxing. A therapist had once told him to dream someplace fun. It wasn't working. He cleared his throat. "I come here to work. Speaking of which, I am in the middle of something, and I'm glad I could help, but if—"

The man whipped around, fast enough that the edges of his tattered jacket came in second place. "I have to say, in the spirit of full disclosure, they thought I might be crazy."

The author pushed his head forward and thought, *What the fuck are you talking about?* But out loud he asked, "Excuse me?"

The man tilted his head, then laughed and brushed his hand through the air, as if waving away the comment. "At my work, I mean. There's always someone raising a ruckus. Still, they let me go. Or let me leave, I should say, because I wasn't a suspect in the murder. I was careful to make sure."

The author went pale.

"After all," the man continued, "how many people run into a police station covered in blood, screaming, *'It's not my blood,'* and then have to backtrack and explain what the hell happened that you have 'not your blood' on you, right?"

The man pulled his lips into a sharp grin, as if he had asked a twisted rhetorical question.

Compelled to answer, the author pulled in an anxious breath. His voice cracked, and he shut his eyes for a second, hating how his larynx betrayed him right then and there. "Murder?"

The man pursed his lips and squinted. "Did I say *murder?*"

The author furrowed his brow and wiped his moist hands on his corduroy pants, running his thumbnail down one of the brown grooves. "Didn't you?"

The man tilted his head and looked at the vaulted, crossbeam ceiling. "Humph, maybe I did," he admitted. "I mean, they couldn't have me snooping around a case I was so close to. They saw to that. But I still called and checked in and asked questions." He shook his head. "I lost friends I didn't work with and friends I used to work with. After all, murder"—he nodded toward the author—"is an awful thing to have to deal with. I mean, talk about messy!"

The man's throaty laugh ended with a snort and snot. He wiped his nose with his cheap coat sleeve, a certainly most disgusting habit, and the author felt puke rise in his throat.

"So," the man went on, "I tried to find out if there were any ideas, *real* ideas, about who they thought might have done it. I mean, is there such a thing as a perfect murder?"

The author choked down a small, dry swallow. He stared back at the man, silent.

"Oh, that's a question for you," the man clarified, staring back with an *"I'm waiting"* look.

The author looked down, then up and around the room, like he might be trying to find the answer from some external source, or perhaps free a thought locked deep down inside. Anything, even a canned answer, to end this.

"I don't know," was all he came up with.

"But it seems like you might," the man said in a singsong sort of way. "As a writer. Isn't it a real talent to be able to plan and plot and work out every detail in advance? After copious amounts of research, of course."

The author raised an eyebrow. In the tiniest of ways, he was offended. "You make it sound easy."

"Isn't it?"

That struck a nerve, any unease the author felt morphing into a tingle of annoyance. "If I had a nickel for every time someone thought what I did was easy. Do you know how hard it is to fill a blank page with words that didn't exist until you thought them up? Ideas that might have been floating around in the universe but had to be snatched by you, at the right time and right place; broken down and put back together in just the right way to ensure that what you hope to say actually says that? And then hope that people read it. And then that people will care?"

The man nodded lightly. "I hadn't thought about it that way."

"No one ever does." The author pursed his lips.

"I suppose then," the man offered, "one could say solving a murder is just like writing one. All the facts have to be laid out—all the possibilities, the myriad reasons of who, what, where, when, and why. The why isn't always the conundrum. It's usually sex or money."

The author laughed. "Not always. People kill for a lot of reasons."

"See!" The man perked up, clapping his hands together. "I knew you had it in you. But, yes, I'm sure there are other reasons." He chewed his lip. "Revenge, that's always a good one. Still, once you know who the victim is, and maybe even the how along with the what and the why, that doesn't mean you've cracked the case. The dead are still dead, and that has many meanings in my current line of work. Or hobby, I guess. I don't know what you call exactly what it is I'm doing."

The nervousness came back, flooding the author's veins with adrenaline and his stomach with bile. Even if he wanted to, he couldn't help but sound concerned. "And what is it you're doing?"

"You know," the man said. "I think you knew my wife."

Hot blood raced through the author from toes to the tip-tops of his ears. He grabbed his stomach as the empty feeling within filled itself with an emotional trigger. Shovelfuls of dirt had been forced into the cavities of his body. He hated what the man said—some horrible insinuation. And for the first time since this meddler had infected his writing bubble, the author felt truly afraid.

Worse, he watched the man grin. It was more than a smile, for that would have occurred with a sense of joy. This look came warped with malice, upset, anger.

"You'd like me to leave, I know," the man said in such a casual way. "And you also know I'm not going to."

The author looked at the avocado-green telephone, almost imperceptibly. If only.

"Go ahead, I won't stop you. Call the police. Call anybody." The man stepped forward, the look of a madman in his eyes. "I'll wait."

The author's eyes shot back and forth, then refocused on the man, who nodded and stepped closer.

Never once taking his eyes off the man, the author reached for the phone slowly, gripped the receiver, and pulled it up to his ear.

His eyes closed. His lips turned down.

No dial tone. *Fuckfuckfuck.*

"What do you want from me?" the author asked as he opened his eyes.

Then he screamed. A high-pitched squeal—a sound of fear one would not have imagined could come from a man his size, a man with his success. He merely caught glimpses of what happened next:

The man's open mouth yelling.

His left hand reaching.

His right, holding something that moved toward the
     author's neck.

A syringe.

The world, the man, and all the glassy eyes of dead animals
     faded into a creamy mist.

Then they were all gone.

*   *   *

The author's eyes fluttered open as he awoke on his back outside, mounds of snow around him, underneath him. The sting of cold on red cheeks and bluing lips. *I'mAliveI'mAliveI'mAlive!* He stared upward into the night sky as white crystals swirled and fell. *How fun,* he thought, *to catch them on my tongue.* He smiled at the notion, only to realize he wasn't smiling. Couldn't smile. His face was frozen. He reached to touch himself, but his hand didn't budge. He tried to move his other hand, an arm, his head. Nothing. He blinked, eyes darting back and forth, and that at least felt like something.

"Are you ready?" The man popped into his field of vision, upside down.

What have you done to me? the author screamed, but the noise never went further than his own mind.

"I can see the wheels spinning in your mind. I just wish I could see your fear," the man said. "It's a special cocktail. One you know well."

The author panicked. He knew. Oh, how he knew! The drug he had used on so many when his days were full of careless glee. And murder. Yes, yes, yes, all the murder. The special cocktail that went in with the prick of a needle and lulled the recipient into a dreamless sleep, allowing them to wake up, see, hear, and understand, but not move. All except the eyes. He never knew why, never cared. In fact, his victims watching him watch them was succulent reverse voyeurism. Now, juices of worry turned in his stomach when he remembered what the sweetness, as he used to call it, of that drug also allowed.

The man's voice filled the author's ears. "And you'll be able to feel it all, to thoroughly experience what you have put so many through." He grinned. "It's very exciting. See, you hurt me, so I am going to hurt you. Really. Really. Hurt. You."

The man disappeared and the author tried to force himself to move, to wiggle, to turn his head to see where his tormentor had gone. Nothing except the quick and quiet warmth of tears down the side of his temple. Then, even the solace that he was still in there, somewhere, went cold.

Please, please, please! He wept, he yelled, he pleaded without moving his lips. Without a hint of sound passing his lips. *I'm sorry. What can I do? don't hurt me!* He sounded like a baby, this he knew. The voice, his pleading, whiny voice, echoed within his mind and was itself an echo—

Of the young girl picking daisies at the park, whose arms were never found.

Of the supermarket checker named Lily, who learned the pain of playing skin the cat.

Of the high school track star whose head spun on his parents' record player surrounded by rose petals.

Finally, of the woman in the lilac dress, walking through the park just after sunset, all alone. The one they had to piece back together just to bury something.

All of them had *Please*'d and *Don't hurt me*'d and *Sorry*'d themselves to the point of their death. Now, the author, who'd found solace in their suffering and money in their murders as he spun the stories of their real-life killings into page-turning fiction, would at last understand what it all meant. How it all felt. And why the fear of death looked so enticing to a captor.

The high-pitched whirring sound began before the pain, but that came soon enough. A burning, ripping, wretched feeling as the man who came to confront his wife's killer drilled the top of the author's left foot with a serrated attachment. Blood sprayed in droplets, a pink mist.

No one could hear the author's screams because they remained in the anguished confines of his mind, the place where he had never given a thought to right or wrong or karma or comeuppance until now. He hoped he might pass out from the shredding of his foot, but that was not in the stars. And his foot, he knew, was just the beginning. *The prologue,* he thought, and wished he could laugh because the situation, this karmic reversal, was all too crazy.

More unheard screams and at least a few visible tears matched the hacking off of his right leg. He could see the ax raise and lower, followed by the squishy landing of metal in flesh and searing hurt. As the weapon came up, so did pieces of him, stringy and dangling, skin covered in blood and mixed with chunks of bubbly fat.

As the man worked hard, he spoke, though the author only heard words here and there, in between his loud but not real screaming.

"You took her," and "You're paying," and "You're going to rot," and a bunch of other things that started with *you*, which made the author realize he sure had been a busy little beaver. Maybe it wasn't a life so ill-spent after all, to have this kind of impact, this reach. Sure, it wasn't for everyone, clearly, when he heard a pop, then a crack. Small potatoes—*a finger, must be a finger*—but it seemed that the man was having fun.

Joy to the world. Sure, the author admitted, he did very bad things, but the glee with which the man currently did worse things showed the author that the student had become the teacher. He wished he could tell the man to stop—show him how to use a blade, make better cuts. Understand that slicing into a person was art before it became commerce.

Then the unexpected happened: he felt a separation. More than when pieces of him, toenails to scalp, had been ripped away. A warmth flooded the author's body and mind, a sensation stronger than the horrors of a hacksaw carving into his jiggling gut. *Back and forth, blood and gore, splish splash, I was taking a bath,* he thought, and he might actually be smiling. The author imagined himself pushing past legs and bumping knees to run down the aisle as a contestant in his very own game show, a dark and twisted program in the depths of a hellscape called *This Is Your Death.* His head lolled to one side, and he witnessed the thick red that used to be his, flowing onto, joining with, melting the snow in rivulets and swirls. The red and white designing delicious patterns of murder.

Candy Cane, he thought. *If I wrote this book, I'd call me Candy Cane.*

EGGNOG

Kristi DeMeester

I T'S MIDNIGHT, AND I've eaten half a tray of brownies. I've dribbled batter down the front of the oversized, stained T-shirt Theo
has given up on calling his. I've adopted most of his T-shirts. This
new, strange body I don't recognize doesn't fit in anything on my
side of the closet. Even the maternity jeans and blouses that once
cradled my belly wrinkle awkwardly at my waist and make me look
stupid for trying to cling to the glow of pregnancy when the baby is
outside of me and two months old.

Somehow, I anticipated this. Bought extra sugar and eggs and
chocolate plus a bag of walnuts because I knew I wouldn't be able
to stop myself, even though the brownies are for Theo's company
Holiday party.

This year, they decided to go with something simpler. Their
focus word for the year was *community*, and they wanted to embody
it in all things. No more open bars on rooftops or rented event
spaces with a live band playing jazzier renditions of Christmas clas-
sics in the background.

And so this year's party became a potluck. The sort of thing
meant to create conversation but was really a burden. Community,
my ass. Theo would have brought something store bought, and so,
last minute, here I am standing over my failure of a contribution
when I once would have made something more extravagant. Lady
fingers soaked in a mixture of Bailey's and espresso. Hand-whipped
mascarpone. Crème brulé in their tiny pots, with perfectly caramel-
ized crusts. Lavender-scented shortbreads with a lemon glaze. Dim

reminders of my old life. The pastry chef I used to be instead of the soggy-shirted mother I've become.

I swipe a finger through the batter before licking it off. The sugar coats my teeth, and even though I feel sick, I can't stop myself. The high is the only thing keeping me going at this point. The baby is due for another feeding in twenty minutes. Just enough time to hustle the brownies out of the oven and onto the cooling rack, then hurry down to the nursery before the screaming starts.

My nipples ache, and I pop a walnut into my mouth instead of thinking how good it would feel to wrench those godforsaken milk tubes from my body. Let them rest for just a bit. Between the cluster feeding and the pumping to increase my supply, I'm raw and tender. Shocked there isn't blood in those tiny bottles every time I hook myself to the breast pump. Like a fucking animal. A milk machine. Nothing else. Certainly not a woman. I can't remember the last time I felt anything other than this newfound awareness that I was the thing that had sheltered a child. The husk our child wore for forty-one weeks and then abandoned.

By the time I've nursed the baby, cut the now cooled brownies, put them in the Pyrex dish I'll take with us to the party, and shoved them in the refrigerator that's dying for a clean out, it's going on two. I have an hour until the next feed. An hour to try and close my eyes and pretend that my very body isn't a weight I can no longer carry.

*   *   *

I feel Theo kiss me goodbye. He smells of cedar. Of smoke. The cologne I bought him last Christmas.

"My mom will be here at seven. Don't forget to pump extra so she can feed him. We have the formula, but I know you'd rather not use it," he says, and I want to bury myself further in the sheets. Motherhood is learning all the ways your body can be a failure. Never enough milk. Enough time. Enough sleep. Never enough. Theo doesn't mean for the reminder to cut, but it does.

I make a noise that's as close to an affirmation as I can, and he's gone, moving past the nursery with a whispered "Love you, spud.

Take care of Mama." Even through the darkness that has stitched itself to me, I glow. Theo is a good dad. A good husband. We are still so new at this. Still working it all out. How to be a family.

Mercifully, the baby sleeps for another hour, and I go through the motions of the day. Feeding. Diaper changes. Clothing changes after two spit-ups and a blowout. A load of laundry I know will sit in the dryer for at least two days before I get around to folding it. Two extra rounds of pumping that yield the most pathetic amount of milk, and I break down in tears. We've avoided formula this entire time—the Greek chorus of *"Breast is best!"* on loop in my head—but looking in the refrigerator at the scant four ounces I've managed to produce leaves me in despair. Barely enough for a single feeding. Even if I let him nurse as much as he wants from now until we leave for the party, it won't be enough to get him through the night.

I sob in the shower while the baby naps. Cut it off at twenty minutes and then quickly blow-dry my hair, my gaze locked on the monitor the entire time. I can feel how swollen my eyes are. Know that no amount of foundation or concealer or powder will manage to cover the dark circles under them. But I put it all on anyway, hoping the contour stick I bought on impulse at Target will do something to conceal the baby weight still clinging to my chin. Eyeliner and mascara and lipstick, and my face is done.

I dress while the baby watches me from his bouncer. The hunter-green sweater I thought would be festive is too tight. Too hot. I swipe a palm over the collected sweat in the small of my back and tug on yet another pair of maternity jeans. The excess material rumples under the sweater, but it's thick enough to somewhat disguise that I'm not in normal jeans yet. A pair of boots. The diamond studs Theo gave me on our wedding day. The baby coos and waves his hands. Mama looks . . . better. Dare I even say, *pretty*. My hair falling dark and thick over my shoulders. My skin brightened with the blush. Eyes sparkling. Something like the woman I used to be. Even if I am slightly uncomfortable in my clothes, it doesn't matter. This will be my first night out since the baby was born. Our first night without the baby. Just us. A few hours to be a couple again.

I dance over to the baby, who flaps his hands and coos as I lift him from the bouncer. "Try not to throw up on Mama, okay?" I say. He responds by gumming my shoulder. Theo comes in like a whirlwind. "Sorry. Meeting ran long. Twenty minutes," he says, shedding clothing on his way to the bathroom for a shower. I try for one last pump and manage two more ounces. Six ounces total. A small victory.

Forty-five minutes later, we've both kissed the baby far too many times and gone through the checklist with Theo's mother as many times too.

"Go," she says, shooing us out the door. "We'll be fine. Have fun." Her emphasis on the *fun* is directed at me. A command not to fret or worry or do any of the things my brain is already telling myself to do as the door closes.

Theo takes a work call on the drive, and I occupy myself with my phone. Scroll social media and its targeted ads for swaddling blankets and tiny plastic cylinders that let you suck snot out of tiny noses that can't blow themselves yet. Tell myself not to open the baby monitor app and stare at it. I put my phone back inside its little slot in the backpack that holds the pump and now doubles as my purse. It's fine. Everything is fine. I'm dressed in an outfit not covered with spit-up. I remembered to grab the brownies. The baby is with his grandmother, and there might just be enough pumped milk to see him through until we come home. It's *fine*.

The office has decorated the entrance. Twinkling icicle lights and garland wind over the glass doors. Poinsettias on either side. A cheeky twist of mistletoe over the door. Community, indeed.

"You look great," Theo says as I check my lipstick one more time.

I let him open my door for me and loop my arm through his as we make our way to the entrance. In the distance, I can make out the strains of Queen Mariah belting out that she doesn't want a lot for Christmas.

We're almost to the door when I realize I forgot the brownies. "Shit," I say turning back to the car. "The brownies."

"I can get them," Theo says, but I wave him on.

"It's your party. Go on in. I'll find you," I say, proud of myself for being so independent. For not needing him as an emotional crutch in a room full of people I don't know. He hands off the keys and drops a kiss on my cheek.

"I'll be at the bar. Unless they decided to axe that too," he says, and heads inside as I turn back to the car.

I lose my balance reaching into the back seat and tip sideways as the pump backpack slides off one shoulder. The maternity panel on my jeans bunches up under the sweater, and I have to put the brownies on top of the car and heave the backpack off to readjust all while hoping no one sees sweaty, pudgy me struggling to fix it. I can feel my hair starting to frizz, and wish, like I do every winter, that December in Georgia meant snow instead of sixty-five-degree days, rain, and humidity.

I dab at the sweat that's clinging to my upper lip and hope my makeup hasn't started to melt off my face. I'm starting to wonder if a sweater was a bad idea.

When I enter into a blast of heat, I know a sweater was a bad idea.

A center table at the back overflows with dishes covered in aluminum foil, and I make my way to it, placing the brownies on the far left with a sad, plastic package of those store-bought iced cookies everyone claims to love but actually taste like plastic. Islands of people float here and there, some with plates in their hands, but the grand majority of the office is clustered around a makeshift bar. At least they sprung for someone to play bartender, even if the drinks he's making are two-ingredient cocktails that feature copious amounts of bourbon. There are multiple bottles of red wine scattered over the bar, and my mouth waters. It feels like decades since I've had a glass of wine, and my fingers itch for the sensation of the glass.

I've heard stories of mothers having their husbands bring them a six-pack of beer or sushi or a sub sandwich for after the delivery.

And it's not as if I didn't consider those things. Theo would have done it if I'd asked. But between the emergency C-section and the tears because the baby wouldn't latch, it didn't happen. Since then, it's been a whirlwind of diapers and feedings, and somehow I never had that celebratory postnatal drink or treat.

I could, though. Tonight. Give myself permission to pump and dump. Could I do that? Go home without any guilt? It's not as if I'm pumping enough for a full feed as it is, and would it really be so bad if the baby has a bottle of formula?

I spy Theo among the crowd, a tumbler filled with amber liquid in his hand, and weave toward him. He lifts his glass, toasting a person I can't yet see, and laughs.

I push past a group of gray-haired, cardigan-draped women, excusing myself as I take in mouthfuls of their hairspray, and then I'm finally in front of the bar. Breathless. Smiling and holding back an excited giggle.

"Could I get a glass of the red please?"

The bartender smiles. Nods. "Easiest order of the night," he says, tossing me a wink as he pours heavy and slides the glass to me.

I know it's likely a cheap blend, but I don't care. That first sip burns through my chest, and it's bliss. Another sip, and I feel myself loosen. Feel myself bloom.

I make my way toward Theo, waiting for him to look up, to see me, but he is deep in conversation. I take another deeper sip of wine. Remind myself to go slow. To savor. Avoid being an embarrassment. Avoid being the new mom sloppy off two glasses of wine at her husband's company holiday party.

Theo is laughing. His head is thrown back, and I can see the stubble he missed shaving. The woman he is talking to steps forward. Puts her hand on his arm. Laughs along with him.

And I burn. In my sweater and maternity jeans, I burn.

Because she is beautiful. Tall. Strawberry blonde. A perfect sprinkle of freckles over her nose and cheeks. Even under her simple burgundy sheath, you can see the Pilates-honed muscle. The ballerina grace of her movements. The sharp angle of her jaw and collarbone. Fluid. Breathtaking.

I freeze, and it's in that moment that Theo looks up. That he sees me. His pudgy wife.

"There you are! Thought I'd lost you to the brownies," he says, and I smile and smile because what else would I do? But I'm not looking at him. I'm looking at the strawberry blonde who *is* looking at him, and I think I could die right here. Burst into flames, the wineglass shattering against the floor, staining this perfect woman and my husband in his best button-down.

"This is Elise. We worked on the Decatur job this summer, remember?" he says, and Elise extends her hand.

"So glad to finally meet you, Julie. How wonderful you were able to get a night away from the baby!" There's an accent there, faint but distinctly French. "My sister refused to leave home for the first six months after her son was born. Said she would never have that time with him back. They are so sweet at that age, and they grow so quickly." She sighs, sips delicately at her own drink, an opaque cream concoction I can only imagine is eggnog.

"They do. Grow so quickly. And it's Gillian," I say, and she reaches for me. Runs her fingers over the sleeve of my sweater.

"Of course! Gillian. And this sweater. So festive! I wish I could do wool, but it's too thick. Makes me feel like a beast. Hulking around." She drops her hand. Bares her teeth into what she must imagine is a smile. "But it works for you. Shorter frame and all. I can't carry that sort of weight. The wool, I mean."

I grip the wineglass instead of throwing it at her perfect face.

She grasps Theo's arm once more. "I should tell you Jul— *Gillian*—that I might have to steal your husband away at some point tonight. They've got me stuck on this job down in Valdosta, and I have no one to gossip with anymore. You remember how you used to bring me coffee every morning, and we'd spend at least twenty minutes talking shit before anyone else was on site? I miss that." She pouts her lips like a little girl, and I know that move. That sick combination of innocence and sexy that's supposed to make men feral. Like that old Love's Baby Soft commercial that was gross even when it came out. Like how porn made men expect us to wax ourselves prepubescent hairless.

"The coffeepot was right there. It was only polite," Theo says. It was the right thing for him to say, but her hand is still on his arm, and it's too hot in the room, the air too thick and fake pine and cinnamon scented. I want to gag. I want to run away. Back to the car. Back home to the safe den I've created with our child.

Somehow, I've finished the wine. I bring the glass to my lips again, my tongue desperate for even the smallest trace, and Theo reaches for it.

"Another?" he asks, and I nod. One more glass. That's all.

"Me too?" Elise stretches between us, and I can smell her perfume. Gourmand. Honey and cinnamon and something darker that my nose tells me is likely labdanum. She smells like something you would want to eat.

"Of course," Theo says. "Eggnog?"

"The one in the glass jar," she says, and then I am alone with her. Her fingernails are almond shaped. The color of blood on snow. She's probably never picked at them. I curl my own fingers into my palm so she won't see my destroyed cuticles.

"Made it myself. The eggnog," she explains. "With oat milk. I don't do dairy."

Of course she fucking doesn't. Probably also doesn't do sugar, refined carbohydrates, red dye, or anything resembling food that actually tastes good.

"I couldn't live without butter," I say, the wine loosening my tongue. "It should be its own food group."

I expect at least a polite laugh, but all she does is stare back at me. "That's right. Theo mentioned something about baking. You made cakes? Like the birthday ones you get at the grocery store?"

I try and fail to keep the edge out of my voice. "Pastry chef. A little more than just cake."

"But you're home now? With the baby?"

"For now. Haven't decided yet if I'll go back to work."

She gives a little sigh and shakes her head. "Such a shame how women rush back to work when they have such delicious babies and husbands to care for. If I had a Theo at home, I wouldn't be able to bring myself to leave. How lucky that you somehow snatched him up!"

I'm ready to tear out her throat with my teeth, but Theo is back, his hands full with our drinks plus three of my brownies on a tiny paper plate.

"A little treat," he says, holding them out. I take the wine first and then one of the brownies.

"Not for me," Elise says.

"Your loss. Gillian can do things with chocolate that are inhuman." He finishes his brownie in two bites and lifts his hand toward someone who has just entered the party. "That's Robertson. I should say hello. You're good here?"

Nodding, I gulp my wine and remind myself to kiss him later. For making sure to compliment me. For checking that I'm okay before stranding me with this woman who has cast herself as his work wife.

He leans in and presses his lips to my temple, his breath warm in the cup of my ear as he whispers, "Sorry. She's such a pain in the ass."

Even though I trust Theo, know he would never hurt me in such a way, the relief is instant and pure. For a moment, I am no longer burning. I take a bite of the brownie, and the rush of sugar is divine. I finish it quickly and ball the napkin in my fist.

Elise turns the glass of eggnog in her hands and watches him hurry across the room before swinging her gaze back to me.

"Big night out, then?" She gestures to my wine. "You aren't nursing?"

"Oh," I glance down at the glass. "No. I mean, yes. I am."

She raises a perfectly waxed eyebrow. "Sorry, I just assumed—"

"I pumped extra for tonight," I say, hating myself for telling her something so personal when it's absolutely none of her fucking business how I feed my child. But I can't stop myself. Can feel the pressure building behind my teeth. The need to explain. To justify. To embody the new role of mother for this woman who has never known the unique pain of her body stretching to accommodate another. How it's almost like slipping your skin inside out.

"Won't it go into the milk—the wine? My sister nursed. Wouldn't touch spicy food. Was forever saying *'What mommy eats, baby eats.'* I don't think she drank for the first three years." Elise glances about the room. Probably wondering how much longer she'll have to pretend she wants to talk to me instead of Theo.

I tug at the straps on my shoulders. The backpack that has suddenly grown heavy with the pump I'm still carrying. "Pump and dump. Back to normal tomorrow morning."

"I see." She purses her lips. Glances away. I try to follow her gaze, to see if she's looking at Theo, giving him a look that says, *"If you left her, I would never do anything but produce bounteous amounts of pure cream for our child,"* but the room has gotten crowded. There's no way to tell for certain.

And then there are my boobs that, at the mention of the pump, have begun to ache.

"Excuse me," I mumble. "Restroom."

Elise nods. "Of course. I'll find Theo. Keep an eye on him for you." She winks and waves a hand over her shoulder before disappearing into the crowd. If my tits weren't hard as rocks, I'd follow her. Maybe grab her by the hair and scratch her eyes out. But those are fantasies, and even if she deserves it, there are no such indulgences possible at this polite, refined company holiday party. At least, none outside of the food and drink.

The restrooms are tucked away at the end of a hallway that branches off the main space, and it's a tiny, three-stall affair that reeks of a septic issue left unresolved. There's no mother's room. This is a male-dominated industry, so if a woman dares to find herself with child, she'll have to make do with balancing the pump on her knees as she teeters on the edge of a toilet seat and waits for the heavy, tingling sensation of her letdown.

This is how I find myself. Woozy from the wine and hooked to the pump, slightly embarrassed by the telltale hiss as the machine pulls at my nipples. Praying a line doesn't form, some angry, tipsy woman pounding against the door and wondering exactly what the hell I'm doing in there, and could I please hurry the fuck up before she literally pisses herself?

I pull my phone from the backpack and open Instagram. Elise isn't hard to find. Her profile is filled with photos of her looking glamourous in various locations. Bikini pics beside turquoise water. Posed at the edge of a cliff, the sun behind her so the light flares around her like something sainted. Holy. Several of her in a hard hat and bright lipstick, at ground breakings and ribbon cuttings.

I can feel my wine wanting to come up. I swallow and wish the burn of it could wash me clean.

I scroll further, and then I see him: Theo. A video. I turn the volume up, not caring if there's someone else in the restroom with me. Not caring that they might hear. This woman has a video of *my* husband on *her* Instagram.

He is serious. Staring at his phone. Playing over the video is the theme to *Jaws*. A hand flashes in frame, and then Elise is giggling over the swell of music as she snatches his phone. The camera pans away as Theo frowns.

"I think he's tired of my shenanigans," the caption reads, followed by the kissy face emoji.

I curl my fingers around my phone as the video plays again and again. As the wine-poisoned milk rushes out of me. Collects in the tiny bottles I'm meant to feed my baby but will instead dump down the toilet and flush.

Bitch-shh, bitch-shhh, bitch-shh.

My thoughts fall into rhythm with the hiss of milk hitting the side of the bottle. I scroll further, but there are no other posts involving Theo.

After twelve minutes, the milk stops. After twelve minutes, I have not yet found the bottom of my disgust for Elise. I am not a woman prone to hatred, but that is the word I want to use. *Hate.*

On autopilot, I unhook the pump. Disassemble its parts and pack it away, the milk I cannot give my baby secured with its little screw top and stored in its separate ice pack lined, insulated bag. I'll dump it later. Clean all those tiny parts and let them air dry. A good mother. A responsible mother.

I don't wash my hands. Push my way out of the restroom and back into the party. As I suspected, Elise has found Theo and is holding court with him and another man wearing a blazer blinking with battery powered lights whom I can only assume is Robertson. I don't join them. Instead, I swing back to the bar. Ask for a refill for Theo and another glass of red. Because really, really, fuck it now, right? The milk is all wasted. One more glass. Two more hours that I'm an unreliable source of nutrients. We likely won't be home by then anyway. And I need the courage the wine will give me to face Elise and keep my hands from squeezing her lovely throat.

I take down half the glass in two swallows and wander to the table stacked with the food. There's a suspicious gray dip. A bag of chips. A plastic tray of pinwheel sandwiches. More dip. A crockpot filled with meatballs that smell overly sweet. I smile when I see there are no brownies left and snag a handful of chips. Let the salt cut through the wine.

I almost don't see the glass jar. It's been shoved to the back along with the two liters of off-brand Coke and stacks of paper napkins. There is a handwritten placard in front of it—Eggnog (Dairy-Free)—and it's still three-quarters filled with thin, clouded liquid.

"Because of course it is. No one wants to drink that shit," I mumble, pushing the jar so the liquid sloshes. "Looks like fucking cum."

I want to hurt her. Embarrass her in the way she's embarrassed me. Even if she doesn't know it. Even if she doesn't feel it. The desire to see her brought low swallows me alive, and I writhe with that need.

Everyone is crowded around the bar now, and I'm alone at the table when I pull a plastic cup from its precarious stack and pour it half full of this culinary abomination. No one sees when I hoist the backpack from my shoulders and unzip the little insulated bag with its two tiny bottles.

"What a *bitch*," I say, and I giggle when I fill the rest of the cup with my soiled breastmilk. Stir it with an unwashed finger. Drain my wine and make my way across the room to my husband and his merry band of idiots.

"Up to no good?" I say, looping my arm through Theo's and snuggling into his side, which forces Elise to take a step backward. Her face remains calm, but her eyes narrow. If my legs weren't wine heavy, I would have stepped on her foot.

"Not with this one around," Theo slaps Robertson on the back, who laughs and reaches for my hand.

"Glad to meet you, Gillian. Even more glad I snagged a brownie before they disappeared. Probably better for me there weren't more," he says, rubbing his stomach.

"Thank you so much," I say, and then hold the drinks out. "Figured y'all would be wanting refills."

"How thoughtful," Elise says, accepting the cup. "You really ought to bring her out more, Theo. I swear if she weren't here, I wouldn't believe she existed! Did he ever tell you what a shameless flirt I was the first two weeks? Was practically throwing myself at him before I figured out he was married. Thought he was dense but turns out he was just a gentleman."

I feel Theo tense next to me, and I give him a reassuring pat. "Better keep an eye on this one," I say to Robertson, my tone light. Joking. The good-humored wife. "Sounds like an HR nightmare waiting to happen."

Robertson gives an uncomfortable laugh. Elise sips her eggnog, but her eyes are murderous. And I smile. Smile as I watch her take down another mouthful. And then another, and God, it's better than butter. Better than chocolate. I want to open her mouth, cram my fist past her teeth, and pour the rest down her throat.

Instead, I stand there prettily next to my husband and tell Robertson how much I love his jacket. So fun! And he tells me that his daughters got it for him last Christmas and insist he wear it to any and all holiday festivities.

He's showing me the battery pack when the retching starts. A dense, wet sound. As if Elise's body is heaving itself apart to reveal some malignant growth.

"You okay?" Robertson asks, and Elise lets out another death rattle, the plastic cup falling from her hand. "Oh, Jesus. She's choking," he says. He doesn't notice the eggnog has spilled all over his jacket. Too bad. Such a wonderful gift, ruined.

Her eyes bulge, mascara streaking down her cheeks as she brings a hand to the blotches of red scaling her chest and neck. Scratches at them. Again. Again. Until it's not scratching at all but an animal clawing itself open.

Robertson is shouting as he attempts a piss poor Heimlich, asking for someone to call 911, for someone to bring water, a towel, because Elise is bleeding now, her mouth slack jawed as she drools.

"Elise," Theo says, bending so she can see him. "Did you eat anything with nuts in it?" Her head lolls and snaps forward as Robertson tugs her upward.

"She's severely allergic," he says. "Where's her purse? She should have an Epi-pen."

Some helpful coworker scuttles away to find it, and I step aside, make room for the crush of people trying to help. And I know how I should be feeling. Horrified. Worried. Guilty. Because *what mommy eats, baby eats*. And what Elise ate was my breast milk mixed with her shitty eggnog. With a half a pan of walnut-studded brownies soaked into it.

And the sight of her torn skin, the blood beading along her collarbone, makes me want to smear my hands through it. Lick my fingers clean. Kiss Theo with her blood still on my tongue and laugh in her face. Feral, violent thoughts.

I am not a good, kind mother-woman. I am not the angel in the house. I have carried a child and birthed it into the world. I have bled. I have sharpened my teeth.

Theo steps away when the woman who found Elise's purse comes barreling through. Grips my hand as she and Robertson puzzle through the direction on the Epi-Pen and then jam it into her thigh.

By the time the ambulance arrives, Elise's breathing has returned to normal, and the crowd drops back as the EMTs load her onto a stretcher and wheel her out into the night.

She looks back at me. At Theo. I give a little wave. Mouth, "Bye, bitch" and hope she sees.

"You okay?" Theo pulls me close, his face full of concern, and my heart swells.

I nod.

"Let's go home," he says, and I nod again.

Yes. Home. Where I'll pump and dump the tainted remainders one more time. And then in the morning, I'll feed my child. Pure, clean milk.

A good, kind mother-woman.

THREADS OF EPIPHANY

Sara Tantlinger

SNOW CRUNCHED BENEATH Minna's boots as she walked deeper into the woods. When she'd left home hours ago, snow cascaded down in a gentle fluff. White flakes painted the village with wintertime serenity, but such peace followed no longer on this journey. She'd been cautioned since childhood to stay away from the eastern woods. Bavarian lullabies were warning songs, crooned by parents to infants, with gruesome details of what lurked in the vast forest. Charms only reached and protected so far, and it seemed none came close to keeping *her* away.

The eastern woods belonged to Spinnstubenfrau, the spinning room lady. She had other names, of course. The winter witch. The belly slitter. Every name complete with its own warning song. One rumor whispered from the eastern towns said an enchanted needle existed, one made of a saint's bone; it alone could pierce through the winter witch and bleed her away from this world.

A silly rumor, Minna thought, but wasn't she the fool for chasing after Spinnstubenfrau in the first place? Desperation was a powerful motivator.

She marched on through the snowfall, which thankfully began to lighten. Midwinter remained the most dangerous time to explore these paths. She had tried to stay away, even tried praying to any deity who would listen, but none held her in their court. It was far more likely the winter witch wouldn't help her either, but Minna had to try.

Enormous trees lined what she hoped was a trail. The earlier snowfall covered the worn earth she'd been following. After all, she was not the first villager to break rules and seek out the woman who haunted these woodlands. Prints from deer and wild boar disrupted the otherwise perfect layering of white, but the marks gave Minna some comfort. She wasn't totally alone out here. Animals still roamed, seeking shelter and sustenance around the patches of moss or beneath the many spruce trees and silver firs.

Cold air stabbed into her lungs as she inhaled, hating how winter smelled like old coins. Icicles dangled from the tall trees; their sharp points tinged the faintest blue. How easily one could fall and pierce her flesh, perhaps right through the heart.

Minna shivered. It did no good to linger on thoughts of her own death, especially when she'd taken this journey to prevent such a tragedy. Her dear brother—he was all she had left in this world that had so cruelly taken their parents and sister from them last year. Minna wasn't sure how Thom had survived the illness. She'd never caught it, but Thom's brief battle with such a cough left his heart weak.

Whatever bargain she needed to strike with the winter witch, Minna would do it. The days stretched ever closer to Epiphany Eve, when the witch would come and deal her punishments to the villagers she found lazy. Thom had been too sick to work or help in the small cabin they shared with their aunt and uncle. It wasn't his fault, and he certainly didn't deserve any punishment for his illness.

Unusual colors waited ahead on the path, and Minna sprinted toward them. Shadows and hours stretched on, threatening to paint the forest black as the sun started to set beyond the foothills. Final rays of light sliced through the trees, illuminating the fabric waving near what Minna assumed was an altar. A crude cross had been shaped by animal bones, then planted into the ground. She gently touched the uneven ridges on the surface, likely from rodent teeth marks.

The place where people came to worship Spinnstubenfrau. What better gift for the spinning room lady than threads and ribbon?

She kneeled on the freezing ground, snow soaking through the long skirt of her dirndl. It was a pretty dress with a decorative bodice Minna had made with her mother two years ago. No one could sew like Mama, and Minna had learned everything she could from her. They'd worked together to add fancy buttons to the otherwise common dress, and ribbons of rare colors that Mama had received from a wealthy lady. On top of the payment, the lady had given Mama fabric of treasured colors. There was one ribbon Minna and her mother had loved the most.

Violent shivers forced her gloved hands to tremble, but Minna carefully pulled out the purple ribbon. Her heart ached as she tied the fabric around the bone cross to join the other offerings. How rare, this imperial shade. She didn't like to think about the fates of the snails used to dye such a color, but she couldn't help marveling at its beauty.

The ground shook beneath the bone altar, and Minna jumped up, fighting the instinct to run far away from these woods. Then, something slurped up the purple ribbon, as if the ground possessed a hungry tongue. The earth split behind the bone altar, and from the fracture rose the skull of . . . of a . . . what *was* that?

The skull wasn't human, but as the creature emerged more fully, Minna recognized the equine features. A long muzzle and forehead glowed white despite the darkening sky. Huge, empty eye sockets stared back at Minna, and she couldn't take her gaze away from rows of teeth.

Attached to the skull, a woman's figure appeared. Covered in a long black mourning dress, the creature glided closer. A high collar hid the neck.

Spinnstubenfrau. Belly slitter. Whatever she was, she paused. Minna's purple ribbon appeared between the horse's teeth, caught in the large incisors. She'd expected the mouth to be sticky with rot, but the huge teeth remained off-white, with a gentle bite on the ribbon. The witch then slid the ribbon out and tied the offering to where a mane would have been on a living horse. This mane sprouted from the skull's smooth top, a mix of brown hair and colorful fabrics that flowed past the creature's hips.

An acceptance of the offering.

Small orbs of light flew out of the skull's mouth and hovered around the clearing, giving some luminance to the dark forest.

"Such a nice gift," the woman-creature cooed, and stroked the ribbon. "What does the human wish for in return?"

Minna's words died in her throat, and she shivered so hard from the cold, it was difficult to speak. She thought of Thom, in good care with their relatives, but she missed him so. He had their father's brown eyes and their mother's patience. Despite his heart falling weak, he found a smile for her each day.

Tears formed in her eyes, quickly freezing to her face. "M-my brother. He needs a new heart."

The creature tilted her skull head; empty eyes filled with black, like liquid shadows. "I see. I see the slow way his heart beats. Merely fourteen years old—so much life left to live. You wish for me to replace his heart?"

"Can you do that?"

"I can." The witch crossed her arms. Her voice was oddly sweet and calm despite the terror she sent into Minna's soul. "There exists an ancient power in me, something the villagers can never take away, though they try. I think I see something similar in you."

Minna shook her head. "I'm just Minna. But I'll do anything you wish if it saves Thom."

A laugh erupted from the equine head, like a sudden whinny. "Noble girl. I can replace his dying heart with one of special fabric. It'll sew itself into his body, become one with the veins and blood. I will whisper enchantments of light to keep the darkness away, and your Thom will live a long life, but"—she stepped closer, and Minna didn't dare move an inch—"you will not be a part of his new life. You will never speak to him again. Can you stand that?"

Minna bowed her head and stared at the disturbed snow. Sorrow bloomed deep in her chest; Thom would be so worried about her, likely assumed she'd died. He was strong, though. He'd carry on, and if she knew he was healthy, it'd be good enough.

"I can. What is it you want from me?"

"You will spin for me. Whisper to the fibers. Twist them to create perfect yarn. Every thread is important, you see. After Epiphany, we bring out the loom. I collect the offerings for me, from the dealmakers below ground, and from the villagers above ground. If

I am not pleased, I must punish. If you please me, though"—the witch caressed Minna's cheek with her bony hand—"you may join me at the loom for creating a rather special tapestry."

A tapestry for a heart. Thom's heart.

The witch offered her hand, and Minna grasped it, sealing the bargain. The orbs of light fluttered around her head, blurring away her vision as the ground trembled again. Nothing rose out of the fracture this time; rather, she was swallowed into the earth. Below winter's ground, she vanished with Spinnstubenfrau.

* * *

Magic was strange. Minna couldn't decide if she was intrigued or repulsed by it. Maybe a little of both. Below the earth, she wandered from a room with a bed to a tiny kitchen, to an even smaller room supplied with two spinning wheels and a ton of wool that needed to be spun into yarn. She'd spent most of the past three days in this room, stationed at the first spinning wheel. Her progress had been good, and each day she got more comfortable operating the different parts of the wheel. The one she'd worked with in the village was older, with a ricketier treadle and knobs that threatened to fall off. This wheel had no flaws. It was almost too perfect to command, but Minna persisted.

Spin and sleep. It became her pattern, along with quick breaks for porridge or a dinner of meat and bread. She needed to create enough yarn to please the winter witch, but she didn't know exactly how much, so she kept spinning.

On the fourth morning, another girl joined Minna in the small room.

"Hello," she said, her voice a croak from having spoken to no one since her bargain with Spinnstubenfrau.

The girl, a few years younger than Minna's twenty years, said nothing. Her golden head merely turned and stared outside of the enchanted window. Only dirt waited outside of these walls, but the window painted a pretty scene of a forever sunny snowfall. At night, the sun changed into a full moon. Minna had grown rather fond of the window and its spells.

Minna worked, not bothering the new girl again. The routine provided comfort. *Guide the leader yarn. Get everything in place to spin the fibers. Foot to the treadle. Keep an eye on the twist.*

For Thom, she'd spend a thousand lifetimes doing this over and over if it saved him.

"Eat."

Minna startled at the witch's voice as she slid into the room, black dress pristine and the purple ribbon on the skull's mane perfectly in place. The woman handed a bowl to Minna and to the new girl. Heat spread from the sides, pleasantly warming up her numb hands.

"May I ask you something?"

The witch tilted her head, and without eyes or a facial expression, Minna had no idea what it meant, but she continued.

"The skull," her voice shook as she suddenly wondered where she'd found the courage, or stupidity, to casually chat with her captor. "Did the horse belong to you?"

Laughter echoed through the hollow cavern of a mouth, ricocheting around the teeth. "Daring girl. Who asks me questions in this underground except for when they ask for favors? No one. No one." She crossed her arms and leaned against the brick wall. "Yes. My beloved mare. When I was human, we were inseparable. She was the truest creature I have ever known."

"You were human once?" Minna couldn't help the question from coming out, but she knew she better watch herself. The winter witch was not her friend.

She nodded though, and took a breath, as if to say more, but then a wooden bowl of gruel and fish splattered against her beloved mare's skull.

Heavy breathing behind her. Minna turned and eyed the new girl. Poor thing, she looked equally angry and terrified. Still, she said nothing.

Food stuck in the mane and ribbons, slopping down onto the witch's black gown. Those eye sockets once again filled with liquid shadows. Empty gaze focused on the girl with such intensity, the very air in the room shifted. A tangible storm brewed, every inch of

Spinnstubenfrau growing angrier like a thunder cloud, waiting to direct a lightning bolt.

Then she simply turned and left. The new girl sobbed.

Minna worked. *Guide the leader yarn. Get everything in place to spin the fibers. Foot to the treadle. Keep an eye on the twist. Repeat.*

*   *   *

Minna hadn't expected to see the new girl again, but she waited in the work room, propped up in the corner. There was a reason why Spinnstubenfrau was sometimes referred to as the belly slitter.

A scream clawed upward in Minna's throat, but she clamped her mouth down. Distressed moans forcing their way past her shut lips.

"Oh gods." She paced, blinked away tears at the sight of the poor, wretched girl.

Slit from belly to ear, the disemboweled child remained in the corner. Straw poked out from where the insides would have been. Like she'd morphed into some sick scarecrow. Silver coins covered the eyes. The stench of it . . . Minna gagged, stumbled. How could she work in here?

Then, the clicking of heels as Spinnstubenfrau approached. Her dress was perfectly black again, and not a speck of gruel remained on the mane's bright ribbons.

"She was a stupid girl, and now she will watch for eternity as women come and go to spin in the room, accomplishing what she never did. Let's hope her replacement has at least half a brain."

Another new girl. Minna did not turn to look, but sat at her spinning wheel, understanding that she needed to work in this room. With a corpse in the corner.

The young woman sat at the other spinning wheel and guided the leader yarn. Perhaps she had been warned of the human scarecrow, because she didn't even gasp as she took her place near Minna.

Smart girl. She must have made an important bargain too. Maybe she understood what Minna did: the power of desperation. Of hope.

*   *   *

"I'm Helene," the stranger said, breaking the comfortable quiet Minna had enjoyed the past two days.

She sighed. "My name is Minna. I'm sorry, but I must keep working."

"Of course." Helene fiddled with her spinning wheel, and Minna stole a quick glance. They were closer in age than she was to the dead girl still in the corner. Dark curls were pulled away from Helene's pale face, and tied with a frayed ribbon.

Silence accompanied the sounds of their wheels at work for most of the day. Minna tidied her station and felt oddly proud of all the yarn she'd spun.

"Do you like the witch?" Helene followed Minna out the door.

She lingered in the hall, anxious to return to the solace of her bedroom. Tiny as it was, she preferred sleeping alone and away from the other workers. Helene asked too many questions.

"It's not about liking someone or something. Whatever she truly is. It's about the bargain. Aren't you here because you made a deal?"

Helene shrugged. "Sort of."

Ghosts danced in the woman's eyes. Minna knew that haunted look. Maybe she was being too harsh. "Look, are you here to save someone? I am. I made a deal, and I intend to see it through." She turned to leave.

"I am here to save someone," Helene whispered. "I'm here to save us all."

A familiar click of heels down the hall. Spinnstubenfrau approached, checking the rooms and making sure the workers had gone to bed.

Minna bid Helene goodnight and rushed down the brick corridor to her room.

*   *   *

"What did you mean yesterday, that you're here to save us all?" Minna had been bursting to ask the question all night.

"Well, except for her." Helene pointed to the rotting corpse. The stench seemed to have reached its peak the other day. Minna had weirdly grown used to the smell. "And others like her. My village sent me here for a reason. I've been chosen." She grinned, looking awfully proud.

Minna organized her threads, then checked her wheel for any broken bits or hidden clumps of wool. Taking care of the wheel had become like looking after a friend. Plus, Helene didn't need much prompting.

"You see," the woman continued, "last year, the witch killed three of our clergy. Slit each man from belly to chin, then ear to ear. She strung them up on ropes made from their own intestines and left them hanging in the church."

Minna didn't particularly care for clergymen, but the whole affair did sound ghastly. Still, she kept working, and Helene kept talking.

"She even claimed they deserved it. It was quite the rumor, people pondering what terrible things those men could have done, but look at what the witch did to that poor girl. What could she have done to deserve it?"

"She threw gruel at Spinnstubenfrau, messed up her ribbons."

"What is wrong with you?" Disgust made itself clear on Helene's face.

Minna paused, cleared her throat. "I mean, it's horrible. She was so young." She'd never say it aloud, but she could've sworn the scarecrow girl had smiled during the story of the clergymen being ripped apart.

Helene rolled her eyes. Not working. Not twisting thread. "Anyway. My village chose me to stop the witch, and I intend to do it. Shouldn't be too hard. She was foolish enough to take my fake plea and get me down here."

"How would you even go about it? She's powerful, and not exactly human in case the horse skull didn't give that away."

Helene scoffed and made a tangle of the wool she worked with.

What a mess, Minna thought. Those threads would never do.

"You'll see," Helene said, and then she pulled something out from a hidden pocket in her skirt, flashed it briefly for Minna to see.

"A bone needle?"

Helene nodded. "The bone of a saint."

Of course. All those rumors she'd heard before about an enchanted needle. What could stop a creature who proudly bore the bones of a horse as her own head? Only another bone, one taken from a pure saint and carved into the sharpest needle.

Sadness bloomed within Minna, taking her by surprise. Before the witch was known as Spinnstubenfrau, she'd been known as other things. As something bright, a guardian between worlds who illuminated a path forward for those in the between spaces. But men had arrived on these lands, men like the clergy who demanded a new way forward that all must follow. Stories of the old gods faded, or were perverted into gruesome stories. Maybe, Minna thought, those stories had been told for so long, what choice did the witch have but to become what those people feared?

"Minna," Helene said, interrupting her thoughts, "whatever you're thinking, get out of your head. It does no good in a place like this."

"I need her," she said, and stopped spinning, losing precious time. "I need her to save my brother."

Helene had the decency to look sorry, but when she spoke her apologies, they meant nothing. Maybe she could steal the needle, hide it or destroy it before Helene even got the chance to attack the witch.

Click. Click. Click.

Too late. She was coming.

"If you say anything, I'll take all of your yarn to the kitchen and turn it into soup."

Minna believed her, but her mind raced as Spinnstubenfrau walked slowly into the room.

It happened in a blur. The witch started a sentence, but words barely had time to move through the horse bones before Helene jumped up and darted toward their keeper. Sainted bone needle in hand, she scraped bone against bone, slashing across the empty eye sockets.

Blood. Crimson as a holiday ribbon. It bubbled and spurted from the equine skull.

The rumor of the needle was real. It could hurt Spinnstuben-frau, and Helene wouldn't stop until the woman-creature was dead. Thom's sweet face pulsed in Minna's mind as she searched the room, the familiar feeling of desperation rising up in her chest. Yarn. It would have to do, have to be strong enough. She grabbed a few strands of the rigid fibers, held them tight in each hand, and then placed it over Helene's head. Flush against her throat.

From behind Helene, she pulled the yarn tight. Hoping it would be enough to scare the woman into stopping. Just enough to leave Spinnstubenfrau alone.

"I'm sorry," she said with a sob. "I have to save my brother. Please stop."

Surprising strength hid beneath Helene's thin frame. She struggled, and one of the threads snapped. Minna held tight to the second thread.

"I'm sorry. I'm so sorry." Tears blurred Minna's eyes. She nearly lost her footing and almost freed Helene until a gentle touch grabbed hold of her shoulder.

"I will finish this." The winter witch moved in front of Helene and plunged a hand through the young woman's ribcage. Bones snapped like twigs, and blood seeped from the cavity onto the stone ground.

Minna yelped, let go of the yarn, and retreated to a small corner of the room. Diagonally across from her, the decomposing scarecrow girl watched. What did she see behind those silver coin eyes?

"You made an interesting choice," Spinnstubenfrau said as she lifted a black sleeve up to her still-bleeding bone face. Helene's heart shone with a slick glaze in the witch's other hand. A prize.

"I told you, I'd do anything to save Thom."

"Then you should go back to your spinning." She kicked Helene's corpse into the corner next to the other girl. Minna swallowed down the rising vomit in her throat, kept her eyes focused on her spinning wheel, and twisted the threads.

*   *   *

Epiphany Eve.

Minna had completed so much work, twisted so many threads from the endless wool. Today would be the last.

A gasp escaped her lips. Helene's body lay alone in the corner. The straw-filled girl was gone, moved . . . elsewhere. Rather than straw, red thread glistened from Helene's slit open torso. The color so vibrant, Minna thought of fresh cherries and roses.

"What do you think?" Spinnstubenfrau said, and walked into the work room.

Minna did not turn around. Her eyes couldn't be parted from tracing the intricate ties of the thread. They'd been shaped into organs. Veins. Muscles. All the inner workings of a body. If the winter witch wanted, she could bring it all to life and restore Helene, but Minna knew that this was something else. Something special.

A gift.

"It's . . . strangely beautiful."

An inhale behind her as the witch hovered. "Thank you. Some of my finest work, I think."

Uncomfortable thoughts danced in Minna's head. Had she really called this massacre a thing of beauty?

"I should get to work."

"No." Spinnstubenfrau put both of her cold hands on Minna's shoulders and made her look into the empty eyes of her skull. The socket Helene had slashed with the bone needle was mostly healed, but a tiny scar remained. "You have completed your work."

Minna's heart thumped, anxious. "You mean, I've done enough for Thom?"

"I replaced his heart last night as an early gift. He is doing well."

"I don't know what to say." Minna hated how tears formed again in her eyes. Tears of relief that this had all been worth it. "Thank you. I wish I could see him."

The witch moved away and paced around the spinning wheels. "I will allow you to return to your village for one night, to say good-bye. Consider it a personal gift. You did try to save me, after all." Her left hand disappeared into a skirt pocket, and she produced a small white cloth. "I can't even touch the sainted needle with my bare hand. Perhaps you'd hang onto it?"

"Why not destroy it?" Minna accepted the cloth, unsure of what else to do. How could something so small and light create such a threat?

"Balance is necessary. Every immortal should have a flaw. This is mine, but I have many years left before some foolish girl from the village tries to kill me again. One day, though, I might need to be destroyed."

Minna absorbed the words, feeling like she'd need a lifetime to truly understand all of this. "What will happen to me after I return from seeing my brother?"

"You can start a new life. A new village. Maybe you'll stay here, in the enchanted underground."

Minna's heart raced, and the excitement of the offer startled her. She should be more disturbed, but instead she was . . . tempted. "What would I do here?"

"You could learn to do this." The witch cried her peculiar black tears from empty eyes, then placed a finger in the liquid. She smeared it across Minna's lips.

A vision took hold, showed Minna something she could have never dreamed. She saw Thom, flush with life and color, talking to their aunt and uncle. Wondering where his sister had gone. Then, she saw inside of him. His new heart. How it glowed with beautiful threads of scarlet and gold. Fabric whispered to his blood, to his mind, connecting all things.

She sobbed. "It's so beautiful."

"You could make something like that too, something just as delicate." Spinnstubenfrau reached up to her mane and untied the purple ribbon. Minna's ribbon. Mama's ribbon. She reached forward, took a tress of Minna's hair, and braided the ribbon into her curls.

How could she return to any normal life after this?

"Come with me this Epiphany Eve, Minna. And I can show you extraordinary things. You have a gift with more than needle and thread. You could sew life."

"But would I have to take life too?" She thought of Helene, of the nameless girl she'd been so callously calling the scarecrow.

"Balance," Spinnstubenfrau whispered. "The exchange of violence for moments of rarest beauty."

"What would I need to do?"

"Let me remake you. Let me sew you into something like me. Something even more remarkable than you already are. We will sew life. Weave stunning tapestries. Tonight, we collect energy. Tomorrow, we create."

Minna saw it then, somewhere in the passion of the witch's words, this creature she didn't even have a true name for. She saw the beauty. The striking black of the dress. The perfect, silken ribbons of the mane. How clean the bone remained. The faint threads connecting horse skull and flesh beneath the dress's high collar. How she had once been a goddess, shining bright.

She took Spinnstubenfrau's hand and followed her into the spinning rooms, where endless colorful threads waited.

What will I become? Minna wondered, and she smiled as her mind began to fashion powerful possibilities.

THE LADIES' SOCIETY FOR THE DEAD

Darcy Coates

SNOW FELL ACROSS eleven figures as they converged on the house at the end of Notary Lane.

They were all women. For many, arthritis had twisted their fingers and stooped their backs, and cataracts turned their eyes into sheer pools of white. They descended like wraiths on the two-story home, its windows lit up in sinewy yellow candlelight.

"Come in, quickly now," Maude Byers called, holding the door open as her guests shuffled through the snow. "There's a fire in the parlor. We'll be starting soon."

The women shed their hats and cloaks, hanging them on hooks by the front door. Some of the younger attendants tilted their heads back, admiring a space they were seeing for the first time. There were briefly shared greetings, but no voices rose past a murmur.

Maude closed the door against the cold and pushed through the throng of guests. "This way," she called.

The house had been decorated for Christmas. Garlands hung from the walls, the stairs, and the mantelpiece. Baubles reflected the light from dozens of candles. The parlor was already small, but the dense decorations and smell of fresh pine made the air thick and heady.

Maude stood in front of the fireplace as they took their seats. She was one of the older ladies, her hair a dense gray and her dress buttoned to her throat, her weathered hands clasped ahead of her chest. Her voice was commanding enough to pierce the still night air and silence the final whispers of conversation. "Welcome, members of the Ladies' Society for the Dead, to our annual communion."

There was a murmur of acknowledgment from the gathered forms.

"We're all well familiar with what we do here," Maude said, "although we wish to welcome our newest member. This is your first year with us, but you understand how the night works, don't you, Anna?"

All eyes flicked to the youngest girl. She was pale and spindly and seemed to wither under the scrutiny. She gave a tentative, unblinking nod.

"We have some time until midnight," Maude said, one hand raised to gesture to the clock on the mantel behind her. It was blocky and ornate, the second hand meting out a *click* with each shift, counting down the dwindling time like heartbeats. "It is traditional for the society to start the gathering with ghost stories. *Our* ghost stories. And since we have a new addition in our midst, it only seems appropriate that she should be allowed to share."

Her focus turned to Anna, but the girl's eyes were wild and terror-stricken.

Maude gave her a fleeting wisp of a smile. "Not everyone is comfortable with being called on first. Perhaps we should let one of our other members take the lead, to show how it is done. Who is prepared to share?"

A hand rose. One of the women closer to the fire, all gentle curves and soft eyes, glanced about for approval. "It's been a few years since I've told mine."

"Go ahead," Maude said.

The woman adjusted her pose. She clasped her hands, her thumbs pressing together hard enough that the knuckles shone white in the flickering firelight. "I want to tell you about the ghost of Dunn Bridge.

"A long time ago, a young couple lived in my town. The husband had smiling blue eyes and the wife had rosy cheeks. They were about as happy as you could expect them to be for the first two years of their marriage, and then the husband fell on a rusted nail while crossing the bridge near their house. First, he lost his fingers, then he lost his arm, and finally he lost his life.

"His wife grieved so hard she thought she would never survive it. On a cold and wet day, she walked to the length of rotting planks and creaking railing that had claimed her husband's life: Dunn Bridge.

"The woman leaned over the side and howled her misery into the water below. As her tears flowed, she thought she saw something in the ripples: her husband's smiling blue eyes, looking up at her.

"She reached over the railing, trying to snatch him out of the water, but the image was gone before she could reach him. She stayed there, looking into the river, until it was dark. And then returned the next day and the next, so hungry and desperate for even a glimpse of the man she loved.

"It took weeks before she saw him again, on a cold day on the edge of winter. But there he was, right at dusk: a glimpse of his eyes, a flash of his gentle smile, rippling through the water. She wasn't going to let him slip from her grasp again. She spilled over the railing and plunged into the water below, her arms outstretched. It wasn't until four days later that her bloated body was found, washed far downriver and tangled in reeds, the hands still reaching overhead, the fingers searching for her lover, even in death.

"She never found him. Her spirit lingers, alone for eternity. When the townspeople cross the bridge late at night, they say they hear the echo of an extra pair of footsteps. On foggy days, when the rotting planks are hard to see, a shrouded form stands at the crossing, warding people away.

"The townspeople repair the bridge whenever its wood begins to crumble, but they refuse to tear it down. That's what my ghost is waiting for, though. For the bridge to be torn apart, completely and forever. And that is why I am a part of your society. That is why I am here tonight. To have Dunn Bridge erased at last."

Some of the women closest to the one telling the story reached out, their hands grasping hers, a voiceless expression of unity.

"All of us in the Society share a unique gifting to reach the other side." Maude spread her hands, gesturing to the women around her. "To cross the barrier between the living and the dead. To commune and to pass on messages that would otherwise be lost to the grave. Every woman here has a story to share. Every woman here is seeking closure, or perhaps justice, for someone."

Murmurs rose from the group, faint but feverish and eager. Glassy eyes reflected the candles' lights like constellations. Heavy lines marked gaunt faces, and skin hung like loose crepe paper across their arms.

"The winter solstice is a special time," Maude continued, and her voice seemed to reverberate back from every corner of the oppressive room. "In this day of darkness and cold, at the heart of midnight, the veil thins to its most vulnerable. We meet each year with the goal to pierce it. To bring some sliver of the dead back into the realm of the living, Lord willing."

Above them all, the old clock ticked, its heartbeat loud and unforgiving as it drew them closer to its zenith.

"And now you," Maude said, turning to Anna. "Our newest member. You are here because of a haunting; now is the time to share it with us."

Anna's back was rigidly straight. She didn't seem able to meet any of their eyes as she opened her mouth and closed it again.

The woman to her left leaned closer, one arthritic hand clasping over the girl's like a claw. "It helps if you tell it like it's a fairy tale."

Anna swallowed. Her voice was faint and wavered at the edges, but the room was quiet enough for the women to hear every whisper. "There was a young woman who lived at home with her siblings and parents. Their home was an hour's walk to the ocean, and when the girl had an afternoon free, she would follow the empty roads to look at the water.

"There wasn't much of a beach, but there were caves—lots of them. They opened like mouths into the cliff walls, and when she was feeling bold, the girl would climb into them to explore.

"One day near the end of winter, the girl told her parents she was going to town. As she walked the road, she changed her mind and turned toward the ocean instead. It was a cold and wet day, but she was happy. She found little bones littering the dirty sand and followed a crab across the rocks. She strayed farther than she'd gone before and found a new cave in the rock wall.

"Inside, the tunnel seemed to go on forever. The girl kept a box of matches in her pocket and lit one as she stepped inside. The walls were wet and dripping, and she had to crawl on her knees to get through a squeeze. The cave kept going, and it was one of the most beautiful she'd seen, and every time her match burnt out, she would light another.

"And then she slipped and dropped the matches. They vanished into the pools of water in the cave's floor. The girl only had the match left in her hand, and she turned and tried to run back to the cave's entrance, but it burnt out against her fingers before she could escape.

"The cave was the darkest place the girl had ever known. The tunnel had twisted so many times that no light from the beach made it inside. The girl searched desperately for the way out in the dark, scratching her hands across the slimy rocks, but she couldn't find it. The tide began to rise. Up to her knees, and then her waist, and when it got to her shoulders, she realized she was going to die."

Anna paused. Her voice was ragged. None of her companions interrupted as they waited for her to regain her composure.

"The girl is still there. No one's found the cave, and no one's found her bones.

"On days like the day she died—when it is cold and overcast and threatening rain—she will walk the beach, looking for someone who can save her. She screams, and her voice sounds like the wind tearing over the bluffs. She cries, and it's like the water bubbling through the rocks. She wants to be found. She wants to be buried. And that"—she clasped her hands and then released them again—"is why I'm here."

Maude took a slow, heavy breath. "As you know, it requires the twelve of us working in tandem to cross the barrier, and we only have this very narrow window, on solstice night." Above her, the clock's hands were inching closer to midnight. "Each year, we give our full attention to one member. If her séance is successful, she will gracefully exit from the Ladies' Society for the Dead to make room for a new member. If the commune is unsuccessful, she must wait for another turn. Some of our party have been waiting a very, very long time."

Several figures nodded, their eyes milky, their gums receding past the roots of their teeth.

"Your turn will come," Maude said to Anna. "But not this night. Tonight, my number has been drawn, and it is now my turn to tell you all a ghost story. And not just a ghost story, but the story of a murder, set in the room where it took place.

"A long time ago, a bank manager named Thomas owned this house. His wife was proud of herself and her home, and although she and her husband no longer shared a bed, she considered herself a good woman. She served their meals on time; she looked after their neighbors; she kept their home well and their family respectable.

"But unbeknownst to her, her husband had begun an affair with a woman in the town. She was younger and more yielding to his wishes; she said she loved him. He told her his wife was a nag, a sour wretch, a creature he had never wanted to be shackled to. They were cruel words, meant to quell the anxieties of a girl who thought she was in love, but the more he repeated those thoughts, the more he began to believe them himself.

"The young woman was expected to be married. She gave Thomas an ultimatum: if he wanted them to be together forever, he would need to find a way to rid them of his wife. If he couldn't, he would never see his lover again.

"That night, Thomas's wife was mending a torn shirt in the parlor when he entered behind her. She saw the axe reflected in her thimble and moved just as he brought it down on her. It cut into her arm, right here"—Maude gestured to her own forearm—"but she was still alive.

"She fought for her life. She left scratches on his arms and his face. But he was stronger, and he had the axe, and it came down again and again until she stopped flinching.

"Her body was strewn across the floor. Thomas left the axe lying in her blood, washed his face and hands, hid his stained jacket, and then ran into the streets. He cried that a stranger had broken into the house and killed his wife. He said he had tried to fight off the attacker and pointed to the scratches on his face as proof.

"Some doubted his story. No one had seen another person enter or leave the home, and the axe had come from a neighbor's shed. But he was respected and trusted as their banker. Many considered him a friend. He put on such a good show of grief that they exclaimed it was impossible for him to commit a murder so vicious.

"The wife was buried. Although a few still suspected the husband, his life continued uninterrupted. Four months after his wife was put into the ground, he married his secret lover.

"His dead wife had left something of herself behind, though. Her blood and bone splinters found home between the floorboards, her breath in the air. The fury from her heart filled the rafters. She watched as the mistress took over the house and all its furnishings as her own. And the wife's anger was so great that she began to break things. The fine china shattered when the new bride tried to use it. Holes formed in the linen. The wallpaper began to peel off in jagged strips.

"The young bride tried to fight back. She bought new plates and new linen. She repapered the walls and mended the windows when they cracked. She covered the mirrors when Thomas swore he could see the dead wife's face staring at him through the reflections.

"After six months, the dread grew too great, and the new wife convinced her husband that they must leave. The house was abandoned for nearly a year before a fresh family came to settle, and then another family after that.

"The wife's ghost no longer breaks the plates or tears the wallpaper, but no family has lasted in this house for more than three years. They can feel her presence. Sometimes, when the veil is thin, she can be seen in their mirrors. She is still angry. And so, this solstice we meet to bring her peace, if such a thing is possible."

Maude paused to draw breath. Her companions shifted imperceptibly, heads tilted to glance at the floorboards beneath their feet, searching for the traces of long-dried blood and slivers of pale bone fragments inside the cracks.

"We are conducting the séance at the scene of death, and I will be the conduit," Maude said. She did not need to look at the floorboards. She had stared at them for many hours already. "I pray that it will be enough to pierce the veil and bring my ghost peace. Ladies, if you would."

The clock meted out seconds. Its hands inched toward their peak: five minutes to midnight.

As one, the gathered women rose from their chairs. They all shifted onto the floor, forming a circle around the bare patch of floorboards. Worn bones clicked and scraped, but no one flinched as they took to their knees.

The firelight threw long, jagged shadows as Maude stepped into the circle's center. She knelt as well, her back ramrod straight as she gazed at the eleven figures surrounding her. The silence lasted a breath, where the only sound came from the crackling fire. Then Maude said, "Let us begin."

The women forming the circle bent forward and reached their hands out, palms down, to press them into the floor. Their smallest fingers touched, forming a connected loop. They would not move from that position until the séance was complete, no matter how much they ached.

Above them, the click clicked down another minute. Four to midnight.

"We carry a message," Maude began. Her breathing was fast, and it could have been excitement, but it sounded more like fear. "We seek this hour to bridge the world of the living with the realm of the dead."

Around her, the kneeling figures began to chant: "Exaudi voces nostras. Nuntium accipere a mortuis."

The closest candle flickered, sending pinwheels of light over the baubles behind it.

"Exaudi voces nostras," the women said again. Maude joined them. "Nuntium accipere a mortuis."

Maude reached into the gray knot of hair at the back of her head. She pulled an object free—a hairpin, four inches long, wickedly sharp at its tip.

"Exaudi voces nostras."

Maude clasped the pin between both hands, point toward the floor, like a knife preparing for a sacrifice. The clock above them counted down another minute. Three to midnight.

"Nuntium accipere a mortuis."

The wind whistled against the house's outside. Blinding white snow smothered across the windows as a chill invaded the room.

The voices grew louder. The women began to sway like seaweed undulating in a tide. Their hands didn't move. None dared break the connection.

Maude tilted her head back. Her eyes were closed. With each repetition of their chant, wisps of mist rose from her lips as the fire at her back began to wither.

"Exaudi voces nostras."

One of the candles flickered and died, quickly followed by a second. The shadows were growing longer. Stranger. They stretched up the walls, like the trunks of a dead forest, and crowded across the ceiling. The room seemed to grow smaller. Heavier. Colder.

The minute hand on the clock shifted again. Two to midnight. Another candle died.

Sounds began to bleed into the room. Somewhere deeper in the house, a door slammed.

"Nuntium accipere a mortuis."

The wind rose another notch. It screamed across the house's exterior. The windows rattled, battering inside their frames. The doors groaned. Beneath all of that, it was nearly possible to miss the slow, aching thuds that moved down the hallway's staircase.

Perspiration shone across Maude's forehead. Her eyes were pressed tightly closed, her brows creasing as they pulled together,

her hands shaking and white as she gripped her hairpin. Rows of yellowed teeth bared as her voice rose still louder.

"Exaudi voces nostras!"

The thudding sound on the stairs grew nearer. The very bones of the house seemed to shake with it. The circle of swaying women didn't pause, didn't even look up as the parlor door sluggishly drew open. The entryway was too dark to see what might be behind it, if anything.

The clock lost another minute. Just one remained.

"Exaudi voces nostras!"

The women shouted in unison, the chant growing fast and frenzied, spittle flying from between teeth, muscles taut.

"Nuntium accipere a mortuis!"

The patterned wallpaper began to wither, peeling up at the edges, turning to shreds beneath the garlands.

"Hear us!" Maude's words were a hoarse scream, lost beneath the howling wind and shuddering, creaking floor. Her eyes shot open, but pupil and iris were gone. Nothing remained but sheer white beneath fluttering lashes. "Receive our message!"

The final candles around the room's edges stuttered and then perished at once. The fire vanished in a hiss of dying embers and wisps of smoke. The unseen presence in the doorway moved closer, a floorboard groaning under its weight.

The clock struck midnight.

Maude plunged her hairpin down into the ancient floorboards. She scratched, her movements frenzied, her eyes a sickly white. Bubbles of blood rose from beneath the implement with every scrape. The women around her chanted and swayed, near exhaustion, shivers wracking them.

At the room's back, something released a low, rattling breath.

The tendons in Maude's arms bulged as she dug and dug and dug, the sharp tip of her hairpin scoring through the old floor. Strings of brittle wood split up like threads being pulled free. The oozing blood smeared across her hands. The wind screamed around them, drowning out their voices, whiting out every window, as though determined to bury them.

And then the clock ticked over once more, past midnight, spilling them into the freshly birthed morning.

Maude slumped back. Her dark dress pooled around her, as limp as the skin on her face.

The seeping blood vanished, shrinking back into the floorboards as their séance concluded. A second passed, then another. The candles' lights came back from the dead, their flames blooming slowly, tentatively. The fireplace's dead embers crackled to life. The flames started as careful wisps, but as the Ladies' Society for the Dead let the silence hang, the fires grew bolder, lighting the walls and the baubles and the faces once more.

Ahead of Maude's pooled dress, in the center of their circle, words had been scratched into the old flooring.

"It worked," one of the women said, her weathered hands reaching out to graze across the fine-spun scrapes. Each mark was no thicker than a gossamer thread, but Maude had been frantic and fast, and dozens of scars overlapped to form each line of the message.

They had achieved it. A message brought from the realm of the dead and spat back for the living to marvel over.

"Will it be enough?" another of the guests asked.

Their voices were low, hushed. As though speaking too loudly might break the magic that had presided over them for that precious midnight minute.

"Let us hope it is," Maude said. Her hands trembled as the other women took them and helped her to her feet. "Let us hope this will conclude the business."

They stood, all silent wraiths, as they looked down at the words they'd so desperately clawed forth.

THOMAS
KILLED
MAUDE

With midnight passed, there was nothing more they could do. One at a time, they left the séance circle and trailed back into the hallway. The sighing phantom was gone, vanished again as the veil grew heavy once more. They passed on gentle feet to the hooks just inside the doorway and took up their cloaks.

"Thank you," Maude said simply. "I wish you the strongest of luck next year, my friends."

The Ladies' Society for the Dead stepped into the icy, gusting wind outside and let its flakes dissolve their forms and snatch them away like a gasp of warm air on a freezing night.

BEING NICE

Jeff Strand

"WHOOPSIE!" I EXCLAIMED as I stepped into my living room. Normally, I was not the kind of person who would say "Whoopsie," but since I'd just walked in on Santa Claus, I didn't think "Holy shit!" was appropriate.

He turned around to face me. "Oh, hello, Adam. Didn't expect to see you at 3:14 AM."

"I couldn't sleep."

Santa Claus shrugged. "It happens." He dropped a small package into the stocking I'd haphazardly hung by the chimney. "I'll see you next year. Actually, no, I won't. You turn eighteen next year, so this is my final visit."

"Right," I said. I couldn't believe I was actually staring at Santa Claus in the flesh. He looked exactly the way he did on the Coke cans. "It's an honor to meet you, sir. Uh, was that my only present?"

"Yes."

"Seems kind of tiny."

Santa nodded. "Indeed."

"Is it a check?"

"No, Adam, it is not. Do you want me to spoil the surprise?"

"Okay."

"It's a lump of coal."

"What?" I asked. "That's not possible! There must be some kind of mistake!"

"Oh, sure, sure," said Santa. "Blame me instead of taking responsibility for your own actions."

"I wasn't blaming you. It could've been the elves!"

"The elves aren't involved in that part of the process." Santa Claus sighed. "I don't appreciate your insinuation that I'm doing sloppy work. The Naughty or Nice lists are accurate, every single time, based on a very specific set of criteria."

"I never said you were doing sloppy work," I insisted. "This just doesn't make any sense!"

"Do you know how much work it is to figure this stuff out?" asked Santa. "It's not just about sorting kids into the Naughty and Nice categories, which is a massive undertaking on its own. I also have to make sure the families actually celebrate Christmas, so that I'm not searching for milk and cookies next to the menorah. Then I have to make sure the presents are appropriate for that particular family's socioeconomic status. It's a *lot* to keep track of."

"Right! I agree! That's why I'm saying there could have been a mistake!"

"Look, Adam, nobody is saying you're bound for eternal hell-fire," Santa told me. "You missed the cutoff for Nice by a bit, and so you get a lump of coal this year. It happens. You'll still get into college."

"But what did I do?"

"For starters, you had sex with your girlfriend . . ."

"That's not allowed?" I asked. "Trent had sex with his girlfriend last year and got a PlayStation!"

"You focused on your own pleasure instead of hers. You're a taker, not a giver. That's naughty."

"I get coal for that?"

"There was also the small matter of the hit-and-run," Santa said.

"What hit-and-run?" I asked. "What the hell are you talking about?"

"I'm just kidding," said Santa. "I did that to bring up the larger point that you lack a sense of humor, which would be fine if you were neurodivergent, but you're not. And you take it upon yourself to be the arbiter of what is and is not appropriate material to joke about. That's also naughty."

"For real? I get coal for pointing out that some subjects should be off-limits for comedy regardless of the context?"

"Not that alone, no. It's all cumulative. You don't please your girlfriend and you're a humor scold. That's mostly it for the bad things you do. There's a lot of masturbation, but that's really more of a Jesus issue. The real reason you got coal is that you haven't done much in the way of good things this year."

"I've done plenty of good things!" I said.

"Name one."

"I kept up my grades!"

Santa shook his head. "That's how you get your parents to buy you a car. It's irrelevant for the Naughty or Nice list. Have you done any volunteer work? Have you helped anybody in need? Think about it, Adam. What have you done this year to make the world a better place?"

"I . . ." I wracked my brain to come up with something. *"Fudge."*

"You don't have to say fudge," Santa told me. "Cursing is fine."

"Do you curse?" I asked.

"Oh goodness, no. I use 'Ho ho ho' instead. But we're not talking about me. I get that you're disappointed, but as we say at the North Pole, tough noogies."

He turned toward the chimney.

"Wait!" I said.

Santa looked back at me. "What? In case you weren't aware, I'm kind of busy tonight."

"You said I missed the cutoff for being nice by a bit. It's still Christmas. Is there time to redeem myself?"

"Hmm." Santa thoughtfully stroked his thick white beard. "It's not standard operating procedure, but I suppose you could try to get yourself off the Naughty list."

"Thank you! Then that's what I'll do!"

"However," said Santa, "sneaking out of the house so you can bring your girlfriend to orgasm won't do it."

"That's not what I was thinking," I said. (It very much was what I was thinking.)

"And you just lied to Santa Claus's face, so you're a little further in the hole."

"Fuck!"

"You just cost yourself another point," Santa informed me.

"Why? You said cursing was okay!"

"It is, but I didn't like your tone."

"Then from the bottom of my heart, I truly apologize, Mr. Claus," I said.

"Sarcasm is naughty," said Santa.

"That wasn't sarcastic!"

"Sounded sarcastic to me."

"Even if it was sarcastic, which it wasn't, you said that I was naughty for not having a sense of humor!"

"Are you really trying to get on the Nice list by arguing with Santa Claus?"

I decided to stop talking.

"I'm going to get back to work," said Santa. "Knock yourself out."

Santa tapped the side of his nose, transformed into a tarantula, and scurried up the chimney. I'd always wondered how the jolly fat man got into people's homes, but that wasn't on my list of top guesses.

I wasn't going to settle for a lump of coal. Not on my final Christmas before adulthood. Screw that. My conversation with Santa Claus apparently hadn't woken up my parents, so I was going to put on my winter clothes, quietly leave the house, and earn my rightful place on the Nice list!

I walked down the sidewalk, ice crunching under my boots, and wondered how I could make the world a better place at three thirty in the morning. Maybe there'd be a lost puppy or an old lady who'd accidentally locked herself out of her house and was clawing helplessly at her front door, desperately trying to get back into the warmth.

I looked around and didn't see any puppies or old ladies.

I wished I lived in New York City instead of Leafy Bush, Tennessee. There'd be a lot more going on. My street was eerily quiet, and even if I walked a few blocks to Main Street, there wasn't likely to be anybody in need of rescue.

Maybe there'd be some vandalism I could repair.

Or an axe-wielding psychopath in a Santa suit I could subdue.

Did shoveling driveways count? How many driveways would I need to shovel to earn a place on the Nice list? Why couldn't Santa be more transparent about what was required? If I'd known the guidelines, when Monica asked me to reciprocate, I would've said "Sure!" instead of making a face and going "Ew."

I walked around the block, hoping to find a stranded motorist, but the neighborhood was at peace. I'd just have to start shoveling driveways and hope that was enough.

I fetched my shovel out of the shed, then walked down the street until I saw a driveway that could use my assistance. It belonged to Mr. Tanner—not old by Santa Claus standards, but old by mine. He was about forty, and I bet his back hurt sometimes.

I began to shovel his driveway.

Ugh. This sucked. I hated manual labor. Why couldn't he just pour salt on it? Or hire somebody? Why didn't he take care of his own driveway instead of waiting for me to do it? *He* should be on the Naughty list, not me!

Ugh. Ugh. Ugh. I was cold and bored and tired.

The front porch light came on, and the door opened. Mr. Tanner stepped outside in his pajamas. "What's going on here?" he asked.

I waved. "Hi! It's Adam."

"Adam? What are you doing?"

"Shoveling your driveway," I said.

"It's the middle of the night!"

"I know. Just thought I'd do something nice for a neighbor."

Mr. Tanner walked toward me. "Have you been smoking marijuana or eating marijuana-laced brownies or popping those marijuana gummies I've heard so much about?"

"No, sir. Just shoveling your driveway."

"Liar! Who goes out and shovels a driveway at three forty-five on Christmas morning? Did you have a mushroom before you came out here?" He waved his hand in the air. "Am I leaving a colorful trail?"

"Nothing like that," I insisted. "I just—"

Mr. Tanner slipped on a patch of ice, fell, and bashed his head. It would've been nice if his head had landed on a fluffy patch of snow, but instead it landed on the exposed concrete I'd just shoveled.

"Are you okay?" I asked, even though the expanding pool of blood seemed to answer that question.

Santa Claus appeared right next to me, almost making me jump out of my skin. "Hmm. I'm not sure you understood the assignment."

"I didn't do it on purpose!" I said.

Mr. Tanner rolled over and moaned.

"Do I get credit for taking him to the emergency room?" I asked.

Santa shook his head. "C'mon, Adam. That would be like giving you credit for saving kids from a burning orphanage that you set on fire."

"Then what am I supposed to do?"

Mr. Tanner spat out some blood.

"Well," said Santa, "you certainly shouldn't stand here and watch him suffer."

I slammed the shovel into Mr. Tanner's skull, again and again, until his head was a gory, pulpy mess.

"That is most definitely not what I meant," said Santa.

"I put him out of his misery! Isn't that what you wanted?"

"No! I wanted you to take him to the emergency room!"

"You said that didn't count!"

"So what? It's not all about the presents!"

"Oh." I looked down at the evidence of my heinous crime. "Can't you bring him back to life?"

"No, I can't bring him back to life!" said Santa. "Are you crazy?"

"But you're Santa Claus!"

"Do you know how many children sit on my lap in a department store and tell me that all they want for Christmas is for me to bring their mommy or daddy back to life? I hear it constantly, and it rips my soul out every single time. If I had the power to bring people back from the dead, do you really think I'd waste my time delivering presents? I'm omniscient, not omnipotent."

"Hey!" somebody shouted from across the street. "What's going on over there?"

I recognized the voice. It was Mrs. Brown, a crabby old lady who used to be my second-grade teacher. She tied the belt of her pink bathrobe, then began to walk toward me.

I hurriedly scooped up a shovelful of snow and poured it over Mr. Tanner's head. The snow immediately turned red, so I repeated the process a few more times as Mrs. Brown stormed over.

Santa Claus had disappeared. Fucking coward.

"What have you done?" Mrs. Brown demanded.

"Not a thing," I said.

"Why is he lying on the ground?"

"I found him like this."

"Why is there blood dripping from your shovel?" Mrs. Brown asked.

"Why is there blood dripping from *your* shovel?" I asked, recognizing right away that it wasn't a very good attempt to talk my way out of this.

"I always knew there was evil in your heart, Adam," she said. "I knew it from the first day you stepped into my classroom. I have never received a stronger Satan vibe than I did when you sipped from that juice box."

I bashed Mrs. Brown in the face with the shovel. Her body dropped to the ground.

"You're racking up quite a body count," Santa told me.

"How many driveways do I have to shovel to balance this out?"

"Oh, you're not getting any presents. That ship has sailed. Your only concern right now should be to avoid getting caught."

A police car turned onto the street, red and blue lights flashing.

"Here," I said, handing Santa Claus the shovel.

"I'm sorry, but did you really just give me this shovel so that you could frame me for your crimes?"

"It was him!" I shouted, pointing to Santa. "He's gone berserk! Please, save me from his psychotic wrath!"

The car screeched to a halt right in front of us, and two police officers got out, guns drawn.

"Put down the shovel, Santa!" one of them ordered.

"Ho ho ho," said Santa. "This is all one big misunderstanding!"

"We said, drop it!"

"I'm not the one who—"

The cops opened fire, pumping several bullets each into Santa's chest. He dropped the shovel and stumbled backward.

His suit was red.

Of course, his suit had already been red. There were a lot of holes in the fabric, but nothing was spurting out of them.

"I break into millions of homes every year," Santa informed me. "You really think I'm not bulletproof?"

Since he'd accused me of not having a sense of humor, I tried to lighten up the situation. "So, I guess I'm still on the Naughty list, huh?" I asked.

"A little worse than that."

The ground cracked open beneath me. Crimson light spilled forth, and scaly clawed hands reached for me. My body burst into flames, and I shrieked in eternal terror as the demons pulled me down into the pits of hell.

What I'm trying to say is that last Christmas wasn't great for me. Satan did get me a present, but I *really* didn't like it.

GHOSTED

Mercedes M. Yardley

MOIRA LOVED THIS dark time of year. The wind howled and demanded entrance to her home. It promised to sneak in through the cracks in the house boards. It would shatter her windows entirely. It would gather in corners of her room and linger when she came down with a nasty cold. That would teach her, the wind sniffed. Moira would pay it the respect it deserved.

Time was when she would laugh back. She would tease the wind, threatening to banish it with cozy fires in the hearth and the smell of oranges and mulled wine. She'd make one of Granny Witch's poultices for her throat and feel right as rain. The wind would be cast outdoors where it ought to be, and she would be snuggled inside like a content woman in a holiday romance movie. Her name would be Noelle or Chrissy or Candy. She'd have hot chocolate ready for carolers.

But that only happened in movies. In reality, she had neither cocoa nor carolers nor holiday cheer. Her name was Moira, and it meant "bitter."

Jak had been dead for two years. Each holiday party, each get-together was incredibly painful.

"Thinking of you," the gold-foil cards said.

"Merry Christmas, Jak and Moira!"

"Have a blessed New Years, Moira."

"Happy Yule to you."

She could see the hesitancy in her friends' handwriting, the way they struggled to write simply *Moira* instead of *Jak and Moira*. Or writing *Jak* before crossing it out. Or writing *MOIRA* in all caps as if shouting her name made up for the lack of his.

Her oldest friend was no better.

"I didn't know what to say," Sasha said. "Do I send you a picture of my family when you don't have any family left?"

"I'm always happy to see your family," Moira said.

"How do I tell you to have a magnificent Christmas when you're all alone?" she continued.

"I'm not alone." Moira's smile was rigid. "I have wonderful friends like you."

"But lying in your room night after night, reaching out for his side of the bed. It must be—"

"You always send the perfect cards, and I'll be delighted to receive one. But I really must go."

Moira put the phone down and sighed.

"I miss you more than life, Jak," she whispered. "I hate every second of it."

I know, the wind whispered back in Jak's voice, but then again, the wind always said silly things.

*   *   *

Winter is a time of ghost stories and gifts and laughter and acute, stabbing loneliness. Moira didn't decorate the house or put up a tree. She had a few wrapped gifts from friends tossed on the counter, with the unpaid bills and junk mail.

This evening she sat in front of the fire, wrapped in one of Jak's old flannel shirts that didn't smell like him any longer.

"What do I do, baby?" she asked aloud. "I don't know how to do this without you."

She had worked with Jak. Lived with Jak. Their lives had become intertwined so quickly and so completely that she couldn't unravel them. Even though he was dead, they were still knotted together.

"I wish you were here," she said. "I've tried wishing on stars and on the moon and on the northern lights, like a fool, in order to have you back."

"God looks out for fools and children," a faint voice said on the wind. Moira wiped her eyes and looked up. She saw a shimmering outline forming in front of her. "Maybe your wishes count after all."

Moira covered her eyes and calmed her breathing. This was a dream or a psychotic break. Ghosts existed in Dickens's novels and fairy tales, not in isolated Canadian towns. She peeked through her fingers.

"Peekaboo. I see you," Jak said, just as he always had.

*   *   *

Sasha was throwing a party and Moira was invited—nay, *commanded*—to come. She sat at her vanity, staring at her hair. It looked fine. Her clothes were fine. She dusted a little pink powder on her cheeks because she looked sallow, but now that was fine too.

"You look like the dead," Jak said behind her. He rested his fingertips lightly on her shoulders like he always had.

"That isn't funny, Jak."

"Sure, it is. Now we match."

Moira closed her eyes, hard, and covered them. She counted to ten. When she opened her eyes, there was no ghostly dead husband or hallucinations brought on by mental illness or unchecked grief. She met her gaze in the mirror.

"I can do this," she told herself firmly.

Sasha's house was a place of curated beauty. Everything had been carefully chosen by an expensive designer who knew nothing of Sasha's personality. The house was cream and beige and boring. Perhaps the designer did understand Sasha's personality after all.

"Moira." Sasha beamed. "I'm so glad you're here. Bradford will take your coat."

"Hi, Brad," Moira said. She handed her coat to Moira's husband. "Coat duty?"

He smiled a long-suffering smile. "I'm useful and yet not underfoot. Just how she likes it." His eyes changed, and Moira tried not to stiffen. "How are you doing, Moira? You still seem sad."

"I am still sad. I thought I'd be used to it by now, but I guess not."

Brad leaned closer and lowered his voice. "Listen, I think you should know—"

"Bradford," Sasha called, and Brad flinched. "Don't commandeer her. Share her with the rest of us. Moira, come inside."

"You've outdone yourself," she told Sasha, and meant it. The room was full of dazzling gold. Baubles, candelabras, golden sashes, and bows hung from the inside balconies and railings. A cluster of tall, tastefully decorated evergreens dominated the room. Moira smelled pine and cinnamon. She smiled.

"That's what I wanted to see," Sasha said, and pressed a champagne glass into her hand. "Relax. Mingle. Take a break from sadness and just live for a while."

A break from sadness. Moira's jaw clenched, but Sasha was already gone.

She didn't mean it, Moira told herself, and sipped from her glass. She could do this. She could do hard things.

* * *

She chatted and socialized and even briefly danced, although it was with Sasha's young nephew who was trying to earn a badge toward his Eagle Scout. Somehow "being kind to widows" gave him a point somewhere on his do-good list. Moira didn't mind because he was sweet and awkward and didn't know how to dance at all, but was trying terribly hard.

"I never thought I'd see you with another man," Jak murmured into her hair. He was pressed into her back, his arms around her, swaying back and forth with her and her adorable dance partner. "He'll be a Lothario when his acne clears. I'd better watch out."

Moira laughed and the nephew looked delighted.

"You can check off another good thing on your list," Moira assured him, and he grinned.

The party wasn't winding down, but Moira was. She drifted toward Sasha to say her goodbyes.

"Not yet," Sasha said, and grabbed her hand. "I have someone to introduce you to, first."

"Oh no, I'd really rather not," Moira said, pulling her hand back gently. "I'm worn out."

Sasha didn't release her grip.

"I thought you two would meet here on your own, but I have to step in, as always."

Brad appeared at Sasha's side.

"Perhaps tonight isn't the best time," he said. "Moira looks pretty spent."

"We already discussed this, Brad." Sasha was smiling but her voice was venomous. "It's the only thing that will help."

"I don't think it will help at all," he insisted. "I think it's none of our business."

"What are you talking about?" Moira yanked her hand back, but Sasha still held on.

"Moira," she snapped. "Stop being ridiculous. You're acting like a child."

"I don't understand why you're so adamant that I meet somebody, Sasha. I can do it another time. I just want to go home."

Sasha's brown eyes flashed. "Go home and what? Curl up in your gloomy little bed and cry? Think about Jak and how things could have been? How they should have been?"

"Stop it," Brad said. Sasha ignored him.

"He's been dead for three years now."

"Two," Moira corrected automatically.

Sasha rolled her eyes. "Two, then. Long enough. You've been mourning him so hard that you've forgotten the rest of us."

"Sasha," Brad warned.

"Do you even see yourself? Have you looked in a mirror lately? Look at you." She jabbed her finger into Moira's chest so hard it hurt. "Wasting away and prettily wrapping up in a smug little blanket of sorrow?"

"Sasha, that's enough," Brad said, but Sasha pushed him with both hands.

"Oh, you're on her side? I thought you agreed to this."

"Agreed to what?" Moira's head was on a swivel, looking between Sasha and Brad. "What did you agree to?"

"This won't be good for you," Jak spoke quietly into her ear. "Turn around and walk out, honey."

"I didn't agree to anything," Brad said, but his voice was lost in the cacophony. Sasha was saying something in the cutting, nasal way she had, and Brad was vowing he had nothing to do with this, whatever *this* was, and Jak was urging her to escape. The holiday music swirled around her, and laughter floated on the air. The cinnamon and pine, so Christmassy before, was overpowered by spilled alcohol and heavy cologne and Moira's fear.

It was too much—too hot, too loud, too bright. The sparkling ornaments and glittery dresses overstimulated her. Her eyes didn't have anywhere to land, so she shut them and covered them with her hands.

"Peekaboo," Jak said. "I see you."

"You're introducing me to another man, aren't you?" she said aloud. "You want me to get over Jak so you're introducing me to someone else. I'm not ready for that. I might never be ready."

"Moira," Sasha said, harshly. "Stop being dramatic and open your eyes."

"Moira," Brad said, taking her elbow. "I'll help you leave."

"Just go away," Moira said. "Everybody stop saying my name."

"Moira, go with Brad," Jak told her.

"Moira?" asked a voice she didn't recognize. She held her breath until the room stopped swirling. She uncovered her eyes.

A woman stood in front of her, small and beautiful with wide eyes and a perfectly shaped rosebud mouth.

She opened her sweet lips and spoke again. "Am I correct? You're Moira?"

"Yes," Moira mumbled. Sasha folded her arms triumphantly. Brad looked ill. "Who are you?"

The woman blinked. "I'm Analee. I was sleeping with your husband."

"Oh," Moira responded, and she meant to say something else then, but the hungry look on Jak's face as he stared at this woman told her it was true.

"Jak," she managed to say, and as he slowly tore his eyes from Analee to look at her, the Christmas party came crashing around her as she slipped to the ground.

* * *

She remembered little after that. Sasha argued with Brad while Jak spoke quickly without any sound. Brad took her home and helped her inside. She fell on the couch because she couldn't make it all the way to the bedroom.

The aurora borealis shone in the sky that night. She wondered if it had exuded the same splendor the first time Analee slept with her husband. She thought maybe it had.

* * *

"It wasn't like that," Jak assured her. He leaned against the wall, smoking a cigarette as ghostly as himself.

"It was exactly like that," she answered. There was a water stain on the ceiling she needed to deal with. Jak always handled those things. He took care of everything, every need. Analee's needs, apparently.

"She's lying," he said. His words evaporated like the smoke. "It isn't true."

"We both know it is," Moira answered, and they were quiet for a while. For the next two days, if you want to be precise, and Moira didn't.

She lay on the couch for so long that it bruised her body. It pushed into the muscles on her back and legs and thighs. The cushions touched her wrists and her slender neck. They trailed kisses down to her collarbone until she realized it wasn't the couch at all, but Jak's ghost.

"Stop it," she said, and slid to the icy floor. There would be no chance she could mistake its coldness for Jak's ethereal lips. Yes, this is where she would stay. It was safer here.

"Moira."

Leave me alone, Jak.

He called her name more insistently.

Leave me alone, Jak!

Jak hauled her onto the couch. She fought back, but she didn't have the strength and simply gave up.

"I would never give up," Jak said. He lazed on the arm of the couch. "That's the difference between us. I'm still here now, aren't I?"

"When's the last time you had something to eat? To drink? Bradford! Get her some water."

It wasn't Jak at all. He watched her from the other side of the couch. Moira peered at Sasha.

"What are you doing here?" she asked.

"Saving your life, apparently. You're still in your party dress. Haven't you even changed since then? It was a week ago."

Brad returned with a glass of water. Moira hadn't realized she was thirsty. He handed her some crackers, and she took a bite.

"Bradford, go start her a bath. She's filthy and freezing. Ugh, you're always such a mess."

"I don't want your help," Moira said, but soon she was down the hall and in the bathtub.

She wrapped her arms around her legs and rested her chin on her knees while Sasha scrubbed at her back.

"What would you do without me?" she groused. "You'd die, that's what. You would have died on the floor."

"Why not let me?" Moira said under her breath, but Sasha's sharp ears caught it.

"Really?" she said, leaning to face her. "Are you being serious right now?"

She poured shampoo on Moira's hair and pulled at it roughly. Moira's eyes filled with tears, and it wasn't just because of the pain.

"Why would you do something so cruel?" she finally asked.

The barrage on her hair slowed.

"It wasn't cruel," Sasha said. "It was a kindness."

Moira snorted. "A kindness? How could that possibly be kind?" She pressed her forehead to her knees.

Sasha's hands were gentler now. "I don't regret telling you, but Bradford said . . . well, he said maybe I didn't go about it the right way. Like maybe I should have told you in private."

"I already knew."

Sasha went still. "You knew? About Analee?"

"Not specifically. But I knew it was someone."

"You did? But you were grieving Jak so hard."

Moira turned to face her. "Sasha, it made it even more complicated when he died. You of all people should understand how thorny it is when your husband cheats."

Sasha shifted uncomfortably. "That was a long time ago. We worked through it. Why would you even bring it up?"

"Why would you?"

Sasha handed Moira a towel. "I know Jak's death broke you. It was so sudden, and you couldn't seem to process it. I thought if you knew about the affair, you'd get over him faster. Get your life back. You're such a chore when you're like this."

"It's not your place to tell me when to stop grieving. It isn't your place to tell me any of this."

"I wouldn't have had to if you hadn't hidden your knowledge of the affair. You just make things harder for me."

Moira stepped out of the tub and wrapped herself in the towel. "Thank you for coming to check on me. I'm feeling better now. I promise to eat dinner and go to bed safely."

Sasha glared. "That's it? You're just going to kick me out? After everything I've done?"

"Precisely because of everything you've done. Don't make me ask Brad to drag you outside."

"You've never been worth my time. We are done, do you understand? You don't deserve my help. Bradford! We're leaving."

"Your help always hurt me," Moira told the empty room. "Goodbye."

Ghostly fingers slid down her shoulders and knotted in her wet hair.

"I thought she'd never leave." Jak nuzzled her ear. "It's about time you cut her off."

Moira pulled a silk robe over her body. Her eyes were on the moon outside.

"I don't need you here either, Jak. You're no better for me than she is."

He stilled. His breath would have moved her hair if he had breath. His hands would have warmed her if he had warmth.

"What are you saying?" he asked.

She turned to face him, looking at him fully. His mouth still crooked the same way, and his hair still tumbled into his face, but death had changed his solidity, changed his eyes. If she took a deep breath and blew, she was certain he would fade away like mist.

Maybe it was time he did.

"You don't belong here anymore, Jak. It's time for you to leave."

He frowned. "Is it because of Analee?"

She hated the way the other woman's name sounded in his mouth. It was too familiar. He had said it a hundred times. A thousand.

"Maybe it was Analee when you were alive. Maybe we could have worked through it, or maybe not. But that isn't an option anymore, and neither are you. I can't hole up in this house wondering if you're a ghost or simply madness."

He drifted closer. "Darling, I love you. I don't want to leave you alone."

Moira rubbed her arms, chilled by his nearness. "You left me alone two years ago. It's time to go. I'm better off without you."

He stood there in his casual, self-assured way. She was going to miss him terribly. She already had, for years, and it hadn't killed her yet.

"Please go away, my love," she said, and closed her eyes. She covered them with her hands. When she opened them, he was gone.

Peekaboo. I can't see you.

Grief is a funny thing. It tastes bitter and sweet and makes you hold your mouth in a certain way. But relief? It tastes like freedom.

She walked to the balcony doors, flung them open, and stepped outside into the cold. Her frozen town was alight with Christmas lights and candles shining brightly in windows. The pesky little wind who used to tease her all those holidays ago came bounding inside, bringing in flurries of snow. It buzzed around her bedposts and her closet. It buried itself in her coats and played with her lipsticks. Then it zipped outside to join Moira as she tipped her face up to the bleak midwinter sky, awash with lights.

BRUISER

Jamie Flanagan

1

Tisha Page walked her evening rounds on the second floor of Harmony Nursing and Rehabilitation, hands in her pockets, when she heard the glass shatter.

She craned her head over one hulking shoulder. The hallway stretched behind her in a mute row of white doors to the left, caged moonlit windows to the right, paneled ceiling above, and checkered floor below. Shadows swayed gently on the wall, cast by frost-covered trees in the parking lot. For a moment, they almost looked like a man.

Tisha was wary. Wary that Mr. Skaft, her supervisor, would be standing there—white jacket flowing and snide smile shining—with his arms folded. Wary she'd lose this job in the same fashion she'd lost the previous one—for once again mooning when she should have been working, as her Aunt Tabby would say.

The sound of glass scattering on tile drifted through the halls once more, accompanied by the distant murmur of old Mr. Thompson reciting the Gettysburg Address, as was his wont.

Tisha knocked twice on the door marked 213. "Mr. Blunt?"

"Fine. S'fine," came the bellowing reply.

"Mister Blunt, it's Tisha. You break something?" Tisha reached for the oversized key ring that dangled from the belt of her uniform. "Mr. Blunt, I'm coming in. Okay?"

Tisha slipped the key into the lock. Gave it a turn. Let out a deep sigh when she realized someone was pressing on the door from the other side. "Sir?"

The opposing force doubled in response.

Tisha leaned her considerable weight against the door. Finally, it gave way.

The room was like any other at Harmony. Small. Single bed. Antique dresser. Exposed sink. But unlike the other rooms, the floor of room 213 was now covered in angry glass shards and a generous dusting of particles. Nathaniel Blunt sat in the far corner with his arms resting on his knees, a crag of a man with gray-blond hair, a matching beard, and skin steeped too long in the sun.

"Are you in need of assistance?" asked Tisha, half-hooded eyes betraying her apathy.

"Oh, fuck off," said Nathaniel.

Tisha glanced at the shards. Followed them to the window, where the glass pane had once been. A chill rustled the drapes, ushering snowflakes into the room. Tisha gestured vaguely toward the mess. "Needed some air?"

Nathaniel Blunt made no reply.

Tisha placed her hands on her hips. "Let me see your hands."

Nathaniel made no movement.

"Hands," repeated Tisha.

Nathaniel covered his face with his large left hand. Splayed the fingers open.

"And the other one," said Tisha.

He raised his right hand—a pulp of lacerations, dripping red.

2

Suturing materials—peroxide, gauze, iodine, butterfly closures— sat in line atop white padding, atop a sterling metal tray. Tisha left the fluorescent lights of the infirmary off, preferring the softer glow of the desk lamp.

Nathaniel winced as she threaded another stitch. "Shouldn't Cathy be doing this?"

"Cathy's shift ended at midnight." Tisha clipped the suture and began to tie it off. "If you wanted to get patched up by the pretty one, you should've tried this at a more godly hour."

Nathaniel stared ahead while Tisha applied gauze.

"Grace is gone," said Nathaniel.

Tisha paused, then continued to wrap the gauze, now a bit more gently. "Yes. Yes, she is."

Not gone in the sense that one would knock on Grace Louise Pangborn's door to no answer, Tisha knew, or that the old woman wouldn't be poised in her wheelchair at the daily pill-cocktail happy hour. But Grace *had* left them. Had departed in a manner both cruel and common. Just yesterday, Tisha had looked into hazel eyes flecked with blue and white and been greeted by the gentle warmth for which Grace was known. This morning, Tisha stared into those same eyes only to realize they were not the same. Grace had gone, leaving behind only medicated longevity. The pharmaceutical fountain of youth. And here sat Nathaniel Blunt—his mourning as out of proportion as Nathaniel himself inside the small infirmary.

Tisha sat back in her chair. Some mechanism groaned beneath her. She was no counselor and she'd never been much good at *people*, so she waited for him to speak. Seemed only proper.

"Do you feel," asked Nathaniel, adjusting one of his new bandages, "that you fit?"

"How do you mean?"

"In the world. They make it in your size?"

Tisha fought the urge to snicker and make some self-deprecating comment. For all her life, she'd been what her Aunt Tabby called a "Big Girl"—and that was probably the most flattering way anyone had ever put it. Most statements about Tisha's size had been punctuated with shame. But this wasn't an attack, and grief deserved honesty.

Tisha shook her head. "No."

Nathaniel nodded then stared at his feet—large, hairy, slippered.

Tisha glanced down at her own, the dark skin swallowed in oversized crocs.

"There was a time," said Nathaniel, "when people like you and me—bruisers, you know—had a place. And a purpose. But now—" He shook his head and indicated vaguely the room around him. Then he exhaled, long and slow, into silence.

Tisha shifted her weight on the stool. Being in a room with grief—real grief—is a lot like sitting on a hot plate. Few can stay long in comfort who haven't already built up some scar tissue on their backside.

Nathaniel continued staring at his feet.

"Mr. Blunt?"

No response. Tisha had seen three guests go this month—three minds slip silently away—and now Nathaniel's head drooped, and his fingers had gone lax. Would this be four?

She placed a hand on his shoulder. "Nathaniel?"

"An anarchist works at the Louvre," he muttered. Then he seemed to come back a little. "I'd like to see her." He blinked a few more times than Tisha would have liked, working to find his bearings. "I'd like to see Grace."

3

Though it was against policy at this hour, Tisha allowed the unscheduled visit. *Grace won't know the difference,* she reasoned. *Doubtful she'll know he's there at all.* Besides, it gave Tisha an opportunity to set Nathaniel's room to rights before the day shift returned. Tisha understood outbursts at any age, but Skaft had a penchant for order. "We're a house of rest," he'd often say, "and rest is sedentary." One aggressive swipe of Skaft's pen on pad, and the target patient would need a bib for the next week to catch the drool from whatever sedative he'd prescribe.

They should be allowed their anger. Tisha carefully swept the busted glass from Nathaniel's window into a dustpan, using a hard bristled brush. *They've known the world a long time. Familiarity breeds contempt. They've earned it. They've earned their rage . . .*

Down the hall, she could hear the faint mumblings of a man speaking. Mr. Thompson, she knew. What was left of his wits seemed to be a small chunk of the Gettysburg Address, which he had no doubt been forced to memorize at some point. These days, it was all that slipped through his lips.

4

Sometime later, Tisha returned to Grace's door. She knocked gently, letting Nathaniel know his clandestine visit had come to an end. She had no need to go inside. Grace's room was identical to Nathaniel's, only where that man dwelled in chaos, Grace lingered in serenity. For each item in Grace's room there was a place. For each picture, a frame.

Tisha glanced down the corridor. Silence, moonlight, and shifting patterns of windswept shadows stared back. Tisha didn't much care for the Weeping Hall, as she'd come to call it during her time at Harmony. Every so often, those shadows would trick her, blending into something upright, with form and figure.

Something that seemed capable of haunting regard.

Tisha relaxed against the doorframe. Listened to the muted tones of Nathaniel's voice as it reverberated through the wood. The words were unintelligible (all well and good, as some things are private), but she could hear his inflections, and those with the cadence of questions brought a heaviness to her chest. Truths left untold are difficult enough, but questions haunt.

Questions become ghosts.

Tisha had learned that early in life.

The handle of the door twisted, the wood began to ease back, and a gentle light stole into the hall. Nathaniel stood in silhouette, tucking something into the pocket of his nightgown. What it was, Tisha couldn't tell.

"I hope she dies," said Nathaniel.

"No, you don't," said Tisha.

5

When the pair returned to Nathaniel's room, Tisha waited in the doorway as the old man situated himself on his bed.

"As her friend," he said, "I hope she dies."

"Death's not a friend."

"Of course it is. Old age, on the other hand—*decay*—that's a sonofabitch of a different color."

"One and the same, I think."

"No," said Nathaniel. Then, not unkindly, "Goodnight, Tisha."

"Goodnight, Nathaniel."

6

In the small hours of morning, when she finally returns to her basement apartment where venetian blinds are her only defense against the sick light that announces the day, Tisha sleeps. And in those scarce hours, she dreams of the Weeping Hall.

It is winter in the Hall.

Always winter.

The windows are sheets of ice, layer upon layer, and what little light steals through is swallowed by the darkness of a night that grows ever longer as the memory of day recedes.

In this feeble light, thin, rough shadows—tree bark impressions—form a piecemeal figure. A patchwork man, shambling down the corridor. Through the halls of Harmony it skulks, replacing what withers with available materials.

A knee from Mr. Thompson. A hip from Miss Jones.

And from an old woman who had always kept her room in quiet order, a mind.

7

The noise that woke her was unpleasant. Far from the gentle crescendo of the afternoon alarm that normally woke her, this was a digital mockery in a major key that Tisha had grown to resent. She retrieved her cell phone from the nightstand. Made a mental note to change the ringtone. Checked the time: 7:22 AM.

She had slept for less than an hour.

She placed the phone to her ear. "Hello?"

"Tisha." Skaft's voice. Freshly risen. Caffeinated. "Cathy called out with the flu. You're on today."

Tisha sighed, then placed her fingers to her temples, struggling to remember the dwindling names on the whiteboard labeled "on call." She tried to wipe the sleep from her left eye, but her vision stayed blurry. "What about Debbie?"

"Flu," said Skaft. "You're on. Get here."

8

Back in the infirmary, flickering halogens hummed overhead as Tisha stitched the open wounds on what had—until recently—been Nathaniel's uninjured hand.

"Shouldn't it be Cathy today?"

"Called out," said Tisha. "Flu."

Nathaniel offered a subverbal grunt.

Tisha continued tending to his hand. "How'd it happen?"

Nathaniel winced, his gaze avoiding Tisha's work. "It was either break some glass or break a man."

"Ah," Tisha nodded and began another stitch. "You and windows." She shook her head. "You're lucky. Most people would break a few bones doing that."

"Guess I'm made of tougher stuff."

"I've often described you as thick," Tisha agreed. "So what did he do?"

Nathaniel made no reply.

Tisha raised her eyebrows. "That bad?"

"We were at breakfast," Nathaniel began, then jerked his hand back and winced.

Tisha took his hand once more, then carefully adjusted the position of the needle. "Stop punching glass, and I won't need to stitch you."

"You went to school for this, didn't you?"

"Certified registered nurse practitioner."

"You're squinting. Can you even see what you're doing?"

Tisha resisted the urge to rub her eyes. Her vision wasn't as blurred as it'd been when she awoke, but she could feel herself straining. "Finish your story."

"We were at breakfast. Skaft was there, and Grace. He was feeding her. Some of it—the egg—got on her blouse, and I said to him, 'Hey, she's got some on her shirt.' He glances at me, and I kinda touch my shirt to indicate where. He ignores me, so I say, 'Hey, asshole, take the woman upstairs, and change her fuckin' shirt.' That got his attention. Then he looked at me—and wiped his fingers on Grace's sleeve."

Tisha sighed. "He's a piece of work . . ."

"Then, when he was cleaning up, about to leave, he reached out—and tousled her hair. And I don't know, I just . . . snapped."

"So you broke a window."

Nathaniel's gaze drifted to the floor. His brow creased.

"Grace would've been able to cow that man with a stare." Nathaniel's words came slow and quiet. "Me? I've never had that sort of strength. So I broke something. Because a moment like that deserves to be marked. A moment like that should leave a bruise."

9

In the Weeping Hall, Tisha walks her rounds. Mr. Thompson's recitation of the Gettysburg Address drifts through the corridor. The shadows of tree branches sway and entwine. Tisha stares at them. Her eyelids feel heavy. For a moment, she sees the figure. Irregular limbs and shifting eyes . . .

Tisha closes her eyes. Inhales. Exhales. Opens them again.

The figure is gone.

Not gone, Tisha assures herself. *Never there.*

Just moonlight and shadows. And the slight blur in the vision of her left eye.

It was never there . . .

10

Skaft typed with a purpose, occasionally referencing files and paperwork strewn across his desk, as a phone rang. A chaos only he could navigate.

"I'm supposed to be home," said Tisha. "I'm supposed to be asleep." She squinted. The dim halogen light in Skaft's office seemed unusually oppressive.

"You think I want to be here?" asked Skaft.

"I've slept two hours. In three days," said Tisha.

Skaft picked up the landline receiver. "Harmony Nursing and Rehabilitation . . . okay, when's the procedure? What time? Your name again? And a contact number where I can reach you?" He scribbled the details onto a legal pad. "Okay, we'll have the van set to take her there and to pick her up after, thank you." Skaft hung up the phone. It rang again. He picked up the receiver, let it hover, then hung up without a word.

"Take the shift," he told Tisha. "Or take your severance. Which—I promise you—won't be much given you'll be fired with cause."

Tisha balked. "What cause?"

The phone rang. Skaft fixed his gaze on Tisha. Smiled. "I'll think of something." Then he gestured toward the door and picked up the receiver.

"Harmony Nursing and Rehabilitation."

11

Tisha's head lulled forward. A sudden sense of vertigo snapped her to attention. She sat in Nathaniel's room. A copy of *People* magazine in her lap, between her lax fingers. She sat up, stretching as her gaze drifted across the barren walls, then at the man himself, tied to the bed with thick padded restraints at the wrists and ankles. Both hands, bandaged like mittens.

Nathaniel peeked at her through eyes half shut. "Nodded off there I see."

"Suppose I did," said Tisha as she unceremoniously flopped the magazine onto the dresser. She had no desire to continue flipping through it. Such magazines only served to remind her of two truths: that there are beautiful people in the world and that she was not one of them.

"Would you mind loosening these a bit?" asked Nathaniel.

"Maybe. You gonna put me in a headlock like you did to Skaft today?"

"Got him to apologize for the other day, at least . . ."

Tisha stood, approached the bed, and began to loosen Nathaniel's restraints.

"So I heard." After a moment of contemplation, Tisha asked, "What did you do? Before Harmony?"

A sly smile crossed Nathaniel's face. He lifted his arms an inch or two, pulling at the restraints. "Before I became a professional vegetable?"

Tisha nodded.

"I was a welder," said Nathaniel. "Among other things."

"You enjoy the work?" Tisha sat back down.

Nathaniel nodded. "Welding's simple. Rewarding. Yeah, I liked it."

"Rewarding how?"

Nathaniel took a moment to consider. "You take two pieces of metal, put 'em to the fire, one of two things happens. You get one thing, stronger than before. Or you ruin them both."

"Like you and Grace? Stronger for knowing each other?"

Nathaniel stared at the ceiling for a long beat. "No. Not much about a woman like that could be improved upon by a man like me."

"So you two were never . . .?" Tisha let the question linger.

"We were friends," said Nathaniel. "At this age, that's enough. At this age, that's the world."

"Ever married?"

"Divorced," said Nathaniel. "You?"

"No. I could never—oh, how'd my Aunt put it?—reconcile what I want with the reality of who I am."

"Your Aunt told you that?"

Tisha nodded, matter-of-factly.

"And what was it you wanted? So crazy, it couldn't be reconciled?"

"I don't know." Tisha retrieved the magazine. Thumbed through gloss and glamour. "Something. Or nothing. I don't know."

Nathaniel didn't ask a follow-up question.

In the quiet of her mind, Tisha thanked him.

"Good magazine?" Nathaniel asked after a moment or two of silence.

"I guess. Gossip columns. Stories. Advice. Self-help techniques. Visualization."

"Yeah?"

"Mm-hmm. They say, 'just close your eyes and imagine' or 'picture yourself,' and there you are. Manifesting."

"Huh," said Nathaniel.

"Therapeutic," said Tisha. She flipped a few more pages. Models with bright white smiles stared back at her. "Then there's the pretty people. Lots of them in here too."

"Ah," said Nathaniel. "You ever heard of—oh, what did Grace call it?—tectonic? No, platonic. Platonic theory?"

Tisha shook her head.

"Theory during the Renaissance. Theory was: What's beautiful outside is beautiful inside."

"That's a shit theory," said Tisha.

"It was the thinkers of the time," Nathaniel continued. "The great minds. They got together, had a sit-down, talked about the soul, and when they stood back up, that's what they'd agreed on. You're beautiful outside, you're beautiful inside."

Tisha offered a noncommittal hum of interest.

"See, when you look at paintings from those times—portraits, you know—they picked all those models for their looks. If you were born ugly, people thought that was just God doing everybody a public service."

"None of this sounds accurate," said Tisha.

"How would you know?"

"I took a class in undergrad. Didn't pay much attention. But are you sure you were picking up what Grace was putting down?"

"Well, that's what I got from it," Nathaniel replied. "Know what the most famous ideal 'Platonic Theory' portrait is? The embodiment of those times? Of that thinking?"

Tisha shook her head.

"She's at the Louvre," said Nathaniel.

"An anarchist works at the Louvre," said Tisha. "Or so I've been told."

"He does indeed."

"Care to elaborate?"

"His name is Padrick. Padrick Carmody." Nathaniel narrowed his gaze. Appraised her. "I could use your help with something. Something important."

"Okay . . ."

"I'd hoped to call Padrick at around eight o'clock in the morning, Paris time. Three or so in the morning, ours. Normally, I wouldn't want to put you out, but the cell phone I intend to use is in the dresser drawer, and as you can see—" Nathaniel pulled against his restraints.

Tisha smirked. But try as she might, she couldn't hide her intrigue.

12

The Weeping Hall is not quiet. There is the distant drone of the Gettysburg Address. The pitter-patter of raindrops against the building. The moaning wind of a violent winter storm. Outside, the trees in the parking lot sway. Their shadow games reach new heights as silhouettes of raindrops streak across windowpanes.

Tisha stands just outside the stairwell, stupefied by her hesitance to enter the Hall. It's the lack of sleep, she knows. The new shadows—the otherworldly patterns of the rain—that make the corridor seem so *alive* tonight, as though the Weeping Hall didn't belong in Harmony at all and had somehow forced itself upon the building. Like a parasite upon a dying animal.

It's three in the morning, she reminds herself. *Some things just seem different at three AM.*

13

The lights in Nathaniel's room were bright. No shadows crept at the periphery. But the sounds of wind and rain had followed Tisha into the man's room. She felt exhausted but aware. Though the world around her seemed increasingly sluggish. Like wading through a marsh.

"Tisha," said Nathaniel. "Top drawer, please."

Tisha opened the drawer, fetched Nathaniel's cell phone. She held it near his hands so he could unlock it, then she navigated through the phone's contacts. It didn't take her long to find Padrick Carmody. There were few names left in Nathaniel's contacts.

"You want this up against your ear, or—"

"Speaker's fine. And Tisha, you can stay for this—if you'd like."

Tisha glanced at Nathaniel. There was a vulnerability to his eyes—a quiver to his voice—that she didn't recognize.

"I would like that," he continued. "If you stayed."

Tisha nodded, then pressed the call button. She put the phone in speaker mode, set it down beside Nathaniel's left arm, then sat in the chair on the opposite side of the room.

The phone rang. Another old man answered. The two began to speak.

14

Padrick Carmody, as Tisha learned in the first few minutes of the call, was an ex-pat who'd lived overseas for almost three decades. Divorced or separated from a longtime partner, if Carmody's comment about "still sending checks" could be followed to its obvious conclusion. Nathaniel, Tisha noticed, drifted in and out of the conversation. More so than usual. Perhaps it was the hour. She hoped it was. Hoped he wasn't beginning to slip down the same hole Grace had fallen.

"So Padrick," said Nathan. "The tools? Did you get my list?"

"The tools." Something in the cadence of Padrick's voice didn't sound promising. "Quite the list, Nathan."

"You couldn't get them?"

"Getting them isn't the problem," Padrick paused. "Nate—there's no easy way to ask this, so I'll just ask."

"I want to deface the Mona Lisa," said Nathaniel.

Padrick Carmody went silent.

"As a testament," Nathaniel continued, a little off kilter, "a memorial to a friend of mine, Grace Pangborn."

"Who's Grace Pangborn?"

"A friend." Nathaniel cleared his throat. The words didn't seem to carry the weight he'd hoped they would. "I've got a tuft of her hair here. I'm gonna mail it to you. What I'd like you to do is burn it down to ash then mix it with lacquer and a bit of acid. Then I want you to burn it into the painting. Into her cheek."

"So the tools—the abrasive jet?"

"That's to cut the glass of the display."

"The rock spike planter?"

"Anchors the abrasive jet."

"Nathan . . ."

"Look, I know I've always been more of a bludgeoner than a thinker, but this could work. I know it, Padrick. It's a tall order, I know. Whatever you've owed me over the years—this settles it. This pays the tab," said Nathaniel.

Tisha—only now noticing how tightly she'd gripped the chair's armrests—shifted uncomfortably. How could she have missed it, how far Nathaniel had drifted? Suddenly she felt sorry for these men. And for herself.

"Nathaniel—no," said Carmody.

"No, what?"

"No."

"Oh," said Nathaniel.

Tisha watched as confusion collided with disappointment on Nathaniel's brow. "Well, that's alright. Got a backup. Jesus, where'd I . . . Tisha—"

She stood up slowly.

"There's a notepad in the drawer. Same one the cell phone was in—mind grabbing that? Holding it up for me?"

"Nathan?" said Carmody.

"I'm here, Padrick."

"Nate, is there someone else in the room with you?"

"Yes. My friend, Tisha. She's helping me out."

"Okay, Nate, I need you to put Tisha on the line, okay?"

"What—why?"

"Just to make sure she's on the up and up."

Tisha placed a cushion on Nathaniel's chest, and the open notepad atop the cushion. Nathaniel offered a nod of gratitude. "I'll vouch for her, but you two go ahead. I'll look over my notes here, and then we'll pick up where we left off."

"I'll only be a sec." Tisha retrieved the phone from beside Nathaniel, then slipped into the hallway, closing the door—all but a crack of light—behind her. She put her back against it, staring at the familiar shadows as they danced and cavorted. She set the cell phone off speaker mode, then lifted it to her ear. "This is Tisha."

"Hi, Tisha. Are you an orderly? A nurse?"

"Nurse," said Tisha.

"Good. Great, okay, look—Nathan isn't himself."

"I'm aware," said Tisha.

"Alright, um—I need to break whatever fantasy he has going on in his head, but gently. And if that doesn't take, then not so gently. And I need to know someone's going to be there for him. After."

"Yeah," she said, "I understand."

"So I can rely on you? If I need some backup in there?"

Tisha didn't respond. She was staring into the Weeping Hall. Staring at the shadows.

"Tisha?"

A few faint words of the Gettysburg Address teased through the hall. Tisha felt her gaze drawn toward the darkness. She blinked. "Yeah, I'm here. I'm putting you back on speaker, Mr. Carmody."

She backed into Nathaniel's room, slowly closing the door, leaving it open a crack to peek out into the hallway one last time before pulling it shut.

"Nate?" Padrick's voice cracked as Tisha set the phone down on the nightstand.

"Yep," said Nathaniel. "Tisha pass muster?"

"With flying colors, Nate." Padrick cleared his throat.

"So the backup plan is a bit simpler," Nathaniel said. "There's a temperature control system, so if cutting the glass would take too long, we could always just use the vents. Coat the thing in a mist of sorts."

"Nathaniel," said Padrick, "I can't do anything to the painting. I'm sorry."

Nathaniel squinted at the phone, chuckled, and rolled his eyes at Tisha. "Says the man who mixed napalm for the Catonsville Nine."

"For burning draft documents."

"I'm not burning anything."

"You asked for acid, Nathan."

"It's diluted."

"I know this isn't what you want to hear—"

"Padrick, I need to do this."

"I'm sorry about your friend."

"Sorry doesn't pay old debts."

"I haven't forgotten," Padrick replied, and Tisha could hear regret in his voice. Sincere, if reluctant. "There was a time you could have asked me to tear God off his throne, and I wouldn't have flinched, but what you're trying to do—time did it for you."

Nathaniel went silent. Tisha listened to rain patter against the window.

"Alright, let's try a little history." Padrick started. "Way back in the day, early 1900s, she was kidnapped by a Louvre employee. He'd hidden with her in a broom closet until after closing time, then walked right out the front door and off to Italy. Made a killing selling replicas before he was eventually arrested for trying to sell her to a gallery in Florence. Around the 1950s, she was doused with acid—"

"We don't need to douse her," Nathaniel interrupted. "It'll help bond the—"

"That same year," Padrick continued, undeterred, "a Bolivian pegged her with a rock."

"That's not—that isn't the point here," Nathaniel shook his head.

"Now those are just a few causes of wear and tear she's suffered over the years, which speaks nothing to the fact that she's rounding her five hundredth birthday. Her paint is cracking; she's getting darker and less distinct with each layer of lacquer we slap on in order to preserve her; she's got a mean scar down her forehead that's held together by two butterfly supports—she's losing bits and pieces every day. Her beech crosspieces got infested with insects and had to be replaced with sycamore, so in terms of defacing her, time did the job for you, Nathan. But you know what she still has?"

Nathaniel snickered. "Please don't say what I think you're going to say."

"She still has that smile," said Padrick.

Nathaniel sighed.

"And there's something to that, Nate. Something worth preserving."

"You talk like it's a person," said Nathaniel. "It's paint on canvas, Padrick."

"Yes—and brother—she'll outlive us both."

For a few moments, neither man spoke. Tisha stared sadly at her friend, whose jaw hung slightly open. Whose resigned gaze seemed very far away. Then Nathaniel—in a voice no louder than a whisper—managed, "I'd like to sleep now . . ."

"Nate—" Padrick began, only to be cut off by Nathaniel.

"Good night, Padrick."

15

After the call ended, Tisha tucked Nathaniel in for the night, undoing his restraints. She should have far sooner, she knew. But Tisha's empathy—though reliable—sometimes warmed more slowly than she cared for. She may have to answer to Skaft for releasing the old man's limbs. But for what Nathaniel had just lost, he deserved the comfort of turning on his side. Of curling into a ball, pulling the covers around himself, and shutting out the world. Even if only for a short rest.

She felt tired. More than tired. Almost inebriated. As though she were slipping into sleep, only to awaken, moment by moment. Tisha leaned against the wall for support, then lurched her way to the door, sliding her hand blindly against the wall to find the light switch. Flipping it down.

As she stepped out of the room, she heard Nathaniel's faraway voice. "Tisha?"

"Yes?" said Tisha, sure her voice slurred.

"Leave it open," he said. "I want to watch the shadows. Hear the storm."

Tisha grunted in agreement, then stepped out of the room, leaving the door ajar. And she wished—dearly wished—that he'd asked for anything else.

16

The Weeping Hall is a funhouse tunnel, its shadows bending in violent, impossible ways, as Tisha stands at the threshold, staring dazed into the corridor, as the full consequences of three consecutive days without sleep finally take their toll.

First, her vision clouds. Next comes the sensation of vertigo.

Her knees buckle, the pit of her stomach drops, and all at once, Tisha Page is crying. Worse still, she does not know why. Tisha hasn't wept since she was a child.

It's only when she sees her own sobs hanging visible in the air that she realizes how cold she's become.

She takes a single step into the Hall, and the wind cries with her. She takes another step, and the shadows wave her on. The sting of chilled air permeates her shoes, as she sinks, seasick, into snow where tile should be. Her hand finds the wall for support—rough and cold beneath her palm, like ice—and she tells herself it's only her imagination when she feels it move beneath her touch.

There's a sound missing tonight. Mr. Thompson's recitation. And though she's immobilized, grieving a loss she can't put to words, Tisha finds herself outside his door, not quite knowing how she came to be there. She opens it, and there—standing at the foot of Mr. Thompson's bed—is the figure.

Its skin is tree bark.

Its limbs, mismatched.

But it's the eyes that hold her. One rheumy and blind, white as frost. The other—discordantly human, blue, aware—regards her. Then the figure hobbles forward, the stench of decay wafting from it, and its twiglike fingers are in her left eye socket.

Its roots dig in behind her eye.

Then Tisha sees nothing at all.

17

The noise that woke her was unpleasant. It was not the gentle crescendo of her afternoon alarm, but that same horrid ringtone she had meant to change. And had—of course—forgotten to do so.

As she retrieved the illuminated cell phone from her nightstand, Tisha had no idea for how long she'd slept. Or how she'd gotten home last night. Or when she'd left Harmony. She placed the phone to her ear.

"We need you again," croaked Skaft. "The flu's knocked out just about everybody."

"I can't come in," said Tisha.

"We need you today. You're coming in."

"I can't," said Tisha.

"Oh? And may I ask why not?"

"Because I can't see out of my left eye."

18

"Macular degeneration," said the man in the white coat. Tisha sat in the black leather exam chair, wincing as the strange metallic mask lifted from her face. "Rare for someone your age, but not unheard of. Good news is your right eye's doing great. Bad news is, it'll likely catch up with your left, eventually. It's the blood vessels of your macula. Think of them as roots."

Tisha found that easier to imagine than she would have liked. "Basically, the roots are destroying the pavement. Your blood vessels are the roots. The walls and receptor cells are the pavement."

"So what are my options?"

"We'll talk those through. But this is progressive. It's just something, in your case, that's going to degenerate with time. Your quality of life won't be greatly affected to begin with, not until the right eye starts to show signs of wear. But when that happens, we'll have to develop a plan to ease you into life without sight."

"Just age and time," said Tisha.

The man nodded. "Just age and time."

19

Tisha didn't return for work that evening. Skaft was not pleased, having to cover the nightshift himself, but Tisha couldn't be bothered. News like this deserved time to take in. And rest. Undisturbed rest. Rest with dreams that took place anywhere but in hallways full of wind, shadows, and whispers of decay.

Aunt Tabby proved surprisingly supportive when Tisha sat her down to break the news.

"You already know," Tabby had said, "I've all but lost these to arthritis." She held up two hands, knotted at the joints. "And that's just time, Tisha. Every year past is another closer to a world without you or me in it. That's just how it goes."

20

A year passed before Tisha returned to Harmony Nursing and Rehabilitation. By then, her position had been terminated, and a replacement found. Tisha didn't mind. These were no longer halls she wished to walk.

The atmosphere of the place felt more welcoming as a visitor. She wore her own clothes. She strode past people undertaking tasks she once dreaded. She took her time greeting and mingling with guests, fearing no reprisals for tardiness.

Nathaniel was in his room. No longer restrained. That was far from necessary these days. He lounged in a wheelchair, eyes vacant. His hair had a more groomed appearance, as did his clothing, save for the stain of egg yolk on his shirt, the sight of which brought a deep sigh from Tisha.

Tisha took a moment to wipe a small glob of spittle from the corner of his lips, the skin cracked and dry.

Nathaniel's room smelled of urine and body odor. Of scorched metal. Of ionized air rising from a red grill of a lone space heater feebly struggling against the oppressive chill of winter.

Tisha sat on Nathaniel's bed.

She leaned toward Nathaniel's chair, took his hand—which felt thin and skeletal—into her own, and whispered . . .

21

Picture yourself . . .

In Harmony Nursing and Rehabilitation.

It's three in the morning. We're in your room. You finish your phone call with Padrick Carmody. Padrick's a disappointment, but that doesn't matter. We know how to get things done. A couple of bruisers like us . . .

We take what we need. Say goodbye to Grace. March past the orderlies, past the doctors, the folks at the front desk. Something in our stride says, "Stand back," and they do.

We stop by Grace's son's to get some stuff we need—like a photograph of Grace before the years took the good and saddled her with the bad—and to get her son's blessing. He knows you. Grace, of course, had written about her friend.

We hop a plane bound for France. My ticket maxes out my credit card. Your ticket maxes out my other credit card—the one I'd hoped to shift my debt onto later in life. You can laugh at that, if you can hear me. I hope you're laughing. You don't need to show me.

Our plane has a layover in Spain, and we see Madrid. You, Nathaniel Blunt, have officially taken me beyond all the places I've ever known. My Aunt Tabby calls to let me know that Skaft is after us. And the police. And the CIA and FBI. Because when a couple of bruisers get together to do something, the world shakes.

We reboard, fly two hours to Orly Airport in Paris, exchange our money, grab a baguette. Maybe some coffee. Pick up a bottle of Johnny Walker Blue, then we hop the RER C train toward Champs de Mars-Tour Eiffel. See? All the little details you never thought about, I took care of. You won't have to do any of this alone.

We find ourselves at Padrick's place, and the old man finds his spine and comes through. He delivers a duffel bag full of all the things we'll need. You thank him with the bottle of JW, and we sit and drink a night away in Paris, we three anarchists.

Morning comes, and we take the 27 bus at Saint-Michel–Notre-Dame, get off in front of that glass pyramid thingy, then walk into the Sully Wing of the Louvre. Padrick, working security, gets our duffel bag through.

And there she is, Nathaniel. At the end of a hallway. Down a glossy lane of parquet wood floors, behind a layer of bulletproof glass, in a temperature-controlled world all her own. In a place protected from wind, rain, shadows, and time.

You approach with the duffel bag. Consider your tools—the rock spike planter, the abrasive jet. You laugh at yourself because you never needed either. You walk up to the glass and pull back your fist. It shatters before you swing. Glass knows you by reputation, and where you go, it breaks.

You take out the lock of Grace's hair, a cigarette lighter, and a small tin. You fill the tin with diluted acid. You burn the hair with the lighter and add the ashes to the tin.

At this point, you're probably worried about security. Don't be. Because even half blind, I hold my own.

You take the acid and the ashes and add it to the lacquer. You dip your thumb into the lacquer, and it burns. That's a good thing. You approach the Mona Lisa, extend your hand, and drag your thumb down her cheek—a slow, dark bruise. It sets there, the weak acid eating in just enough to make it permanent.

And there Grace stays, and a bit of you. In a place the cold will never find. Preserved, attended, admired. Remembered.

You return to Harmony. You have to. That's just how these things go. And yes, decay finds you. That thing will take its due . . .

But hopefully, the other's following not too far behind. That silence. That peace. The friend that soothes your fears, drowns your hopes, and begs to lift your burden.

ACKNOWLEDGMENTS

T HANK YOU TO my editor Melissa Rechter and her team at Crooked Lane Books, and to my agent, Italia Gandolfo.

ABOUT
GEORGE C. ROMERO

G EORGE C. ROMERO is a producer, film director, comic writer, and contributor to the futureverse of *Heavy Metal Magazine*. The son of legendary film director George A. Romeo (*Night of the Living Dead*), he is one half of Romero Pictures with Rebecca Romero. The two also founded the Veterans' Compound, a nonprofit organization designed to help veterans process their experiences through the visual arts of filmmaking and deliver the career training necessary for veterans to find a new home in the film industry.

With almost two dozen films and hundreds of commercial campaigns under his belt, George's most recent releases are the "Cold Dead War" and "The Rise" comics through *Heavy Metal Magazine*. Both inaugural issues went to second printings almost immediately after release.

He has written, produced and/or directed, and arranged financing for more than 35 film, television, and streaming projects, and serves as a business consultant and mentor for young and new filmmakers, content creators, and entrepreneurs, to help them navigate the turbulence of the entertainment industry.

Romero also works as a set/production designer for small, independent short films and feature-length projects, overseeing and executing the design and construction of sets, props, and design pieces with his son.

His early and comprehensive exposure to the film industry and the process of filmmaking offered Romero the opportunity to learn the intimate details of production at a granular level while nurturing his own creative endeavors. This has led Romero to his current career stage and afforded him the experience necessary to provide a steady and guiding hand to those he works with and mentors.

ABOUT THE EDITOR

CALLED A "CHAMPION for women's voices in horror" by *Shelf Awareness*, LINDY RYAN is the Bram Stoker Awards®–nominated and Silver Falchion Award–winning editor of *Into the Forest: Tales of the Baba Yaga*. She has been named one of horror's most masterful anthology curators, alongside Ellen Datlow and Christopher Golden; is the current author-in-residence at *Rue Morgue*; and was a 2020 *Publishers Weekly* Star Watch Honoree for her work at Black Spot Books, an independent press focused on amplifying underrepresented voices in horror. She is the author of *Bless Your Heart*, *Cold Snap*, and more, as well as an award-winning short film director for her children's-picture-book-turned-animated-short, *Trick or Treat, Alistair Gray*.

www.LindyRyanWrites.com

ABOUT THE ARTISTS

Jessica McHugh is a two-time Bram Stoker Awards®–nominated poet, a multi-genre novelist, and an internationally produced playwright who spends her days surrounded by artistic inspiration at a Maryland tattoo shop. She's had thirty books published in fifteen years, including her Elgin Award–nominated blackout poetry collection, *A Complex Accident of Life*; her sci-fi bizarro romp, *The Green Kangaroos*; and her cross-generational horror series, *The Gardening Guidebooks Trilogy*. Explore the growing worlds of Jessica McHugh at McHughniverse.com.

Mister Sam Shearon is a British born "dark artist" based in Los Angeles. Specializing in the unexplained, horror, and science fiction, his work often includes elements inspired by ancient cultures, folklore, legend, and the occult.

Sam has created artwork for a variety of clients in both the rock and metal music scene and the world of the comic book and graphic novels, creating album covers, merchandise, and comic-book covers for a variety of clients, including Jason Charles Miller, Rob Zombie, Slayer, Pantera, Ministry, Rammstein, Filter, Iron Maiden, KISS, Powerman 5000, HIM, Orgy, Doyle, American Head Charge, Clive Barker, Stan Lee, IDW publishing, Boom Studios, The X-Files and Fangoria. He has also produced a number of alternate promotional posters for the movie *Nandor Fodor and the Talking Mongoose*, directed by Adam Sigal and starring Simon Pegg, Minnie Driver, and Christopher Lloyd, with Neil Gaiman providing the voice of the mongoose himself. More at www.mistersamshearon.com.

ABOUT THE AUTHORS

Josh Malerman is a *New York Times* bestselling author and one of two singer/songwriters for the rock band The High Strung, whose song "The Luck You Got" can be heard as the theme song to the Showtime show *Shameless*. His book *Bird Box* was made into a Netflix film of the same name, starring Sandra Bullock and John Malkovich.

Jamie Flanagan is a Bram Stoker Awards®–winning writer and actor. Writing credits include Netflix's *The Haunting of Bly Manor*, *Midnight Mass*, *The Midnight Club*, *The Fall of the House of Usher*, and AMC Shudder's *Creepshow*.

Rachel Harrison is the national bestselling author of *Black Sheep*, *Such Sharp Teeth*, *Cackle*, and *The Return*, and was nominated for the Bram Stoker Award for Superior Achievement in a First Novel. Her short fiction has appeared in *Guernica*, *Electric Literature*'s Recommended Reading, as an Audible Original, and in her debut story collection *Bad Dolls*.

Jeff Strand is the Bram Stoker Awards®–winning author of almost sixty books, most of them horror/comedy. He's definitely getting coal in his stocking this year. You can visit his Gleefully Macabre website at www.JeffStrand.com.

Gwendolyn Kiste is the three-time Bram Stoker Awards®–winning author of *The Rust Maidens*, *Reluctant Immortals*, *Boneset & Feathers*, *Pretty Marys All in a Row*, and *The Haunting of*

Velkwood. Her short fiction and nonfiction have appeared in outlets including *Lit Hub*, *Nightmare*, *Best American Science Fiction and Fantasy*, *Vastarien*, Tor Nightfire, Titan Books, and *The Dark*. She's a Lambda Literary Award winner, and her fiction has also received the This Is Horror Award for Novel of the Year, as well as nominations for the Premios Kelvin 505 and Ignotus awards. Originally from Ohio, she now resides on an abandoned horse farm outside of Pittsburgh with her husband, their excitable calico cat, and not nearly enough ghosts. Find her online at gwendolynkiste.com.

Tim Waggoner has published over fifty novels and seven collections of short stories. He's a four-time winner of the Bram Stoker Award, a one-time winner of the Scribe Award, and a finalist for the Shirley Jackson Award and the Splatterpunk Award. Tim is the author of the acclaimed horror-writing guide *Writing in the Dark*, and he's a full-time tenured professor who teaches creative writing and composition at Sinclair College in Dayton, Ohio. His papers are collected by the University of Pittsburgh's Horror Studies Program.

Darcy Coates is the *USA Today* bestselling author of more than a dozen horror and suspense novels. She lives in the Central Coast of Australia with her family, cat, and a collection of chickens. Her home is surrounded by rolling wilderness on all sides, and she wouldn't have it any other way.

Thommy Hutson is a screenwriter, producer, and bestselling author. He has written or produced film and television projects in multiple genres—horror, thriller, holiday, animation, and documentary—that have been released on Netflix, Hulu, Audible, Shudder, Hallmark, Lifetime, Syfy, Bio Channel, and more. In addition, he has written two novels and a nonfiction book. A member of the Producers Guild of America and the Horror Writers Association, and a Saturn and Home Media Magazine award winner, Thommy holds an MFA in creative writing from the University of British Columbia.

Christopher Brooks is a freelance writer and editor with a background in small press publishing and theater; he also had a brief stint as a truck driver—which is to say his art degree got him nowhere. He grew up in New England and lives in Oregon with his wife and two children.

Christopher Golden is the *New York Times* bestselling author of such novels as *Road of Bones*, *All Hallows*, and *The House of Last Resort*. His work in comics includes cocreating multiple series with Mike Mignola, including Baltimore and Joe Golem: Occult Detective. He has also written for film, television, audio drama, animation, and video games. As an editor, his anthologies include *The New Dead*, *Hex Life*, *Hark the Herald Angels Scream*, and the Shirley Jackson Award–winning *The Twisted Book of Shadows*. Golden has been nominated for the Bram Stoker Award ten times in eight different categories, and won twice, including Best Novel for Ararat. His work has also been nominated for the British Fantasy Award, the Eisner Award, the Locus Award, and multiple Shirley Jackson Awards.

Clay McLeod Chapman writes books, comic books, and children's books for film/TV. You can find him at www.claymcleodchapman .com.

Kristi DeMeester is the author of *Such a Pretty Smile*, *Beneath*, and the short fiction collection *Everything That's Underneath*. Her short stories have appeared in *Black Static* and *The Dark*, among other magazines, and she's had stories included in several volumes of Ellen Datlow's *The Best Horror of the Year* and *Year's Best Weird Fiction*, as well as Stephen Jones's *Best New Horror*. She is at work on her next novel. Find her online at www.kristidemeester.com.

Hailey Piper is the Bram Stoker Awards®–winning author of *Queen of Teeth* and *A Light Most Hateful*, The Worm and His Kings Series, and other books of horror. She's also the author of over one hundred short stories appearing in *Weird Tales*, *Pseudopod*, *Vastarien*, and many other publications. She lives with her wife in Maryland, where their occult rituals are secret. Find Hailey at www.haileypiper.com.

Nat Cassidy writes horror for the page, stage, and screen. His debut, *Mary: An Awakening of Terror*, was named one of the best horror novels of 2022 by Esquire, Paste Magazine, Harper's Bazaar, and more. His follow-up, *Nestlings*, was named one of the best horror novels of 2023 by Esquire, NPR, the NY Public Library, and more. Also an established actor on stage and television (usually playing monsters and villains on shows such as *Blue Bloods, Bull, Quantico, FBI, Law & Order: SVU*, and others), Nat was commissioned by the Kennedy Center to write the libretto for a short opera about the end of the world, and he won the New York Innovative Theatre Award for his one-man show about H. P. Lovecraft. He lives in New York City with his wife.

Eric LaRocca *(he/they)* is the Bram Stoker Awards®–nominated and Splatterpunk Award–winning author of the viral sensation *Things Have Gotten Worse Since We Last Spoke*. A lover of luxury fashion and an admirer of European musical theatre, Eric can often be found roaming the streets of his home city, Boston, Massachusetts, for inspiration. For more information, please visit ericlarocca.com.

Tim Lebbon is a *New York Times*–bestselling writer from South Wales. He's had over forty novels published to date, and hundreds of novellas and short stories. He has won four British Fantasy Awards, as well as the Bram Stoker, Scribe, and Dragon awards, and has been shortlisted for World Fantasy, International Horror Guild, and Shirley Jackson awards. He's recently worked on the new computer game *Resurgence* and acted as lead writer on a major Audible audio drama, and he's cowriting his first comic for Dark Horse. The movie of his novel *The Silence* debuted on Netflix in April 2019, and *Pay the Ghost* was released Hallowe'en 2015. Tim is currently developing more novels, short stories, audio dramas, and projects for TV and the big screen.

Sara Tantlinger is the author of the Bram Stoker Awards®–winning *The Devil's Dreamland: Poetry Inspired by H. H. Holmes,* and the Stoker-nominated works *To Be Devoured* and *Cradleland of Parasites.* She is an active HWA member and participates in the HWA Pittsburgh Chapter. She embraces all things macabre and can be found lurking in graveyards or at saratantlinger.com.

Mary Rickert has worked as kindergarten teacher, coffee-shop barista, Disneyland balloon vendor, and personnel assistant in Sequoia National Park. She is the winner of the Locus Award, Crawford Award, World Fantasy Award, and Shirley Jackson Award. Her novel, *The Shipbuilder of BellFairie,* was published by Undertow Publications in 2021. Her novella, *Lucky Girl, How I Became a Horror Writer: A Krampus Story,* was published by Tor.com in 2022. Her short story "A Geography of Innocence" is included in the fall issue of *Weird Horror* magazine, and another chilly short story of hers will appear in *Christmas and Other Horrors: An Anthology of Solstice Horror.* This is Rickert's first year growing pumpkins, and by the time you read this, she hopes to be roasting the seeds and making a pie.

Cynthia Pelayo is a Bram Stoker Awards®– and International Latino Book Award–winning author and poet. Her works include *Children of Chicago, Into the Forest and All the Way Through, The Shoemaker's Magician, Crime Scene,* and *Loteria.* Her latest novel, *Forgotten Sisters,* is inspired by Hans Christian Andersen's "The Little Mermaid." She lives in Chicago with her husband and children.

Lee Murray a writer, editor, poet, essayist, and screenwriter from Aotearoa New Zealand. A *USA Today* bestselling author, her titles include the Taine McKenna Adventures, supernatural crime-noir series The Path of Ra (with Dan Rabarts), fiction collection *Grotesque: Monster Stories,* and several books for children. Her many anthologies include *Hellhole, Black Cranes* (with Geneve Flynn), *Unquiet Spirits* (with Angela Yuriko Smith), and *Under Her Eye* (with Lindy Ryan), and her short fiction appears in prestigious venues such as *Weird Tales, Space and Time*, and *Grimdark Magazine*. A five-time Bram Stoker Awards® winner, and multiple winner of Australian Shadows & Sir Julius Vogel Awards, Lee is New Zealand's only recipient of the Shirley Jackson Award. She is an NZSA Honorary Literary Fellow, a Grimshaw Sargeson Fellow, 2023 NZSA Laura Solomon Cuba Press Prize winner for her prose-poetry manuscript *Fox Spirit on a Distant Cloud*, and a recent winner of New Zealand's Prime Minister's Award for Literary Achievement in Fiction. Read more at leemurray.info.

Mercedes M. Yardley is a whimsical dark fantasist who wears red lipstick and poisonous flowers in her hair. She is the author of numerous works, including *Darling*, the Stabby Award–winning *Apocalyptic Montessa and Nuclear Lulu: A Tale of Atomic Love*, *Pretty Little Dead Girls*, *Love is a Crematorium*, and *Nameless*. She won the Bram Stoker Award for her stories "Little Dead Red" and "Fracture," and was nominated for "Loving You Darkly" and editing "Arterial Bloom." Mercedes lives and works in Las Vegas. You can find her at mercedesmyardley.com.

Stephanie M. Wytovich is an American poet, novelist, and essayist. Her work has been showcased in numerous magazines and anthologies, such as *Weird Tales, Nightmare Magazine, Southwest Review, Year's Best Hardcore Horror: Volume 2, The Best Horror of the Year: Volume 8 & 15*, as well as many others. Wytovich is the poetry editor for Raw Dog Screaming Press, and an adjunct at Western Connecticut State University, Southern New Hampshire University, and Point Park University. She is a recipient of the Elizabeth Matchett Stover Memorial Award and the 2021 Ladies of Horror Fiction Writers Grant, and has received the Rocky Wood Memorial Scholarship for nonfiction writing. Wytovich is a member of the Science Fiction and Fantasy Poetry Association, an active member of the Horror Writers Association, and a graduate of Seton Hill University's MFA program for Writing Popular Fiction. Her Bram Stoker Awards®–winning poetry collection, *Brothel*, earned a home with Raw Dog Screaming Press alongside her collections

Hysteria: A Collection of Madness, *Mourning Jewelry*, *An Exorcism of Angels*, *Sheet Music to My Acoustic Nightmare*, *The Apocalyptic Mannequin*, and most recently, *On the Subject of Blackberries*. Her debut novel, *The Eighth*, is published with Dark Regions Press, and her nonfiction craft book for speculative poetry, *Writing Poetry in the Dark*, is available now.

Kelsea Yu is the Shirley Jackson Award–nominated author of *Bound Feet* and *It's Only a Game*. She has over a dozen short stories and essays published in *Clarkesworld*, *Fantasy*, *PseudoPod*, and elsewhere. Find her on Instagram or Twitter as @anovelescape, or visit her website kelseayu.com. Kelsea lives in the Pacific Northwest with her husband, children, and a pile of art supplies.